PASSAGE

~TO~

MOOREA

The Thomas Scoundrel Novels

Vol. # 1
Scoundrel in the Thick

Vol. #2
Passage to Moorea

PASSAGE ~TO~ MOOREA

Vol. #2

The Life & Times

of

Colonel Thomas Edward Scoundrel, USA, Ret.

B.R. O'HAGAN

PEDEE CREEK PRESS
Hilton Head Island • South Carolina

PEDEE CREEK PRESS

Hilton Head Island • South Carolina

Passage to Moorea is a work of historical fiction. Apart from the well-known actual people, events, and locales that figure in the narrative, all names, characters, places, and incidents are the products of the author's imagination or are used fictitiously. Any resemblance to current events or locales, or to living persons, is entirely coincidental.

Printed in the United States of America

ISBN: 978-1-7342263-4-8

For inquiries about volume orders please contact:

admin@brohagan.com

Cover Illustration

Thomas Scoundrel in Paradise

by Tyler Jacobson

© Pedee Creek Press

For Kai Douglas. Pick up the torch, my boy,
I have done my best and now the adventure is yours.

Jules Verne

44 Boulevard Longueville
Amiens, France

My dear Thomas,
Greetings from Amiens, and the deck of the St. Michel, which,
alas, is moored to the dock in the River Somme instead of defying
the wind and waves in the Channel. The sketch below is my
poor attempt to show her to you.

I have had occasion of late to reflect upon the extraordinary art
Museum opening we attended in New York last December.
Watching you swing from the drapes and fly down from the
balcony with no less than a dozen club-weilding Polynesian
warriors in pursuit was pure exhileration for me, and I dare say,
for every one of the stuffed shirt aristocrats who held their breath
as you and those brutes battled your way to the museum's front
doors.

I have been unable to stop that scene from playing over and
over in my mind, and so have I have determined(with your kind
permission, I pray) to incorporate it into my latest Voyage
Extraordinaire, to be published in the Magasin d'Éducation et de
Récréation in September. I will send you a pre-publication draft
to review.

Make plans to visit soon. The key to my wine cellar awaits
you!

~ PROLOGUE ~

Above Kealakekua Bay, Hawai'i
January 1872

A ring of torches flickered deep into the night sky above the temple complex, where the only sounds were the lapping of waves on the rocky shore two hundred feet below and the sobbing of the pale skinned American who was lashed to a post beside a flat rock on which lay a freshly caught *aku* tuna.

The priest smiled. In his grandfather's time the *makahiki* ceremonies and processions lasted from October through February. An intricately carved image of the god *Lono* was paraded in clockwise fashion around the perimeter of the island to accept tribute from every village, and a *kapu* proclamation warned the people against waging war or doing most kinds of work. Instead, they engaged in ritualized sports and games and assisted the priests in expanding the holy sites.

He had taken the name of Pa'ao after the high priest who arrived in Hawai'i from Polynesia six hundred years earlier and set about transforming every aspect of Hawaiian religious life. Pa'ao introduced new gods to the people, created a highly independent and hereditary priest class and started the practice of carving wooden images to place in *luakini* temples and sacred sites. As he watched the American struggle against the reed ties that held him fast to the post, he also recalled that his namesake had made human sacrifice an important part of most major ceremonies.

The newly constructed temple in which Pa'ao and three dozen of his followers were recreating the ancient ritual had been built on a hilltop directly above the original rock walled *Hikiau heiau* on the leeward coast of Hawai'i at Kealakekua Bay. It was the exact spot where the priest's great grandfather watched a group of islanders attack the English explorer Captain James Cook's landing party a century earlier. Cook's men believed the Hawaiians had stolen one of *Discovery*'s shore boats, and in the ensuing argument the sailors fired their muskets into a crowd that had gathered along the shore, killing one of the chiefs.

In response, dozens of Hawaiians armed with knives and warclubs swarmed the English sailors, and during the skirmish Cook was stabbed in the neck with a stone dagger, clubbed mercilessly, and then stabbed repeatedly as he lay face down in the surf.

When Cook's men realized the battle was lost and retreated to their ship, the Hawaiians baked the captain's body in an underground oven so they could easily remove his flesh before carefully and respectfully washing and wrapping his bones, as befit a powerful man who possessed great *mana*. They did not eat Cook's flesh, as Europeans later claimed, though it was true that Pa'ao's great grandfather and some of his friends came upon the explorer's heart two days later in the crook of a tree where it had been placed to dry. The children thought it was a pig heart and feasted on the delicacy, much to the dismay of their families.

Pa'ao reflected on this as the moon reached its peak and shadows darted along the chamber walls. When the time was right he moved to the center of the platform and signaled for the tuna to be brought before him. It always came back to Captain Cook he thought, as two men carefully and with great dignity lifted the fish and began to walk towards him. In the years since his ancestors had slaughtered the famous explorer on the beach below, European and American businessmen and Christian missionaries had swarmed the islands like flies on a bloated corpse. They took a knife to Hawaiian culture, despoiled its women, refashioned its governing traditions, and gutted its ancient religion.

Until a few years ago, Hawai'i had been the whaling capitol of the world. Pa'ao himself had worked on the docks as a young man, helping to provision the hundreds of ships that docked in Honolulu and Lahaina. As petroleum products began to replace whale oil and the great whaling ships were scuttled or sold for scrap, America's growing hunger for sweets of all kinds ignited the explosive growth of the sugar business. With a total population of less than 60,000 people, however, the islands did not have a large enough labor force to harvest and transport the cane, and for decades sugar cane growers had been importing low wage workers from China, Japan, and the Philippines.

The results of that policy had been devastating. Most of the children Pa'ao now encountered on the street were mixed race *hapa haoles*, neither Hawaiian or American, a fact that further enraged him and fueled his desire to evict the interlopers and lead Hawaii back to its old ways. Those who shared his beliefs were few in number, but his greatest strength was his patience, and each day more converts made their hearts known to him. He would grow his following year by year and strike down the colonial masters when the gods told him the time was right.

Pa'ao smelled seaweed and sandalwood on the breeze, good omens for the business at hand. He raised his head to the sky and saw a canvas of stars sparkling on black velvet above the *heiau*, and when he cast his eyes beyond the cliff on which the temple sat, he could see winter moonlight dancing across the placid waters of the bay. The hour had come.

He adjusted his feathered headdress and lowered his gaze to the floor. The men carrying the tuna knelt, kissed the woven mat in front of the alter, and then stood up at attention and held the *aku* out at chest height.

"In the times before the great disruptions, our ancestors gathered on the shore below this temple to mark the end of the games and processions of the *makahiki*," Pa'ao said to the assembly. "With the end of the rituals the *kapu* prohibitions would be lifted, and villages would plant new crops and return to the sea to fish. Wives would lay with their husbands, and children would come into the world to ensure the continuation of our way of life."

Heads nodded all around the chamber.

"But our brethren have forgotten the old ways, and our children are not taught about them. Our kings have grown weak, more interested in politics and profits than in restoring Hawaii to its rightful place among all the peoples of the islands that stretch across the seas."

"Tonight, we gather to honor our ancestors, and we cry out to the gods who existed before creation to prepare a path for us to follow, especially to *Lono*, god of storms, the harvest, and fertility, the very reason *makahiki* is celebrated. Our task shall not be complete until every European, American, and Asian has left our shores, until every one of their banks and churches and warehouses have been burnt to the ground and the ashes have been scattered in the sea."

Cheers and war cries echoed across the chamber and were lifted into the night sky. Hawai'i for Hawaiians. Who could imagine a better destiny?

Pa'ao lifted a sharp-edged spoon that had been resting on a stone pillar. He raised it above his head and said, "Every year the *makahiki* procession ended its four-month journey here, on the shore of our bay. To mark the end of the *kapu* against eating the *aku* tuna, the priest performed a three-part ritual. First, he would recite the *Kumulipo*, in honor of *Kalimamao* who created peace for all when he was born. Then…"

He leaned forward, extended his arm, and placed the edge of the spoon below one of the tuna's lidless black eyes. He stuck the spoon deep into the corner of the eye, pushed it across and to the left and gouged the eyeball from its socket. Then he held the spoon high for everyone to see.

"Tonight, we welcome *aku* back to the coals of our fires. May he nourish our bodies and our spirits."

With that, Pa'ao lowered the spoon to his lips, opened his mouth and swallowed the lifeless eyeball. The men holding the fish stepped back, turned, and walked to the fire pit in the center of the chamber that had been burning down to embers since that morning. They dropped the fish into the flames and then took up positions on either side of the

American.

The pale, fleshy man had not stopped crying since the ceremony began. His thinning blond hair and crisp white shirt were soaked in sweat, and the front of his light linen trousers were stained with urine.

Pa'ao was not surprised at the American's display of weakness; this is who they are the priest thought, and this is why they will be easy to defeat.

He approached the American and looked him directly in the eyes. "Your people did not take the time to see us as we really were when they came to ravage our islands. When you look at us today you see only cane field laborers and prostitutes. Your willful blindness is an afront to the gods. It can only be appeased through sacrifice and fire."

Pa'ao stood close to the American as his followers formed a circle around the pole and began to chant an ancient song. Shadows flitted across the faces of the carved wooden gods that lined the timber walls and the smell of fresh straw rose from the newly woven mats covering the dirt floor.

"As it was for the centuries, so shall it be again," intoned Pa'ao. "Thus, do we honor *Lono* and pledge to him that he shall be honored until the forever times. The invaders shall be driven from our shores and Hawai'i will be cleansed for generations of our families."

The priest raised the ceremonial spoon in front of the American's face. He tried to slump to the ground, but his restraints held, and he could only bend his neck and breathe in short, racking sobs as the two men standing beside him came closer. One wrapped an arm around the American's neck, the other placed his hands on either side of his head to prevent him from moving.

"In the land of the blind only a one-eyed man can help his people see the truth," said Pa'ao.

The volume and tempo of the chanting increased, and the priest placed the edge of the spoon just below the American's right eye. Then, as he had done with the great tuna, he shoved the spoon deep into the right side of the man's eye socket, pulled it to the left, and ripped the eyeball from its cavity. Before the American could react Pa'ao pulled a knife from his waist band and severed the tangle of nerves and tissue that held the dangling eye in place.

The men holding the American stepped back, but he did not scream or try to run; the shock of what had just been done to him was too great. As Pa'ao raised his arm towards the heavens and watched the light of a dozen torches glisten off the fresh-plucked eyeball and the gore dripping down his sleeve, a deep, primal moan rose from the American's throat.

"I pledge to you my brothers," Pa'ao cried, "that we will make them see. Our land will be cleansed, and Hawai'i will be reborn!"

The American looked on in horror with his remaining eye as the Hawaiian priest lowered his arm and calmly spooned the eyeball into his mouth.

Then the one-eyed man's head slumped to his chest, and he went still.

Pa'ao reached behind a flat stone and retrieved a covered glass jar. He opened it, spit the eyeball into the noxious liquid and quickly closed it up.

Lono would be pleased.

~ ONE ~

San Francisco, California
January 1872

Thomas was drifting off with his feet perched on the edge of a roll-top desk when a brick smashed through the front window of the *Chronicle* office and hit his editor on the head. It was probably intended for him, Thomas thought as he jumped to his feet. Everyone knew he sat at the window desk in the afternoons because he liked to observe the parade of well-fed pols who spilled out of city hall on their way to the saloons and chop houses that lined the muddy street in both directions.

Today, however, Andrew Whitton had arrived early and laid claim to the front desk. The long-time editor of the paper had a feeling in his bones; something bad was going to happen as a consequence of publishing Thomas's blistering exposé of Colin P. Stafford, one of the richest and most powerful men in California. He settled into Thomas's chair, poured his fourth cup of coffee, and added a slug of brandy for medicinal purposes. Then he unfolded yesterday's edition of the *Chronicle* and shook his head at the audacious banner headline he himself had written:

Captain of Industry, Or Nefarious Villain?
Who is the Real Colin P. Stafford?
Special to the Chronicle from TES Bayside

The editor splashed another finger of brandy into his coffee and read Thomas's article for the tenth time. He had hesitated to hire the young reporter, mostly because of the fame he had garnered at the Battle of Pebble Creek Ridge in the last week of the war. A celebrity with no journalistic skill was the last thing the struggling daily newspaper needed. Retired Colonel Thomas Edward Scoundrel was a household name, recipient of the Congressional Medal of Honor, confidant of President Ulysses S. Grant, and the luckiest damn-fool gambler Whitton had ever known. He also had an appetite for fine food, rare wine, and finely turned ankles that the gray-haired newspaperman was certain would be his undoing.

When Thomas mounted the wooden steps to the newspaper's cluttered office that first morning, however, Whitton made a quick head-to-toe assessment and figured the smart thing to do would be to tell the ex-soldier that the reporter position had been filled. It wasn't so much his dress or general demeanor that caused the editor to bite down hard on the cold stub of cigar that always dangled from his mouth. In fact, his wife would probably have found the lean, broad-shouldered fellow with wavy brown hair, dark hazel eyes and tanned, open face to be downright handsome. Whitton allowed as how he would cede that point to her.

The editor didn't give a damn what he looked like, but when Thomas opened the door and walked towards him with a pronounced limp, alarm bells went off in Whitton's head. There was no profit in hiring cripples. A moment later he discerned that the former soldier could barely raise his left arm, and his decision was complete. He cleared his throat and prepared to deliver the bad news. Then, almost as if he knew what was coming, Thomas reached out to take Whitton's hand. He shook his head slowly and a sly smile creased his face. The editor was a good judge of character; he saw cleverness and confidence in the young colonel's eyes, two of the most important traits a good reporter should possess. Whitton had been in the newspaper business long enough to know that no amount of education or formal training could instill or hone those qualities in a person. You either had them at birth or you didn't. Perhaps there was more to Thomas Scoundrel after all.

They sat down, and Thomas immediately told the editor that his physical impairments were temporary. He'd gotten busted up three weeks ago when his horse was spooked by a rattlesnake and bucked him off into a scramble of rocks and sagebrush in the Sierra foothills. Broke his collarbone, cracked a few ribs, and sustained a clean fracture of his lower right leg. Compared to the wounds he suffered in the war, it wasn't much, he assured the newspaper man. And damned if Whitton didn't find himself nodding in agreement.

And so, despite his serious reservations about the colonel's fitness for the job, he offered to give Scoundrel a trial. Of course, he half expected that the man would grab his hat and head out the door when he learned about the meager salary, grueling hours, and short deadlines he would have to accept. That's what most of the other applicants had done.

Not Thomas. He set about learning everything he could from Whitton and the other *Chronicle* reporters, peppering them with such a flurry of questions for the first few days that the editor finally sent him out on his first assignment just to get some peace.

"I won't let you down," Thomas promised. He grabbed a notebook and a handful of pencils and limped out the door towards city hall, where the origins of every good tale of corruption, greed, lust, and general calumny was waiting to be discovered by those wily enough to pry information out of the hangers-on who skittered like cockroaches towards the smallest tidbits of gossip.

For the next several weeks Thomas tramped every street, alley, hill, and neighborhood in the booming city. He met with silver miners who struck it rich in the Comstock Lode and with stock speculators who became even richer by trading shares in mining concerns without once dirtying their hands. He lunched in private clubs with shipping magnates and drank and gambled in waterfront saloons with the sailors who manned the square-rigged China trade clippers they owned. From bar rooms to bedposts, and from a Chinese restaurant owned by a chef trained in classic French cuisine to the dockside taverns frequented by the burly stevedores who offloaded hundreds of tons of cargo from ships each day, Thomas learned to view the living, breathing city of San Francisco through the eyes of a journalist in search of the next big story.

Whitton was pleased to see how quickly his new reporter was learning to navigate the tangle of information, people, and places that made up the city. And he came to trust Scoundrel, even though he never believed that his injuries had been caused by a fall from a horse. That conclusion was cemented after seeing Thomas ride a lightning-fast thoroughbred to victory in the 4th of July Founder's Race. Busted up or not, Thomas could teach the Comanche a thing or two about horse-manship, which was the most complimentary thing you could say about a man's saddle skills in the West.

Whitton had a hunch about where Thomas's instincts could best be employed, and from day one he sent the fledgling reporter to comb the seedy underbelly of the city for stories that would shock and titillate readers from the mansions on Nob Hill to the raucous saloons in the Tenderloin. To hide Thomas's real identity, they assigned him a byline to use in articles in place of his real name. The readers of San Francisco's second largest daily newspaper came to know him simply as TES Bayside.

The Bayside series about the Christmas Eve murder of three prostitutes in the warehouse district and the frantic search for their killer was the first indication of how popular Thomas was going to be. He followed those stories up with an article about arson fires in Chinatown and the arrest of a police captain who managed to embarrass the city's corrupt police commissioner with the amount of protection money he squeezed from small businesses.

Whitton was impressed by Thomas's snappy, energetic prose style and tongue-in-cheek wit. *Chronicle* readers felt the same way and the editor was delighted by the steady increase in sales. The publication of yesterday's front-page article about Colin P. Stafford saw two special editions of the paper sell out in a matter of hours.

As he re-read Thomas's scathing detail of Stafford's ties to all manner of criminal activity, he was also painfully aware of the personal and professional liability he had opened himself up to when he gave the go-ahead for Thomas to spend two months researching and writing the story. The article detailed how Stafford fixed railroad freight prices, how he brutally crushed competitors in timber, cattle ranching, mining, sugar processing, and shipping, and it alluded to the cadre of judges, sheriffs, and legislators who were on his payroll.

Stafford also owned *The Evening Standard*, the only other newspaper in town. The editor had no doubt the *Standard* would rebut every word of Thomas's article in today's edition, but, for the moment at least, the Chronicle owned the news business in San Francisco. He was turning to congratulate his star reporter when the red brick shattered the window and knocked him out of his chair.

Thomas drew a .36 caliber Pocket Navy revolver from inside his jacket and raced to the broken window. He looked up and down the wide boardwalk, but there was no one in sight. A typesetter rushed into the office from the back room, followed by the paper's distribution and sales manager. Thomas motioned for them to retreat into their offices and then kneeled beside Whitton.

The editor lay curled on his side with one arm crooked protectively around his head. The brick struck him squarely on the crown and a stream of blood was flowing onto the wooden floor. Thomas had seen plenty of head wounds in the war and he knew that because the skin under the scalp was so thin there was no relationship between the amount of blood and the severity of the injury. He pulled a handkerchief from his coat and pressed in against the gash while keeping his revolver at the ready.

"What the hell was that," mumbled Whitton.

"Take your pick," Thomas replied. "Jealous husband, a barman we owe money to, or…"

"Stafford," said the editor. "Help me get up."

Thomas slipped his revolver into his coat and helped Whitton to his chair. He kept the cloth pressed against the wound and whistled for the men in the backroom to join them. A minute later the typesetter was trotting down the boardwalk to fetch a doctor.

Thomas held the brandy-laced coffee to the editor's mouth and watched him take a deep drink. Whitton's eyes were clear, and he didn't seem confused, both good signs that he had not suffered a brain injury. He'd have one hell of a headache, but that and a few stitches would be the worst of it—for now, at least.

"Apparently, we have our first review of the article you did about Stafford," said Whitton as he took the handkerchief from Thomas and held it against his wound.

"Were you expecting this?"

Whitton managed a weak smile. "I once watched a bull elk in full rut take on two cows, one right after the other. It was a beautiful October morning, everything orange and green. Quiet as a church, too, until that bull decided it was time to scratch his itch and began to bugle. He peed all over himself to make his perfume irresistible to the ladies, then he mounted one, thrust a few times, and then sidled right over and climbed on board the other one. I was behind a bush about 50 yards from them. All of a sudden, I let out a loud sneeze, and damned if that monster didn't swing his antlers in my direction whilst he was still giving it to the second cow. The look in his eyes told me that the instant he climbed down off her rump I was going to have seven hundred pounds of angry elk trampling my own backside. I made it to where my horse was tied in about three seconds and flew out of there."

"And you think Stafford is like that bull elk?"

"He is in his prime, and when it comes to the way he attacks his competitors, yes, he is always in the rut, although when he is done with them, they don't have quite the same smile on their faces that those cows did."

Whitton looked into Thomas' eyes. "The big difference is that Stafford didn't have to pee on himself. We did that for him."

Thomas sat down and laid his hand on Whitton's forearm. "I have placed you and everyone here in danger," he said. "I was so eager to get the goods on that bastard that I didn't think about the possible consequences. I am sorry, my friend."

Whitton snorted. "We're newspapermen, Thomas. Our job is to ferret out the truth and tell it as best we can to the people of this city. Sometimes that means taking a few lumps."

"And now you have taken yours. I just don't want to see you bashed in the head again."

Whitton opened a desk drawer and pulled out a fresh handkerchief. He dropped the blood-soaked rag in a wastebasket and held the clean cloth against the wound.

"My wife and Stafford's wife are first cousins," said the editor. "They're good friends—at least they were until your article—and they mix in the same society circles. No, I won't be the target of Stafford's revenge. We both know you should have been sitting here at this desk today. The brick was supposed to take you out. So, I want you to disappear for a while. Lay low…and watch your back."

The front door swung open, and the typesetter rushed in with a doctor in tow.

Thomas patted the revolver in his jacket. "I'll be cautious," he said. "But I'll also be close by.

~ TWO ~

Kam Sung Kwan buttoned the starched double-breasted jacket he wore over houndstooth-patterned trousers before securing the t*oque blanche* on his head. The placement of the classic *chef de cuisine's* hat atop the diminutive restaurant owner's head was the signal to the staff in the hot, crowded kitchen that it was time to shift gears.

Each day from noon until six they served heaping plates of Chinese noodles and steamed dumplings to working men and small business owners in the street-side Canton Restaurant. Then at 6:15 sharp they locked the door and began the transformation of the prep area from a chop suey shop into a finely tuned professional kitchen that could hold its own against the finest French restaurants in New York City.

Kwan's highly trained *brigade de cuisine* had one hour to change out every pot, saucepan, serving platter, broiler configuration and plate before carriages began to line up at the alley side door to drop off the crème of San Francisco for an evening of fine dining in the small but elegantly appointed *La Rue de Paris* restaurant, located directly behind the Canton and accessible only from the side entrance.

The young Hong Kong-born chef and his wife were among the 40,000 people from around the world who flocked to San Francisco in 1849 as word of the California gold rush set the world on fire with promises of easy overnight riches. Kwan had no illusions that a Chinaman would be allowed to do anything other than menial labor in the gold fields and placer mines, but he knew that every miner, settler, merchant, and sailor needed to eat, and with gold dust lining their pockets he would never have a shortage of customers.

He and his wife opened their first Chinese kitchen under a makeshift canvas tent in Portsmouth Square the next year. It was a block from the bay on the exact spot where Captain John Montgomery sailed over from Sausalito three years earlier with seventy American soldiers and raised the American flag, claiming the small settlement of Yerba Buena for the United States. Two decades and three buildings later, the Kwan's two restaurants served a city that had grown to over 150,000.

The chef smiled as he watched his staff begin the frenetic transition from filling huge platters with stir-fried vegetables and boiled noodles to preparing small plates of rich, buttery foie gras. He nodded approval to his new *sous-chef*, a promising lad from the American Midwest who had worked his way up from dishwasher to second in command, and when his saucier appeared and asked Kwan to taste the light, lemon-infused mousseline sauce he was preparing for tonight's fresh fish, he took a slow sip, smacked his lips, and suggested he add more cream. Then he snapped his fingers impatiently at a group of junior cooks and apprentices who weren't moving fast enough, and waved encouragement to the chef de partie who would be overseeing tonight's special offerings. Finally, he adjusted his cap, pulled his jacket straight and went through the double doors into the dining area to speak to his wife and the hostess about tonight's guests.

Dinner service at *La Rue de Paris* was limited to no more than thirty-six people each evening, and no one was seated without a reservation. A steady stream of messengers and servants came into the restaurant foyer each evening to arrange future dining dates for their employers, many of whom lived in the growing cluster of mansions that crowned Nob Hill. As Kwan scanned the list for this evening, he recognized the names of one prominent businessman after another, as well as a handful of politicians whose expensive meals, Kwan knew, would be unwittingly subsidized by their over-taxed constituents.

At the bottom of the list of tonight's guests was one name that was decidedly not from Nob Hill: Colonel Thomas Scoundrel, US Army, retired. Kwan liked the young man, but he had no idea how someone in his 20s could be retired from anything. And the colonel was something of a mystery for another reason; he dined with Kwan three or four times a month, and yet he always came alone. The chef knew from other restaurant owners that Scoundrel often arrived at their establishments with one beautiful woman or another on his arm. Kwan doubted that Thomas came alone for lack of money; perhaps this evening he would have an opportunity to broach the question. For now, it was time to go into the kitchen and prepare his signature curry from scratch. That spice mixture and his wife's extraordinarily popular pot sticker sauce were used to make small appetizers that were the only non-French items on the *Rue de Paris* menu. The chef allowed himself a quiet laugh: after twenty-five years of marriage his wife still refused to share her sauce recipe with him. 'Marriage insurance,' she called it.

The hostess led Thomas across the crowded restaurant to a small corner table set for one. He smiled when he saw a bottle of Hamilton Crabb's Hermosa Vineyards zinfandel next to the brass candle lantern in the center of the crisp linen tablecloth. The tables, at which his fellow diners sat in their finest dinner clothing, were graced with arrangements of fresh flowers. Given that it was January, that was no small feat. It wasn't that Mrs. Kwan thought Thomas would not enjoy a bouquet; instead, she knew he would appreciate a bottle of their best wine much more. The first time the young colonel brought a young lady with him, she determined fresh flowers would precede the wine. But not until then.

Thomas looked around the candle lit dining room and strained to hear what people were talking about. He had no doubt that his *Chronicle* article about Colin Stafford was the main topic at every table. Scandal had always been the coin of the realm for high society gossip, and the

Stafford story was packed full of the sort of delicious tidbits that would satisfy even the most jaded among San Francisco's monied class. He wondered: if they knew that the author of the sensational piece was seated amongst them, would he be greeted with applause, or summarily tossed into the street?

Before he could answer, Mrs. Kwan materialized beside his table. She pulled a wine opener from her apron, deftly removed the cork from the zinfandel and handed it to Thomas to inspect. He took a quick sniff, set the cork down and smiled. That was the signal for her to pour a taste.

He had only recently discovered the wine that was becoming so popular in California and around the country. He typically preferred the darker, bolder flavors of cabernet or merlot, but the tannins and high acidity and alcohol content of zinfandel had captured his attention. And he liked the flavors of cherry, dark plum, and tobacco that lingered on the tongue.

Mrs. Kwan watched the expression on his face as he sipped. She filled his glass and left the bottle on the table before bustling off. A moment later her husband came over. Even with his tall chef's hat, Mr. Kwan barely came eyeball to eyeball with his seated guest.

"Welcome home," said the chef. "The wine is to your liking?"

Thomas nodded and raised his glass.

"May I recommend the oxtail bourguignonne in Beaujolais?" asked Kwan. "We simmer the stew in wine all day with garlic, potatoes, carrots, shallots, mushrooms, onions, and bacon. It is served in a bowl with a plate of French mashed potatoes made with creme fraiche, cheese, and garlic-butter."

Thomas felt his eyebrows raise.

"You will not go home hungry, my friend," said Kwan with a wide smile. "And with your coffee we will serve a tarte Tatin made with caramelized apples and puff pastry."

"That sounds just right. And to open…"

Kwan cut him off. "A few of my wife's potstickers?"

Thomas raised his hands, palms up. "You know me too well."

The chef went off to place the dinner order and a busboy appeared with a covered basket containing fresh-baked crusty bread and a small ramekin of whipped butter. He sliced a piece of the warm bread, slathered it with butter and sat back and relaxed for the first time in days. The two-week lead up to the publication of the Stafford article had been a non-stop whirlwind of fact-checking and editing. Keeping it secret had also been a major undertaking, but it was the brick through the window that convinced him that the downstream effects of thearticle had only just begun to be felt. A tidal wave would probably follow.

His editor was right; he should get out of town for a few weeks. Whitton's family connection to Stafford should save him from harm, but Thomas enjoyed no such natural immunity.

It would be hard to leave the only place he had called home since the war ended seven years earlier. From the day he was discharged from Mt. Pleasant military hospital in Washington D.C. until he walked into the *Chronicle* office a year ago, he had been a wanderer. He lived comfortably on the pension he received after mustering out at the rank of full colonel, and with a month's advance notice, he could collect his money at any army outpost, post office or federal office in the country. He briefly settled in Chicago, then St. Louis, and most recently, New Orleans. He liked the energy and wide-open feel of La Nouvelle-Orléans, where the danger and distractions of exotic cuisine, high-stakes gaming and aristocratic belle femmes were everyday occurrences.

A powerful man had forced him to leave that city, too, he mused as he absentmindedly rubbed his leg where the pistol ball shattered his thigh bone. He winced at the memory of the ball tearing through his flesh and the gasps of the crowd gathered on the mossy lake bank behind Henri Lavelle's antebellum estate. The late-night duel of honor that played out between the young Yankee colonel and the patrician businessman in the sticky August heat might have been the highlight of the summer season for the onlookers, but Thomas regarded it as the low point of his life. He escaped New Orleans with his life, the clothes on his back, and wounds that took six months to heal.

He was so deep in memories that he barely noticed the young woman setting a small plate of pot stickers and a tiny bowl of dipping sauce on the table. He forked one of the delicacies onto his plate and considered his current predicament. Colin Stafford's reach extended around the country. If he was going to lie low for a few weeks it meant heading somewhere Stafford wouldn't be able to look, like the thick forest slopes of the Sierra Nevada. That meant buying a pack horse and supplies and steeling himself for the unpredictable weather.

All around him, happy diners were chattering on about the day's events while marveling at the gourmet bounty pouring forth from Kwan's kitchen. He sighed and reached for another potsticker. It would be beans, bacon, and sourdough for the next few weeks.

He poured more of the excellent zinfandel and was contemplating adding a *pâté de foie gras* to his order when he noticed the door to the kitchen fly open. Mr. Kwan stepped out, only to have an arm reach from inside the kitchen and yank him back so violently that his chef cap flew off and landed on the floor. Thomas swung his head around the restaurant but saw nothing out of place. None of the other diners or staff seemed to have noticed their host being pulled back.

Thomas dropped his linen napkin on the table and strode quickly to the kitchen entrance. He pulled his revolver from his pocket and swung the door open.

Inside, water was boiling over on one of the stoves and he could smell food burning in a pan. A woman was sobbing, and three unfamiliar men with clubs in their hands were herding the workers over against the shelves that lined the back wall. A fourth man, who Thomas vaguely recognized from one of the waterfront taverns he had visited for a story, was holding Mr. Kwan tightly by the front of his jacket, suspended in the air above the open flame of a sauté stove. By the looks of it, the man was about to drop Kwan onto the fire.

As Thomas stepped forward, he saw Mrs. Kwan lying face down on the floor beside the stove over which her husband was dangling. She was moaning softly, and a small puddle of blood was forming alongside her head.

Thomas was five feet from the stove. He raised his revolver and pointed it at the man holding Chef Kwan. "Turk," he thought to himself. That was the man's name. A thug for hire in a town where there was never a shortage of demand for his line of work.

"Put him DOWN," commanded Thomas.

Turk clutched the tiny chef against his chest and turned his head in Thomas' direction. A look of recognition crossed his face, and he swung Kwan away from the stove and dumped him in a heap on the floor beside his wife.

"Well now, you stupid Chinee' dwarf," said Turk, "why didn't you just tell me the sumbitch was already here? Would've saved your old lady a knock upside the head."

Kwan muttered something in Mandarin. Thomas was pretty sure it wasn't a warm greeting. Then he sat up and pulled his wife's head onto his lap.

"Turk, isn't it?" asked Thomas.

The man who had just led an invasion into Kwan's kitchen looked neither surprised nor scared by the revolver pointed at his face. Just irritated.

"Foley, Manuel," Turk shouted to his men across the large kitchen. "We got our boy."

"And I got me a sweet Chinese titty," said the man who was gripping a young woman tightly from behind. Thomas could see that he was grinding against the girl's backside.

"No time for that, Reg…. maybe later," replied Turk as he took a step towards Thomas.

No point in drawing this out thought Thomas. He fired a shot across the kitchen that whizzed only two inches from Turk's face. The bullet smashed through a pile of plates and lodged in the wall. Thomas stepped back and waved the gun at the men holding the kitchen staff in the corner.

Turk slapped his hands against his head to feel if he had been hit. But he was smart enough to stand still.

"You men back away from those people," said Thomas. "Raise your hands and come over here beside your boss. Hurry it up; I'm hungry and I promise my next shot will send one of you to hell."

Turk's men walked slowly over beside their boss with their hands in the air.

"Keep them up," growled Thomas. He looked down at Kwan and his wife. "You OK?" he asked.

"We will be," replied Kwan. He helped his wife to her feet and motioned for her to join their employees at the back of the kitchen. Then the chef lifted a razor-sharp meat cleaver off a butcher block.

"If you miss anyone, I will take off his head," he said with a deadly smile.

Thomas had no doubt Kwan meant it. From the looks on Turk and his men's faces, they believed it, too. Their hands remained high in the air.

"I wish we could," said Thomas. "It would do us both good to put these dogs down. Unfortunately, the only crime they have committed so far is assaulting your wife."

"And you want me to let that go without punishment?" asked the chef.

"No," Thomas answered. "But the punishment must fit the crime."

He looked at Turk. "Put your hands down at your side and step over towards me. If you so much as move a muscle the wrong way I will put a round through your skull. Understand?"

Turk nodded. He dropped his hands to his side and walked over to within three feet of Thomas and Kwan. It was silent in the kitchen except for the sounds of sizzling food, steam rising from the warming table, and the soft murmurs of conversation out in the restaurant. Mrs. Kwan and the staff were riveted on her husband and Thomas.

Thomas finally spoke. "Mr. Kwan," he simply said in a soft, matter-of-fact voice.

Kwan smiled. He set down the cleaver and lifted a heavy copper saucepan from the table. Then he used both hands to swing it behind his shoulder and smash Turk squarely in the face. Turk lurched backwards and dropped to his knees, pressing his hands on his broken nose and jaw.

Thomas winced, but still managed a slight grin.

Kwan barked instructions in Chinese and two strapping young men stepped over beside him. He handed each of them a long slicing knife. "Do what my sons tell you," Kwan said to Turk and his men, "or I promise you will be on tomorrow night's menu."

One son went to the alleyway door and swung it open. The other got behind the men to make sure they went where they were told.

"Turk," said Thomas as they headed for the door. "Tell Stafford that his brick failed, and so did you."

Turk grunted and pulled the hem of his jacket up to his swelling, bloody face. He would be out of commission for a long time.

As soon as Kwan's sons led the men outside, Mrs. Kwan came over to her husband's side. Her lip was split, and her eye was blackening, but that seemed to be the worst of it.

"My sons will take them down the block to where the policeman is stationed. Given who our customers are, we always have a cop nearby. He will see that they don't come back."

Thomas' adrenaline level was subsiding. He looked around the kitchen at the staff, and then at the Kwans.

"I am so sorry for this," he said. "They came for me. This should never have happened to you."

Mrs. Kwan held a kitchen towel to her lip. "Why, Thomas?"

"Did you read the *Chronicle* article about Colin Stafford?"

"Yes, of course," said Kwan. "Everyone is talking about it."

Thomas looked the chef in the eye and saw a glimmer of recognition.

"You are TES Bayside?" asked Kwan.

Thomas nodded.

Mrs. Kwan came over beside him and put her hand on his shoulder.

"We do not hold any blame against you, Colonel," she said. "I am only sorry you did not get your meal."

Kwan's head snapped up. "Your meal!" He clapped his hands to get the staff's attention. "Our guests have been unattended for ten minutes. Quickly. Recook their meals and take a bottle of the best champagne to each table with our apologies."

"What do we tell them?" asked the young woman who had been

groped by Turk's man.

Thomas smiled. "Tell them you were resolving a customer complaint."

As the kitchen exploded into activity around him, he scooped up Kwan's hat, set it on the chef's head, and went out through the side door into the darkness.

It was bitterly cold, and the wind-swept drizzle blowing off the bay made it seem even colder. He turned up his collar and set off towards his hotel. Whatever else tonight meant, he knew that he was going to have to disappear for much longer than he had originally planned.

He bent into the wind and walked for a block under the flickering gas streetlamps. A few moments later he heard hurried footsteps and felt a tap on his back. It was the young woman who had served him earlier that evening. She smiled and handed him a cloth bag that smelled like heaven.

"Food," she said in broken English. The she kissed him on the cheek, pulled her cloak tight, and scurried back towards the restaurant in the black rain.

~ THREE ~

Thomas stepped out of the alley and walked for a block along the wood- plank sidewalk up to Broadway Street. He pulled his collar tight against the sleeting rain and headed east for a mile until he reached Octavia Street, checking frequently to see if anyone was following him. Stafford was not a man who took bad news well, and Thomas was certain that Turk's men would keep searching the muddy streets and hills of the city until they found him and delivered their boss's message to him in person.

He turned south on Octavia and pushed through the wind and rain for three blocks until he saw the silhouettes of trees in Lafayette Park. He paused under a black iron streetlamp and looked at the scrub-covered hill that separated the park from Chinatown. At only 376 feet above sea level, California Hill offered the best views of San Francisco Bay, and in the last six months construction had begun there on three palatial homes, including Colin P. Stafford's newest mansion. Though the homes were still only wooden frames, locals had begun to call California Hill 'Nob' Hill, a contraction of Hindu word nabob, or wealthy person. It was a perfect moniker, and Thomas hoped the term would stick.

His hotel was located one block south of the park. The modest three-story building was ablaze with gas lamps, and a stream of people were going in and out of its beveled glass doors. A line of carriages waited beside the sidewalk to take guests to restaurants, gambling halls, or for those seeking more intimate entertainment, to one of the three dozen brothels that dotted Chinatown. The discrete hand-lettered signs hanging above the doors of those establishments only hinted at the delights that lay within; his favorite sign simply read: *Mother's Best.* A piece of blue paper pasted in the window needed only five characters to advertise the complete satisfaction that awaited the randy traveler. In tall block letters it said: '$3.50.' No further description of services was required.

Next door, a small chalkboard affixed to the door of the Happy Minute boasted competitively about their '*$1 Happy Time.*' Thomas had been told that the madam used a sand filled minute glass to enforce a strict sixty-second rule for the $1 adventure, which had to leave many of her bargain-seeking customers in a condition that was far from happy.

His plan was simple; he would pen a note to his editor, pack a bag, and take a carriage south to a small inn at the outskirts of the city. Tomorrow he would purchase a coach ticket to Los Angeles, where his friend and fellow Civil War officer John Hayden had recently moved from Ohio. From there…who knew.

He stood behind an iron hitch post a half block from the hotel and scanned the people huddled against the weather under a broad canvas awning. It only took a moment to catch sight of two of Stafford's men, the ones Turk had referred to as Reg and Manuel. Turk was not with them; he was probably waiting somewhere for a doctor to tend to his broken jaw and nose.

Would the men stay there for long, or would they move on to search the gaming houses and saloons that Thomas was known to frequent? As a gust of wind battered his rain-soaked overcoat, Thomas hoped they were tiring of the cat and mouse game. During the winter the local taverns served pewter tankards of hot buttered rum, and right now that had to sound good to Stafford's men. He wouldn't mind one himself.

Then a carriage pulled up, and three rough-looking men tumbled out onto the sidewalk. They acknowledged Reg and Manual with a nod and walked briskly through the heavy glass doors into the lobby.

Thomas cursed under his breath; it looked like Stafford's men intended to wait as long as it took for him to return to his room.

He pulled his hat tight, secured the top button of his coat and headed back towards the bay. There wouldn't be a hotel, inn, coach stop or whorehouse for miles around that wasn't being watched tonight. Such was the power and reach of the man he had wronged.

It took fifteen minutes to reach the bay front. Mercifully, the rain and wind blowing off the water were relenting, replaced by a gentle drizzle. He knew he was close to the ocean when he heard water lapping softly against the rock seawall where the Stockton and Alameda ferries were docked. He turned south on East Street and walked for a half mile through a jumble of warehouses, piers, and rigging repair shops. When he reached the Oregon and Mexican Steamships wharf, he could see Rincon Point, and beyond that, the wharves where the giant steamers bound for China and Panama berthed. As a distant clock tower chimed ten o'clock, Thomas considered his plan one last time. No place in the city was safe tonight. If Stafford's men didn't find him, there would be even more searchers on his trail in the morning. His plan was foolhardy, but he couldn't come up with an alternative that made more sense.

The rain picked up again and a biting wind cut through his sodden overcoat and set his teeth chattering. It was time. He walked onto a deserted pier and climbed down a ladder to the dock where a half dozen dinghies were tied to mooring posts. One of the boat owners had forgotten to carry his oars away with him, and Thomas untied its mooring line and slipped onto the narrow seat. He set each oar into an open oarlock and pushed the eight-foot boat away from the dock with his foot.

He peered through the rain and darkness to a point thee hundred yards out in the bay where he could just make out the stern and bow lights of his destination.

"This is crazy," he thought. Then he gripped the oars, leaned forward, and dipped them into the dark green water.

~ FOUR ~

San Francisco Bay

Great sheets of freezing rain swept across the bay. Thomas struggled to hold the dinghy on course, fighting the wind and spray from the white-capped waves and a growing sense that he had made a huge error in judgment.

Only a month earlier, he had joined a crowd of onlookers on a pier where the remains of a fisherman were being winched out of the water in a braided rope net. According to the captain of the boat, the poor fool had downed one tankard of rum too many and fallen overboard while taking a leak. He banged his head against the side of the vessel as he went down, opening a gash on his head that attracted a pair of sharks before the crew could fish him out. The sharks ripped and tore at the man's body as he screamed for help. Mercifully, his cries lasted only a minute before the sharks pulled him below to finish their feast. When the sharks had their fill, smaller fish and a swarm of crabs picked most of the remaining flesh from the man's body. As Thomas turned away from the grisly sight dangling from the winch post, a fisherman standing beside him pulled the pipe from his mouth and said to his friend, "They won't be needing much more than a lady's hat box to bury what's left of the poor old sod."

His arms were leaden and aching and his lower back was on fire from the exertion of rowing against the wind and the waves and the tide. For every ten yards he advanced, he was pushed back five. In calmer seas it would have taken about twenty minutes to reach his target. As he leaned forward for the hundredth time to dip the oars into the unforgiving water and sweep them back, he estimated he had been battling San Francisco Bay for at least an hour.

Thick gray clouds covered the moon and stars. The bow and stern lights, faint and flickering in the distance, were his only guide. He lost sight of the lights twice and had to swing the dinghy around in circles until the lights reappeared as tiny pinpoints in the inky blackness.

When he was within 100 yards of the lights, his boat was broadsided by a ten-foot swell that rose out of nowhere. The boat was lifted upwards, the oars popped out of the water, and the dinghy tilted 45 degrees to port. Thomas shifted his weight to the right, pulled the left oar in, and bore down with all his remaining strength on the right oar to counterbalance the surging wave. Then the swirling bay current threw an even bigger wave against him from the right, and he found himself sliding down a trough between the two massive waves.

He could not stop what happened next. The bow of the dinghy was plunged deep into the water, which flipped the stern up into the air and sent him flying forward into the icy water. A wave swept over his head, and then another. He turned in the water, desperate to get back into the dinghy, but the sirens of the deep were drawing the hapless boat into the depths with the sweetness of their song, and a few seconds later it was gone.

Thomas fought back a crushing sense of despair. He knew two things: the cold would drag him down with his boat if he did not keep moving, and the great white sharks were probably assembling for their next meal. Another swell came in from the west, raising him eight or ten feet. He rode the crest, treaded water, and spun slowly around in search of the only hope there might be to escape a watery grave.

The wind began to relent and the wall of rain that had been pummeling him moved towards shore. He turned in the water one more time and saw the outline of the armored frigate fifty yards ahead. The bow and stern lights were clearly visible now, as was the pale light spilling from lamps in several of the square canon openings just above the waterline. He could hear rigging lines slapping against the ironclad's hull as the ship swayed in the waves and when he looked up, he could make out the warship's twin steam funnels and the cross bars of its three wooden masts.

He began a slow crawl towards the side of the ship. Fifty yards. There were two permanent ladders attached amidships, he recalled. He had to find one quickly and pull himself out of the frozen water of the bay. There would be dry clothing, a tot of whiskey and food. Most of all, there would be warmth—if he wasn't smashed to bits against the iron hull by another set of waves. His body was numb from his waist down. His mind willed his legs to kick but he wasn't sure they were moving. He stretched his left arm out towards the ship, lowered his head to the top of the water, and used his right arm to push back against the swells. Slowly, slowly, he could feel he was moving in the right direction, but those 50 yards might as well have been 50 miles. He was losing control of his muscles; his brain was screaming for rest and a voice deep inside his mind was beginning to murmur about how calm and restful it would be if he simply allowed himself to slip below the water and accept the embrace of the sirens. He had read Homer's *Odyssey* as a boy, and the description of the mermaid-like creatures singing in perfect harmony to lure sailors to their deaths captivated him as few other myths had done. It would be easy to let go, to give up the fight, and to accept what waited for him below.

An image of the skeleton of the sailor being pulled from the bay arose in his mind. To hell with that, he thought. He had just turned 23. He wasn't going to have his bones picked clean by hordes of seagoing scavengers.

He sucked in his breath and willed his legs to move, his arm to move, his lungs to breathe. He forced himself to focus on the ship he was going to reach. Was it only three nights ago that he had joined his editor and leading businesspeople of the city in the officer's mess aboard the *SMS König Wilhelm* as Kapitän Ehrhardt Schmidt's dinner guest?

The *Wilhelm* was anchored in the Bay as part of its round-the-world goodwill tour. The flagship of the German navy was a monster; 368 feet long, 60 feet wide at the beam, displacing 9,700 tons. The First Officer gave the guests a tour before dinner, and like the others, Thomas found himself shaking his head at the firepower packed below the teak main deck. It's 18 9-inch guns could lob shells up to three miles away, while its wrought iron plating over teak backing could withstand heavy enemy broadsides. And with or without its sails unfurled, the ships horizontal, two-cylinder single-expansion steam engine could propel the frigate at speeds up to 14 knots.

He was almost close enough now to touch the side of the ship. The swells had calmed, but he was still bobbing up and down like a cork. Then he banged against the iron hull. He instinctively reached both arms up for a handhold but felt only smooth iron and one-inch rivets. As the swells began to push him harder against the hull, he marshalled his strength and began to swim along the port side. The rain was returning, and he could hear the wind picking up out over the open ocean. It would be only a matter of minutes before the cold killed him or a rogue wave smashed him to death against the frigate's hull.

His left hand banged into something sticking out from the side of the frigate. A wave lifted him a foot, and he grabbed ahold of the metal with both hands. It was the bottom rung of one of the two amidships boarding ladders. From the water line to the deck above was about 25 feet. First, he had to find the strength to pull himself up out of the freezing water and onto the ladder. Then he would have to pull his body hand-over-hand up to the deck.

He waited for the next swell and when it lifted him up several feet, he reached as high as he could and grabbed the sides of the iron ladder. He shook his head, strained to make his legs obey his brain, and pulled with every ounce of strength he had left. Then the swell subsided, and he suddenly found himself out of the water and clinging to the ladder.

His legs felt like rubber and his arms ached with exhaustion. He wearily raised one arm to the rung above, and then the other. His legs and feet screamed with pain at a sensation like being pierced by hundreds of needles, and to add to his discomfort, he began to vomit what little dinner he had been enjoying with the Kwan's only a few hours ago.

He almost laughed when he thought about the apology he would have to make to Mrs. Kwan for losing her savory pot-stickers like this, and that thought powered him to reach up one rung higher. The roar of the wind was increasing, and the spray from the swells hit him like bee stings. He was halfway up the ladder, and his arms and legs were moving in an almost subconscious rhythm that he knew he could not allow to slow or stop. The sirens were purring to him from the depths more seductively than ever and their promise of eternal rest and warmth was getting harder to resist.

When his right hand reached for the next rung, he felt the underside of a smooth wooden railing. He was at the top of the ladder, only a few feet from the deck. What now?

Thomas found the strength to swing his legs over the teak rail and a moment later he dropped onto the deck in a shivering heap beside a coil of rope. There would be an evening watch, of course, but he had no idea if they remained at a station or walked the length and breadth of the ship to look for intruders. It was peacetime and they were guests of the American government, so Thomas figured the duty sailors would not be on high alert.

And if they did find him? Would they dry him out and immediately return him to the shore for Stafford's men to find him and mete out their boss's punishment? He would have to figure that out in the morning. His original plan had been to row out to the *König Wilhelm*, tie his dinghy to the side and take refuge in one of the small launches the warship carried on deck. Then he would awaken before first light and row back to shore where he would find a way to sneak back into his hotel and pack a bag for the coach to Los Angeles.

Freezing rain enveloped him and the wind picked up and rocked the ship gently from side to side. *My escape plan is sitting on the bottom of the bay,* he thought. He would have to find another small boat to make his way back to shore. Right now, he needed a place to get out of the weather. He had to rest.

He recalled from the tour that *König Wilhelm* carried several smaller boats on its deck, including two picket boats, two launches, a pinnace, two cutters, two yawls, and a dinghy. The pinnace would be his choice to hide in until dawn. It was used to ferry passengers and mail and could also double as a lifeboat. That meant there would be water and supplies on board.

A bell clanged on the foredeck signaling the beginning of the midnight to 4 AM middle watch, but no sailors were patrolling the deck where he was hiding. Most of the crew would be asleep in their cabins. It was time to move.

He stretched his legs to get some warmth flowing through his cramped muscles and pushed himself up. Then, under the lamplight streaming from the center of each of the three masts, he began to walk the length of the deck, taking care to stay close to the railing and avoid the boxes, barrels, coiled ropes, and folded tarps that covered most the open deck space.

He came to the dinghy first. It was uncovered and held fast by two lines. If he could find a hatchet or knife, he could cut the lines and roll the tiny vessel over the side of the ship just before dawn. Then he would climb down the ladder and row away before anyone on board saw him.

A wave of exhaustion engulfed him as he made his way along the deck to where the pinnace was secured on an elevated platform. Canvas sailcloth was stretched over the top, but it was loose enough to get his head and shoulders under. He climbed onto the platform, looked around to see that no one was approaching, and pushed his upper body under the canvas. Then he hopped up, swung his legs over the side, and dropped into the boat.

The first thing he noticed was the absence of rain, cold, or wind. He got on his knees and felt around in the pitch darkness until he touched the haft of a rigging pole. He wedged one end of the pole against the left side of the boat and the other against a section of the canvas tarp to make a small opening where a little lamp light could spill in. Then he began to rummage through the two oblong boxes that were attached to the boat's ribs. The first box contained a folded sail, mending gear and rigging. In the second box, he found a jug of fresh water, a pile of blankets, and a half dozen heavy wool peacoats.

Thomas shrugged off his wet clothing and wrapped himself in a peacoat. He laid his clothing out in the bow to dry and spread a blanket and several more of the thick winter coats on the floor for a mattress. Then he pulled down the pole holding open the canvas top and stowed it away.

He took a long drink of water, laid down and pulled two more blankets on top of him. Then, inside the small boat perched on the deck of a German warship, he fell into a deep sleep.

~ FIVE ~

His dream was all wrong. Not because it didn't reflect real events from his life, but because it dealt with the wrong events, moments so mundane and ordinary that one would not consider them worthy of dreaming about again and again. What he should have dreamed about was the ride he took to the top of Pebble Creek Ridge on a bright April morning seven years ago.

When he awoke that morning, he was a lowly seventeen-year-old private named Thomas Scandréll, cook's assistant with the 109th Ohio. Five hours later when he was carried broken and bleeding off the ridge by Captain Hayden's men, he was a full colonel with a new last name: Scoundrel. And he was the last Union hero of the Civil War.

But he did not dream about being shot off Cornwall's back in a hail of Johnny Reb fire as he galloped along the ridge or of the weeks he spent recuperating in the federal hospital outside Washington, DC. He did not dream about the poet, Walt Whitman, who spent hours reading to him at his bedside, or about beautiful Angela, his first love, who nursed him back to health and helped him find the courage to live. He had never dreamed about the day the Secretary of War pinned the   Congressional Medal of Honor on his jacket to the thunderous applause of a room packed with reporters, politicians, and more than a few envious army officers, either.

Instead, he dreamed about oatmeal. And coffee. Each morning at 3 AM, Sergeant O'Hanlon roused Thomas and the other cooks to stir the coals from last night's cookfires and stoke them with seasoned wood. Then they suspended a dozen giant iron pots over the trench fires and half-filled them with water. Most mornings they made gallons of bland corn-meal mush. On special occasions they made oatmeal, and in the summer and fall they tossed in any apples, peaches, or berries they could scavenge or buy from local farmers. By the time the regiment woke at 5 AM they were carting five-gallon buckets of mush or oatmeal, piles of hot corn muffins and steaming pots of black coffee to each company. Then they turned to boiling beef or pork for the evening meal and preparing mountains of hardtack biscuits and salt pork for soldiers to put in their knapsacks.

The sequence of the dream was always the same; O'Hanlon stood behind him reciting instructions on making a perfect serving of cooked oats. Then, lines of hungry, blue-coated soldiers swarmed the outdoor kitchen to fill their tin bowls and coffee cups. Many of them slapped Thomas on the back to thank him for elevating their breakfasts from the goopy slop served by so many other outfits to a superb oatmeal that was fit for President Lincoln's own table.

Thomas was no expert on the workings of the subconscious mind, but he knew why he dreamt about being a cook and not the gallant hero the world believed him to be. He had been catapulted to the rank of colonel by a corrupt general who was being paid handsomely to keep the sons of the wealthy and powerful out of harm's way. General Yoke kept the regiment on the move, taking extraordinary care to keep his charges miles away from any fighting. When his scheme began to unravel in the final days of the war, he concocted a desperate plan to cover his tracks in the event the War Department ever investigated the rumors about the ghost-regiment he had been profiting from for years.

Yoke's plan required the slaughter of an entire company of men, and their commanding officer. Thomas was selected to play the role of a regimental colonel because he was a nobody who looked like he could pass for an officer. He had been summoned before dawn to collect dirty dishes from General Yoke's command tent. A half hour later he was wearing a new uniform, his hair was freshly cut, and, in a twist of fate that changed his life forever, a partially deaf clerk scribbled the name Scoundrel instead of Scandréll in the regimental record book.

Then Thomas was put on the general's personal horse and ordered to take command of the regiment's only company of experienced fighters, 100 men who did not come from family's wealthy enough to pay for Yoke's protection. He was to lead them up Pebble Creek Ridge, where, according to the part of the plan the general did not share with him, they would be wiped out by a far superior Confederate force coming up from the heavily forested river valley to the north. For the general, the death of Thomas and every man in B Company was a small price to pay for the wealth he and his subordinate conspirators would realize for their treachery.

Fate, however, was not so accommodating to the general's plans. When Yoke and his staff rode to safety, Thomas spent a few minutes getting into character. Then, instead of leading B Company up the ridge, he ordered Captain Hayden to hold back while he reconnoitered the ridge alone. The general had assured him there would be only a handful of Rebs up there, and said they were coming to surrender to the Union soldiers, not to fight them. Who knows, he thought, perhaps he would get a commendation for capturing the Rebs by himself.

He took the American flag from one of Hayden's men and rode up the ridge on the general's horse, cresting the hill as the sun broke over a thick canopy of oaks. Instead of finding a handful of Johnnies peacefully waiting to surrender as the general had promised, however, he was immediately swarmed by dozens of Confederate riders, and every damn one of the butternuts immediately opened fire on him.

He whirled Cornwall around and raced for the safety of a line of trees, but a half dozen Reb bullets found their marks, slamming into his legs, abdomen and back. At the base of the ridge Captain Hayden and his men saw the riders catch up to Thomas. Their new colonel was clutching one hand over his stomach wound while holding the flag out away from his body with his other hand. Cornwall sensed that something was wrong. He broke his gallop, stopped, and reared back on his hind legs. For a moment, Thomas and Cornwall and the waving flag were suspended in mid-air, appearing as dark silhouettes against the rising sun. Then Thomas toppled out of his saddle into the folds of the flag and fell to the ground. Cornwall had also been hit by rebel fire. His front legs buckled, and he collapsed beside his new master.

Captain Hayden and his men froze for a moment as they watched the astonishing tableau play out on the ridge above them. Then they raced up the brushy hill and used their new Spencer repeating rifles to drive the Rebs back down into the valley. They carried Thomas to an ambulance wagon and transported him to Mt. Pleasant hospital, fifteen miles away in Washington.

The newspapers trumpeted B Company's victory and lavished praise on the newly minted hero Colonel Scoundrel, but General Yoke did not join in the celebration. To protect himself from being exposed and tried for treason, Yoke arranged for former private Scandréll to be mustered out of the Army at the rank of full colonel, with a handsome pension and medical benefits for life.

At first Thomas had no inkling that he had been an unwitting pawn in Yoke's crimes. But the more he learned, the more people he talked to, the more he became convinced of the depth of the general's treachery. He wanted to report the crime, but Walt Whitman counseled against going to the War Department or the newspapers. In all likelihood, the poet argued, you will end up being charged as a co-conspirator and spend the rest of your life in prison, while Yoke would be protected by the politicians he had been bribing for years. Fade into the background, Whitman advised. Live your life and put this behind you.

And so, he wandered for seven years, drifting from his family home in Ohio to Cuernavaca, where he did a stint with the Mexican Army before moving on to the rowdy gambling halls of St. Louis. He sharpened his gunfighting skills on the wide-open streets of Abilene and lingered at Fort Dodge in Kansas before signing on as a riverboat dealer along the Mississippi. Then he boarded a Mississippi paddle wheeler to New Orleans, where a fiery affair with a stunning Creole beauty led to the bayou duel that nearly ended his life.

Wherever he traveled, his sense of shame for the role he played at Pebble Creek Ridge gnawed at his gut. His remorse multiplied on the one-year anniversary of the battle when a Midwest brewing company commissioned a noted artist to produce a 4' x 8' painting that dramatized the moment the valiant Colonel Scoundrel reared back on his mighty steed before charging headlong into the Rebel horde. The painting was accurate in one regard, Thomas mused when he first saw it: like him, it was a magnificent fraud. A year later a business syndicate got permission to sell reproductions of the painting, and whiskey drummers and beer companies hung the brightly colored heroic scene above back bars in saloons, restaurants, whorehouses, and faro parlors from Maine to Oregon. He did not have to revisit that part of his past in dreams; it slapped him in the face every time he pushed through a set of saloon doors.

No, there was nothing about fame and adulation that Thomas cared to dream about. That's why oatmeal made sense: his job as a cook was the one thing in life he looked back on with pride.

The dream was no different tonight, at least until the moment when O'Hanlon normally congratulated him on his culinary skills. This time, instead of delivering an affectionate slap on the back, the towering sergeant pulled the striker rope on a solid brass ship's bell eight times, and then stepped back.

Thomas sat bolt upright in the pitch-black boat. Eight bells. 4:00 AM. He fumbled to find his clothes in the darkness and shivered as he pulled his still-wet shirt and trousers on. Then he slipped into his boots and put the pea coat back on. He would find a way to have it sent back to the ship later.

The sun wouldn't be up for two more hours, but he knew the crew would be stirring soon. He had to find a knife to cut away the lines holding the dingy on deck, and somehow muscle it over the railing and into the sea. As he readied himself to climb out of the boat, he found himself murmuring Psalm 89:9, his mother's favorite prayer. *"You rule over the surging sea…"* it began, *"when its waves mount up, you still them."* If last night's storm was still roiling the waters of San Francisco Bay, he was going to need every bit of help he could find to get the dinghy overboard and make it to land.

He knelt on a storage box, reached up, and carefully raised a corner of the tarp covering the pinnace. Then he eased his head and shoulders out from under the canvas and looked around the darkened ship.

Something was wrong. The rain had stopped, and thankfully there was no wind. That was all well and good. But then he felt a vibration rising from deep inside the ship, and he saw boiler steam billowing in thick clouds from its two giant funnels. The side of the ship he had climbed onto last night was oriented due east towards San Francisco, but he could not see any of the lights that should be burning in the city, even at this hour. There was nothing on the horizon, only darkness. Then the vibration was joined by a deep, rhythmic thrumming. Thomas's heart sank; that was the sound of a steam engine fully engaging. The warship was moving.

He collapsed back onto the pile of blankets on the floor of the pinnace. He had no idea how long they had been underway; they could be 500 yards from shore, or five miles. It didn't really matter; his plan to steal a dinghy and row to shore was done for. He did not have the strength to fight the unpredictable current in the bay again.

Thomas pulled off his wet clothing and re-wrapped himself in a blanket and peacoat. A moment ago he had been a temporary if unwelcome guest. Now he was a stowaway on a foreign warship that was picking up speed and moving out into the open ocean. Worst of all, he had no idea where the *König Wilhelm* was headed.

~ SIX ~

espair was a foreign emotion to Thomas. His French-born father had lived by a devil-may-care attitude that suited his shady business dealings and carousing, while his Irish mother faced life's struggles with a Catholic fatalism that imagined the worst possible outcomes in even the sunniest situations.

His parents' personalities blended in him in the form of frequent bouts of melancholy, which he dealt with by diving headlong into adventure of any kind, from high stakes gambling to short-lived romantic encounters. But the sense of hopelessness and depression that was enveloping him now as he huddled for warmth in the dark pinnace was something he had never experienced, and he knew he had to shake it off before it overwhelmed him and prevented him from doing whatever it took to get out of this mess.

He leaned back against the side of the boat and concentrated on what he must do right now. For starters, he needed to relieve himself. Then he would need food, more water, and most of all, he had to find out where the hell the *König Wilhelm's* next goodwill tour port of call would be. Vladivostok, Russia, was one possibility. The main Russian naval base for the Pacific had just been moved there. Following the end of the Franco-Prussian War and the unification of the German states into a single political entity a year earlier, it made sense that Germany would want to cement better ties with Alexander II.

Thomas struggled to do the calculations in his head. Would it take two weeks to reach the Russian coast? Three? How could he survive during a voyage of that length? And even if he did, how would he get off the ship, and how would he explain his status to Russian customs officials when he presented himself with no papers, no luggage, and no money?

Another possibility was that the König Wilhelm was heading south, along the coasts of Mexico and South America, past Tierra del Fuego, and around Cape Horn and into the Atlantic Ocean for the journey back to Europe. Thomas had heard stories about the ferocious weather around the Cape. But the seasons were reversed below the equator, and South America would be in the middle of the summer season. A southerly voyage might not be so bad.

What if they were headed to Japan, or even China? He slammed his fist against the side of the boat in frustration and willed himself to stop speculating. He had to face the fact that there were an endless number of possible destinations for the German warship. He had to act. Now.

It was approaching 4:30 AM, and the early watch would soon be waking the ship's 700 sailors and 36 officers to have breakfast and set about their morning duties. For the second time in 30 minutes, Thomas put on his damp clothing. Then he popped his head out from under the canvas tarp and peered up and down the length of the deck. The air was still, and the glow from the mast lamps cast pale yellow shadows of the funnels across the teak decking. But no sailors were in sight.

He clambered out of the pinnace and went swiftly over to the railing to relieve himself into the ocean. Then, as he turned to climb back into the small boat, he caught the unmistakable aroma of fresh-baked bread, followed by voices and the sound of footsteps coming up the stairs from below decks. He ducked behind a stack of wooden crates and waited. A moment later two forms appeared out of the darkness and walked right past him. Each of the young sailors was carrying a baking rack loaded with several dozen loaves of bread. They set the racks down on a long bench close by the main mast, and then hurried back down the stairs to fetch more bread to cool in the morning air.

As soon as the bakers disappeared, Thomas dashed over to the racks and scooped up four loaves. Then he returned to the pinnace, shoved the bread under the tarp, and climbed back in.

The smell of warm bread filled the boat and cheered his spirits. He tore right in, marveling at the flavor and the quality of the ingredients the ship's bakers used. By the time he finished a full loaf, the boat had come to life around him. Sailors were chattering as they passed the pinnace on the way to their duty stations, and he heard crates being moved and the clanging of metal against the masts. It sounded as if they might be getting ready to unfurl some of the ship's 28,000 square feet of sail to supplement the power from the steam engine.

Then, two sailors came to a halt next to the pinnace and began talking in animated voices. Thomas's father had taught him French, and he knew a bit of Latin, but he could only make out a few of the German words. He sorted out a few of the more colorful terms for women's anatomy including *die muschi* and *der arsch* but heard no mention of any geographical location that might hint at the ship's destination. A moment later one of the sailor's laughed at a joke his friend had made, and they moved on.

Thomas settled back in the boat and willed himself to come up with a plan. First, he knew he could not abide remaining in the dark boat for more than one more day. He was going to have to find a hold or storage room where he could hide until late night, when he would stealthily roam the boat in search of food and information about their destination. Once he knew where they were going, he could formulate a real plan— but not until then. He made a pillow with two of the wool peacoats, and as the great warship steamed steadily somewhere, the gentle dipping and rising of the 368-foot ironclad plowing through the waves helped him to fall asleep.

Dappled sunlight filtered through the sail cloth canvas covering the pinnace at mid-day, and he woke with a hopeful attitude. There was enough light to go through both storage benches again, where he found a German- Bible and first aid supplies, including a bottle of opium-laced laudanum, surgical scissors, and scalpels. Then he noticed there was a third storage compartment built into the bow of the little boat. Inside were two bottles wrapped in burlap, a ceramic chamber pot with a lid and a box of candles and matches. One of the bottles contained pear brandy, the other was filled with korn, a grain spirit fermented from a mash of wheat, rye, buckwheat, barley, or oats that he had been introduced to by a German born cook in the 109th. He uncorked the brandy, tore off a piece of bread, and celebrated his good fortune. A few minutes later he was fast asleep.

He woke to the sound of the ship's bell ringing the start of the midnight to 4 AM middle watch. He stretched to loosen his aching muscles and was pleased to note that his clothing was finally dry. He slipped on his boots, buttoned his coat, and poked his head out from under the tarp. The sails were furled, and the ship's twin funnels were exhaling a steady stream of cotton-ball clouds that glowed blue and silver under the light of the full moon before wisping away into the night. No one was on deck, and he took a moment to marvel at the stars glittering in the velvet dome of the sky. That's when he spotted the planet Mars almost directly over the main mast. The star Vega was above the horizon and to his left, and he could make out the distinct glow of Jupiter just off the starboard beam. Also clearly visible were January's brightest constellations, Orion, Canis Major and Minor, and Gemini.

Thomas had studied the heavens since he was a child on the farm in Ohio. Given the warship's position relative to Mars, Vega, and Jupiter, there was no doubt about their heading: the *König Wilhelm* was steaming to the southwest. That eliminated Russia as a possible destination, and Japan and China, as well. The most likely possibility now would be Australia, which was over 7,000 miles and three weeks from San Francisco Bay.

He ducked back into the pinnace and packed a cotton bag with bread, brandy and korn, and the candles and matches. Then he put the laudanum and surgical scissors in his coat pocket, climbed down out of the boat and crouched behind a water barrel. Despite his bleak circumstance, he was feeling better about his prospects. He would find a way to survive the voyage and get past the Australian authorities. It was an English-speaking nation, after all, and if he could make his way to a military base there would certainly be officers who knew the history of the American Civil War who would be familiar with his name and story. He was sure they would help him find a way to return to America. The honor of the worldwide fraternity of professional military men would demand no less.

Walt Whitman had told him that his fame—undeserved and unwanted as it might have been—would open doors for him for the rest of his life. As he swung the bag over his shoulder and stole quietly along the rail towards the bow of the ship to find an entrance to the front hold, he couldn't help but smile at the irony.

~ SEVEN ~

At Sea

The pinnace was lashed to a platform between the aft and main masts in front of the command bridge, directly across from one of the warship's two deckhouses. A brass lantern cast a pale glow through the grimy deckhouse windows and Thomas could see that the sailor on watch was asleep in his chair. That was a hanging offense in wartime and would merit at least a good lashing and confinement in the brig in peacetime if the fellow was caught.

He kept to the rail as he passed the steam funnels. The amidship deckhouse sat to the left of the forward funnel and he could see that the sailor on watch was awake and scanning the horizon with a brass telescope. He ducked low and scrambled past the deckhouse to the foremast, where he crouched down and listened for footsteps or voices, but the only sounds in the still night air were the rumble of the steam engine, the creaking of rigging swaying in the soft breeze, and the splash of waves against the ship's hull as it cut across a north-south current.

Ten feet beyond the mast were stairs leading down to the foredeck. He took them in two strides, taking care to avoid the coils of rope and metal winching gear that covered much of the deck. His objective lay just ahead of the drum-shaped capstan, a three-foot square hatch cover over the entrance to the forward hold. He remembered from the tour of the ship a week ago that this hold was used to store spare parts for the engine, along with ropes, cables, and rigging to replace any that might be lost or damaged in foul weather. Odds were that the hold would remain closed for the duration of the voyage, and he could hide in safety.

He knelt beside the hatch and was pleased to find how easily it raised on its well-oiled hinges. It was pitch black below, but he could not risk lighting a candle in the open where it might be seen from the deckhouse. He pulled a candle and the matches from his bag and slipped them in his pocket before slinging the bag over his shoulder and stepping carefully onto the first metal rung. He took two more steps, turned, and pulled the hatch back down over his head. As dark as the interior of the pinnace had been this was an even deeper blackness. The air was damp and musty, and the sound of the bow slicing through the waves was so loud he could have been tied to a bowsprit with his face only inches from the water.

He lit a candle, climbed down into the hold, and set his bag on the floor before wedging a second candle behind a crossbar so that it was held in place against the hull. The flickering light cast shadows around the hold, where four oil lanterns dangled on a twisted metal cable just above his head. He took one down, removed the chimney, and lit the wick. When he lit a second lantern, the hold was illuminated as brightly as a parlor in a Nob Hill mansion. He was about to extinguish one of the lanterns to conserve fuel when he saw a stack of five-gallon cans secured against the bulkhead. That was enough oil to light the hold for months.

To celebrate this tiny bit of good fortune Thomas pulled the bottle of korn from his bag, took a deep drink, and fired up the other lanterns so he could explore his new home. Stacked among the wooden crates of machine parts and rigging lines were two rolled up mattresses, a pile of wool blankets, a box of books, and a collection of cast iron cooking pots with lids. He wouldn't be doing any cooking, but the larger Dutch ovens would do fine as chamber pots. He took another drink of the korn and wondered what his mother would think of that sacrilege. She was famous for the stews, roasts, bread, and cakes she produced in her Dutch ovens, but what he was going to fill them with would not be suitable for anyone's table.

Ah, he thought as the liquor began to warm his insides, but she would be the first to forgive me.

He slept until midday, and then pried open the box of books and rummaged through for any that might be in English or French. He was pleased to find an English version of the British naturalist Alfred Russel Wallace's two volume work, *The Malay Archipelago: The Land of the Orang-utan and the Bird of Paradise* wrapped tightly in an oilcloth wrapper. It had been on his reading list since its publication three years earlier, but he had never found the time to sit down with it. He tore a loaf of bread in half and set it on a box beside a lamp. Then he made himself comfortable on a folded blanket and opened Wallace's book. Time, it seemed, was no longer an issue.

He fell into a routine over the next three days as the *König Wilhelm* steamed towards its next destination. He woke when the ship's bell signaled the 4 AM watch and waited a half hour before climbing out of the hold. Then he made his way up to the main deck and hid until the bakers appeared with their racks of fresh warm bread. On the second morning they also set out a tray of sweet rolls to cool in the damp predawn air, which brought some much-needed variety to his diet.

With his food secured, he returned to the hold, ate breakfast, and slept into the late afternoon. Then, to the sounds of the deep Pacific flowing past his windowless stateroom, he settled in with Wallace's book, delving deep into the naturalist's remarkable account of his years studying the natural history, geography, and peoples scattered across the Malay Archipelago.

On his fourth morning at sea, the bakers did not appear on deck at the usual time. He waited for ten minutes, then turned to steal back to the forward hold before the crew's workday began.

He had only taken a few steps when four shapes emerged out of the darkness. Rough hands grabbed his arms from behind and a sailor wearing a cap with a leather visor held a lantern up to his face. He struggled to free himself, but his captors held him in an iron grip that only got stronger the more he fought. Then a massive fist smashed into his back, driving him down to his knees.

"*Sprich, wer bist du?*" demanded the man holding the lantern. "*Was tun Sie hier?*"

Thomas tried to catch his breath, but before he could say anything a boot slammed into his back, and he was pushed flat onto the deck.

"*Sprich!*" repeated the man. "*Jetzt!*"

Thomas pulled himself to his knees. All he could see in the darkness was a forest of legs. "I am an American," he finally said. "I don't speak German."

"*Amerikanisch? Was zur Hölle?*" a voice said.

Another man stepped forward and slapped Thomas hard across the face with the back of his hand. He wiped blood from the corner of his mouth and said, "Thanks for that, you bastard, but I still don't speak your gutter tongue."

"Ah, but now you have had your first lesson," said the man holding the lantern in heavily accented English. "As for Kurd, who you have just insulted, I will forgive you this time because he actually is a bastard, born the illegitimate son of some minor nobleman in Prussia. Even so, I suggest you do not disparage his lineage again. Being the son of the town whore left him with a wicked temper."

The man chuckled at his own joke and then said, "*Helmuth, Karl, steh ihn auf.*"

Two men broke through the knot of sailors surrounding Thomas and helped him to stand. Then the man with the lantern nodded to another sailor, who approached with a rope. The sailors holding his arms pulled him back and lashed him to the side of a wooden crate.

The man giving orders said, "You are a stowaway on an Imperial Warship in international waters. And you are a thief. Did you think we would not notice our bread and sweet rolls disappearing these past few mornings? *Der Kapitän* will have many questions for you, my friend. In your favor, he is a man who enjoys a good yarn. I hope your story will amuse him….in the German navy it is customary to throw stowaways to the sharks." Then he started to walk away.

"One question, please," said Thomas.

His captor turned and raised his eyebrows.

"Where are we going?"

The man shook his head and left without answering. But even in the darkness Thomas could tell that he was smiling.

The sun broke the horizon astern of the ship a few minutes later. They were headed west, Thomas thought. The sunlight felt good after spending five days in darkness, even in his present circumstance. *König Wilhelm* came to life around him as sailors appeared from below to scrub decks, work with lines and gear, and prepare to unfurl the sails to supplement the single propeller steam engine. The sailors were young, many of them in their teens, but when they passed Thomas tied to the crate, they paid him no more attention than they would to a monkey in a zoo. Rules of conduct aboard a ship of war were rigid and unbending and corporal punishment for even the smallest infractions was swift and harsh, even for an American war hero. His time would come, he was certain of that.

Three piercing whistles interrupted his reflection, and sailors answered the call by swarming around the masts. He had never seen sails raised on a three-mast giant like the *Wilhelm*. At an officer's command dozens of sailors leapt into action at each mast, and for the next 20 minutes Thomas watched the organized chaos of lines being turned and hoisted, men mounting the rigging and scrambling from station to station, and the great sails unfurling to catch the wind.

"Impressive, isn't it?"

Thomas turned his head. It was the man who had been holding the lantern. He wore the light wool coat and cap of an officer, and his face was decorated with a heavy mustache. Thomas nodded his head.

"I am First Officer Hans Stoch. Kapitän Schmidt sends his compliments, Colonel. He sent his aide out this morning to look you over and he recognized you as part of the delegation that visited the ship last week."

"Yes, I was here," replied Thomas, "although it was a much warmer welcome than this one."

Stoch smiled. "You weren't committing a crime last time, Colonel."

Thomas could only shake his head. The First Officer was right. In fact, at this point, his situation had all the makings of an international incident. He could imagine the headline his editor at the *Chronicle* would write:

Hero of Pebble Creek Ridge Tried as Stowaway on German Warship: Colonel T.E. Scoundrel Flogged & Imprisoned. Ambassador Demands Immediate Release.

"We are on a long voyage, and we have many days of steaming ahead," Stoch went on. "We do have a brig, of course, and you could be confined there for the duration, but the Kapitän has a different proposal, if you are willing."

"I'm listening."

"If you will give us your word as a military officer that you will follow our instructions and not attempt any more mischief, we will untie you. You will be treated decently, and you will be free to move around the ship. Do you agree?"

"Yes."

Stoch summoned a seaman to undo the ropes holding Thomas to the crate. He rubbed his wrists to get the blood flowing and thanked the First Officer.

"This sailor will take you below to clean up and get fresh clothing," said Stoch. "And he will get you some food. After four days of eating only bread you are probably ready for something different."

"I am, thank you."

"After you eat, you will be taken to a duty officer who will assign you a berth and line out your duties. I hope you appreciate that you must earn your keep. This is a ship of war after all, not a pleasure cruise."

Having something to do to occupy his mind sounded just right to Thomas. "Of course," he answered.

"The Kapitän requests that you join him and the officers for dinner this evening. He may choose to share our destination with you at that time."

"I know that we are headed west by southwest," replied Thomas, "So I have a general idea." His remark was half-truth and half bravado, but it was time for him to behave like a senior army officer, not a prisoner.

To his surprise Stoch seemed pleased both by his observation and his confident attitude. "Perhaps you should have considered a career in the American navy," he said. Then he left Thomas in the sailor's custody and returned to his duties.

An hour later Thomas had bathed, changed into clean clothing, and gobbled down two bowls of excellent beef stew. His escort led him to a canvas-covered area on the main deck that served as the duty officer's open-air office.

"Can you work rigging lines?" the officer asked from behind a cluttered table.

Thomas shook his head.

"Do you know anything about steam engines?"

Again, Thomas shook his head.

The officer continued down a list of possible duties, from assisting with the ship's carpenter to helping clean and maintain the ship's guns. Thomas was almost embarrassed at his own lack of practical skills.

When the officer had exhausted his list of higher order duties he lit a cigarette, took several puffs, and then asked, "Can you perhaps paint?"

Thomas replied with a sheepish grin. He could paint.

The officer barked a command and two sailors appeared with a bucket of wire brushes and iron scrapers.

"First you scrape, Colonel. Then you paint. Not exactly the kind of command duty you are used to, but it is honest work." He shared a bemused smile with the sailors before he stood and turned to leave.

"Viel Glück, Herr Oberst," he chuckled as he walked away.

Thomas sighed and pulled a wire brush from the bucket. Then he followed the sailors to a rusting metal storage shed located near the stern.

"Viel Glück," he thought to himself as he began to scrape away the flaking paint. He was pretty sure it meant good luck.

<h1 style="text-align:center">~ EIGHT ~</h1>

The captain's mess aboard the *König Wilhelm* was ablaze with the light of oil lamps and crystal chandeliers. The flagship of the German fleet carried a complement of 46 officers, most of whom were taking their seats around polished mahogany tables in a room large enough to hold a dance.

Four portholes along the starboard wall were cranked open to bring in cool air and help exhaust cigar and cigarette fumes, and ornate walnut buffets were laden with silver tureens, displays of fresh fruit, and a variety of wines and liquors. A dozen aproned stewards were settling officers and guests as Thomas was directed to a seat next to First Officer Stoch. Captain Schmidt's chair at the head of the center table was still empty.

The captain's personal steward had seen to the cleaning and pressing of the dinner clothing Thomas was wearing the night he rushed out of Kwan's restaurant, stole a dinghy, and rowed out into the storm-churned San Francisco Bay. The steward also brought him a shaving kit and saw that his shoes were cleaned and polished.

As another steward snapped a crisp linen napkin onto his lap, Thomas nodded to Stoch and looked around the room; most of his fellow diners had a drink in hand before their napkins were open. He heard a smattering of French in the buzz of conversation and a little English but for the most part everyone was speaking German.

A wine steward appeared at his elbow with a bottle of red wine and Thomas happily accepted a full glass. He was pleased to see that the German navy used large leaded glass goblets, not the tiny crystal stems preferred by the Americans and French.

Then a voice rang out: *"Deine Aufmerksamkeit!"* The call to attention brought the *Wilhelm's* officers to their feet. Thomas joined them as Captain Schmidt entered the room, took his seat, and motioned for everyone to sit. A moment later conversation resumed, and stewards began ladling soup into bowls of bone china that featured the warship's crest.

The captain was in his 50s, with close-cropped gray hair, a ruddy face, and stocky build. Thomas noted that he smiled easily and used his hands expansively as he talked with the Catholic priest with intense eyes and a carefully trimmed beard seated next to him. An older gentleman—perhaps a diplomat or businessman—sat on the captain's other side, nursing a glass of sherry.

Stoch turned towards him. "You look refreshed, colonel, and I am glad to see they were able to save your clothing. I am anxious to hear your story, but I will have to defer to the Kapitän, who, I suspect, will want to hear the tale in some detail…ah, the soup," he said as a steward ladled clear broth into their bowls.

Stoch saw the look on Thomas's face as he regarded the thin soup. "Do not worry my friend," he laughed," this is simply to cleanse the palate. I promise you will not leave the table hungry—or thirsty."

At those words two bottles of wine, one white and one red, were placed on the table between Stoch and him. He watched as stewards went around the table with two bottles for every two people.

"Do you eat like this every night?" he asked the first officer.

"Oh, would that were true, colonel. There are two officer's messes on the deck below us where we take most of our meals. But it is a tradition that we have a formal dinner on the fourth or fifth night at sea during any voyage that lasts more than ten days." He raised his glass to Thomas and said, "Good on you for being found out when you were, or you would be eating an ordinary seaman's rations for the duration."

Thomas lifted his glass in reply; Sergeant O'Hanlon used to say that in war, acting, and lovemaking, precise timing was the greatest asset a man could possess. The promise of tonight's meal proved the fatherly

Irish mess cook right yet again.

Captain Schmidt noticed their toast and tapped a fork against his wine glass for attention.

"Gentlemen," he began in English in a deep baritone voice as the room fell silent, "we have an unexpected guest of some renown with us this evening. Colonel Thomas Scoundrel, whose name many of you know from his exploits during the American Civil War, apparently joined our company the night we debarked from San Francisco. How he did that, and more importantly why, should prove to be a fascinating story to accompany our coffee and dessert. Now, please enjoy your meal."

The captain raised his glass to his officers, and then to Thomas.

Over the next hour and a half, the stewards pulled a steady stream of food out of a pair of dumbwaiters that were hoisted up from the kitchen two decks below. As each new dish was set before them on the table, First Officer Stoch described it in some detail. First up were small plates of *Kartoffelpuffer*, shallow pan-fried pancakes made from grated potatoes mixed with flour, egg, onion, and seasoning. They were followed by bowls of *Käsespätzle* egg noodles made from wheat flour and egg and topped with cheese and roasted onions. Then the stewards cleared room for large silver platters piled high with tonight's main course. Thomas had never eaten *Rouladen*, but the delicately seasoned variation of the classic dish using veal wrapped with bacon, onions, mustard, and pickles soon upended everything he thought he knew about German cuisine. He enjoyed three helpings with sides of dumplings, mashed potatoes, cooked red cabbage, and red wine gravy before he had to surrender and push his plate aside, much to Officer Stoch's amusement.

The white wine was an aromatic, almost flowery *Schloss Johannisberg Riesling* that came from 700-year-old vineyards planted around a Benedictine monastery. For the Rouladen course, Stoch chose a pinot noir from the Burg Ravensburg winery, which had been producing *Spätburgunder pinots* since 1251. Thomas had only been drinking wine for a few years, but he had learned enough to appreciate that the flavors of cherry and mountain strawberry present in this pinot marked it as an exceptional selection. If he was ever able to return to San Francisco, he would find a case of the remarkable vintage to give to Chef Kwan at the *Rue de Paris*.

The food and wine were so good, and the dinner conversation so lively, that he nearly forgot Captain Schmidt's pronouncement about telling his story during dessert. So when the stewards set coffee, brandy, and a six-layer chocolate and whipped cream cake shot through with cherries before him (*"Schwarzwälder Kirschtorte"* Stoch called it), he was momentarily surprised when his first bite was interrupted by the captain tapping his spoon on the table.

"Officers and guests of the *König Wilhelm*," said the captain, whose cheeks, Thomas noted, had taken on a reddish glow with the wine, "I hope you have enjoyed our traditional mid-voyage feast. My compliments to Hans Lothar and his most excellent kitchen staff." There was a brief round of applause as wine and brandy glasses were raised in salute.

"We are not at war today, thank God, though our memory of the conflict with France that ended one year ago this week is still fresh. Raise your glasses, please, to King Wilhelm, Chancellor Bismarck, and the new Union of Germany. *Ein prost!*"

The officers stood and raised their glasses to the portrait of the king hanging behind the captain. Then they settled in to listen to their captain interrogate the stowaway American colonel.

"Meine offizieres" the captain began, "our mess has been graced this evening with the presence of three distinguished guests." He turned to his right to introduce the older gentleman who had remained quiet for most of the meal. "Herr Wallenstein is the first official representative of the new Union to His Majesty Kamehameha V of the Kingdom of Hawai'i. Weather permitting, we will deliver Herr Wallenstein to the royal palace in Honolulu in seven days."

Thomas's head shot up. Hawai'i! He had not foreseen that exotic place as a possible destination for the *Wilhelm*. What would that mean for him? Would he be welcomed by the local authorities, or slapped into jail until they could sort out his story? His mind went a dozen places in an instant. He knew almost nothing about Hawai'i except that Christian missionaries had been traveling there for a half century. Wasn't it the source of sugar and pineapples? It had been a whaling center, too, until the whale oil used for lamps and soap was replaced by petroleum-based products. Damn, why didn't he know more?

Stoch noticed his discomfort and elbowed Thomas in the ribs. "Don't fear, my friend," he whispered. "The women are beautiful, the weather is perfect, and everyone naps for two hours in the afternoon. The food is shit but there are a few hotels in Honolulu that serve a decent meal."

Captain Schmidt was now introducing his other guest, the priest with the intense expression. "Father Joseph Damien joined us in San Francisco after a trip to the mainland to visit his family. He has been in service to God in Hawai'i since, is it seven years now, Father?"

The priest nodded.

"Father Damien will also debark in Honolulu, where, I understand, he will prepare to travel to the isolated settlement of Kalawao on Moloka'i Island. There, may God and the Saints protect him, he will minister to the needs of the leper colony which is maintained from afar by the Hawaiian authorities."

An audible gasp went up around the room. Lepers. The unclean carriers of a flesh-rotting disease for which there was no cure, very little understanding, and almost no compassion save from the likes of Damien.

Thomas felt his skin crawl, almost as if a rattlesnake had slithered from beneath his seat and wrapped itself around his neck. All around him the officers of the *Wilhelm* clutched their brandy snifters and stared hard at the tabletop. Lepers. No other word in any language evoked such an immediate, visceral reaction.

Father Damien felt the chill run through the room as Captain Schmidt spoke. His own family and friends had responded the same way when he declared his intention to go to Moloka'i. He cleared his throat and said, "Thank you, Captain, for your hospitality.

I understand how difficult it is for healthy young men like your officers to contemplate life among the lepers, but I assure you the situation is not entirely bleak. Only last month a Norwegian scientist named Gerhard Hansen identified and described the bacillus responsible for leprosy. No cure yet, sadly, but there will be. In God's own time there will be."

The room fell silent, and Damien slowly sipped at his brandy. Word of his mission would spread among the crew like wildfire and even though he was not infected, not one of the 700 souls aboard the warship—many of them Catholic—would so much as shake his hand or ask to be confessed. This was the painful reality of the vocation he had chosen to follow.

It was time to change the subject. Captain Schmidt called for the stewards to refill glasses, and then stood to address the room. "We have another guest this evening, a gentleman who materialized out of a winter gale in San Francisco Bay and dropped onto the deck of the *Wilhelm*. The reason for his presence, I confess, is a true mystery." He raised his glass in Thomas's direction. "Gentlemen, meet Colonel Thomas Scoundrel. For those of you who are not familiar with his last name, in Deutsch it is '*Schurke*.'"

A sprinkle of laughter erupted around the table.

"Yes, but in the good colonel's defense, I expect there may be a tale behind the name that is every bit as intriguing as the reason he chose to stowaway on the *Wilhelm*."

Thomas raised his glass to the captain and managed a wan smile.

Schmidt returned to his seat and lit a cigar. "And therefore, my friends," he continued, "the first question I shall put to *Herr* Scoundrel is done out of respect to both his rank and his reputation: how do you prefer to be addressed?"

Thomas understood that he was about to be formally interrogated, and so he stood and faced the captain. A sea of faces turned towards him with expressions ranging from bemusement to wariness. Germany and the United States maintained cordial relations, but, retired or not, he was a senior American military officer who had boarded a foreign warship without permission and stolen from its crew to boot. He had to be careful. Despite his friendly demeanor Captain Schmidt had every right under maritime law to have Thomas hung from the mast. In fact, the wonderful food he had just enjoyed could well have been a condemned man's last meal.

He pushed his chair in, cleared his voice, and rested his hands on the back of the chair. "Let me first thank you Captain, for the invitation to join you and your officers and guests this evening. I would be surprised if any restaurant in Berlin could match the quality of the food we have just enjoyed. In fact, I had the pleasure of dining at the White House with President Grant recently and I assure you his chef would be jealous of what your kitchen staff can prepare on the high seas." He raised his glass in the direction of the serving staff as the captain and his officers applauded.

"As to your query about my surname; I was not christened with the name Scoundrel. My family name is Scandréll, which is French. An error made by a partially deaf clerk resulted in the official Army rolls recording my name as Scoundrel, and as I am sure is true in the military of all nations, once an official document is recorded it is nigh unto impossible to get it changed."

Heads around the room nodded. Language and protocols aside, most of them had experienced the colossal power wielded by imperious clerks and ossified records managers.

First Officer Stoch exhaled a cloud of cigar smoke and in a serious tone, said, "Let us hope that we never receive orders to go to war with Persia, for I fear our scribes would probably write 'Perdition' instead." He paused for effect and added, "…and the German navy follows orders to the letter!"

Those who understood English began to laugh, and when his comment was translated for the German-only speakers, the room erupted in gales of laughter.

The Duty Officer now rose to his feet and lifted his glass towards the head of the table. "The officers and sailors of the *Wilhelm* are prepared to follow you to Persia's shore or Perdition's gate Kapitän Schmidt, no matter what destination the fuzzy-heads scrawl upon our orders."

The captain beamed, and his officers slammed their brandy glasses on the table in approval. Father Damien took the opportunity provided by Stoch's joke to redeem himself in the eyes of Schmidt and his men. "You know," he began solemnly, "the ancients believed that Hades was accessible by water, as Charon demonstrated by rowing the souls of the damned across the Acheron. Legend has it that the river was bottomless, and thus I think it reasonable to conclude that the Wilhem could indeed steam right up to the gates of hell itself. Interesting thought...."

Captain Schmidt cast an icy glance at the priest that Damien was certain was a rebuke. The dining room quieted. Schmidt was famous for his volcanic temper, and every officer at the table had witnessed him transform from amiable to furious at the drop of a hat. Suddenly, to everyone's surprise, Schmidt clapped the Belgian priest on the back and laughed. Then he raised his glass and toasted: "To hell!"

His men raised their glasses in reply and Stoch exclaimed, "And back again, if you please, Kapitän," which set the assembled officers to laughing again.

Thomas had never experienced this level of exuberant camaraderie between officers and a senior commander in his own army. Would the lighthearted atmosphere that filled the room carry over to his circumstance? The contemplative gaze that Captain Schmidt leveled at him suggested he was about to learn whether he would be strung from the *Wilhelm's* yardarm or handed over to Hawaiian authorities to be returned to California and the wrath of Colin P. Stafford.

The tables had been cleared and bottles of brandy and boxes of cigars were distributed. At a signal from the First Officer, the stewards retreated from the mess, leaving only the captain, his officers, Father Damien, and the diplomat to oversee whatever proceeding the captain had in mind to determine Thomas's fate.

Schmidt clipped the tip from a fresh cigar and accepted a light from the Second Officer. Then he leaned forward with his hands clasped on the table. "The floor is yours, Colonel Scoundrel. Why did you flee San Francisco? Why did you row across the bay in the middle of a gale-force storm and why did you hide onboard the *Wilhelm* when you had no idea where we were bound?"

Thomas remained standing. The captain's expression was sober, serious, and impossible to misinterpret—he expected complete honesty from the American stowaway. As brutal as the consequences of delivering such honesty might be, Thomas had no doubt that offering anything less than the truth would most likely find him swinging from a rope above the Wilhelm's aft deck before sunset tomorrow.

He looked around the room to gauge the temper of the officers sipping at their brandy but saw only cool, dispassionate expressions. They were professionals who would support whatever decision their captain made about the American; he had neither friend nor enemy among the group.

Stoch tapped Thomas's foot with his boot. "You must answer the Kapitän now," he said in a stage whisper, which drew quiet laughter from several officers.

Thomas gripped the back of his chair and let his eyes make a final sweep of the room before he nodded to the captain and began to speak.

"I am a newspaper reporter," he began. "I search out and tell important stories, even if doing so puts me in peril of reprisals from the powerful people I sometimes write about."

At the mention of powerful people, the diplomat's head came up and his eyes widened. Perhaps this evening's performance would provide some tidbit of gossip to add to his vast collection of information about people, princes, and government officials that could be useful at some point. Successful diplomacy wasn't just conducted by pinstriped functionaries speaking in vague generalizations. Sometimes more practical leverage was needed to accomplish a nation's ends and he had learned over the years how to transform human frailty, greed, lust, and a host of other sins and scandal into powerful negotiating tools. As he took the measure of the young American colonel, he had no doubt he was about to be immersed in the kind of tawdry stew that made his profession so very enjoyable.

Thomas felt the diplomat's demeanor shift from bored politeness at the usual post-dinner banter to a sudden, acute interest in what he was about to share. He shook off the urge to figure out what that was all about and continued speaking. "Several months ago, I happened upon a story that revolved around one of the richest and most powerful men in America…"

The diplomat could not help but smile. This was his kind of story.

"My research was meticulous, and my sources were above reproach," Thomas was saying. "What I learned was that Colin P. Stafford, probably the richest man in California, is involved in a number of highly questionable, if not outright illegal, activities."

He went on to describe the breadth and depth of Stafford's empire, how he had purchased the loyalty of judges and politicians, and the lives and businesses he had destroyed in his rise to power. When he finished describing the article, he told the captain and his officers and guests about the events the day he fled the city and rowed out to the *Wilhelm*. From the dinner at Kwan's to the chase to his hotel, down to the docks and out into the stormy bay, he detailed every step he took and exactly why he made the choices he did along the way.

"I had no intention of staying more than one night here on the *Wilhelm*," Thomas said. "I was going to take a dinghy and row back to shore before dawn. And, yes," he added, "I would have seen that the dinghy was returned to you the same day." He looked at Captain Schmidt: "I admit that I came aboard without permission and that I stole food and provisions. I apologize for that, and I give you my word I will make whatever restitution you may feel to be in order." He waited a moment, and then sat down.

Stoch turned to him and whispered, "That was a fine tale, colonel… let us see what the Kapitän makes of it."

Captain Schmidt had smoked his cigar down to a nub while

Thomas told his story. He poured another brandy and sat back in his chair with his chin in his hand, and when he began to speak, it was with a professorial tone, almost as if he was evaluating a graduate student's term paper.

"So, you have done harm to a powerful man, someone like a *prinz* in my homeland. You have threatened his kingdom, dirtied his reputation, and embarrassed him, as well. Since this man owns the law—is the law, to be more precise—he is free to mete out whatever punishment he feels is suitable."

Thomas nodded.

"Had we found you and returned you to the authorities in the city the night you came aboard you would probably have ended up at the bottom of the bay with a weight around your neck. Is that your contention?"

"It is."

"And now that we are transiting international waters on our way to the Kingdom of Hawai'i, we are outside the jurisdiction of California laws and courts but unfortunately, we are not out of the jurisdiction of the international laws and treaties to which Germany is a signatory. Is that not correct Herr Wallenstein?"

The diplomat canted his head to the side and raised his eyebrows as if he was carefully considering a matter of grave consequence. Inside, though, he was grinning; he had met the great Colin Stafford, and he could not wait to obtain a copy of Thomas's article to add to his collection of blackmail instruments.

"That law, Colonel Scoundrel, compels me to hand you over to the Hawaiian government at Honolulu, who will then contact San Francisco and ask for instructions. There is no telegraph between the mainland and the islands, of course, and so it could be several months before your fate is announced, though, if what you say about Stafford is true, there can be little doubt as to what is waiting for you."

Thomas could not dispute a single point the captain was making. Schmidt was a command officer, bound both to the law and his duty.

"You bested the fates by surviving your excursion across the bay to the *Wilhelm*," added the captain. "Perhaps they will look upon you with favor once again. In the meantime, you will resume your labors at the direction of the duty officer. We should arrive in Honolulu in seven days at which time we shall resolve this matter so far as the German navy is concerned. Thank you for being frank."

The captain stood and his officers rose, saluted, and then waited for him to leave the room before they began filing out to their cabins and stations.

Stoch grabbed a bottle of brandy and two glasses. "Join me on the foredeck," he said to Thomas. "There is thinking drinking to be done."

~ NINE ~

Off Honolulu, February 1872

At twelve noon precisely, Captain Schmidt stood on the foredeck in front of a half dozen officers and a score of sailors. The *Wilhelm* was anchored 300 yards outside Honolulu Harbor, which, despite all the recent dredging and rock wall work, was still little more than a small, reefed basin created by the natural flow of freshwater from the streams of Nuʻuanu Valley.

He served his apprenticeship 30 years earlier aboard a three-masted schooner when the entrance to the harbor was narrow and lined on either side with reefs. The fact that the channel into the harbor had a northeasterly alignment and the Tradewinds blew from the northeast made Honolulu Harbor difficult to enter prior to the introduction of steam power ships that could easily slice across the wind and the current.

And now we can go anywhere mused the captain as he considered his decision about the American colonel for the third time this morning. The seas had been charted, the deserts had been traversed, even the deepest jungles of Africa and southeast Asia were being mapped. Progress, to be sure, he thought. But at a price. Everything was getting more complicated, and today's proceeding was proof of that. A situation that should have called for nothing more than a direct application of maritime law as it related to stowaways had become a diplomatic and legal minefield.

If the decision he had reached about Colonel Scoundrel was adjudged by a board of inquiry to have been wrong, he could lose his command and his pension. And if it was correct, the colonel could lose his life. Hobson's choice, he thought as he adjusted his cap to shield his eyes from the tropical sun. He began to speak as the ship rolled over a swell and the German flag snapped brightly in the breeze across the bow.

"Last night we transited the channel between Hawai'i and Mau'i and this morning we anchored at this temporary mooring to conclude some important business. I know that you are anxious to enjoy your shore leave, and I will make this proceeding as brief as possible."

He motioned to First Officer Stoch, who nudged Thomas and pointed towards the captain. Thomas walked up the stairs and stood at attention in front of Schmidt, who was standing between Father Damien and the diplomat. The fact that he wasn't shackled and his hands hadn't been bound meant he wasn't going to be hung—he hoped. But neither Stoch nor any of the sailors he had befriended in the past week had given him any indication that they knew what the captain had in store for him. He tried to focus on the sharp, cloud- shrouded mountains that rose out of the sea behind and around the town of Honolulu.

"Colonel Thomas Scoundrel," the captain said, "your presence on this vessel raises a host of legal and diplomatic issues that only get thornier the more I consider them. If you were an ordinary citizen, I would hand you over to the Honolulu constabulary and let them sort it out with the United States Legation. However, you are a senior command officer in the United States military and thus could be required to stand trial before a German Maritime Court where, if found guilty, you could face years in prison, or even execution."

The captain let those words sink in. Whatever was about to happen, Thomas was certain it was not going to be pleasant.

"An already complicated situation is compounded many times over by the fact that you are not only a stowaway on His Majesty's flagship, but you may also be a fugitive from justice in the American state of California. I found your story of the after-effects of the article you wrote about Mr. Stafford to be both compelling and truthful but that does not lessen the probability that both Mr. Stafford and the legal authorities both wish to," he paused and cleared his throat, "ahem, bring you into their custody."

The captain shifted his stance and clasped his hands behind his back. The wind was picking up and the sound of breakers crashing on the shore and the cries of seagulls wheeling in the sky above the ship forced him to raise his voice.

"There are two legal paths I could follow," said the captain. "Under maritime law I could take you back to Germany to await trial as a stowaway on a foreign warship. That course of action is so fraught with layers of possible diplomatic chaos that I shudder to think of following through with it. A famous American war hero and all—the newspapers would have a field day with the story and Herr Wallenstein would be buried under diplomatic cables from your ambassador for months." He looked over to the diplomat, who nodded somberly in agreement. Arresting Scoundrel would not benefit his career in any way, that much was certain.

"Still," the captain went on, "I do have that option under the law and would be completely justified in clapping you in irons today and being done with it."

Thomas searched Stoch's face for some clue as to where the captain was headed, but the First Officer's face was a stone wall.

"The alternative is to have you taken ashore at Honolulu and remanded to the local authorities. The Kingdom of Hawai'i would take on the responsibility of communication with American authorities and, once again, my part would be done." He shook his head, and a half smile crossed his face.

"Unfortunately, if I hand you over here, I will also have to file a formal report that Herr Wallenstein would then have to send on to Germany. The matter would take many months to resolve on both the American and the German ends and your State Department and our Foreign Ministry would have no end of questions and concerns. I prefer sailoring over negotiating, Colonel—meaning no disrespect of course, Herr Wallenstein."

Why did you have to row out to my ship the captain thought with a sigh before he offered his third possible solution.

"There may be another way out of our mutual quandary, Colonel," he finally said. "It was presented to me at breakfast this morning by Father Damien."

The priest nodded to Thomas, but his facial expression volunteered nothing. What could a priest know about such matters, Thomas wondered. Good lord, he wasn't going to suggest that he be set ashore at the leper colony on Moloka'i?

Schmidt saw the cloud cross Thomas' face. It was time to get this over with.

"It is my decision that you will not be transported to Berlin to stand trial, Colonel. Nor will you be handed over to the Hawaiian government. That being the case and mindful that my next action must resolve this matter to the complete satisfaction of the Imperial Navy, I have decided...." he paused a moment..."to throw you back to the sea from whence you came—not unlike what the great fish did when he vomited forth Jonah after three days and nights in his belly."

Thomas was bewildered. He was to be 'vomited forth?'

Captain Schmidt raised his hand and four of his tallest, strongest seamen came up alongside Thomas. They lifted him by his arms, carried him to the railing and tossed him over the side into the gray, foam-flecked sea.

Before dismissing the crew Schmidt turned to Wallenstein.

"You disapprove?" he asked.

The diplomat struggled to maintain his professional composure. Then he said, "Did it occur to anyone to ask the colonel if he could swim?"

The captain walked to the railing and looked over the side of the ship.

"*Gott im Himmel* let us hope so, my friend," he said softly to himself. "There is nothing more I can do for you."

~ TEN ~

Near Honolulu Harbor

Thomas hit the water feet first and immediately began kicking to propel himself upwards. When his head broke the surface five feet from the starboard bow of the *Wilhelm*, he began to tread water and look around. Twenty feet above him the captain was leaning over the railing. Schmidt made brief eye contact and then turned and walked away.

He had been dumped overboard like a sack of garbage, but this was not the time to try to figure out why. When the *Wilhelm's* engines fired up and its seven-foot propeller began to churn it would suck him in and chop him into shark bait. He turned in the water and looked towards land, where he could make out a thicket of schooner masts and the tops of several buildings, including a church spire. Craggy mountain peaks dominated the horizon, running north to south on the eastern side of Honolulu. The *Wilhelm's* quartermaster, who was something of an amateur geologist and naturalist, had told Thomas that Oahu's Ko'olau Range wasn't really a mountain range in the usual sense because it had originally formed as a single volcanic mountain. What we see today is just the western half of the original volcano that remained after the eastern half tumbled into the oceans millions of years ago, he said. They form Oahu's windward coast, rising high behind the leeward- facing town of Honolulu. If he swam towards the Ko'olau, Thomas knew, it would be impossible for him to stray off course.

Then, a voice called out. "Colonel…Thomas…up here."

He looked up to see Stoch, who was resting a large pouch on the railing where the captain had stood a moment before.

"Catch," shouted Stoch as he tossed down the bag. Thomas swam a few feet and grabbed the pouch by its strap. It was thick, yellow-brown and appeared to be made from waterproof material.

"Seal skin," yelled Stoch. "There is a fresh set of clothing, a pair of boots and shaving gear inside. And the men took up a collection and raised $100 American to help you get started in Honolulu."

Thomas pulled the strap over his shoulder and touched his hand to his forehead in salute. Considering Captain Schmidt's limited options for dealing with his stowaway, tossing the problem over the side was probably the best solution to the German naval officer's dilemma. If he survived the swim to shore the captain could simply shrug his shoulders and tell the authorities that no one should have been surprised that his stowaway chose to risk his life in the open water rather than face possible imprisonment or death. And if the sharks got him before he reached land, so much the better; the sea would have rendered her own justice, and there would be no need for further investigation. Thomas had to admit that it was quite a neat solution.

Stoch said there were boots inside the bag, so he pulled one leg at a time to the surface, slipped off the pair he was wearing and watched as they slowly drifted to the bottom. Then he leaned forward in the water and began to swim towards the harbor. The wind was soft, and the warm, gentle ocean swells were drifting in the direction he was going. With luck he would make land in under an hour.

"One last thing, colonel," Stoch shouted. "Keep to your right as you get to the harbor. The first buildings you will see will be on a small sand islet on your left. Avoid the place. It's called Quarantine Island, built with debris that piled up when they dredged the harbor. It's used to isolate ships that carry contagious diseases. If you go ashore there, they will keep you in isolation for a month. *Viel Glück!* "

Thomas raised his right hand out of the water and waved behind his head. *Viel Glück*—again. After a week working and sharing meals with the German crew, he knew it really did mean 'good luck.'

The morning sun was warm for February, at least compared to what he was used to in San Francisco. It also felt more intense than he had ever experienced, no doubt because the Hawaiian Islands were closer to the equator and the angle of the sun was correspondingly steeper. The air was perfumed with the musty aroma of seaweed and the scent of massed plants and trees on the island rising out of the sea in front of him, and he felt strangely invigorated despite his circumstance. He wasn't worried about having to swim nearly a mile to land; the hard physical labor he had been doing onboard the *Wilhelm* had helped to prepare him for this exertion.

Each time an incoming swell raised him up he could make out more details along the coastline. A half dozen schooners sat at anchor in the harbor, with several more lined up along a row of wharves built parallel to the land. Two piers jutted out into the water near a floating lighthouse and a buoy, and he could see a gang of stevedores offloading crates from one of the parked schooners. The way the men carried the boxes reminded him of Henri Lavelle's employees, who slung 132-pound burlap bags filled with South American coffee beans over their shoulders and carried them from the ship's hold to Lavelle's dockside warehouse in New Orleans.

A twinge coursed through his leg at the thought of Lavelle. The aristocratic planter-merchant was a better shot than Thomas, and, as it happened, also a better judge of women. The crack of a flintlock pistol on the mossy bank of the creek behind Lavelle's mansion proved both those points. Thomas would never forget the oppressive thickness of the bayou air, the clouds slipping across the bright yellow moon above the cypress trees, or the surprise he felt when Lavelle's pistol ball tore into his leg and spun him to the ground. And he would always remember the expression that crossed Delphine's face as he crumpled to the ground. "I've made my choice," her eyes said, "and it's not you."

A trio of gulls swooped low over his head and a long dark shadow slid through the blue water a few feet beneath him. Shark, or dolphin? If he continued to stew in memories of Lavelle and Delphine, the shark might be his preferred choice for a swimming partner.

He paused for a moment to switch the seal-skin satchel to his left shoulder. As he treaded water, he noticed how clear the ocean had become; he could make out his feet now and dark clusters of something-perhaps coral or rocks-on the seabed 20 or 30 feet below. Ahead to his left was the sand island Stoch had warned him about. He could also make out the top of a rock jetty that extended halfway across the harbor entrance and he could hear where lines of breakers were forming and crashing. Were they cresting over coral reefs? He couldn't be sure, but he was going to take care to swim between the lines of overlapping breakers so he would not be flung down onto rows of razor-sharp coral fans.

He swam steady and rhythmically towards the harbor entrance. If I ever meet Captain Stoch again, I am going to thank him for the hearty food and exercise that gave me the strength to make it this far, he thought. Right before I punch him in the nose.

The sea grew warmer as he neared shore. He swam through a patch of calm water between the long, rolling lines of waves breaking outside the jetty. His theory that they were crashing only over areas where there was coral or rock on the sea bottom had better hold; he did not want to be pushed down by a cresting wave to whatever unpleasant surprises were waiting in the depths.

He passed the jetty and veered to the right towards the first wooden pier in the harbor. Two small boats were tied to the pilings and just beyond was the schooner being offloaded. In the distance he could see a stretch of mud flats and a scattering of trees, warehouse buildings, and mountains, but beyond that his view of downtown Honolulu was blocked. There were certainly no hints of the tropical paradise that Stoch had promised. No waterfalls, no flowers, and not a single exotic maiden.

When he was within a few yards of the pier he felt sandpaper scrape against his left leg and then a gray head popped up two feet from his face. It had cat-like whiskers, black liquid eyes, and a wide mouth that was formed into a permanent grin. Thomas was so startled that he almost let the pouch slip off his shoulder.

The seal was equally surprised; it snapped its head back, barked twice, and dipped back into the water.

Thomas shook off the encounter and swam the few remaining feet to the pier. The pilings on each side were three feet in diameter, spaced about 20 feet apart. He made his way to the third piling where a makeshift wooden ladder was fastened and felt relief when his hand grasped a wooden cross-piece. He waited for a swell to raise him up a few inches, grabbed hold of a rung and pulled himself out of the water.

Until that moment he hadn't appreciated how much the swim had taken out of him. He mustered his strength and began the slow climb to the top, 15 feet above the harbor surface. He stopped to rest a few feet below the sun-drenched pier railing, hoping no one would see him when he appeared out of the ocean like Jonah from the whale. Then he climbed the last step and placed his hand on top of the railing, but before he could pull himself over, a huge form blotted out the sun and a pair of giant brown hands reached down and grabbed hold of the back of his shirt. An instant later he was lifted off the ladder and dropped in a heap on the pier's rough wood deck.

Thomas held his hand up to block the sun so he could see who had plucked him off the ladder as easily as if he was lifting an egg from a hen's nest. The fellow was enormous, almost as square as he was tall. He wore a loose cotton shirt and trousers, a ragged-brim straw hat, and leather sandals. Standing beside him was a boy of about ten, dressed exactly like his father.

The man placed his hands on his hips and looked down at Thomas, unsure of what to make of the situation. Then he wrapped a massive arm around his son's shoulders and in a serious tone said, "The gods would make us laugh, Kou. We come to fish for *aku* for tonight's supper, and instead we haul in a *kanaka keʻokeʻo*."

Had he just been yanked from the sea by the same tribe of cannibals that killed and boiled Captain James Cook in 1779, Thomas wondered?

The man let out a great belly laugh. "Have no fear, my friend," he said. "You are far too skinny to go into tonight's stewpot." As his son burst into laughter, the man extended a hand and helped Thomas stand.

"Come with us to our home. You can dry your clothing and tell your story." With that the giant fisherman and his boy turned and walked away.

Thomas opened his bag and pulled on the boots Stoch gave him. Then he slipped the bag over his shoulder and trotted down the pier in the direction of the dusty town beyond the warehouses.

ELEVEN

San Francisco, February 1872

Fitch Donegan had come to the Stafford mansion several times, but never at night, and never through the front door.

His line of work wasn't exactly respectable, and almost always involved breaking as many laws as he broke heads, which is why his clients typically preferred that he come in through the service entrance.

He smoothed his jacket and adjusted his tie before removing his bowler and brushing a few raindrops from the brim. Then he rapped the brass door knocker and waited for a servant to admit him into the great man's home.

His work for Stafford had been routine; he collected debts, 'persuaded' business competitors to find other places to ply their wares, and reminded politicians who Stafford had bribed that once bought they were going to stay bought. He liked Stafford about as much as you could like anyone on whose behalf you cracked skulls and burned down buildings, but only because the man paid well and on time.

The servant led him across the marble foyer to a set of inlaid walnut pocket doors near the ornate staircase. She tapped once and slid the doors open, closing them as soon as Donegan stepped into the library.

Colin P. Stafford was standing beside his desk riffling through a pile of papers. A fire burned in a grate in the corner and a wall clock ticked softly. He was dressed in formal evening clothes: a knee length chesterfield coat edged with braid and silk velvet facings, a four-in-hand tie, a silk cravat fastened with a stickpin, and a gold watch chain strung across his waist.

He knew what Donegan was wondering. "Opera," he said. "Out of New York by way of St. Louis and Denver. Damned if this town isn't becoming cultured."

Donegan nodded. He was not being asked to engage in a conversation, of course, so he stood quietly, turning his hat over and over in his hands until Stafford dropped the papers onto his desk and motioned for Donegan to take a seat. As he settled in, Fitch took the measure of the man many believed could become the next president of the United States. He was of average build and height, with close cropped muttonchop whiskers and thick, graying hair. He had unruly eyebrows, a piercing gaze, and, most prominently, a port-wine stain that spread from his left cheek and down across his neck.

The businessman removed the stopper from a crystal decanter and poured two brandies. He slid a glass across to Donegan and raised his own. "To a mutually profitable negotiation," he said.

Negotiation? Donegan was perplexed. Since when was a negotiation needed for the kind of work he did. Stafford knew the rates: if he wanted someone beaten up it would cost him $35. Beaten and left with a few broken bones might double the fee, and if the message Stafford wanted to deliver was to be of a permanent nature, Donegan charged $200. Debts were recovered for a percentage of the take, plus travel expenses when necessary. For jobs that required a bit more creativity, Donegan typically presented a bill for 'personal services.' Stafford had never objected.

"I would like to talk to you about a long-term arrangement," Stafford began. "Exclusive call on your services for at least one month, and perhaps longer. Might you be amenable to such an offer?"

"That would be an unusual sort of deal for me, Mr. Stafford. I take work as it comes; it's really the only way I can safely navigate through lean times."

"And by 'lean times' I suppose you mean peaceful times, when there are not enough heads that need to be knocked together," replied Stafford with a chuckle.

"Let's just say that things like the opera coming to town don't bode well for my profession."

"I understand precisely what you mean, Mr. Donegan. Civilization is an enemy of both our business endeavors. It's for that very reason that my proposition might interest you."

"I'm listening."

Stafford picked up the copy of the *Chronicle* newspaper that was sitting on the edge of his desk. Donegan could see that the page had been handled and turned so many times that it was almost worn through.

"Did you read this?" asked Stafford, pointing to the frontpage banner headline that Andrew Whitton had penned about him.

"I did, though to be blunt, I don't put much stock in them rags."

"Sadly, that is not the prevailing view among my friends, my peers, or my competitors. They read, and they believe."

"Your own newspaper fired back...." Donegan began.

"Oh, of course," replied Stafford. "We did a three-day series refuting every spurious claim the reporter made, and I think we have successfully tamped down the worst of the fires he set."

"But not all of them," Donegan said in a quiet voice. Of course, he thought to himself, or why else would you ask to see me?

"No, not all of them. And as with all lies, some of the dirt can never be washed away. It will stick. Damage has been done that will cost more by far than money."

Donegan raised his eyebrows.

"It will cost me respect, Mr. Donegan. I have spent years building a reputation as someone who is worthy of respect..."

"And fear?" added Donegan.

"Yes," said Stafford with a shake of his head. "Fear. If I am not feared, then new rivals will pop up like weeds in an abandoned field. I will have to spend more and more of my time pulling those weeds, and less time tending to my businesses."

There was a tap on the library door. The servant poked her head in. "The carriage will be ready in ten minutes, sir."

"High-brow music followed by dinner with the mayor," sighed

Stafford.

"And every one of the swells sitting in the private boxes will be taking the measure of me, trying to figure out if Colin P. Stafford is beginning to crack, if he is starting to lose control of his empire."

He finished his brandy and refilled both their glasses.

"You are part of my response to those bastards, Mr. Donegan."

"Sir?"

"You are going to find the reporter who wrote the article about me, this TES Bayside. Find him and kill him in so spectacular and painful a fashion that years from now people will still shiver at the thought of how he met his end."

Donegan did not respond. Stafford was asking him to shut down a lucrative enterprise where he alone called the shots, just to do one job.

Stafford saw the hesitation in Donegan's eyes. "In exchange for your commitment to this job I will give you a $1,000 retainer tonight. I will pay you an additional $20 per day, plus expenses, for every day you work for me, and I will pay you a full month in advance tonight. Let's call it $1,600?"

Stafford slid an envelope across the desk. Donegan knew if he picked it up, he was both accepting the job and shutting his existing business down. On the plus side, Stafford's offer was twice what he made in a typical month, and it meant cracking only one skull instead of the usual half dozen or so.

"That's a generous proposition," Donegan finally said. "But I wouldn't know where to begin. I don't even know who it is I am looking for."

"Ah, but I do," replied Stafford with a smile, "and he is far too famous to be able to simply disappear. He will lead you right to his front door. He can't help himself."

Donegan lifted the envelope from the desk and placed it in his jacket pocket.

"Where do I begin?" he asked his new employer.

~ TWELVE ~

Honolulu, Kingdom of Hawai'i

Every saloon in the world looks the same, Thomas thought. He mounted the stairs to the covered porch that wrapped around the two-story clapboard building and skirted a pair of scrawny dogs loitering next to the swinging doors. When he stepped inside, he was greeted with the familiar aromas of beer and cigar smoke and the energy of animated conversation.

His new friend, Henry Kakaako, had laughed when Thomas asked for directions to the best card game to be found in the town of 20,000. "I pluck you out of the sea only to throw you to the sharks?" grinned the huge fisherman. He shook his head. "The Oahu Palace is the only place to find a real game. Ranchers from the big island come at auction time, and it's where the sugar plantation owners and merchants meet to do business. Bankers, too, and more than a few officers from ships moored in the harbor. *Haoles* only."

"*Haoles?*" asked Thomas.

Henry smiled and took another drink of rum. "You. Anyone who is not *kama'aina*—an islander."

"I have a lot to learn."

"We are an ancient people, my friend, but the number of Hawaiians like myself who are descended from full-blood stock is steadily dwindling. Probably half of the 50,000 people who make up the islands today were brought from Japan, China, and the Philippines to harvest sugarcane. Plus, your people, of course…the missionaries."

"I am a lot of things," replied Thomas in an earnest tone, "but I assure you no one has ever mistaken me for a missionary."

Henry laughed and slapped him on the back. "We will hold your things for you until you return. Good luck."

Thomas left the small frame house and stepped over a low coral wall and onto the hard-packed dirt street. Each house on the street had a similar kind of wall, but none had gates, he noticed. A scattering of stubby palm trees lined the way, and, in the distance, he could see thinner, taller palms sweeping up the foothills below the cloud-shrouded mountains that ringed the city. The first cross street he passed boasted the Kingdom's only two-story government buildings, including the Royal Guard's Iolani Barracks, a place Henry called Hale Koa. Turn left there, the fisherman told him, and walk three blocks past the Catholic Church and the Kapiolani Hotel. The Oahu Palace was the only building on its block.

The weather was pleasant, and the people he passed in the street seemed indifferent to his presence, a sign that Honolulu was a town where encounters with strangers were the norm. Was the Wilhelm at anchor in the harbor by now, he wondered as he pushed open the saloon doors? And if it was, how should he greet the warship's officers or crew if he ran into them?

He pushed those thoughts aside and stepped into the high-ceilinged saloon. Three fans pushed cool air around, and a bank of windows on the west wall was open to catch breezes drifting off the ocean. A half-dozen oval tables dotted the sawdust-sprinkled floor, but at this early afternoon hour only three were occupied. Five men were seated at the largest table, deep into a game of cards. The men at the other tables were drinking and talking, and as Thomas passed one of their tables, he felt a man in a broad-brimmed straw hat give him a thorough once over.

The barman watched the tall young American come through the door. His clothes were decent enough quality, but the arms on the linen jacket were three inches too long, and the legs on his trousers were three inches too short. The barkeep fancied himself a student of human personality, and he watched carefully as the handsome character in the ill-fitting suit walked towards him with a confidence that bordered on swagger. There was a story here, thought the barman as he finished sizing up his new customer.

Thomas dropped two bits on the bar and asked for a beer.

"New to Honolulu?" asked the barman.

Thomas managed a half smile. "You could say that. I was dropped off this morning."

"You in need of a hotel?"

"I'm staying with friends now, but, yes, I would like to find a place."

"We have a few rooms," said the bartender, "but if you are looking for something nicer…"

Thomas took a sip of beer. "I am," he replied, "And if they have a first-class kitchen, so much the better."

"That would be the Merchant, three blocks east. Daily laundry, and the only decent food between here and San Francisco. Tell them Robert at the Palace referred you."

Thomas nodded, and then looked in the direction of the poker game and asked, "Is that an open game?"

"Fifty-dollar buy-in if they'll have you," said the barman. "A little rich for most folks around here."

And for me, too, thought Thomas, but the $100 collected by First Officer Stoch and the crew wouldn't get him far, and was nowhere near enough to get back to California. He could register to collect his Army pension through the office of the US Consulate, but that would take months. It was going to have to be cards.

He thanked the barman and went over to the gaming table. When the active hand closed, he asked the dealer if he could sit in. The man looked Thomas up and down, clearly not impressed by what he saw. Still, it was early in the day, and one more player meant a little more rake for him. "Five card stud, $50 to join, and I make the calls. All of them. That work for you?"

"It does. And who am I playing against?"

The dealer seemed surprised by the question, but he shrugged and made a circle around the table with his finger: "Turtleman, Hopwell, Terrance, and Devris," he said. "And you are?"

"Scandréll. From Ohio."

The dealer took Thomas's money and motioned to an empty chair. "Gentlemen, meet Mr. Scandréll. How's about we play some stud?"

Thomas waved the bartender over and asked him to bring drinks to his fellow players. When the drinks arrived, the players raised their glasses to the man from Ohio and the game began in earnest.

Thomas once told a novice gambler that the act of playing cards was like living through a summer day in the Midwest. Inside an hour the weather could change from clear and cool to cloudy and blazing hot, and if the atmospheric conditions lined up just so, a wind-whipped frenzy of rain, lightning, and hail could appear without warning and send you scrambling for safe cover.

He made it a habit to study his opponents when he first took his place at the table. Three of the four players today were businessmen; their soft hands and ample bellies told him their playing would be sober and deliberate. They had money but they would be a cautious lot who set limits on themselves before they walked through the saloon doors. These were not his main opponents.

The fourth man, Hopwell, had calloused hands and sunburnt skin, and though he was taller by a head than the other three, he was at least 20 pounds lighter than any of them. *He works for a living,* Thomas thought. Perhaps he was a warehouse owner or plantation manager. Whatever he did, he was the player to beat.

In the variant of stud they were playing, each player started with one private card dealt face down and one card face up. The player with the lowest card visible was forced to open betting with a small amount, and betting for that round continued until all but one folded or until all bets were called. If necessary, three more rounds would begin with one card dealt face up to each player, and then betting would ensue. During these rounds, the action started on the player with the best hand showing.

If a showdown was necessary at the end of all the rounds of betting, each remaining player would show his down card and the player with the best five card hand would win.

Thomas did his best to play by a fixed set of rules: if he could not beat what other players had showing up on the table, or was not comfortable bluffing, he folded. And he carefully watched and measured every move his opponents made. One of the worst mistakes you could make was to stay in a pot looking for a card an opponent folded two minutes ago. He knew that to win money in this game he had to weigh both the amount of the ante and the dealer rake. If the ante was large—and he needed that to be the case if he was going to get off this island—he would need to be aggressive about bluffing at additional pots when he had virtually nothing to back the bluff up. To build to the bluff he would play a tight, conservative game for the first few hours, and then change his playing style when his opponents thought they had him figured out.

The light began to soften and deepen as late afternoon spilled into evening. The saloon filled up and Thomas thought he heard rain, but his entire focus was on the game. When a boy brought a bucket of sandwiches to the table, the players took a five-minute break to eat before settling back in. Each game had its own personality and energy, and Thomas was pleased that the businessmen found the action to be compelling enough—including the promise of winning what was becoming a very substantial pot—that they stayed well into the evening. By midnight, though, the call of morning business and the probability of angry wives waiting at their front doors found the three men ready to call it a day.

Thomas knew without counting that he had amassed about $500. After the businessmen made their goodbyes, he slid a $20 gold piece across to the dealer and asked if he would stay if Hopwell wanted to play on. Hopwell—who Thomas had learned was half owner of a sugar plantation on the island of Lana'i—agreed, but only if they upped the ante on their remaining games and no one else was allowed to sit in.

The man's intention was clear; he needed the $500 Thomas had won, and anything else he might have in his pocket. A needful attitude was a formidable burden to carry into a game of chance, thought Thomas, but since he, too, was desperate for cash he would have to steel himself to play without letting emotion get the best of his judgment.

The dealer swept Hopwell and Thomas's winnings into two piles at the center of the table. The plantation owner plucked a twenty-dollar bill from his winnings and handed it to the dealer.

"Let's get to it," he growled.

The dealer nodded and broke open a fresh deck of cards.

When Thomas stepped onto the dirt street in front of the O'ahu Palace at daybreak it had rained a little, and the air was clean and crisp. A small pig trotted across the street, and a chicken pecked her way down the road towards the waterfront. The mountains were filled with morning shadows and the clouds that had obscured the foothills yesterday had lifted and he could see deep into the compressed green and brown folds that pinched the mountain walls like the edge of a pie crust.

"Step aside," a voice called, and he scooted to the left as a woman stepped out of the bar and emptied a five-gallon slop bucket into the dirt. Every saloon in the world was the same.

He was hungry, and a cup of coffee sounded good. He would walk up to the Merchant Hotel and have breakfast before taking a room. Then he'd visit Henry to gather up his few possessions and to thank the fisherman for his kindness.

After that? He patted his jacket pocket, where $870 in cash and a freshly signed bill of sale were secured in his wallet. After that he would find a tailor, enjoy a fine meal with a great bottle of wine, and take a long bath.

~ **THIRTEEN** ~

L et me make sure I understand correctly," said the banker as he read the bill of sale for the third time. "Martin Hopwell signed over his interest in the plantation to you as a way of covering his losses at cards?"

Thomas nodded and tried again not to stare at the cloth eye patch that covered the banker's right eye. The injury looked fresh; the skin around the patch was red and swollen, and the tall, pale American kept dabbing at it with the tip of his handkerchief.

"That's right," Thomas said, "and as you can see the document is signed by Hopwell, the owner of the Oahu Palace, and the dealer who managed the game."

"Oh, I know Hopwell's signature," replied the banker. "I do not doubt the authenticity of the bill, but I hope you can appreciate that this is a highly irregular way of transferring ownership of one's business."

"Does he owe your bank any money?" asked Thomas.

"He and his partner, William Fortnite, have been extended a line of credit on occasion, which they repay at harvest time." He looked down at the ledger book on his desk and flipped through several pages. "You will be pleased to know that there is no debt outstanding at present."

'Not as pleased as I am sure you are,' Thomas thought.

Stafford closed the book and said, "I don't suppose Hopwell described their current struggles?"

"He did not."

The banker sat back in his swivel chair. "Sugar cane is a thirsty crop, Colonel. It takes 2,000 pounds of water to produce a single pound of sugar, and the combined production of all the plantations on the islands will exceed 16 million pounds this year. Your plantation on Lana'i depends on a network of flumes to bring water from the hills, and they must be maintained and cleared constantly. That is expensive. And, unlike the plantations on O'ahu, Kaua'i, Mauii and Hawai'i, there is no sugar refinery on your island, so you have to transport your cane to the other islands, which is also a considerable expense."

"The truth is, when you also consider the shortage of labor needed to harvest and haul your cane, I cannot help but suggest that you may have won yourself the proverbial pig in a poke."

Thomas quietly considered the banker's comments. Hopwell had told him where he banked when he signed over his half of the plantation, but when Thomas learned the banker's name was Stafford, he nearly tore the bill of sale in half and cancelled the deal. Doing business with someone who might be related to Colin P. Stafford in California would be an open invitation to the assassins to show up in the islands and finish the job that Colin had begun.

Until the moment he was ushered into the banker's office the next morning, he was prepared to reverse course and figure out some other way to make enough money to get back to California. When the man got out of his chair, however, Thomas instantly knew he was not related to the San Francisco Stafford. Colin was short and dark; banker Wallace was tall and fair. And during their introductions, the banker mentioned that his family hailed from Pennsylvania, not California. Their last names were a simple coincidence.

"Is the business profitable?" Thomas asked.

The banker shrugged. "Your new partner is not, how best to say it, a man who places much value in the details. That was Hopwell's strength. Gambling was his great weakness, as you yourself can now attest. I suppose the best I can say is that the plantation could be profitable with better management, more labor availability, and a better than average rainy season."

"In other words, equal parts hard work and luck."

The banker dabbed at a rivulet of fluid seeping from under the corner of his eye patch. "As is true with everything we do in life, wouldn't you agree?"

Thomas nodded and stood to go. The banker shook his hand and said, "My bank is prepared to work with you in any way that we can, Colonel. I will prepare a letter of introduction that you can take to our local merchants and equipment suppliers, and I will inform the Island Sugar Council of the ownership change. You will find them a good resource on everything from sourcing labor to upcoming changes in production and processing costs."

"You want me to look to my competitors for help?"

The banker smiled. "You will need what they have to offer, and they need all the members they can get. Demand for sugar in the U.S. is booming, and the growers and processors have figured out that presenting a united front to customers on sugar pricing benefits everyone. I wouldn't recommend going it alone in this business, Colonel."

The notion of this kind of cooperative effort among rivals was a foreign notion to Thomas, but this wasn't the time to ask for more information. He had to get to Lana'i. So, he simply nodded and said, "I understand. Thank you."

The banker leaned against his desk and took several deep breaths. The man is still not recovered from whatever kind of accident took his eye, Thomas thought.

Stafford stood up straight and cleared his throat. "And now, Colonel, if you don't mind, may I ask a personal question?"

"Yes?"

"People come to the islands for many reasons, these days almost always related to the sugar business. Some say that Hawai'i could become a destination for holiday-goers one day, though that is difficult to believe. As busy as our harbor may appear, few ships remain in port for longer than a day or two—just long enough to load and offload cargo. Given that, Colonel, may I ask what brought someone of your fame and prominence here? It appears you do not know anyone, nor do you seem to have had business ambitions before winning the plantation in a poker game. Again, forgive my being blunt but if we are to do business, I would like to know something about you."

'Why am I here,' thought Thomas. He looked into the banker's good eye and lied; "Adventure, Mr. Stafford. The western frontier in America has closed, and we have become civilized from coast to coast."

He walked to the door and pulled it open. "This is the frontier now."

"And when the islands are no longer wild?" asked Stafford. "Where will you go then?"

"It's a big world," Thomas answered with a smile. "I'll find someplace."

The sprawling Merchant Hotel at the corner of Hotel and Richards Streets had an antebellum style main structure with a dozen flower-covered cottages spread across four manicured acres. With open-air verandas, thick stands of tropical foliage and trees and sweeping views of the Nu'uanu Mountains, the hotel was both peaceful and exotic.

His dinner the first night was a perfect blend of cultures; his waiter insisted that he sample a few local dishes before ordering a main course, including poi, a thick, starchy, and slightly sour pudding made from taro root, and laulau, delicately seasoned bits of pork wrapped in taro leaves that had been slow cooked for hours in an underground rock oven. Poi would be an acquired taste, he decided, but the pork was exceptional, and the half bottle of *Moet & Chandon* Imperial Green Seal Champagne his waiter recommended was the perfect accompaniment.

The menu featured several fish dishes and the usual roasted chicken found in every hotel restaurant back home, but his waiter urged him to consider a grilled rib eye steak from beef grown on the Parker Ranch on the big island. Thomas was surprised to learn that a cattle ranch had been operating in Hawai'i for over a quarter century, and that the cow hands who worked the herds were Mexican vaqueros the locals called paniolos who had been imported by King Kamehameha III.

It really had been a season for surprises, he thought as he sipped the first-rate champagne and savored its unique notes of white peach, apple, and pear. When he woke up yesterday, he was a penniless stowaway on a German warship, and a candidate for hanging. Tonight, he was the co-owner of a sugar plantation enjoying a fine meal at an elegant Hawaiian restaurant with a panoramic view of the evening sky above the Pacific Ocean. He had on a new suit of clothing, courtesy of the haberdashery at the hotel, with several more shirts, trousers and boots being prepared for him to pick up in the coming days. Tomorrow he would visit Henry Kakaako to thank him for his kindness, and then find the best place to purchase work clothing, a revolver and assorted gear for his trip to Lana'i.

When the sommelier appeared with a wine to accompany his steak, Thomas was pleased to see that it was a Schamsberger Burgundy from St. Helena, California, close to the Napa County vineyards where his favorite, black-skinned zinfandel grapes were grown. As he finished his second glass of the velvety dark wine, the waiter placed a perfectly cooked steak, a plate of sliced tomatoes, and a side of steamed asparagus on the table.

He raised his crystal goblet to the star-swept sky and silently toasted his good fortune.

~ FOURTEEN ~

Kaiwi Channel, Hawaiian Islands

Three days after his meeting with Wallace Stafford, Thomas stood at the bow rail outside the wheelhouse of the steam packet, *Lela M.* The 80' wooden coaster was heading out of Honolulu harbor and into the sunrise on a sea that was surprisingly calm for February. The Kaiwi Channel it would be crossing on the short voyage to Moloka'i was notorious for strong winds, vicious currents, and unpredictably large swells, but this morning the channel was a shimmering blue mirror with not so much as a breeze to ripple its surface. The sky was cloudless, and from his vantage point on the upper deck, Thomas could make out the northwestern tip of Moloka'i, and to the south, his destination, the island of Lana'i.

He had boarded with about two dozen other passengers, many of them laborers bound for work on O'ahu or the big island. It was possible that some might even be headed for his sugar cane fields on Lana'i. The boat sat low in the water, packed with groceries, dry goods, machine parts, mail, and other supplies.

At his feet a waxed canvas carryall was packed with his clothing and supplies, including the newest model Colt revolver. He had been reluctant to consider buying anything other than his favorite model 1858 Remington, but he was impressed with the Colt's open top design and construction and when he went out back of the general store with the salesclerk to test fire the gun, he had to admit that it was far superior to the revolver he had carried since the end of the war. A $20 gold piece paid for the gun, a holster, and 100 .44 caliber metallic cartridges.

He paid a visit to Henry Kakaako after meeting the banker to thank the fisherman for his hospitality. When he placed $50 in the giant man's hand, though, his gift was refused. That was what Henry earned in a good month, but he would not take money for simply doing what was right. Henry rebuffed all Thomas's arguments as to why he should keep the money until Thomas finally said, "Good enough, then, don't take the money for yourself. How about taking it for your son? He could use some new clothing, schoolbooks, and maybe a new bed and a real kitchen table." With the issue of his pride accounted for, Henry grudgingly accepted the money and then poured two glasses of dark rum.

"The *kō* you will be growing on your plantation is useful for much more than sugar, my friend," said Henry.

"*Kō?*"

"Sugar cane, Colonel. Molasses is a by-product of the manufacturing process, and it is the base for all rums." Henry raised his glass and toasted Thomas. "May your enterprise be profitable, and may your bed be always free of cane rats."

Thomas took a drink and shook his head. "I'm sorry, did you say rats?"

"By the tens of thousands," replied the Hawaiian. "They gnaw through the rind of the cane stalk to eat the sweet, juicy tissue inside. Kō can grow to 30 feet, but if a rat eats into just six inches the stalk will die. And what the rats don't get the insects will when they bore into the places the rat has been eating."

Thomas held out his glass for Henry to fill again. "Rats and insects," he said in a quiet voice. "There's something to look forward to."

Henry laughed. "And drought, and a shortage of labor, along with diseases that can sweep like forest fires through the camp. Dealing with the missionary bankers and the sugar brokers will be the worst, though: you will probably prefer the company of the sugar rats to those greedy bastards."

"Why the hell does anyone go into the business?"

"Oh, you can make money, Colonel. Piles of it. *Kō* is new to Lana'i, but the world craves sweets, and you will never want for customers."

"Once I get past the rats and the bankers you mean."

Henry poured more rum. "Who are really one and the same...."

The men enjoyed a laugh and then Henry became serious. "One other thing, Thomas. You are about to step into a world in which laborers are treated as poorly as the slaves your nation fought to free in your Civil War. That is the nature of the business. You will have children as young as eight weeding the fields in brutally hot weather, and when a worker is no longer strong enough to clear, plant, and harvest, they are discarded like yesterday's garbage. By the time *kō* harvesters are 15 or 16, they will have lost at least a couple of their fingers. You can't swing a razor-sharp machete thousands of times for 10 or 12 hours a day and not have an accident now and then. And your workers will come from many nations, and most will speak little or no English. The only thing they will hate more than one another is the overseer—and you."

Thomas finished his rum and pushed his glass aside. "If *kō* is only now being introduced to Lana'i, perhaps I can introduce a more enlightened way to manage the workers."

Henry looked into Thomas's eyes. "That is a noble sentiment Colonel Scoundrel." He emptied his own glass and thought to himself: *"One that will probably get you killed."*

"Ah, so it appears that you can swim."

Thomas shook off his reverie and turned towards the heavily accented voice. Father Damien had replaced his priest's cassock with a light linen jacket and shirt and his head was bare. In contrast to his serious demeaner onboard the *König Wilhelm*, the young Belgian priest was grinning as he stepped up to the railing.

"Well enough to bypass the reefs and the sharks," Thomas answered with a smile of his own. "I suppose I should thank you for that."

The priest responded with a quizzical look.

"Just before I was tossed overboard Captain Schmidt said that you were the person who came up with the, ahem, solution to the dilemma of dealing with the stowaway American officer." He extended his hand and shook with Damien. "I preferred that outcome to being hung on the yardarm or tossed into a Hawaiian jail."

A look of confusion crossed the priest's face. "I am sorry," he said slowly, "but my English is…lacking."

"*Je parle français, Père,*" replied Thomas in the priest's native tongue.

"*Oh, mais c'est merveilleux,*" said Damien, his grin widening. "Just wonderful."

"I was saying," Thomas continued in French, "that I preferred your solution to my situation over the others that were presented."

"Well, it did have the advantage of offering you at least some chance of surviving the episode. And here you are."

Thomas looked across the channel to the southeast, where the mountains of Moloka'i loomed high above the sapphire blue sea. "Your destination?" he asked the Belgian.

Damien rested his hands on the polished wooden rail and followed Thomas's gaze. "My destiny," he replied in a soft voice.

"The leper colony."

"*Oui.* My new home. And, no doubt, my last."

"With respect, Father, I must ask: why does one—even a priest—march willingly into what can only be a place of execution? Is the call of your vocation that much stronger than your desire to live?"

"I have no desire to die, Colonel, no more than any other man of 32. I desire simply to serve God where the need is the greatest, and in that role, I hope to live and serve into a ripe old age."

"I suppose I just can't fathom planning my life in such a way," said Thomas. "I have been in battle, and I understand why war must sometimes be waged, but I would never travel halfway around the world to do battle on behalf of people I don't even know."

Damien gave a wistful smile and clasped his hands together on the railing. Seabirds circled in long, lazy circles above the steam packet as it glided upon the surface of the glass smooth channel, and their fellow passengers milled about below on the main deck. "The greatest lesson I have learned," he finally said, "is that we must let go of the life we have planned so that we can accept the one that is waiting for us."

"Even when what is waiting is disease and death?" asked Thomas.

The priest shrugged. "The government of the Kingdom of Hawai'i regards the afflicted who are sent to the village of Kalawao to be officially dead, though many of them will live for years before the disease is done with them." He removed his horn-rimmed glasses and cleaned them with the hem of his shirt. "Why should their new shepherd not come to them under the same sentence of death?"

Thomas had no answer. For a few minutes they stood quietly as the coaster steamed towards the Kalaupapa Peninsula on Molokai's northern shore. The priest would go ashore at Awahua Bay and then hike three miles across the peninsula until he reached the 1,500-foot cliffs and the steep switchback trail that snaked down to the seaside leper colony known as Kalawao.

"The village is almost impossible to reach," the priest said, "and there are only temporary docks for approaches from the sea. The entire settlement consists of just four square miles of rocky soil and brush. Before the site was chosen in 1865, there were small farms raising sweet potatoes and fat hogs and they had a thriving fishing community. But the diseases that ravaged the other islands took the lives of most of the farmers and fishermen, and the few that remained left when the colony was established."

He went on to describe how the village sat in the lee of a cliff, so there was never an early sunrise, and afternoons were short in the summer and almost nonexistent in the winter.

The closer the *Lela M.* got to the island, the more imposing the green furrowed cliffs became. Father Damien was genuinely interested in Thomas's sugar plantation adventure and peppered him with dozens of questions, and when the packet slipped up to the tiny dock, he gathered his things and Thomas walked down to the boarding plank beside him. The priest was the only passenger getting off on Moloka'i.

"I have enjoyed our conversation," Thomas told the priest. "If things were different...."

"Indeed, yes," answered the priest. "The proper thing for me to do would be to extend an invitation to dinner. For a short while at least, I am afraid that my home will be a wool blanket spread under a tree." He smiled and placed a hand on Thomas's shoulder. Then he swung his rucksack across his back and stepped up onto the boarding plank. Before he stepped onto the dock he turned, and with a cheerful smile added, "But I will certainly understand if you choose to pass on my invitation. *Que Dieu te bénisse.*"

With that Father Damien clambered onto the dock and walked briskly to the shore. He turned, set his bag down, and waved a final goodbye to his new American friend.

Thomas returned the wave. *"May God bless you as well, my friend,"* he thought to himself as the packet reversed course and headed back to sea.

~ FIFTEEN ~

Lana'i, March 1872

A Japanese boy held up a bucket of dead cane rats for Thomas to inspect, and when the new plantation owner nodded his approval the eight-year-old stretched out his other hand to collect a peppermint candy. The child was a member of the Third Gang, a work group made up of old people and children whose endless chores included weeding the cane fields and keeping the rat population down. The gap-toothed boy popped the treat into his mouth, grinned his thank you, and raced to the edge of the field to dump his catch onto a growing pile that would be torched when the sun went down.

"Not quite what you envisioned when you played that last hand and found yourself the co-owner of a sugar plantation," observed Kukane, the Hawaiian overseer.

Thomas mopped sweat from his face with the sleeve of his loose-fitting cotton shirt and took a drink from his canteen. He liked Kukane and had grown used to his pointed reflections on plantation life in the five weeks he had been on Lana'i. Where his new partner, William Fortnite, was closed mouth and gloomy, Kukane exuded joy in the simplest daily acts of work and conversation. He had been Thomas's unflagging tutor in all matters to do with growing and harvesting sugar cane, including the history of his partner's family.

Fortnite's grandfather arrived in Jamaica from England in 1810 after inheriting ownership of a sugar cane plantation. With profits built upon the backs of hundreds of enslaved Africans, the elder Fortnite amassed a huge fortune which supported a lavish lifestyle and expensive gambling habit that lasted until 1838. That year the slaves in Jamaica were freed by order of the British government, and Fortnite's former slaves celebrated the occasion by burning his crops and mansion before stringing their former master up on the highest branch of a scarlet-red Poinciana tree.

As a young man, William spent several years working with his grandfather, and after the family's plantations and fortunes were destroyed, he returned to England where he worked for fifteen years as a clerk in the Trade Ministry. He kept his eye on the sugar business worldwide, and when it became apparent that Hawai'i was going to be the next great sugar-producing region, he moved his family to Honolulu and opened a dry goods store, setting the profits aside to buy land on Lana'i to start his own plantation. He lost so much money the first year building irrigation flumes down from the mountains and getting the first crop in that he was forced to take on a partner. And now, after two years of struggling to import labor and plant enough cane to become marginally profitable, his partner had just handed 50% of the ownership to some brash American colonel.

Fortnite's strengths were planning and organizing. When he mapped out the scheme for his sugar cane plantation, he built it on the same model his grandfather had created in Jamaica. He imported workers and their families from Japan, China, and the Philippines and organized them into three 'Gangs.' The First Gang was comprised of young men and women in their teens, who Fortnite knew from experience could do the most intense, back-breaking work for at least ten or twelve years, at which time they would move into the Second Gang, where the excruciating workload was reduced, though only slightly. After as much as twenty years in the Second Gang, the worker, now in his or her 40s, would look decades older than their actual age and have no choice but to move into the Third Gang, also known as the 'Grass Gang', where they would work alongside the children and help keep the irrigation flumes working.

The First and Second Gangs prepared the fields for planting in the early summer, turning over the rich volcanic soil with spades and hoes. In the late-summer and early-autumn the First Gang planted the sugar cane using a process called cane-holing. It was brutal work. Workers marked out six-foot squares, which they dug out to a depth of nine inches. Each First Gang laborer was expected to dig out between 60 and 100 squares between dawn and dusk, moving as much as 1,500 cubic feet of soil. The soil they removed was immediately built up as a retaining bank around each square before two young sugar cane plants were planted in the center.

The worst job came next; First and Second Gang workers balanced large baskets of animal manure on their heads and carried the 80-pound loads from horse-drawn carts to pack around the plants. One woven basket of reeking, dripping dung was sufficient for two holes and four plants. It took over 2,000 pounds of manure to prepare an acre of cane plants.

The first harvest came in February-March, when the cane plants towered over the men and women as they cut down the plants about six inches above the ground using razor sharp, curved billhooks, or 'bills.' Once down, workers cut the top and the leaves off the cane, tied them into bundles, and loaded them onto wagons. Lana'i had no processing facilities, and so wagons of cane were hauled to the coast and placed onboard steam-powered packets for the short journey to the sugar mills and boiling houses on O'ahu.

Thomas turned to Kukane, who was scribbling planting notes in one of his ever-present leather-wrapped journals. "I had no vision when I won this place," he said, "and after a month I'm not sure I ever will. But I do know there is a profit to be made, that is, if we expand our holdings, find more labor, and secure a new line of credit."

The overseer smiled. "That is a lot of maybes, my friend."

Two Third Gang elders crossed the path in front of them carrying wicker baskets filled with freshly sharpened billhooks. They touched fingers to their foreheads in a sign of respect as they passed.

"Will it be a good harvest?" asked Thomas.

"The rains have been plentiful, and we are keeping the rats at bay," answered Kukane. "I would like to have more workers, but we will get by with those we have."

Thomas looked out across a sea of mature cane where dozens of billhooks flashed in the morning light as workers wearing wide-brimmed straw hats cut their way through the thick shocks.

"Why do they come, Kukane? Why do they leave their homes half-way around the world to come here and work themselves to death, and for so little money? Most are in debt to the plantation store where they buy their food and supplies, and many will never leave this little island for as long as they live. I don't understand."

Kukane slipped his pencil into the journal and closed it. "Yes, it is hardly an ideal life, especially for the little ones. But understand, Colonel, that the lives they left behind were infinitely worse than it is here. Starvation, disease, and war is all they knew. Here, they at least have hope that one day their lives will be better."

"A small hope," Thomas replied.

Kukane slapped him on the back. "A small hope is better than a great despair," he said with a grin. "In the short time you have been here, you have treated the workers fairly and with dignity. You have given them more reason to hope."

"But most of them will still never leave this place," said Thomas as he watched the boy he had given candy dart across the field in search of more cane rats.

"A few will," answered Kukane. "And they will be the best among them."

The two men walked down from the knoll overlooking the fields and skirted the path on which several ox-drawn carts were already piled high with bundled sheaves of freshly cut cane.

Kukane turned towards the row of carts waiting to be filled, while Thomas headed uphill to check repairs that had been made on a flume gate the day before. With that done he would return to his small cabin for the morning meal and then ride to the harbor to supervise loading of the season's first harvest onto the freight coaster.

As he rounded a stand of freshly cut cane, a frantic Chinese woman in her early 30s rushed up to him and dropped to her knees.

"My husband, he kill!" she cried. "He kill for my daughter. Help, Mr. Colonel, please help!"

She pointed to the edge of the field 50 yards away where a Chinese man was running towards a grass-thatched hut. The man was holding a billhook high in the air and shouting something in his native tongue.

Thomas dropped his canteen and notebook and raced towards the man, though he had no idea what might be happening. When he was a few yards from the worker, the man tried to wave him off. Thomas was taller and faster and overtook the man easily. He grabbed the worker by his shirt and pulled him to a halt.

"Where are you going?"

The man kept his billhook raised as he replied. His eyes were wild and his face was flushed, as much in rage as from the run Thomas thought.

"The Mr. has my child," he said in halting English. "He take her to his bed. I will kill him now."

The man wrenched away, but Thomas stepped forward and grabbed him by the arm. The 'Mr.' the worker was talking about could only be Fortnite. The fact that he had taken a child into a deserted hut that the laborers were forbidden to enter could only mean one thing.

"No," said Thomas in his strongest command voice. "I will go. You will wait here."

Despair filled the man's eyes. His child had been taken, and it was his responsibility to save her, not the American's. He started to object, but Thomas gripped his arm even harder.

"You cannot do this thing," he said softly. "You will be hung, and what will become of your family then?" Thomas knew that in any legal dispute between a plantation owner and a laborer the courts would always side with the owner. Whatever was happening to the man's daughter inside that hut, just pushing through the door without permission was a guaranteed prison sentence for a cane worker.

The man's shoulders slumped, and he crumpled to the ground and cradled his head in his hands.

"Wait for me. I will bring your daughter to you."

Thomas strode to the door of the hut, not sure how he was going to fulfill the promise he had just made. He was about to knock on the rough wooden door when he heard a child sob, and then cry out. He took three steps back, rushed forward, and threw his shoulder against the wood. The flimsy door shattered off its hinges and Thomas found himself inside.

Light from a single window spilled across the room, where Fortnite was lying back on the bed. He was naked, and he was pleasuring himself. At the foot of the bed was a girl of about 11 or 12. Her shirt had been ripped off, and her loose trousers were down around her ankles. She was crying softly and gripping a bedpost tightly with both hands.

Fortnite's face turned scarlet when he saw Thomas. He whipped a blanket over his body and sat up. The girl tried to cover herself with her hands, and Thomas motioned for her to pull on her clothing and leave. At first, she seemed too terrified to disobey whatever threats Fortnite had used against her, but when Thomas smiled softly and again motioned to the door, she pulled on her shirt and trousers and raced out the door and into her father's arms.

Thomas turned towards his business partner, who was now sitting on the edge of the bed. His face registered neither fear nor shame, only anger at having been interrupted at play. That's because he has done this before, Thomas thought.

"You bastard," were the only words Thomas could form.

"Oh, do set your tiresome Christian pretensions aside," replied Fortnite in a matter-of-fact British accent. "These heathens expect no less, in fact, they deserve no less. Her job is to see to my needs, Colonel, whatever those needs may be. And for the record, I did not put a hand on her. I seldom do actually touch the little tarts."

Thomas fought the urge to do to Fortnite what the Chinese girl's father had intended. "No Christian pretensions are necessary, Fortnite. How about simple decency and compassion? Have you none?"

Fortnite stood and walked over to a side table under the window. He took a cigar from a small box, lit it, and inhaled deeply. When he blew out the smoke he said, "Those are luxuries, my dear colonel, and when you live and work in this flea-bitten backwater long enough you will discover that luxury has no place here. There is no profit in your so-called decency, and compassion is simply another word for weakness. You may choose to be weak; I choose to thrive and survive, where you seem to want to invite failure and death."

Thomas knew that further conversation was pointless. He walked to the door, then turned. "I am going to Honolulu in a few days to speak to our banker about the credit line and to meet with the Sugar Council." He stared hard at his partner. "If you touch that child—or any other—while I am gone, I will hear of it. And I will kill you."

The brief flicker that crossed Fortnite's eyes told Thomas that his message had been received. He walked out of the hut and into the bright morning light where he saw the girl and her parents walking hand in hand over the rise towards the cane fields.

~ SIXTEEN ~

Honolulu

The Principal Personal Secretary to His Majesty King Kamehameha V was as round as he was short, and his face was creased with a perpetual smile.

"You know my friend, Kukane," he said as he scanned the envelope Thomas handed him.

"He is the manager of my plantation on Lana'i," Thomas replied, "and one of the wisest and kindest people I know."

The Secretary beamed even wider. "On that we agree," he said, motioning for Thomas to sit.

As the secretary read Kukane's letter, Thomas looked around the cluttered office on the second floor of the newly constructed Iolani Palace. The three-story concrete block building featured a front façade of arches and columns behind a row of graceful palm trees. The trip from his hotel on the mule-drawn streetcar took only five minutes, and he would have walked if an early morning rain had not turned the wide, dirt street in front of the palace to a sea of mud.

Kukane's name on the envelope was all that Thomas needed to be ushered into the palace by the royal guard, where he was directed up the grand staircase in the foyer, and down a long office-lined hallway.

"So, you have come for tonight's gala?" asked the secretary as he set the letter down on his desk.

"I'm sorry…the gala?"

"Did Kukane not tell you about His Majesty's biggest social event of the year?"

Thomas was mystified. "No, he simply handed me the letter when I was getting on the coaster yesterday with instructions to come to the palace and introduce myself to you. I assumed it had something to do with me meeting more of Hawaii's businesspeople and government officials."

A young woman came into the office and the secretary asked her to bring a tray of coffee and pastries.

"Oh, you will meet them all here tonight, Colonel. I suspect Kukane knew it would be the perfect opportunity to introduce you to Honolulu society."

"May I ask, Mr. Secretary, how it is that the manager of a small sugar plantation is so well known at the palace?"

The secretary chuckled. "Kukane is a second cousin of the King. That in itself is not remarkable, since nearly everyone with a drop of Hawaiian blood is related to some degree to His Majesty. But he and Kukane were raised together, and they still visit regularly."

"And tonight's gala is…?"

The young woman returned with coffee and cakes, and the secretary served Thomas and helped himself before answering between bites.

"Tonight is the annual observance of the ascension to the throne of his grandfather, the first Kamehameha to occupy the throne. Every foreign dignitary in the city will be here, as well as the leading merchants, bankers, planters, distinguished citizens, and the officers of any ships now in the harbor. Do you happen to have dinner clothing?"

"I can make do," replied Thomas.

The King's Secretary licked frosting off his hand before scribbling a note and sliding it across the desk. "Give this to the guards at the front gate tonight after 7," he said. "I will see that you are introduced to His Majesty."

Thomas thanked the secretary and went to the door. As he pulled it open, the secretary asked, "Are you a married man, Colonel?"

Thomas turned. "I am not."

The secretary swallowed another bite of pastry and cleared his throat. "You must pardon my observation, but I believe you are going to make a splash among some of our most lovely and eligible young ladies."

Thomas kept his expression impassive, uncertain about the secretary's intent.

"Do be careful, my dear colonel. The rules of courtship and bedding are quite different here in the islands than they are in your homeland. In fact, it is said that the slopes of the Kīlauea volcano are littered with the bones of men who paid more attention to the firmness of their intended's backsides than to the fire in their fathers' eyes."

Thomas shook his head. "I don't understand," he said slowly.

The secretary's eyes twinkled. "You will, my dear colonel. You will."

A knock on the door interrupted Thomas's reflections on the day's events. A haberdashery employee came into his room with a garment bag and laid it on the bed. Thomas inspected the crisp white shirt with starched collar and the freshly pressed jacket and trousers, tipped the young man, and then sipped a glass of port as he began to dress for the gala.

Before his visit to the palace, he had met with banker Stafford to arrange for a line of credit. The one-eyed man flipped through the account book Thomas set on the desk and asked several questions about the plantation's water supply and labor situation. Then he shut the book and looked up. "Your accounting is accurate? Acres under cultivation, the harvest to date?"

"Yes," Thomas replied. "And here are the preliminary receipts from the warehouse here on O'ahu."

The banker studied the slips of paper that certified how many tons of raw sugar cane had been delivered for processing. "These numbers represent half of your anticipated harvest?"

"Just under half," Thomas replied.

"And you are asking for a line of credit in the amount of…?"

"$50,000."

"To expand operations?"

"Yes," said Thomas, "to buy land, add new irrigation, build more houses for the workers, and secure more warehouse space."

The banker nodded and adjusted the eye patch that had replaced the gauze bandage he was wearing when they first met five weeks earlier. Thomas noted that the redness and swelling were almost completely gone.

"It is a reasonable request," the banker said, "and would seem to be a prudent amount to achieve your goals. I can have the papers drawn up this afternoon for you to sign tomorrow, say, at lunch?"

The small clock on the bedside table chimed 6:00 PM. Thomas checked his tie and then went down the wide marble stairs to the expansive lobby. The plantation-style building was becoming his favorite hotel in the world; from the manicured grounds to the sweeping vistas up into the mist-shrouded mountains ringing the city, everything about it was exotic and grand. That included the open-air restaurant bar, where he took a seat under a gas lamp on the veranda and ordered a half bottle of champagne, a small plate of smokey *laulau* pork wrapped in *taro* leaves, and a salad made with minced guava and mango sprinkled with lime juice.

An hour later he joined a parade of well-dressed people leaving the hotel's front entrance for the short walk to Iolani Palace. The evening was soft, and the light from the full moon and a carpet of stars made for a pleasant stroll. He fell into conversation with an Australian naval officer along the way and wondered again why the King's secretary had warned him of the dangers he could face should he attempt to become too friendly with the local maidens.

Danger or not, it had been months since he had spent time with a beautiful woman, and the prospect of finally meeting one of First Officer Stoch's willing and nubile Polynesian princesses, or *kamāli ' iwahine* as Kukane called them, dampened any concern he had about their overly watchful fathers.

His group arrived at the palace gates, which were festooned with garlands of aromatic plumeria flowers and lit by a row of torches. All three stories of the building were ablaze with light from gas lamps and candle chandeliers, and the strains of a popular waltz being performed by the Royal Hawaiian Band wafted down the stairs and spilled across the fountain-dappled courtyard.

Guests were being ushered through three sets of French doors into the palace ballroom, where small couches were lined against two walls and flower-topped tables and chairs were scattered around the floor. A great chandelier hung from the center of the ceiling, and candle sconces and lamps cast a warm glow around the enormous room.

Thomas estimated there were 200 people in the ballroom, with more streaming steadily in through the front doors. He recognized several members of the Island Sugar Council and quickly spotted his banker, who was deep in conversation with a Captain in the American navy. Four couples were whirling away on the dance floor in front of the orchestra stand and servers snaked their way through the crowd with silver platters bearing champagne, goblets of wine, and sherry. Thomas intercepted a server and took a glass of champagne before walking over to look at the three buffet tables overflowing with fresh fruits, salads, tureens of soup, a baron of beef, and baskets of fresh baked breads and desserts.

"Not bad for a rabble of primitive islanders," said the King's Secretary, who had materialized beside him from out of the crowd.

Thomas raised his glass. "I have yet to discover anything in Hawai'i that I would characterize as primitive," he said, "though I might have recommended a more civilized champagne."

The portly official took Thomas's elbow. "Why don't we share both of those sentiments with His Majesty."

The men made their way across the room to a corner where the Monarch of the Kingdom of Hawai'i was holding court in the middle of a group of businesspeople, islander aristocracy, church leaders, and military officers. The King, Thomas noted, looked to be in his early 40s, with thick black hair and keen, intelligent eyes above a bushy mustache and fashionable muttonchop whiskers. The front of his formal jacket was emblazoned with several burnished gold and silver medallions, and he was leaning his considerable girth against a thick wooden cane.

The King's Secretary noticed Thomas's questioning glance. "Gout," he whispered, "and a few too many sweets."

They approached the knot of people surrounding Kamehameha V and waited to be acknowledged. A moment later the King finished his conversation with the Commodore of the Australian frigate berthed in the harbor and nodded in the direction of his secretary, who guided Thomas up to within a few feet of the King.

"Majesty," began the Secretary, "I have the pleasure of introducing to the court the famous hero of the American War of Rebellion, Colonel Thomas E. Scoundrel."

The King extended his hand and smiled. "And now a sugar plantation owner?" he asked.

Thomas shook the King's hand and nodded. "I am, Your Highness, on the island of Lana'i."

"Where, if I understand correctly, you employ my cousin, Kukane?"

"That is only partly true, Majesty. Kukane has taken me under his wing and taught me everything about *kō*, and about Hawaiian customs and history. He is more a teacher than an overseer."

The King smiled and sipped at his sherry. Then he shifted his weight to get more comfortable and said, "All that in the brief time you have been here? My cousin is a remarkable man, indeed."

"And a product of the mission schools, let us not forget," said a silver-haired American attired in formal dinner wear.

"Never let it be said that Mr. Grimthorpe has ever failed to remind us of our debt to Christian education," replied the King in a weary tone.

"Nor should I," Grimthorpe said, "given that you yourself have also been its beneficiary."

"The laws and ways of my ancestors also had something to do with forming my mind and character," smiled the King as he turned back towards Thomas. "Get to know Mr. Grimthorpe, Colonel, if for no other reason than to experience the extraordinary bounty of his wife's kitchen. I have reveled in that experience myself, and more than a few times as the evidence shows." He patted his stomach with dramatic flair with his free hand to the polite laughter of the small crowd surrounding him.

"A little more *poi*, perhaps uncle, and a little less custard trifle?" said a woman's voice.

Thomas turned his head to see who had the impertinence to address their king in such a fashion. He noticed her dress first; a sleeveless, off the shoulder gown that shimmered with the iridescent luster of pearls and satin as she flowed across the floor. The crowd parted as she neared, and Thomas was able to take her full measure. She was nearly as tall as he was and walked with the grace and control of a ballet dancer. Her dark hair spilled in thick lustrous waves around her shoulders, and the way her turquoise eyes sparkled mischievously told Thomas that teasing her royal uncle was something she did routinely, and with no fear of reproach.

The shape of her finely turned nose, the curves of her full, rose lips, and the soft crème hue of her skin spoke to her mixed Hawaiian and European ancestry, and the confident tilt of her head testified to the strength of her character. She kissed her uncle's cheek, took his arm, and began to greet the guests. When she made eye contact with Thomas, she gave him a quizzical look before nudging her uncle and inclining her head in Thomas's direction.

"Ah," said the King "but I have neglected my introductions. Colonel, if you would?"

Thomas took a few paces until he was standing directly in front of the King and his niece. Before the King spoke, he snatched a tulip of champagne off the tray of a passing waiter and downed it in one gulp. His niece gave a disapproving smile as she retrieved the glass and returned it to the server.

Ignoring the upbraiding, the King said, "Colonel Thomas Scoundrel, let me introduce my niece, the lovely and quite meddlesome Princess Noelani."

Thomas took the Princess's hand as the King continued.

"Noelani, this is the hero of the epic battle of Pebble Creek Ridge in the closing days of the American Civil War. Did you know, colonel, that a magnificent painting of the event hangs above the bar in my private billiard room? "

Thomas groaned inwardly as he–reluctantly–released Noelani's hand. That damn painting again.

A huge Hawaiian for whom the royal tailor had been unable to fashion a fitting shirt collar stepped up beside Noelani and glared at Thomas. As the King turned to shake the giant's hand, his secretary came up alongside.

"See what I meant earlier?" he whispered. "Beware, my friend. These are treacherous shoals."

The rotund bureaucrat's warning went unheeded. Thomas could not tear his eyes away from Noelani. Then a thought struck him; was the massive Hawaiian Noelani's husband, or perhaps her fiancé?

The secretary read his mind. "That is Akoni, her brother and protector," he said softly. "Of all the women you would be well advised to avoid tonight, Noelani should be at the head of your list."

Thomas shrugged off the warning and stretched out his hand to Akoni, whose crushing grip left his hand momentarily frozen. Thomas masked the pain and smiled as if the two were the very best of friends. Then, to everyone's astonishment—including his own—Thomas turned to Noelani. "May I have the pleasure of the next dance?" he blurted out.

Akoni's countenance darkened. He was seething, but he would wait for a signal from the King before he hauled the American out of the palace and tossed him onto the street. For his part, Kamehameha grinned in delight at the hornet's nest that the American colonel had just dropped into the gala. Protocol instructed that the King's Principal Secretary would have prepared a list of men with whom the Princess was allowed to dance days before the event. The colonel was blissfully unaware of such rigid social dictates, the king realized, which made the moment even more delicious. He could approve or forbid the dance, or, he thought with an impish smile, he could repay his niece for her insult about his weight and put the onus for making the right social call on her shoulders. And so, the hereditary Ruler of All the Islands simply smiled and raised his eyebrows at her.

Noelani was up to the challenge. She nodded to her uncle and then to Thomas, who stepped forward and took her arm. He led her to the center of the dance floor to the strains of the opening passage of Beautiful Blue Danube, by Strauss. The princess stood tall and canted her head slightly forward as Thomas took her outstretched left hand in his and placed his right hand on her back at the shoulder blade, with his elbow raised and his arm bent sufficiently to hold her as close as etiquette permitted. He was not nervous; his mother was an accomplished dancer and had instructed him since childhood. By the time she died when he was sixteen, he danced superbly. It was one of the few social skills he enjoyed as often as opportunity afforded.

The American Colonel and the Hawaiian Princess were immediately the center of attention in the crowded ballroom. Several other couples danced around them, but every eye in the room was focused on the tall young couple gliding effortlessly in sweeping circles on the wings of the beautiful waltz.

"He's German, you know," said the Princess as they danced.

"The composer?" answered Thomas, "Yes, he is."

"No, I meant the orchestra conductor," she replied. "We're a funny little kingdom, colonel. European plantation owners, Chinese bankers, German band leaders…."

"And American dance partners," Thomas added.

Noelani looked into his eyes. "Surprisingly gifted dance partners, I must say."

Etiquette forbade drawing too close to one's partner on the floor, but if good manners alone were not enough to keep Thomas the requisite six inches from the Princess's cheeks and bosom, the sight of her hulking brother watching his every move did the trick. He had to reply to her compliment, however, and so he briefly applied a bit more pressure on her back. The message was unmistakable.

Noelani did not reply, nor did the expression on her face change. Instead, she suddenly increased the tempo of her movements, causing

Thomas to miss a step. He compensated so quickly that no one watching noticed, and in a moment, they were slipping effortlessly in a series of ever-widening circles around the wooden floor.

The glow from the chandelier cast golden shadows across Noelani's face, and a tiny bead of perspiration appeared at her décolletage in the company of the scents of night-blooming jasmine and gardenia. Thomas, who was famously relaxed and conversational in the company of beautiful women, found himself unable to speak. The crowded space around the dance floor became a blur of color and motion, and only the Princess and her hauntingly beautiful face came into focus in his eyes.

He was so entranced with the Princess that he did not notice when the music stopped. He took several more steps in the silence before Noelani disengaged from his arms with a soft chuckle and walked off the floor. He blinked and felt his face redden as guests around the ballroom smiled knowingly and chattered on about the thunderstruck American.

Akoni, however, found no amusement in the spectacle. He was embarrassed for his sister, and ashamed that Colonel Scoundrel had been allowed to humiliate the King's niece in such a fashion. He watched his sister rejoin her uncle and his party, and then followed Scoundrel out onto a back terrace where the idiot was no doubt retreating to hide in shame.

Akoni stepped through the doors to find Thomas standing alone beside a fountain near the parapet that overlooked the inner courtyard gardens. He strode quickly up behind the American, laid one massive hand on the colonel's shoulder, and swung him around. Before Thomas could react Akoni grabbed the lapels of his jacket, lifted him a few inches in the air, and pulled him close to his chest.

"You have dishonored my family," the giant hissed between clenched teeth. "And you must be held to account."

Whatever spell Princess Noelani had cast upon Thomas was broken the instant he was whirled around and found himself face to face with Akoni's chest. He reacted instinctively, thrusting both hands with palms up to the underside of Akoni's elbows, striking them with all his strength. Akoni's arms flew back, and Thomas ducked down, slid to the left, and took a few steps backwards.

"All this for a dance?" Thomas thought as he raised his fists and stepped into a fighting stance. Akoni was only momentarily distracted by Thomas's move; he growled, ran his hand through his hair and then tore off his jacket and tossed it onto the steps.

Thomas looked around; they were alone on the terrace, and as the orchestra struck up its next tune, he realized that no one inside would hear him yell after he had taken his best punch and Noelani's brother tossed him over the parapet and into the garden thirty feet below.

"And this is paradise," he thought with a sigh as Akoni began to move around him in a wide circle with his ham-sized fists ready to strike. The fact that Akoni didn't immediately begin throwing blows told Thomas that he was assessing his opponent's fighting ability. That might have been heartening but looking at the Hawaiian's barrel chest and tree-trunk forearms sent a shiver up his back. Why hadn't he brought along his Colt?

The full moon sat directly above the palace and a palm tree creaked in the warm breeze as Akoni chose his battle strategy; he raised both hands above his head, welded his hands together, and prepared to batter Thomas into submission with one great downward blow. But when the King's Secretary stepped out of the shadows and walked up beside them Akoni froze in place.

"The dance is inside, gentlemen," the secretary said. "Perhaps you would care to play out this little drama for His Majesty?"

Akoni lowered his hands. "I will deal with this insult to my family in my own way, *kanaka uuku*. Leave us."

"You call me 'little man,' but it is you who insults the throne and our people," responded the secretary. Then he turned to Thomas, who had yet to drop his fists. "Thank you for coming this evening, Colonel, but I think it best if you took this opportunity to return to your hotel. I will convey your apology for taking leave without notice to His Majesty." Then the secretary pointed down to the end of the veranda. "Those stairs lead into the garden. Follow the path past the stables to the gate. The guard will let you out."

With that the Secretary stepped between Akoni and Thomas to signal that his command was to be obeyed. Akoni clenched his fists at his side but said nothing. Thomas nodded to the secretary and walked slowly across the veranda, made a sidelong glance into the crowded ballroom, and went down the long flight of steps to the garden.

Torches flickered among the flowering bushes and palms in the garden and he followed the winding pea-gravel path past two fountains until he reached a tall green gate. He swung it open and stepped out of the garden to the front of the stables, beyond which he saw a guarded gate leading to a side street. It was barely 9 PM, and he was headed back to his hotel. He supposed he should be grateful that his skull was intact, but the memory of Noelani and their dance sent a wave of melancholy flowing through his being that not even a night of cards was going to suppress.

As he walked past the stable, a voice whispered in the darkness: "Colonel, over here."

He turned and saw one of the two-story wooden doors swinging open. Standing in the doorway, illuminated by torchlight, was Princess Noelani.

"Would you like to go for a swim?" she asked.

~ SEVENTEEN ~

Kukui Hōkū Lagoon

Thomas's legs turned to lead, and he struggled to form a reply.

"Swim?" he finally said. "Here, in the barn?"

Noelani laughed. She had put a short jacket over her gown, and in the dim lamplight her eyes glowed like pale green sapphires.

"No, Colonel. We will take that…"

She pointed to a two-person buggy with a folding top to which a chestnut Hackney stallion had been hitched.

"You can drive?" she asked.

"Of course," he mumbled. He steadied her arm as she stepped up onto the seat before sitting beside her and taking the reins.

"Where are we going?" he asked.

"North along the coast road, about an hour from here. Take us to the left outside the gate and use your lightest touch with the Hackney—he is very well trained."

Thomas snapped the reins gently and the heavily muscled horse eased out of the barn and ambled towards the concrete block wall that surrounded the palace grounds. The guards recognized the Princess and opened the gate, but when Thomas began the turn onto the hard-packed dirt road, he could tell that they were confused to see their Royal Princess in the company of a strange American. *Which is exactly how I am feeling,* Thomas thought.

There was no other traffic on the road, and the light from the moon was all they needed to steer by. When they reached the outskirts of town, Noelani directed him to turn north and follow the winding road that hugged the coastline. The mountains that ringed the city to the northeast loomed black and threatening and made Thomas wonder about the princess's brother. What would he do if he learned that his sister had ridden off with the man he had just tried to crush? But, when he turned his head and took in Noelani's radiant face and shining eyes, his concern evaporated. Then, a thought struck him.

"I don't have a bathing suit," he blurted out as they passed a clump of flowering trees whose branches spilled out onto the road.

Noelani laid her hand on his forearm. "Why ever would you worry about such a small thing?" she asked. "You can swim, can't you?"

Thomas looked into the star-speckled sky before replying. "The last person who asked me that was the captain of the ship that dropped me off at Honolulu," he said. "My swim that morning was over a mile."

"You won't have to swim that far tonight, Thomas. The rock pool in *Kukui Hōkū* Lagoon is only a few hundred feet around. It is a special place, sacred, in fact, and only members of the royal family and their guests are permitted to enter its water."

"Does *Kukui Hōkū* have a special meaning?" he asked.

The Princess squeezed his arm. "The best translation into English would be pool of starlight."

The buggy was riding close to the ocean now, and they could hear the crashing of waves on the shore and smell the salt brine and ripe seaweed along the surf line. The Hackney trotted smoothly, its hooves beating a steady, almost musical rhythm beneath the crowning moon.

Other than a few fisherman's shacks there were no buildings along the road, and they snaked along the contours of several small inlets for the next 30 minutes. Then the road climbed up over a line of sand dunes before winding down through a forest of massive trees whose gnarled roots rose from the water like the bent knees of giants at prayer. When they passed the trees, Noelani pointed to a fork in the road 50 yards ahead. The right fork was marked on each side by a pile of flat stones reaching 20 feet into the night sky. Thomas could not see any carriage or horse tracks going to the right, while the road that continued to the left appeared to be well traveled.

"Your lagoon road?" he asked. Noelani nodded. "Where are the No-Trespass signs and locked gate?"

"Our people respect us," she answered. "We do not need such barriers." She saw the look of disbelief on Thomas's face and added,"Of course, it doesn't hurt that an ancient legend says that anyone other than blood royalty and their guests who violate the sanctity of *Kukui Hōkū* will have their entrails sucked out of their abdomens by a tribe of blood thirsty *menehune*."

"*Menehune*?"

"Little people, Thomas, very little. They come out only at night, and usually to construct temples or other clever structures. Most are kind and gentle, but a handful are quite evil."

"And I suppose your uncle and his ancestors have encouraged those legends to be told to children so that they will be too frightened to ever come out here when they grow older?"

Noelani leaned over and kissed Thomas on the cheek. "Of course," she said, holding back a laugh. "That is far less expensive than building a gate or placing guards around the lagoon, wouldn't you agree?"

The road narrowed beyond the stone piles, and the light from the full moon illuminated rows of delicately arched trees and shrubs that bordered the path. The unmistakable fragrance of jasmine filled the air as they wound through stands of palms and boulders to the sounds of the ocean, and Thomas felt sea spray wafting through the thick mass of greenery between them and the lagoon.

A moment later the Hackney trotted under a tree branch covered with white hibiscus flowers that rippled in the soft breeze like waves on a pond. Then the buggy navigated a sharp turn and came to halt where a line of trees and bushes closed off the way forward.

"I have never seen anything like this place," he said.

"And you haven't really seen it yet, dear Thomas," Noelani replied. She stepped onto the path and walked around to pat the horse on the nose. "He won't go anywhere," she said. Then she took Thomas by the hand and led him through a narrow opening that had been cut into the brush. They made their way for 50 feet along a footpath where the only light came from a scattering of stars directly overhead. When they stepped out of the hedge and into the open, they were in another world.

For the second time that night, Thomas was at a complete loss for words. He searched Noelani's eyes, looking for confirmation that what he was seeing in the light streaming from the buttery moon above their heads was a dream. No earthly place could be this stunning.

Noelani smiled softly and took his arm, recalling her own reaction when she had first seen the lagoon pool as a child. She knew what he was thinking.

"It is real," she whispered.

They were standing on a narrow strip of white sand that swept down to a natural oval-shaped pool about 100 feet in diameter. A line of boulders separated the pool from the main lagoon and the ocean beyond and as he watched, small waves spilled over the rocks, sending ripples of seawater skimming across the pool. To his amazement, the leading edge of the waves phosphoresced with sparkles of translucent blue before merging with the deep green water in the pool. He turned to Noelani for an explanation, but she only smiled and held his arm more tightly.

A mass of delicate jasmine flowers spilled down the rocks to the water, filling the starry night sky with their sweet perfume. "How is that possible?" he asked when he found his tongue. "At night, in March?"

"Jasmine open as far as they can when the temperature drops," replied Noelani. "And they bloom year-round. Look behind them."

Beyond the expanse of jasmine-covered rocks that formed a half circle around the pool were thick vines covered in clumps of hibiscus flowers, and behind them a line of palms swayed gently in the warm breeze. Then Thomas noticed a tree-sheltered waterfall splashing into the pool. Like the waves from the lagoon, when the water from the mountains spilled into the pool a shower of luminescent blue sparks pulsed briefly before being absorbed into the darkness.

"What is that?" he whispered. "Is this some kind of island magic?"

"No, my darling, not magic or *menehunes*. A French biologist who studied the phenomenon years ago said it is caused by a tiny living organism. It only happens a few times a year, and it is spectacular."

Thomas continued to watch the glowing water, completely absorbed in the vision. "There is so much to take in, so much to see," he said.

"More than you realize, sweet Thomas," Noelani replied. "And it's all around you."

He turned to answer, and gasped. Noelani had shrugged off her jacket and dress and was standing beside him completely nude.

Thomas held his breath as the warm moonlight played across her breasts, stomach, and thighs. She stood tall, with her arms relaxed at her sides and a look of complete peace on her face. Then she turned and kissed him on the lips, full and deep.

"We did come to swim," she said in a throaty whisper. Then she ran across the sand and dove into the deep green pool. Her body was instantly wrapped in the blue astral light, and as she began to swim in long, slow strokes, a phosphorescent trail radiated around her.

Thomas watched, entranced by the magical scene. Then, without hurry or hesitation, he removed his boots and clothing and walked out into waist-deep water. He wiggled his toes and watched in amazement as blue sparks formed around his feet, and then he plunged his hands into the water and began to laugh when the iridescent shine rippled along his hands and wrists with every move he made. The wonder of the moment was so overwhelming that he almost forgot that just a few yards away, naked and glowing in the moonlit pool, a royal princess was waiting for him to join her.

He began to swim, following the glittering powder blue trail Noelani left in her wake. She had made it to the other side and climbed onto a smooth boulder directly beneath the waterfall. As he neared, she raised her arms above her head and slowly turned under the pure, cascading flow. Thomas feasted on the sight of water splashing over her shoulders, across her breasts and down to the triangle between her legs. Then her back was towards him, the water a moonlit stream of gleaming crystal caressing her lustrous crème colored derrière. An image of the statue of the Greek goddess of love, Aphrodite Kallipygos, who raises her robe to reveal her perfect backside flashed across his consciousness. But Princess Noelani was a warm-blooded woman, not a cold marble statue.

He reached the boulder and came up beside her. Noelani completed her turn, lowered her arms, and took him in a tight embrace. The sensation of the cool water splashing on his head and shoulders mingled with the rising heat in his body, the fullness of her breasts and nipples, the taut line of her stomach, and the warmth of her inner thighs. His mouth filled with water when he moved to kiss her, but he didn't care. She tasted of ripe berry and honeysuckle, and he trailed his hands down her back to the firm roundness of her buttocks and pulled her against his legs. Noelani shuddered, lowered one hand between his legs and softly stroked him. Then she pulled back, looked deep into his eyes, and dove into the pool.

The game was on. He prepared to dive into the water, only to be distracted by a dark shadow flitting between the trees where the mountain stream reached the edge of the rock before falling into the pool. He stared hard but did not see any more movement. The white light from the moon was casting shadows from the palm trees and bushes across the landscape. No doubt that was all he had seen.

He dove deep and swam to the center of the pool where Noelani was waiting. The water came to just below her breasts and Thomas swam up, wrapped his arms around her waist and began showering her shoulders and breasts with kisses. She held his head in her hands and laughed, and then pulled him up and kissed him again.

"Thomas," she finally said, "now listen, there is something I must tell you."

But he did not listen. Instead, he reached down into the water, put his hands behind her knees, and lifted her up. Then, with one hand under her shoulders and the other beneath her thighs, he lowered her onto her back and began spinning slowly in the water. Blue phosphor trails encircled them, and as they turned, Thomas lowered his head and lavished kisses on her breasts, stomach, thighs, and the warmth between her legs.

Noelani began to laugh and threw her arms out into the water behind her head. Thomas kept spinning and kissing and caressing, marveling at the way her body shone in the water with moonlight from above and phosphorescence from below.

He had never known such joy, or such passion, and he was quickly reaching the point where he had to join with her body. Should he carry her to the beach, or keep her afloat on her back and wrap her legs around his hips?

Noelani solved his dilemma. She rolled off his arms and stood up in the water. Then she put a finger on his lips, and said, "Thomas. Please, my darling, I really do need to talk to you."

She was more beautiful than he could imagine. Several strands of wet hair were plastered across her forehead and cheek, her skin glowed in the light of the moon, and the way her full breasts rose and fell as she spoke mesmerized him. But he nodded that he was ready to listen.

"Good," she said. She kissed him again, and then crossed her arms over her breasts.

"This is all so wonderful," she began, "and all my doing. I want you this minute more than I have ever wanted anything. Please believe me."

Suddenly the water felt cold to Thomas, and the breeze began to chill him. Things weren't moving in quite the direction he had hoped for. "Go ahead," he finally said.

Noelani reached her hands out and took his. "I am Princess of the Kingdom of Hawai'i," she said softly. "My responsibilities are to my people and to my family. When I bear a child there is a good chance that he or she will become the future monarch. My child must be born to a father who has roots in the kingdom and knows our history and customs. There is no other way."

Thomas kept hold of her hands, but to his surprise realized that he was neither angry nor disappointed that they were not going to make love. That was a new sensation for him. But everything about this night had been pure magic, something he knew he would never experience again in his lifetime. That was going to have to be enough.

He felt himself smile. He raised her hands up out of the water and kissed each one. "I understand, Noelani. I do." Then he turned in the water and began to walk to the shore to get dressed.

"Where are you going?" she called after him.

He swung around, a questioning expression in his eyes. *'Why, I'm leaving,'* he thought to himself. *'Isn't that what you wanted?'*

Noelani came up in front of him and reached under the water to caress him between his legs. "Thomas, dear Thomas, I cannot have you inside of me because I cannot become pregnant by you. That's all." Then she lowered her head, and in a demure tone said, "Have you so little imagination that you cannot conceive of other things that we can do together?"

Thomas tilted his head back and laughed. Then he lowered his body into the pool and swam quickly over beneath the waterfall. Noelani followed him and watched as he pulled himself out of the water and lay on his back on the smooth boulder. She stood at the edge of the rock and began caressing and kissing his feet, ankles, calves, and thighs.

"You taste like the ocean," she said with a giggle as her lips trailed up his stomach and chest.

"Not all of me," he whispered. She kissed him, smiled knowingly, and lowered her head to his thighs.

From its perch a quarter million miles above the green lagoon, the moon reached out its arms to wrap the lovers in celestial light. A school of pearl and ruby colored fish danced in phosphorescent circles around the rock beneath the waterfall, and the night-blooming jasmine stretched open its petals to catch the last warming breeze. The palms swayed gently to the rhythm of the waves rolling in from the depths of the great sea, and a flock of birds flowed in unison across the western horizon.

Then a shadow slipped out of its hiding place in the rocks above the waterfall and melted into the darkness.

~ EIGHTEEN ~

Honolulu Harbor

It was 3 AM when he returned to the hotel, but he was unable to sleep. Noelani had napped against his shoulder during the buggy ride back to the palace, and when they parted outside the stable, they said goodbye knowing they would never meet like this again.

He poured a brandy and settled into a chair on the wrought-iron balcony outside his second-story room. The town was asleep under the waning moon, and the light breeze off the ocean was the only thing moving on the island. His encounter with the princess had been extraordinary, unlike anything he had experienced. In fact, magical was the only word he could summon up to describe their swim in the moon-lit pool. But, in a rare moment of self-reflection he had to acknowledge that even magic could not hide the deeper truth gnawing at his gut. Their tryst in the fluorescing water was a once in a lifetime escapade, but it still ended the way all of his short-term romances did; when the fireworks faded, he went home by himself, and the relationship sputtered to an end. Every time. And while the thought of getting married and settling in one place had never entered his mind to a serious degree, this evening's romp, as sensually remarkable as it had been, still left him feeling hollow and unfulfilled.

Or was incomplete a more accurate description, he wondered. Nothing about his life was settled. He had banged around the world since the end of the war like Odysseus after the fall of Troy, and he was as far away from achieving stability and meaning in his life as he had ever been. It wasn't that his life had been without accomplishment or adventure, of course. He was famous, a hero who had made his mark in both the American and Mexican militaries. His skills at cards were world-class, few could match his prowess on horseback, and he had become an excellent reporter who counted among his friends Ulysses S. Grant, President of the United States. Now, at just 23, he was also the co-owner of a sugar plantation with more than 100 employees. A man, he smiled to himself, who had just frolicked in the nude under a tropical waterfall with an authentic royal princess. And yet…

He was also a marked man. Colin Stafford would spare no expense to track him down and kill him. No place in the world would be safe from the wealthy businessman's thirst for revenge after what Thomas had written about him in the *Chronicle*. He would be back on Lana'i tomorrow, but all that separated him from those who were bent on his murder was 3,000 miles of ocean and an eleven-day steamship voyage.

A soft glow behind the mountains encircling the town signaled that sunrise was not far off. Thomas finished his brandy and went back into his room to change and pack his bag. The steam packet to Lana'i wouldn't leave for another six hours, but he couldn't sit still.

He went down to the lobby where a sleepy desk clerk apologized that the restaurant wasn't open yet, although he probably could fetch some biscuits and coffee. Thomas opened the French doors leading out to the veranda and settled at a small table overlooking the hotel gardens where he had his breakfast and watched the world come to life. An hour later he paid his bill, turned down the clerk's offer to call a cab, and slung his bag over his shoulder for the ten-minute walk to the harbor.

The pier where the *Lela M.* would berth to take on passengers for Molokai' and Lana'i was deserted, which suited Thomas's mood just fine. He took a seat on a wooden bench midway down the plank structure and pulled a notebook and pencil from his bag. He had been thinking through the projects he wanted to undertake on the plantation, and it was time to make a final list.

The sun broke the eastern horizon beyond the rock jetty, turning the water in the harbor from gray to pearl blue. He had jotted a few lines when he heard shuffling noises and turned his head to see Noelani's brother Akoni approaching rapidly, accompanied by a much shorter, feral-looking man carrying a wooden club. As Thomas's survival instinct kicked in, the thought occurred to him that Akoni wasn't carrying a club because the giant Hawaiian had no need of a weapon. He was a weapon.

His Colt was packed too deep inside his bag to grab quickly, and it looked like the only other way out of his predicament would be to jump off the pier and make a swim for it. That might buy a minute or two, but Akoni would reach land before he did, and he could not stay in the water all day. He was going to have to fight.

Akoni surged down the pier in his black linen shirt and trousers like a flow of super-heated lava, only to come to a sudden stop a few feet from Thomas. The smaller man kept coming, swinging his club in the air, and yelling in Hawaiian.

Thomas sidestepped the first downward swing, and when the man countered with a sideways slash, Thomas was able to grab the wrist holding the club and use the man's own momentum to slam him against a rough-sawn railing post, knocking the air out of his lungs. Then he swung the man around, punched him in the throat with a chisel fist, and yanked the club from his hand. The man crumpled to the deck, and Thomas whipped around to face Akoni, who had remained stock still while his partner initiated the fight. Smart strategy, Thomas thought. Get your opponent a bit winded and wear down his physical reserves before you wade into the battle yourself.

Akoni raised his fists and stepped closer. Thomas was struck by how calm his opponent was; his eyes were clear and focused, his stance was almost relaxed, and his breathing was normal. All in all, he seemed to be in no hurry to begin bashing the man to death who had so publicly defiled his sister and humiliated his family.

Thomas had to stay out of range of Akoni's tree-trunk sized arms. A single blow or crushing bear hug would be all it would take to render him unconscious, or dead. He shifted to the left and got closer to the light crossbar railing. Someone—probably a fisherman—was moving on the beach, but no one had come out onto the pier. Whatever happened now there would be no witnesses.

He gripped the club and held it at the ready behind his right shoulder as he stepped up against the railing. If things went badly, he might have to hop over the rail and into the water—if he wasn't tossed over first, of course.

Suddenly the rising sun shone directly into Akoni's eyes, and he narrowed them reflexively to block out the glare. Thomas had to act. The instant Akoni began to turn his head away from the direct sunlight, Thomas swung the club against his attacker's left knee.

There was a cracking sound, and Akoni grunted and collapsed to the deck on his broken knee cap. The reprieve only lasted a moment; the towering islander threw back his head, roared, and pulled himself to his feet. Thomas took two steps to the side and positioned his club for the next blow. Now Akoni backed up against the railing, but his expression did not convey fear, only anger at having been bested, if only for an instant. I must make him come to me on his bad leg, Thomas thought. If he winces or halts for even a second, I will take out his other leg.

Before Akoni could move off the railing and strike, Thomas caught a blur of motion in his right eye. It was the partner he had knocked to the deck a few seconds ago. The man lunged at him, but Thomas stepped to the side so quickly that the man stumbled past without making contact. As the man tripped, Thomas smashed his club down onto the center of his back. The combination of the man's own forward velocity and the force of Thomas's blow sent him barreling into Akoni's midsection just as he was about to push off the railing and rejoin the fight.

The smaller attacker hit Akoni hard, and to right himself he threw his arms around Akoni's waist and held on tight. Thomas heard wood shatter under the combined weight and momentum of the two men. A look of surprise crossed Akoni's face as he flailed his arms wildly in an attempt to overcome the laws of physics, but what happened next was inevitable: the railing gave way and both men toppled off the pier towards the water 15 feet below.

Akoni's confederate splashed harmlessly into the harbor, but Noelani's brother smashed his head against a wooden piling three feet above the water line. He careened into the water facedown and went still. His friend gave a sidelong glance at Akoni's lifeless form and decided that trying to save the huge Hawaiian was a waste of time. He swung around in the water and began swimming towards shore.

Then Thomas heard voices and turned to see a half dozen people running onto the pier. He recognized Henry Kakaako, the fisherman who had dredged him out of the water onto this very pier after he'd been tossed into the water by the German naval commander. He looked back down to where Akoni was bobbing with his head half-submerged. If the man wasn't dead yet, it wouldn't be long.

But the drowning man wasn't just his enemy. He was also Noelani's brother, and that changed the life-or-death calculation dramatically. Thomas cursed under his breath, slipped off his boots and jumped through the break in the railing. He went under water for a second, pulled himself up and swam over to where the Hawaiian was still afloat. It took all his strength to get in front of Akoni's body, reach his arms under the giant's shoulders, and turn him over onto his back. There was a long gash across Akoni's forehead, and he was bleeding profusely into the water. Did sharks cross the jetty barrier into the harbor, he wondered?

"Thomas!" a voice shouted. He began to tread water and looked up onto the pier. It was Henry. "Can you pull him to shore?" his friend asked.

"I'll try," he answered.

He knew that Akoni would start to sink the moment the air in his lungs was replaced by seawater, and he had no idea how much the man may have taken in. What he knew for certain was that if Noelani's brother started to go under there was no way he was going to be able to stop the descent to the bottom of the harbor.

He reached under and took hold of the back of Akoni's shirt collar. Then he turned and began to half swim, half paddle towards the shore

40 yards distant. Akoni's unconscious body was partially buoyant, and the gentle swells helped push them in the right direction. When they were 50 feet from shore, Henry and two other men waded in to help drag Akoni up onto the muddy beach.

Thomas collapsed on his back, exhausted. The Harbor Master appeared with a half-pint bottle of brandy and helped him sit up and a small crowd of onlookers milled around as Henry and the others checked to make sure Akoni was breathing. Then Henry came over and told him they were going to take Akoni to Henry's house, two blocks away. Someone rolled a two-wheeled fish cart to the edge of the water, and four men lifted Akoni into the back and began to pull it up off the beach. When Thomas was able to stand, he followed the cart to his friend's house. He came through the door just as the men were laying Akoni down on a straw pallet in the center of the main room.

"Shall I send someone to the palace to alert his family?" Henry asked.

"I don't think that would be a good idea—at least not yet," Thomas replied.

Henry raised his eyebrows.

"Akoni and his friend were trying to kill me," Thomas said in a quiet voice. "That might be hard to explain to his uncle."

"Kill you?" asked Henry. "Then I will send for the constable. He needs to be jailed."

Thomas shook his head. "Before we contact anyone, I want to talk to him. I know he was angry about me spending time with Princess Noelani but killing me for that reason is a little…."

"Excessive?" asked his friend.

Thomas shrugged. "Depending on your perspective, I suppose."

A woman materialized from the kitchen and began cleaning and bandaging Akoni's head wound. When she was done, she left to fetch the doctor. The men who had helped bring Akoni to Henry's said their goodbyes, and Thomas and Henry sat at the table.

"I have four hours until the coaster leaves for Lana'i," Thomas said. "Plenty of time to get dry and maybe even to figure this mess out.

There are already enough people after my hide–I don't need another enemy."

Henry laughed. "From what I saw as I came onto the pier, I'm not so sure saving him was a good idea."

"Couldn't see myself trying to explain that to his sister," Thomas replied.

Henry nodded. "I will make coffee."

Thomas looked up at the brown crockery bottle on the mantle. "How about a little rum instead."

He changed into dry clothes while Henry walked his son over to a friend's house. When the fisherman returned, Akoni was groaning softly where he lay on the pallet. Henry pulled a chair close to the unconscious man and nodded for Thomas to step away.

"Best you aren't the first person he sees when he wakes up," Henry said.

Thomas moved to the doorway that led into the kitchen and waited for the man who wanted to kill him to wake up. It didn't take long; Akoni raised one hand to the bandages on his head, moved his neck from side to side to make sure he was alive, and then slowly sat up. When his eyes cleared, he looked around the room. "Where am I?" he asked Henry. "Who are you?"

"I am Kakaako, the fisherman. You are in my home," replied Henry. "You fell from the pier and smashed into one of the pilings. You are lucky to be alive."

"You saved me?"

Henry pointed to Thomas standing in the shadow of the doorway. "He did."

Akoni swung his head around and immediately recognized his enemy. His face flushed, and he started to pull off his blanket and push himself up, but Henry placed a hand on his shoulder to keep him down.

"You can settle your personal business later, my friend," Henry said.

"But not in my home."

Akoni was too weak to argue. He looked down at the floor and asked, "Why?"

Thomas knew the question was meant for him. "Do you mean why did I jump in and pull you to shore after you and your friend tried to kill me?"

Akoni looked Thomas in the eye. "I would not have done the same for you."

"Perhaps not, but when your friend swam away without trying to help you, I had no choice."

A half-smile creased Akoni's face. "The weasel deserted me?"

"It's their nature," Henry said as he handed Akoni a tin cup of coffee laced with rum. "And to be clear, if I had been in my friend Thomas's place, I would probably have left you to the sharks."

Akoni lifted his cup in acknowledgement and said, "This man insulted my family."

"No," replied Henry, "this man accepted your sister's invitation to go for a swim. That's all. She was clearly not insulted. Only your feelings were hurt."

"Do you have a chair?" asked Akoni.

Henry pulled a chair from the kitchen table and helped Akoni stand. Then he wrapped the blanket around Akoni's shoulders and motioned for Thomas to join them. Thomas was a little wary of getting close to his intended murderer, but Henry was nearly as big as Akoni, and would be able to stop anything before it got out of hand. He slid a chair to within a few feet of the giant and waited.

Noelani's brother took a drink before he spoke. "We—the Hawaiian people—have been conquered. Conquered by the Christian God, by the merchants and bankers, conquered by the whalers and the sugar plantation owners, and by our own fear and superstitions." He gripped his cup tightly with both hands and looked at Thomas. "I could not stand by and watch my own sister fall to another kind of conquest." Then he went silent.

To his own surprise, Thomas found himself nodding in agreement with Akoni's observations. You could only take so much from a man before he fought back in any way he could.

"I did not conquer Noelani," Thomas began in a soft voice. "At least not in the sense you are suggesting. In fact, she made it clear to me the moment we arrived at the pool that she would only share her complete being with the man she would one day marry. It is not easy for me to talk about such things, Akoni, but you need to know that I heard your sister, and I respected her wish."

Akoni shifted in his chair, rubbed his hand on the knee that Thomas had clubbed, and pulled the blanket tighter. Then he sighed, and said, "I must think this through. It is not an easy thing for me."

Thomas chuckled. "And almost being killed was not an easy thing for me."

Akoni raised his head. "For what it is worth, I did not intend to kill you, Colonel. Just to break a few bones and perhaps crush your testicles."

"You'll have to pardon me for not feeling a sense of relief about that," Thomas answered with a laugh.

There was a knock at the door and Henry admitted the doctor. While Akoni's forehead and knee were being attended to, Thomas and Henry waited outside. When the doctor finished the stitches and braced Akoni's leg, he asked Henry to let Akoni rest there for the day before he returned to the palace. Thomas sat down next to the couch where Akoni lay with his head swathed in bandages and his leg elevated on pillows. "The coaster leaves for Lana'i in two hours," Thomas said. "I suppose I wouldn't mind knowing if I should be keeping an eye out for a visit some night from you and your friend."

"About you and my sister…" Akoni began.

"We parted as friends," Thomas said, "and I will treasure her memory always. But her future and mine lay along very different paths."

Akoni nodded. "I understand. As for when you might see me again, Colonel, I promise you this: should I ever come through your door it will be to save your life, not to take it."

He extended a massive hand, and they shook. Then the laudanum the doctor gave him took hold and he drifted off to sleep.

~ NINETEEN ~

San Francisco, April 1872

Fitch Donegan had always chafed under authority and being subjected to criticism from Colin P. Stafford every day for the three months he had been tracking Colonel Scoundrel hadn't done anything to change his outlook.

Oh, the money was fine, in fact it was the most he had ever earned on a regular basis. But a man could only drink so much whiskey and bang so much quim, which were pretty much the only indulgences his limited imagination could come up with for squandering his new-found fortune.

The work itself was tedious; when he left Stafford's home after agreeing to set everything else aside and just search for Scoundrel, he had assembled a team of private investigators, tavern and whorehouse snitches, telegraph operators from Seattle to Los Angeles, beat cops, hotel clerks, even laundry workers. Stafford grudgingly paid for all of them, but as the weeks passed, he became increasingly short-tempered. "A man can't simply disappear," he had shouted the previous evening when Donegan showed up for his weekly report. "It's not possible."

Donegan knew differently. If a man was so inclined and had a little money, he could change his name and live anonymously anywhere he pleased. Colonel Scoundrel's fame notwithstanding, he was probably better equipped than most to vanish and stay that way.

When Donegan woke this morning, he gave serious thought to visiting Stafford and calling it a day. He was tired and frustrated, and if he was being honest with himself, he missed watching wealthy businessmen soil their trousers when he threated to bash in their skulls. And more than that, he missed taking their wives or daughters by force even after their men had begged for mercy and agreed to dance to whatever tune Stafford played. He had no problem paying professional tarts for sex, but it was so much more satisfying to listen to the sound of petticoats and underpants being torn off and to watch the terror in the eyes of a woman when he ripped her legs apart and began to thrust deep inside her, a pleasure that was magnified when he did it in front of a bound and gagged husband.

Giving that life up to become a research assistant and errand boy was not playing well with him. He was prepared to steel himself for a final visit to his employer, who, he was sure, would go into a volcanic rage and perhaps even send someone to teach Donegan himself the futility of crossing a Stafford.

Then, a miracle: the mousey young woman he had hired to search every newspaper she could put her hands on for information about the elusive Colonel Scoundrel showed up at his hotel at lunch wearing a triumphant expression. Donegan was quiet as she sat across from him and unfolded a newspaper.

"My brother works for a steamship line," she said. "He has made two trips to Hawai'i since you hired me, and this is the first newspaper he has brought to me. It's from Honolulu, three weeks ago."

She slid the paper across the table. "Page 3," she simply said. "Left column."

Donegan flipped open the paper and focused his attention on the article on the left side.

Royal Celebration at Iolani Palace

Hawaiian royalty mixed with businessmen, diplomats, dignitaries, visiting naval officers and other distinguished individuals last night at the newly built Iolani Palace to celebrate the anniversary of the ascension to the throne of King Kamehameha V.

Donegan raised his eyebrows.

"Paragraph 5," said the woman.

Among the distinguished visitors to the palace was retired American Army Colonel Thomas E. Scoundrel, hero of the recent American War of Rebellion, who traveled from his sugar cane plantation on Lana'i.

Donegan beamed and slammed the paper on the table. "Does it say anything more about him?" he asked.

"Just that one mention. But according to our deal, that should be enough."

Donegan could barely contain his excitement. He took his wallet out of his vest pocket and handed two $50 bills across the table.

The woman took the money and said, "We agreed to $200."

"I will give you $300 as soon as I confirm this information," he said.

Then, without waiting for a reply, he left his lunch on the table and rushed to hail a cab.

A half hour later, Donegan was at Stafford's front door. The maid informed him that her boss was meeting with a group of investors and ushered him into the library to wait to be called. "Tell Mr. Stafford that he is going to want to leave that meeting now," Donegan told the maid. "Right now."

A moment later an exasperated looking Stafford came into the library. "Well?" he demanded.

Donegan handed over the newspaper and directed his employer to the article about the royal gala. The flush that bloomed on Stafford's cheeks a minute later was visible even through the port wine stain that covered half his face.

"How?" Stafford asked. "Where did you find...."

"You have paid me well to find him, Mr. Stafford. I have been doing my job."

Stafford read the article again and then tossed the newspaper on a chair. He clasped his hands behind his back and began to pace around the book-lined room before coming to a halt in front of a display case filled with the kind of trinkets and treasures that rich men collect on their travels.

"You leave on the next steamship to Honolulu," Stafford said. "I will give you enough cash to make the trip, and a letter of credit to give to my brother at his bank. It will authorize him to provide you with whatever funds you may need for outfitting, travel, and to, ahem, hire whatever local help you may require."

"Of course," replied Donegan. "With respect, Mr. Stafford, I don't believe I knew you had a brother who lived in Hawai'i."

"Same father, different mothers," came the reply. "We are as different as night and day, but from time to time our respective interests cross paths."

He opened the door of the display case and removed a clear glass jar filled with a yellowish liquid. Then he held it up to the light and examined its contents before handing it to Donegan.

The fluid was opaque enough that it was difficult to make out what was inside. Donegan gave the jar a shake and brought it close to his face. At first, he saw nothing. Then, an object appeared out of the swirling, smokey liquid and came to rest directly in front of him. Donegan sucked in his breath. Staring at him from the depths of the embalming fluid was a human eyeball with a pale blue iris and a jangle of nerves stringing out its backside. He lost his balance for a moment and almost dropped the jar.

Stafford took the container from Donegan's trembling hands. "I never trusted my brother, and we didn't see eye to eye on much," he said as he raised the jar to eye level. "Until now, that is."

<h1 style="text-align:center">~ TWENTY ~</h1>

Lana'i, May 1872

Thomas had never worked harder in his life. In the four weeks since his return from Honolulu, he and Kukane mapped out plots for new plantings and supervised the first and second gang workers who laid in the new cane. They built irrigation flumes and cane wagons, cleared 50 acres of brush and trees, constructed more housing for the workers and widened the road to the loading docks on the coast.

They also imported new varieties of sugar cane to plant in test plots. Since it took two years for the cane to reach harvestable size, their experiments might not pay off for several years—if ever. But if they were able to identify higher yield varieties with shorter growing times, it could transform their business and allow for the production of one more crop per year.

Kukane joined Thomas each evening for dinner, and the men talked long into the night about Hawaiian history and culture. The field supervisor's knowledge of Polynesian geography and natural history inspired Thomas to convert the field shack his partner had used as an illicit love nest into a one-room schoolhouse. They placed an advertisement for a teacher in the Honolulu newspaper and hired the first—and only—applicant for the job, a young woman who had been teaching at a mission school on O'ahu but who desired to work in a more pastoral setting. Thomas saw that she had supplies and books, and they built two new rooms in the cabin for her living quarters. They also purchased a one-year pass on the coaster so that she could take the afternoon packet home on Friday afternoons and return on Sunday.

A Catholic priest visited on the first day of class to bless the venture, which he did to the thunderous applause of parents from four different countries. Absent from the celebration was Thomas's partner, William Fortnite. The two men had entered an uneasy truce upon Thomas's return from Honolulu, and now Fortnite focused on managing the accounts and left the day-to-day plantation operation to Thomas. At Thomas's insistence they signed an agreement specifying that the $50,000 line of credit from the bank would be accessed and used only for the purchase of land, new cane plants, equipment, and labor.

At midday on May 20th Thomas was supervising a third gang team as they burned an acre of slash to prepare it for planting. He heard shouts and turned to see a horse and rider bolt out of a stand of trees to the west. The horse was heavily lathered, not a surprise, Thomas thought, given the size of the rider. A minute later he realized that it was Akoni in the saddle.

The King's nephew flew up to the top of the low hill. He was breathing almost as hard as his horse.

"Akoni, what …?" Thomas began.

"You must leave here now Thomas," said Akoni as he swung down off the horse. "There is no time. I have a skiff at the landing."

Kukane handed the huge man a canteen of cool water, and when he had his fill, Thomas asked, "Leave? Why? And where did you come from?"

"I arrived an hour ago from Honolulu and paid the owner of the general merchandise store a few dollars to borrow his horse. We don't have much time, maybe one hour."

"To do what?" Thomas asked.

"To save your life," Akoni answered.

Kukane tapped his pipe on the bottom of his boot. "Perhaps you would like to explain the situation?"

"I'm sorry," Akoni answered. He gathered his breath and continued.

"Thomas, four men will be arriving on the packet in about an hour. One is named Donegan. Does that name mean anything to you?"

Thomas shook his head.

"He is an assassin, employed by a man named Stafford in San Francisco. He arrived in Honolulu three days ago and hired three layabouts to come here with him and kill you."

"That name I know," Thomas replied.

"The one you told me about?" asked Kukane. "The one you wrote about in your article?"

Thomas nodded, and then shook his head. "How the hell did he track me here?" he said in a low voice.

"I have some idea," answered Akoni, "and I will tell you when we leave the island."

"To go where?" asked Thomas.

Akoni shook his head. "That I do not know. When we get the sail up, we can decide. Right now, we need to leave."

"One hour, you said?"

"Maybe less. One hour to get the harbor, one hour to get here."

Thomas briefly considered making a stand against the men. With Akoni and Kukane beside him the odds would be about even. Then he looked out across the fields and saw dozens of workers and children scattered around the cane plots. When the bullets started flying, they would all become targets.

"My cabin is over there," he said, pointing to a small structure at the edge of the field 300 yards down the valley. "Let me take your horse so I can go and pack, and you two get over there as quickly as you can."

Without waiting for a response Thomas stepped up into the saddle and put his heels to the horse's flanks. It felt good to ride, even under these circumstances. He galloped at full speed to his cabin and tethered the horse to a post. Then he went inside and began throwing clothing into his satchel. He was slipping his Colt revolver into his belt when Kukane and Akoni stepped through the door.

"I sent a boy to the main house to saddle a horse for you, Thomas," said Kukane. "I will gather it up at the landing later."

Thomas opened a desk drawer and took out an envelope. "This is for you, my friend," he told Kukane. "If anything happens to me, my 50% ownership of the plantation belongs to you. That includes the right to make draws against the credit line."

Kukane took the envelope and slipped it into his shirt pocket. "Let us hope it does not come to that."

Then Thomas walked to the corner of the room, pried up a floorboard, and lifted out a small metal box. He took out a stack of paper money tied with a string before handing the box to Kukane. "Here is $2,000. See to it that the schoolteacher is paid and use the rest as you see fit."

Kukane's eyes were misting as he took the box. "You will be back tomorrow, Thomas. I know you will."

Thomas laid his hand on Kukane's shoulder. "I guess we both know that won't be happening," he replied.

They heard the sound of a horse approaching, and went out under a warm, cloudless sky. Thomas breathed in the scent of burning cane and felt a soft breeze spill through the tree line. He could see planting crews in the distance, and when he strained his ears, he could just make out the song they were singing. He turned to Kukane and embraced him. Then he mounted his horse, gripped his satchel with one hand, and galloped off towards the coast behind Akoni.

The tiller pulled gently in Akoni's experienced hands, and when he released it the 17-foot single sail skiff rounded up easily into the eye of the wind and accelerated briskly away from the landing. Thomas had sailed enough to know that the press of a breeze would tend to twist the sail and lift the after end of the boom, which was something experienced sailors worked to avoid. The triangle formed by the spirit boom, the sail's foot, and the mast took care of that problem, Akoni had explained when he set the mast and sail after their gallop from the plantation. There was still, however, the question of where they were going.

"Moloka'i," said Thomas. "Northeast into the Kolohi Channel, then hug the coast and make for Halawa Bay. We'll anchor there and figure out our next move."

Akoni nodded and concentrated on navigating the craft across the choppy waters of the channel. The southern coast of Moloka'i was 15 nautical miles from the wooden pier at Lana'i and Thomas estimated they would arrive in under two hours. With fair winds and a following sea they could take shelter on Molokai's northeast coast before sunset.

He was learning that Akoni was not a particularly conversational man, and so he sat quietly in the bilge and tried to enjoy the journey. The Hawaiian handled the little boat skillfully, snugging up on the halyard and snouter to give more fullness to the sail when the wind was brisk, and slacking off on them when the wind eased up. Thomas wanted to ask if Noelani had been sailing the islands since childhood like her brother, but he decided not to poke that bear quite yet. The more immediate issue was what to do about Stafford's assassin. Donegan had steamed 3,000 miles to do his master's bidding, which meant that Stafford would not relent until the job was done, no matter what it cost or how long it took, and, if Donegan was worthy of his pay, he would leave no stone unturned to track Scoundrel down and kill him. Except for one, Thomas thought. He looked back at Akoni and wondered what he was going to think of the idea that was beginning to form in his mind.

The southern coast of Moloka'i had been visible since they departed Lana'i, and 90 minutes later they could make out the entry to Kalaeloa Harbor. Rugged, green-shrouded mountains swept up from behind the little harbor, where Thomas counted three small boats at anchor.

"From here until we get to the northeast peninsula, it is fishponds and reef all the way," said Akoni. "We'll stay well clear of the reefs until we get to Kapuupoi, which is the easternmost promontory on the island. From there it is just a few miles to the west along the shore to a small landing at Kapaliloa. I overnighted in a deserted fisherman's shack during a storm last year. We'll make for there."

"You sail the islands a lot," said Thomas.

Akoni pushed his hair back off his forehead and drank from the crockery jug he had packed. "Since I was a child," he replied. "A few years ago, I began mapping some of the reefs and shoals that were overlooked by Captain Cook in 1784, and by the missionaries in the 1840s. Even your American navy chose not to survey them in detail during the big topographical expedition after the Civil War. I also collect specimens from tide pools that are preserved and shipped to the British Museum of Natural History."

So that is how the nephew of a King spends his time, thought Thomas. "I am impressed," he said as Akoni adjusted the sail to accommodate a shift in the wind's direction. "Will you write a book?'

Akoni simply grinned in reply and pointed to the northeast. "This is as close as we will come to the shoreline until we round Kapuupoi Head. We have been protected from the winds and waves of the open sea by both Mau'i and Lana'i islands, but that will change when we reach the north coast."

When they rounded the islands' northeast head in the late afternoon and slipped close to the shore, the temperature dropped by ten degrees and the surface chop picked up. They swung away from a huge rock at Kapaliloa where it looked as if a giant shark had taken a bite out of the island, and Akoni began to ease the skiff towards a small, cliff-walled inlet. As they came close in, he spilled the wind from the skiff's sail and eased the shallow-draft boat right up on the sand beach. Thomas shook his head and smiled as he stepped out of the skiff onto dry land without getting his boots wet.

An hour later the two men were sitting beside a crackling fire as the sun dropped behind the fisherman's hut. The night was mild, and a blanket of stars spanned the sky across the horizon under a three-quarter moon. The skiff sat on the beach 50 yards away, protected from the tide and winds by thick brush and a line of stubby trees. They dined on the dried pork, biscuits, and fruit Akoni brought, along with a bottle of rum made with island molasses.

When the King's nephew lit a pipe and settled back against a pile of smooth rocks, Thomas decide it was time to talk. "If you are a man who keeps score, Akoni, your rescue today makes us even. My life for yours."

"Yes, I suppose you are right. Of course, this 'rescue' as you call it, is not quite complete." He paused for a moment to relight his pipe and then said, "I told you I would take you wherever you believed you would be safe. Unless you plan to stay on this little beach, we haven't reached that place."

This was the opening Thomas had been waiting for. He looked up into the sky and felt as if an icy wind had gusted off the water. "I know where I need to go," he said in a soft voice. "It's the only place they won't search."

Akoni looked across at him through the flames. "And where might that be, Thomas?"

"Kalawao."

The giant Hawaiian set down his pipe and placed his hands on his knees.

Then, in a voice drained of emotion he said, "You mean the leper colony."

Thomas nodded and stared into the fire.

~ TWENTY-ONE ~

Moloka'i

The skiff slipped effortlessly through the morning chop along Moloka'i's north coast. The breeze was steady under a cloudy sky and Akoni estimated they would reach the eastern shore of the Kalaupapa peninsula by midday. The king's nephew hadn't said more than few words since they broke camp, but Thomas could not just sit quietly in the bilge of the little boat and watch the rugged green coastline slide by in silence.

"You haven't told me how you learned about the men coming to kill me," he finally said.

Akoni slacked off on the halyard before answering. "It seems you have friends in many places. A messenger from the Office of the American Counsel came to the palace with a letter addressed to you. The Counsel saw you at His Majesty's gala and thought someone in the palace might be able to find you. The Principal Secretary gave it to my sister of course, who read the letter and brought it to me. I told her how you saved my life at the pier, and she knew I was in your debt. When I learned the letter's contents, I went to the harbor master for a list of Americans who had recently arrived in Honolulu. A man named Donegan had arrived the previous day, giving the Palace hotel as his destination. From there it only took a quick conversation with a hotel clerk to learn that Donegan had been looking for men to hire onto a job he was going to do on Lana'i. I loaded the skiff immediately and sailed for your plantation."

"For which I will always be grateful," Thomas replied. "You kept the letter?"

"My sister has it in a safe place. We both felt it would be best for me not to be found with it in my possession if what I was going to do would be in violation of the law."

Akoni began a wide sweep around a rocky islet and then angled the skiff closer to the shore before he spoke again. "The letter came from a man in San Francisco named Kwan. Do you know him?"

Thomas smiled and nodded at the mention of his friend and the memory of his wonderful food.

"According to the letter Kwan's niece works as a house maid for the man who hired Donegan to kill you. She overheard them discussing their plans and she rushed to her uncle with the news. He wrote the letter and saw to it that it was on the steamer to Hawai'i the next day. Donegan left two days later."

The wind began to gust and Akoni had to raise his voice to be heard. He pointed to the northwest and said, "There, in the notch between those two cliffs. Can you see the flat area?"

Thomas strained to make out the spot Akoni was indicating, but he could only see cliffs and rocks with a scattering of trees.

"That is Kalawao," said Akoni. "It is only about four square miles in size, but it was once a prosperous farming and fishing village."

"And the leper colony destroyed it?" asked Thomas.

"No, western diseases killed most of the villagers before the government decided this was the perfect place to isolate the lepers. It is a perfectly beautiful and desolate prison."

Thomas took note of the resignation in Akoni's voice and waited a minute before he replied. "I can't see a wharf."

Akoni laughed and snugged up on the lines as the wind grew more intense. "I have been told there is a wharf of sorts, but it must be rebuilt each summer after winter waves tear it apart. If it is standing, I will get you there. If it isn't…"

Thomas sighed at the memory of being tossed off the bow of the German warship outside Honolulu harbor. "If it isn't, I swim for it."

Akoni grinned. "There is another way. We sail around the peninsula, and I drop you at the Kalaupapa wharf. Then you hike the three miles across to the eastern side and make your way down those."

He pointed to the wall of imposing green-clad rock cliffs that rose straight up to the sky behind the tiny settlement. "It's a 1,500-foot descent down a narrow switchback path. I am told people and animals fall off it quite often."

The surface chop picked up, and the skiff began to sway from side to side. Akoni held tight to the tiller and the lines as the little boat got to within 100 yards of the rock-strewn shoreline. Thomas could see five-foot waves whipping around dozens of boulders that paralleled the shore, but he still could not make out a wharf.

"Can you see anything?" he shouted.

Akoni shook his head.

The wind made it difficult for the men to speak without cupping their hands. "Time to go around the peninsula?" Thomas called.

"We can, but you should also know that in a small village like Kalaupapa a stranger will be noticed. If anyone comes looking for you...."

He did not have to finish his sentence. Thomas believed Donegan would be afraid to follow him to the leper colony, but he could not be certain. The man had traveled across the Pacific Ocean to do his job, and it was possible that he would even be willing to risk exposure to leprosy to fulfill his contract. There were no good options.

The skiff began to slide up and down in the troughs between the breaking waves, and the wind blew water and sea foam hard against them.

"It's got to be here then," Thomas yelled. "Can you make it to shore?"

Akoni looked into the sheets of gray water billowing around them. The outlines of boulders were everywhere, and there were probably many more just under the surface of the water that he could not see. Even if he could make it to shore without a rock ripping out the hull, he might not be able to get back out to sea. As for what awaited them in the huts and wooden shacks just off the leper colony's beach, that possibility frightened the giant Hawaiian even more.

He clenched his hand around the tiller and made his decision.

"I will get you as close as I can," he shouted. "When I tell you to jump, you must do it at once. "

Thomas pushed wet hair back from his forehead. "And you?" he called.

"I'll be back in Honolulu before you are dry, my friend."

Thomas wrapped the strap of his sealskin bag around his shoulder and held onto the gunwale as Akoni pointed the skiff at the shore, deftly avoiding one boulder after another by just a few feet. The wind picked up, and it began to rain. When they were fifty yards from land Thomas could make out pinpricks of lamp light glowing in a row of huts in the deepening purple dusk.

"About your sister," he shouted.

"What's that?" answered Akoni without turning his head as he pulled in the sail with one hand and held the tiller with the other.

"Noelani," yelled Thomas. "I'm sorry…."

Akoni could not hear what Thomas was saying. The wind howled and cold rain battered the little boat with such force that it felt like the wooden vessel was going to shatter. Somewhere above them the sun was still shining but its light was unable to penetrate the thickening clouds and rising sea that merged into a dark curtain and spread across the horizon.

Then there was a great cracking noise as the port side of the skiff smashed into a boulder and spun in a half circle. Thomas was nearly thrown from his seat as Akoni fought to right the boat before it capsized. He threw himself against the tiller and leaned his huge body hard to the right, and for a moment it felt like he had succeeded. The skiff leveled and Thomas let out a sigh of relief. They were only 20 yards from shore, close enough for him to jump into the shallow water and walk to dry land. He smiled at Akoni and started to thank him when a wave lifted the back of the skiff and slammed the stern against a boulder.

Thomas fell back against the gunwale as Akoni was launched overboard, but before he could react, the stern of the boat splintered against another boulder, and he was flung over the side and engulfed by a surging wave that pushed him under. He felt his hands strike the rocky seabed, and he fought with all his strength to get into a crouching position and propel his body upward. A moment later his head broke the surface, and he was relieved to discover that the water was only chest deep.

Thomas was desperate to find Akoni. He grasped his bag and spun slowly in the water, shouting Akoni's name into the vortex of sleeting wind and rain until a powerful wave rammed him from behind and tossed him against a boulder like a flimsy piece of driftwood.

'*Damn my stupidity to hell,*' he thought as he went numb and slipped down into the icy darkness.

~ TWENTY-TWO ~

Kalawao

The monster smiled.

It's a sign, Thomas thought. I'm going to live.

He was lying on his back on a cot under a light blanket. The thatched roof above his head looked new, and the pale light streaming through the single window in the small hut told him that it was still daytime. He felt the warmth of a fire and smelled bread baking. Not exactly what one would expect to find in a monster's lair.

When he was able to focus and turn his head, he looked at the creature seated on the stool beside him. It was a man, he quickly realized, but the face was every bit as monstrous as he first thought. He was dressed in a rough cotton shirt and trousers and was holding a mug of tea in the stump of one hand. No fingers, Thomas saw, just three bulbous nubs covered with leathery skin. But the face...it was worse than any battlefield injury Thomas had seen during the war.

The man might have been Polynesian, but so many layers of his facial skin were missing or discolored that his race was impossible to surmise. He had hair on half of his skull, no ears or eyebrows, and where there should have been a nose there was only an oozing indentation. One of his eyes protruded out of its socket and dangled at the top of his cheekbone, while the other was clouded over with a mass of thick gray film. His upper lip was missing, and the skin around it had shrunk up to where his nose used to be, exposing his upper teeth to the roots, and giving the impression that he was grinning. So much for my assumption about him smiling, Thomas thought.

The man grunted something and set the tea down beside the cot. Then he rose from his stool and went to the doorway, which had a heavy woolen blanket in place of a door. He turned and nodded to Thomas and disappeared through the blanket.

A moment later the blanket parted again, and Father Damien De Veuster came into the hut. "I did not actually expect you to take me up on my dinner invitation from that day on the boat," the priest began in French. "And I certainly did not expect you to appear out of the depths of the sea like a flying fish."

"My friend?" asked Thomas.

"He is well and being cared for."

"Who…or what was that in here a minute ago?

Damien pulled the stool close to Thomas's cot and sat down. "One of my flock. A leper who, you will be interested to know, is the same age as you: 23."

Thomas pulled himself into a sitting position and picked up the mug of tea left for him by the leper. It was steeped with lemon and honey and tasted delicious. "Thank you, Father," he said.

"The honey is from my bees, as is the wax in the candles on the bureau. I also keep chickens and pigs and raise vegetables, especially sweet potatoes."

Thomas detected a note of pride in the Flemish priest's voice. "I apologize for my comment about that man, it was just such…"

"A shock?" said Damien with a smile. He removed his broad-brimmed hat and adjusted his spectacles. "The physical indignities visited upon lepers by this terrible affliction truly beggar description."

"And yet they persevere?"

"Some better than others, by the grace of God. Many accept the death sentence imposed by the Hawaiian government when they are banished here and try to retain some semblance of normalcy, others will themselves to die."

"And the disease kills everyone who contracts it?"

"Sadly, yes. Few days go by when we do not bury at least one of the poor souls."

"There are that many people with the disease" asked Thomas. "I had no idea."

"The supply seems endless. In fact, more people have been banished here in the past year than in the first seven years after the colony was established," Damien replied. "The first were brought here just six years ago, 16 of them. Today there are nearly 800."

"Are you also condemned to remain here until you become ill and die, Father? Does your church require that much of you?"

Damien chuckled. "My Lord requires that of me, Thomas. For better or worse, my decision to come to Kalawao was the most significant act of faith I will ever undertake."

Thomas sipped his tea in silence. Outside the hut the wind continued to blow, and darkness was gathering above the sea. He heard shuffling outside the hut and Damien rose to admit a man and woman who were carrying a tray and a wash basin. The man's face was covered with blister-like sores, but his hands and facial features were intact. The woman would have been quite lovely were it not for the large open sores on her forehead and cheeks.

"This is Michael and Helene," said Damien. "They are Hawaiian, husband and wife. They took new names when they were baptized last month. They have a 14-year-old daughter who remarkably has remained free of disease."

"We hope to find a way to get her off this island," said Helene as she set down the basin filled with soapy water.

"Something the law does not allow for," added her husband. He set the tray on the bureau and Father Damien carried a bowl of vegetable stew with pork and a fresh-baked roll over to Thomas.

Michael and Helene left the hut, and Damien sat back down on the stool. "Eat," he said, "and then we will talk."

Thomas wolfed down the excellent stew and when the priest lit an oil lamp and two candles, he stood up and walked gingerly around the room.

"Did you build the hut?" he asked Damien.

"With help, yes. During my first week here I slept on the ground under a tree. Housing is in short supply in Kalawao."

Thomas sat on the edge of the cot and accepted a small glass of brandy from the priest.

"And now, Colonel Scoundrel, perhaps you would indulge me with the tale of how you came to attempt passage to our colony via the sea, and not by the trail across the peninsula. And more importantly, why? This is hardly a place people want to visit for relaxation." Damien lit his pipe and sat back on the stool.

"You will recall the story I shared after dinner aboard the *König Wilhelm* about why I stowed away in San Francisco," Thomas began, "and in our meeting on the coaster three months ago, I explained how I became half owner of a sugar cane plantation."

Damien nodded. "In a game of chance, you said. From what I have learned about you, Colonel, it seems to me that your life has been one long treatise on the role of chance."

Thomas smiled. "In more ways than you can imagine, Father." He went on to share everything that had happened since he arrived on Lana'i and began building up the plantation, including the gala at the palace. He thought best to leave the story of Noelani and the moonlight swim in the lagoon pool aside and concentrated instead on his decision to leave Lana'i when he learned Donegan had been dispatched to kill him.

"You cannot hide from him and Stafford forever, Thomas, and you certainly do not want to remain here any longer than is necessary," Damien said when Thomas had finished his story.

"I have no intention of doing either," replied Thomas. "But I must deal with Stafford in my own way and my own time."

Damien refilled their glasses. "You mean kill him," he said in a soft voice.

Thomas downed the brandy in one gulp but said nothing.

He was rested enough the following day to walk outside the hut and down to the rocky beach where he and Akoni had washed ashore. Pieces of the skiff were strewn around the beach just above the tide line, and someone had salvaged his seal skin bag and laid it on a flat rock. He turned and surveyed the settlement of small houses and outbuildings that were scattered around several acres under the shadow of the great green cliffs. Smoke drifted up out of many of the structures, and in the distance he could make out a group of men working in a field, no doubt planting sweet potatoes for the early fall harvest. "Don't be concerned about coming into direct contact with anyone," Father Damien had told him. "They will do their best to avoid you."

The sky was mostly clear, and the breeze blowing off the ocean was soft. Last night's storm had swept to the east, and it promised to be a pleasant day. Thomas sat on a rock and looked out to sea. What was he going to do? How much longer was he going to be on the run? He missed his friends at the *Chronicle*, and his job. He missed Chef Kwan's cooking, and the warmth of the little French bistro.

"Damn," he suddenly sputtered out loud.

"A fine way to thank the gods for saving your miserable hide," he heard a voice say.

He turned to see that Akoni had come up behind him. The king's nephew was limping, and his right arm was in a sling. There were cuts and bruises on his face and hands, but he was alive, and he was smiling.

"I'm sorry about your skiff," said Thomas as Akoni settled onto a rock beside him. "She was a fine vessel."

"She got the job done," Akoni replied, "and here we are to tell the story."

"Is your arm broken?"

"Cleanly, for which I am thankful. One of the lepers is a fine doctor and he set it quickly."

Thomas looked troubled. "You weren't afraid to have him touch you?"

"It's not as if I had a choice, Thomas. And in any event, that priest has been here for months and is still healthy."

"We can't stay here…" Thomas began.

"And we won't," Akoni continued. "Just long enough to get enough strength back to climb those." He pointed to the cliffs that ringed the village.

"Then back to Honolulu where you will stay with me until we figure out what to do about the assassin."

Thomas had been rummaging in his bag while Akoni spoke. Now he pulled out his Colt and spun the cylinder. "I have some thoughts about that," he said.

Akoni laughed and slapped him on the back. "Let's get something to eat and make our plan."

They stayed beneath the cliffs of Kalawao for a week. Each day Thomas and Akoni walked the rocky beaches and newly planted fields, and each evening they sat around an outside fire pit with Father Damien sharing stories of their lives and travels. Thomas came to admire the priest's ferocious devotion to his ministry, and to appreciate Akoni's zeal for life. He was surprised to learn that Akoni had accompanied his sister to New York the previous year, where she was fêted by society and newspapers alike before traveling down to Washington, D.C. where she met the President and was presented to Congress. The enormous Hawaiian was nonplussed by the attention and the overall experience; "They are unimpressive people," was all he could say about the nabobs of Eastern seaboard society and the politicians who swarmed the Capital like locusts on a field of ripening grain.

On the night before they were set to leave for the hike up the cliff, Michael and Helene appeared out of the darkness and approached the fire. Accompanying them was their 14-year-old daughter, Taiana. She was tall and graceful, with quick, keen eyes and a confident smile.

Her hair was cut unfashionably short above her shoulders, a concession to the disease that Thomas learned was required of all women in the colony. And as far as he could see, she bore no evidence of the leprosy that was slowly consuming her parents who stopped a few feet away from the fire with their daughter and waited for Damien to speak.

"My friends," the priest said to Thomas and Akoni, "we have a request to make of you. I will tell you at the outset that what we are about to ask would put you in violation of Hawaiian law, one that even you, Akoni, would not be forgiven by your uncle for committing."

Thomas looked at Akoni, who appeared to already understand what he was about to be asked to do. Thomas had no such premonition. "And what crime would that be, Father?"

Damien pulled his cloak tight against the evening breeze and sipped his brandy before answering. "The child, Taiana, is disease free. We would like you to take her to Honolulu. Find her a home."

Akoni looked across the fire at Thomas, but his expression did not change. They both knew that once a person was condemned to Kalawao there was no hope of a legal reprieve, and if they were caught trying to smuggle anyone out, they would face long prison sentences.

Akoni finally spoke. "You ask much of us, Father."

"I ask what is right and just. There is no hope for Taiana here. She will eventually contract leprosy, there is no possibility it will pass her by. And then she will fade away, just as her mother and father are doing now."

Thomas knew it was his turn to speak. "You know my situation, Father. I am being stalked by a band of assassins who will follow me around the world, and who will give no thought to killing whoever they find with me."

The priest smiled and reached out for Taiana's hand. She came alongside him and stood quietly. "Taiana has already been sentenced to death. How much more dangerous could her world become?"

"My influence as a member of the royal family will do nothing for her," Akoni said. "Arrangements will have to be made without any involvement on my part."

Taiana's father spoke up. "We have thought about that. Since Colonel Scoundrel is known as the owner of a sugar plantation with hundreds of workers and their families in his care, would it be so unusual for him to inquire in Honolulu about a household position for one of his worker's children?"

Damien turned to Thomas. "Colonel?"

Thomas shook his head and sighed. Then he looked across at Taiana, who held her head high and returned his stare with a level of dignity and strength that surprised him.

"You understand that if you come with us, you will never see your parents again? Are you prepared for that? And are they?"

Taiana slowly nodded her head. Her mother let out a soft sob, but her father remained as stoic as his daughter. "We are prepared, Colonel," he said. "Life awaits our daughter off this island. Here there is only suffering and death."

"You understand that if we allow you to come with us, you must do exactly as we say, with no hesitation," Thomas said to Taiana. "Your life—and ours—might depend upon that."

"I understand, Colonel," Taiana answered in a calm, adult voice. "I will do my part."

"We are agreed then?" asked Father Damien.

Akoni and Thomas exchanged glances.

"We are," Thomas answered.

~ TWENTY-THREE ~

Honolulu

Donegan had never entertained the notion of starting a business. But as he lifted a mug of tepid beer to his mouth in this miserable excuse for a proper whorehouse, he knew that Honolulu was long overdue for the establishment of a first-class sporting venue. More importantly, he was convinced that he was the right man to bring just such a shining example of true civilization to the Hawaiian backwater. The fact that he had some time on his hands also played into his notion.

He had returned from Lana'i yesterday after missing that bastard Scoundrel by less than two hours. When the proprietor of the little wharf-side store told him that he had seen Thomas and another man sail off to the north just before the coaster from O'ahu pulled up to the dock, Donegan got back on the steam packet and returned to Honolulu. He paid an informant to watch the steamship arrivals and departures for any sign of Scoundrel, and since O'ahu was the only island where passage to the mainland was available, he knew that the colonel would have to show up sooner or later. Stafford's brother was honoring the letter of credit by providing him with whatever funds he requested, and so his sense of urgency to complete the job and send Scoundrel to the bottom of the bay was not too great.

The drunks he hired to go to Lana'i with him assured him that the dockside brothel was the finest establishment of its kind on the island, but when he walked through the batwing doors and saw the low ceilings, dark furniture, grimy windows, and beer-soaked floors, he pegged the men as liars and fools. The sole whore available, a toothless, overweight grandmother wearing a stained nightgown and crazed, lop-sided grin who charged a dollar per toss only cemented his conviction. So, he spent the next three days visiting every bar, restaurant, and hotel in town, including O'ahu's only opium den. In the end, he determined the drunks had been truthful.

The fact that a major port of call for hundreds of steamships, deep-ocean clippers and naval vessels didn't offer a selection of brothels for the sailors and longshoremen who poured off their vessels with money in their wallets and hard-ons in their trousers was a real mystery at first.

"Until you realize two things," a barman at the Palace Hotel told him. "The first is that for 50 years after the English and French and Germans and Dutch and every other damn country sent ships to the islands, most every maiden was giving it away for free. They fell on their backs faster than a monkey can shimmy up a coconut tree. Performing the horizontal rumba with a European was all the rage, leastwise until most of the women became infected with one or another of the poxes them sailors were injecting them with."

"And the other thing?" Donegan asked dryly.

The barman filled Donegan's mug and poured himself a shot of whisky. "That would be religion. The missionaries who began flooding the islands 40 years ago made it their business to bring a halt to all the unlicensed fornicating, in the name of their God, of course."

"Some would call that civilization," replied Donegan.

"Maybe that was their intention in the early days. But lo and behold, it wasn't long after the sweet young things started closing their honey pots to every sailor who waltzed past, that the missionaries found themselves a kind of screwing that they did approve of."

Donegan raised his eyebrows.

"These islanders didn't have much of a head for business. And owning raw land didn't interest them at all. That made them ripe for a whole new level of screwing; the missionaries snapped up land for pennies per acre, and sometimes they just stole it. Hell, on Lana'i where you just came from, a Mormon bishop named Gibson used church funds to buy thousands of acres of land a few years ago, and he put it in his name, not the church's."

"How'd that work out" asked Donegan.

"For Gibson? Great. The church demanded he sign the land over to them or be booted out of the fold."

"Don't tell me,"said Donegan with a chuckle. "He chose the dirt over the Book."

"And brother it was a good decision," replied the barman. "My guess is that he will be one of the richest men in the Pacific in a few years."

Donegan pointed to the whisky. "Let me buy you a drink," he said. The barman nodded and tended to another customer before returning.

"Say a fella had in mind opening a first-class whorehouse hereabouts," Donegan began. "Two story, oak backbar, clean rooms and cleaner girls. Good food, too. Who'd fight it—the missionaries??

The barman laughed. "Ten years ago, I would have told you to put that idea out of your head. Today? Things are very different. See them sailors?" He pointed to where two American naval officers were eating dinner in a corner booth. "It's supposed to be some kind of big secret, but the Americans are surveying the area around the Pearl River basin, a big estuary that's about a half day's ride from here. Seems they are thinking of building a naval base there—a big one that would have a permanent staff. Hundreds of sailors and marines, from what I hear."

Donegan smiled. This was exactly the kind of information he had been seeking. He raised his glass to the barman. "And where there's sailors…" The barman clinked his glass against Donegan's and finished the thought, "There's got to be whores!"

The bartender finished his drink, lit the evening lamps around the room, and looked after several other customers before finishing the conversation with Donegan. "Are you serious about opening a place?" he asked, "and do you have the cash to do it?"

"Yes, and yes," Donegan replied. "Do you have something in mind?"

"Aye, I do." The barman leaned over the counter and whispered, "But I would have to be part of the deal."

"In what way?"

The barman looked around to make sure no one could hear them. "A fella from Boston built himself an inn and restaurant last year down near the harbor. Figured he would attract the shippers and merchants who sail through on their way West. Lots of trade going on across the islands. The mistake the bugger made was ignoring the fact that the swells can afford the best hotels in town, with all the amenities. They ain't looking for middle-of-the- road accommodations like his."

"He didn't put out a welcome sign for ordinary seamen?"

The barman snorted. "Hell, he ran 'em off if they so much as put a foot through his doors. He wanted no part of their trade."

Donegan shook his head. "So he went bust?"

"He's about to, word is the bank is going to close him down next week."

"And you think his place would be right for what I have in mind?"

"Friend," said the barman, "his place is perfect. Five bedrooms, a new kitchen, fancy bar, hell it even has stained-glass windows."

Donegan sipped his drink. He'd spent a lifetime working for other men, and he was getting tired, physically, and emotionally. He looked across the bar at his reflection in the mirror and made up his mind: killing Colonel Scoundrel would be the last job he did as anybody's employee. Running an inn couldn't be that difficult, and he couldn't imagine a more enjoyable situation than one that included testing out the occupational skills of a steady stream of new whores.

"What would you want out of this deal?" he asked the barman. "I ain't looking for a partner."

The bartender leaned forward and laid his palms flat on the walnut bar in front of Donegan. "I run the kitchen and the bar. That and a piece of the action, including a special discount on any of them little gals I get a hankering for."

Donegan thought it over. He needed someone who knew the town but had no ambitions beyond being an employee. The barman might fit the bill, but there was one final qualification he would need to meet before he was offered the job.

"Can you find me a dozen whores? Decent looking, young, and with all their teeth?" he asked.

The barman topped off Donegan's drink. "By the boatload," he said with a grin.

~ TWENTY-FOUR ~

Moloka'i / O'ahu
June

The wharf at Kalaupapa was nearly deserted when Thomas, Akoni, and Taiana walked through the dusty village after their three-mile trek across the peninsula from the leper colony at Kalawao. The steam packet for Honolulu would leave at 10 AM for the five-hour transit of Kaiwi Channel and they had planned their arrival as closely as they could to boarding time. Donegan might have paid watchers on the packet wharves of every island, and the less time they spent milling around the tiny port, the better.

They left Kalawao just after dawn, each carrying a single bag. Taiana's parents and Father Damien walked them through the settlement to the base of the switchback trail that had been hewn out of the massive cliffs that walled the colony off from the world.

Thomas held his breath when he leaned back and looked straight up the rocky, shrub-covered escarpment to the soft blue sky floating miles above.

Damien answered the question before he asked it: "One thousand, five-hundred feet," he said. "We pray before we come down or go up. But it does seem to be successful at keeping unwelcome guests away."

"And we lepers in our place," added Taiana's father.

Akoni slung his bag over his shoulder and shook Damien's hand. "We must go," he said quietly.

Thomas embraced the priest and pressed several hundred dollars into his hand. "I would say this is to get some decent furniture for your hut, but I suspect you will find other purposes for it."

Damien smiled and accepted the gift. "God will guide me in its use," he said. "Thank you for taking the child with you."

Taiana had been standing close to her parents, but there would be no embraces shared by them for fear she might contract the dreaded disease. Her father and mother held hands and wept quietly, and then her mother blew her daughter a final kiss. Her father turned to Akoni and said, "We entrust our most precious possession to you and Colonel Thomas. Please keep her safe." Akoni nodded somberly and walked to the base of the switchback path.

"We will not say goodbye, my dearest one," said Taiana's mother, "only *Ke akua hoomaikai oe*, God's blessings." With that she and her husband turned and hurried towards the settlement. They would not look back.

Damien took Taiana's hand and placed a Catholic rosary in her palm. Then she and Thomas joined Akoni to begin the long climb up the cliff.

The trio walked through the scattering of shacks and small buildings that made up the village and stepped onto the wharf just as the coaster appeared on the horizon. When the steam packet docked 15 minutes later, a small crowd was assembling to make the journey to O'ahu. Four men with carts arrived and began offloading supplies as soon as the packet was tied off and fresh coal was loaded. As they worked the pilot circulated among the crowd and sold tickets for the passage. One hour after it docked, the packet slipped away from the wharf and began its 'S' shaped trip around the western coast of Moloka'i, south into the channel and then around the southeastern tip of O'ahu and into Honolulu harbor.

Taiana purchased a jug of coffee and a basket of corn muffins from a vendor on the wharf, and carried then to a bench on the bow of the packet where Thomas and Akoni had settled in. There was a light chop in the channel, and a cool breeze had passengers reaching for jackets and sweaters.

"We'll need to figure that out quickly," Thomas was saying as she sat on a bench opposite the men. "Especially now that we have her to think about."

"And were you going to ask me to weigh in on whatever it is you need to figure out, or does my sex and age exclude me from taking part in that discussion?" she asked.

"*Ālia iki*…hold on, little one," Akoni said with a grin as he reached out for a muffin. "We hadn't come to the part about you yet. Be patient, we will get there, and you can have your say."

Thomas pulled a tin cup from his bag and held it out for Taiana to fill. In agreeing to take her along, he had opened himself up to a whole new world of responsibility. It was time to figure out what that was going to look like. But before he could speak, Taiana leaned forward towards Akoni and said, "I apologize. It's just…," she looked down at the deck for a moment to collect her thoughts, and when she raised her head, her cheeks were flushed.

"It's just that I have been taking care of my parents and myself for two years. I make the meals and do the wash; I mend and sew and collect firewood, and I write letters for them because their hands can no longer hold a pen steady. I suppose I am just not used to…"

"Adults telling you what to do?" Thomas interjected.

He spoke with such softness and sincerity that Taiana burst into laughter before thinking better of her rudeness and covering her mouth with her hand.

"A feeling shared by most young people, I suppose" said Akoni, "although in your case it appears that you have more than earned the right to speak on your own behalf regarding any plans we make. What say you, Thomas?"

He thought for a moment before answering. None of them really knew what they might be coming up against in the next few days. If they were going to get through this quagmire, they needed Taiana to be at her best. In fact, they would probably have to ask more of her than was fair for a child her age.

"Here is what I propose," he finally said. "There are two issues at play: first, I have to deal with the assassin who is chasing me, and then with his boss in San Francisco. I don't want either of you tangled up in that mess. Second, we—meaning Akoni and I—must find a safe and suitable home for you, Taiana."

"There are no boarding schools in the islands, and the only orphanage is for little ones," added Akoni. "We will have to place you in a private home, where, I am sure, you will be expected to earn your keep by performing household duties."

Taiana nodded. "I understand," she said, "I do not want charity."

"And that you won't receive if you are working as a domestic," replied Akoni. "My contacts at the palace should help us find something that will work. But you can never tell anyone where you came from, or about your parents, or anything about Father Damien or Kalawao. We will tell them that you are an orphan from a good family. That will be enough."

A man and woman came over by them to watch a school of dolphin leaping left and right across the bow, and they waited until the couple moved away to resume the conversation.

Thomas took a bite of muffin and said, "Have you given any thought to what you want to do with your life?"

Taiana's eyes lit up. "Oh, yes," she said in a rush, "I am going to write books."

"Write?" asked Akoni with a mystified expression. "Like that fellow, Mark Twain, who wrote the newspaper columns about our islands when he lived here a few years ago?"

"Or perhaps you will become the new William Shakespeare?" said Thomas. "Or better yet, the heir to Charles Dickens. I read *A Tale of Two Cities* several times. Shall we expect to see such work from you?"

"Don't mock me, Thomas," Taiana said in a decidedly adult tone.

"Thomas is it?" asked Akoni. "Was I absent when you asked permission to call him by his first name?"

Taiana looked as if she were about to scold a naughty child.

"You told me," she began before switching her gaze to Thomas, "in fact you both told me, that secrecy was of the utmost importance to hide our true identities. I therefore cannot call him…" her voiced lowered to a whisper, "Colonel Scoundrel, now can I, lest we be found out by a watcher. I suppose I could address him as father, though he clearly is too young to have a 14-year-old daughter. Shall I instead pretend he is my husband, or perhaps my brother? Given all that, Thomas seemed to me to be the best choice to avoid detection."

Akoni looked over at Thomas and winked. "I'd say she has us there, my friend. I cannot fault her reasoning."

Thomas laughed and poured more coffee. The steam powered coaster was well into the channel now, making good time with a following wind and a gentle sea.

"We'll be in Honolulu in four hours," he said. "It's time to make our plan."

~ TWENTY-FIVE ~

Honolulu

Two men on ladders were hanging a freshly painted sign above the entrance to the inn as Thomas and Akoni stepped out of the muddy street and climbed the stairs to the covered porch.

"The Pearl," Akoni read out loud. "Last week this was 'The Wharf.' Decent food, pretty good rooms, too. Owned by a fellow out of Boston."

"Things change," Thomas said as they stepped through an impressive oak door with etched glass windows. The walk from Henry's house to the wharf district took just ten minutes, and it felt good to be in a town again, even though he felt compelled to pull his hat down over his brow to avoid being recognized. Akoni had taken Taiana with him to Iolani Palace earlier that morning, and when he introduced her to Noelani and explained the situation his sister shooed him away and led Taiana into the gardens for a private chat.

Akoni returned to Henry's and suggested he and Thomas go somewhere for lunch to plot out their next moves. When they entered the high-ceilinged Pearl and he saw more workmen hammering away, he was about to turn around and take them elsewhere only to be intercepted by a very enthusiastic barman who assured them the other side of the saloon was quiet. A minute later they were seated in a comfortable booth with menus in their hands.

"New owner"? Akoni asked the attractive young woman who brought a bowl of mixed nuts to their table.

"Brand new," she beamed, "as of a few days ago. Our lunch menu will be available all day, but our specialties of the house won't be ready for a few more hours. I hope you gentlemen will be here to enjoy them." When she turned to go, she took care to wiggle her backside suggestively.

The message was unmistakable. "Your Pearl is a whorehouse?" asked Thomas with a grin.

"Not as of last week," sputtered Akoni. He started to slide out of the booth, but Thomas put a hand on his forearm.

"It's just lunch," he said. "In any event, in my experience there is no better place in the world to hold a private conversation. I'm guessing this place is so new that almost no one in town knows it exists. Hell, we'll probably see a pastor or two come in for a meal before we leave."

Akoni settled back in his seat with a disgruntled expression on his face. "I am no prude, Thomas, but I would rather not see businesses like this sprouting in the open in our capitol city. Hawai'i has been defiled enough."

The barman arrived with two mugs of beer and a plate piled high with sausages, fruit, and cheese. "Compliments of the Pearl, gentlemen. I recommend the boar stew with vegetables and rice for lunch, but if you prefer a sandwich or a steak, we can do that."

Thomas could not help himself. "My friend is a little uneasy about your side business," he said slyly, "especially if your establishment puts more care and attention into your girls than your fare."

The barman looked at Akoni and smiled. "I assure you that we only serve up the finest in the kitchen and the bedrooms." He stared more closely at Akoni. "I know you. You're the king's nephew."

Akoni nodded but did not reply.

"I am Archibald, manager of the bar and the kitchen. I worked for years at the Palace Hotel, which is where I have seen you. You are always welcome here, sir, no matter which parts of our menu you seek to partake. Everything—and everyone here—is of the freshest, finest quality."

The barman turned his attention to Thomas. "But I don't believe I have seen you, sir. Are you new to our island?"

Thomas kept his head down as if he were still reading the menu.

"Just arrived," he said. "And the stew sounds good."

Akoni nodded in agreement and Archibald shuffled off to give their order to the chef.

"What now," Thomas said almost to himself.

Akoni wrapped both hands around his beer and looked off in the distance. "You can stay and fight, but if this man in California is committed to seeing you dead, he will just send another assassin, and another after that."

Thomas looked into his friend's eyes. "Then I must take the fight to him."

They remained quiet until after the waitress delivered their meals. The stew was excellent, and as they were beginning their meal, Thomas chuckled when a collared clergyman came through the door with two respectable looking businessmen.

"See what I mean," he said to Akoni with a wink. "Word hasn't gotten around yet."

Akoni turned and watched the man of the cloth and his associates follow the shapely young waitress to their table. He also noticed that the clergyman's eyes lingered on the young woman's derrière as she walked away. He raised his mug to Thomas, and with a laugh, said, "Or maybe it has!"

A door opened behind the mirrored walnut bar, and a lean, sandy-haired man in his 40s handed a case of whiskey to Archibald. The man looked out over the half-filled dining room and smiled.

"Not a bad lunch crowd for our third day in business," he said. "The barkers you sent around the docks did a good job of spreading the word."

"Aye, some came for the free mug of beer, but I suspect most of them will be back for the upstairs menu," replied the barman. "I tried two of the tarts myself and I promise you, not one of our customers is going to leave with an unhappy pecker."

The owner smiled. His stable of whores was small, but they were young and pleasant looking enough, and in another week, he would have four or five more working the upstairs rooms around the clock. Archibald was now looking to hire an experienced madam to manage the growing enterprise.

"Do you know that giant native fellow at the booth under the window?" he asked. "He's the sort who would make a perfect thumper should we ever need to cool down a customer."

"Believe it or not, that is His Majesty' s nephew, Akoni. Spends his time studying the ocean and drawing pictures of sea creatures, or so they say."

"Hmph. And his friend, the tall fellow with the hat?"

"Him I do not know, Mr. Donegan. Doesn't look like a laborer or shopkeeper, and he surely ain't no sailor. Sugar broker, maybe. Perhaps you should introduce yourself. It's time for Honolulu to get to know the town's newest business leader."

Donegan opened the till and pulled out a wad of cash. "Let me put this in the safe, and then I'll make the rounds."

He went through the back door and walked across the kitchen to the stairs that led up to his office and private quarters. As he put his boot on the first step, a thought hit him. The King's nephew matched the description of the Hawaiian who was seen sailing away from the dock on Lana'i with Scoundrel ten days ago. He'd never seen the Colonel, of course, and did not have a photograph, but the general appearance of the man with Akoni could be a fit. Was it possible that after all this time chasing Scoundrel halfway around the world, the son of a bitch had actually just walked into his establishment?

He trotted up the stairs and threw the money into the safe and then raced back down and went to the window of the door leading into the bar. He could make out the table where Akoni was sitting, but the man across from him had his hat pulled down below his brow, and Donegan could only see the bottom of the man's jaw. Was the fellow embarrassed to be seen in a whorehouse in the middle of the day, or did he have a better reason to conceal his face?

Donegan called over a kitchen worker and sent him out to fetch the girl who had delivered the meal to Akoni's table.

"Did you catch either of their names?" he asked her.

"No sir, but they were real gentlemen, even when I told them about our special menu."

Donegan thought for a moment. Then he pressed a five-dollar bill into the girl's hand and said, "I want you to do something for me, exactly as I tell you. Do you understand?"

The girl looked confused. Five dollars bought a full hour of her time. "Here, sir, in the kitchen? Wouldn't you rather do it in your room?"

Donegan's face flushed with anger. "No, damn it, not that. I simply want you to go out to their table in ten minutes and do what I am about to tell you."

The girl was relieved that she wasn't about to be bent over a greasy butcher block table, but she was still confused. "Of course, sir," she finally managed to reply.

Donegan cracked open the door and signaled for Archibald to join him in the kitchen.

"You have told me that you can round up any people I might need for any kind of job, on the spot, as long as the pay was right."

The barman hesitated. "Yes, I suppose I can."

Donegan nodded. "I need five-no six-of the biggest, strongest stevedores you can find, and I need them in the next fifteen minutes. Tell them I will give them each a $20 gold piece for five minutes of work."

Archibald whistled softly. "That's almost two weeks wages, Mr. Donegan. I'm not asking them to kill somebody, am I?"

The door swung open, and a bus boy carried a tray of dirty dishes over to the sinks.

"No," Donegan replied, "though by the time the job is done they might have preferred I ask them to do that." He pointed through the window. "Your friend Akoni? When he steps out the door, I want him to be held in place for a few minutes while I settle some personal business with his friend."

"Just that? Held in place?"

"Just that," Donegan answered. "Given his size I'm guessing that it will not be an easy thing to do. If he wasn't a member of the royal family, I'd find another way to keep him back, but this will have to do. And another thing: I don't want the men to know I am the one who hired them. Got that?"

The barman didn't get it, but he wasn't about to louse up this plum job over something so small as helping his boss take care of some old business. Dozens of stevedores were working the docks within shouting distance of The Pearl. Finding men willing to take on a few minutes work for that amount of money would be easy.

"Give me the money, and I'll bring the men," he said.

Donegan dug into his vest pocket and pulled out six small gold coins. "Fifteen minutes, no more," he said. Archibald nodded and hustled out the back door to the alley.

If I'm wrong about that being Colonel Scoundrel then I've just blown $120, he thought. But as he turned to go back upstairs to retrieve a pistol, he knew in his heart that his instinct was right. Now he only needed to figure out how to make the murder he was about to commit look like it had been a case of self-defense. He smiled inwardly at the challenge; he didn't know much about innkeeping, but when it came to the business of murdering, he had few equals.

They had come to the Pearl to work out a plan to deal with the assassin hired by Stafford to track Thomas down and kill him, but as they quietly ate their meals, they both knew there was only one way forward: Thomas would have to return to San Francisco and confront Stafford on his own territory. That meant coming to a resolution that both men could live with, or that one man would die for.

Thomas was reaching for his vest wallet to pay their bill when their waitress came to the table. "Now then, you boys weren't going to leave without trying a little dessert, were you?" she cooed.

Akoni almost laughed at her transparent offer. "Another time perhaps, little angel," he said as he stood.

Thomas slid out of the booth and as he handed her the cash for their meal, she looked up under the brim of his hat. "But don't I know you?" she asked. "I worked in the laundry at the Merchant Hotel a few months ago, and I am certain I delivered a cleaned suit to your room. You are Colonel Scoundrel?"

Thomas's face darkened. He did not recall her, and he had purchased a suit at the hotel haberdashery but did not have one cleaned. "Good to see you again," he curtly replied. He ignored Akoni's questioning glance for the moment and walked quickly to the front door. If he had turned around that moment, he would have seen the young woman mouthing the word 'yes;' to the sandy haired man behind the bar.

Before Thomas opened the door to step out onto the covered porch the barman returned. "They're out in the street," he told Donegan. "I could only get five."

Donegan reached inside his vest to make sure his pistol was easy to grab. Then he patted his back pocket where the derringer he was going to slip into Scoundrel's hand after he shot him was located. That would back up his claim of self-defense. It seems the man was desperate for a whore, he would tell the constable, and he went off the rails when he was told he would have to wait a few hours for one to become available. Everyone knew that if left untended, a stiff dick could eventually drive a man to act irrationally. Shame it had to happen during his first week in business when he wasn't up and fully running, but there it was. Oh, the dead man was a war hero? Pity about that, too, but what choice did I have once the fool pointed his pistol at my head? Witnesses? Of course, a barroom full. How many would you like to speak to?

Thomas and Akoni stepped out of the Pearl and onto the wide covered porch. The sun was breaking through the rain clouds gathered around the mountain peaks behind the town, and the hard-packed dirt street was drying out under the warming sky. Carts and buggies carried people and goods from the wharf side warehouses towards the center of town, and stevedores and sailors lined up to offload the half dozen schooners and steamships tied to the Honolulu docks.

Their plan was for Akoni to return to the palace to fetch Taiana and then meet up at Henry Kakaako's home. Taiana would stay with the fisherman until they found a suitable position for her, and the three men would figure out a way to get Thomas on a steamer bound for San Francisco without the port authority's knowledge. His wallet was emptying quickly, but bribes would have to be paid if he was to get off the island unnoticed.

Akoni sensed the trouble first. A knot of five stevedores clad in loose fitting jackets and short-billed caps had formed on the other side of the street. They were a rough-looking bunch in their hob-nail boots and dark wool scarves, and several of the men sported stubby wooden clubs. When they moved as one into the street, Akoni put a hand on Thomas's forearm. "The little tart did her job," he said in a calm voice, "though at who's direction I have no idea. These lads are coming for you, and it's not to ask for the next dance."

Thomas pulled his revolver and held it at his side as an overloaded cart rumbled past them down the center of the street. When the cart passed, the stevedores saw the pistol and came to a halt a few feet from the steps leading up to the Pearl's entrance.

"We're not here for you," one of the stevedores said to Thomas. "We just want a word with your friend."

Thomas shot a questioning glance at Akoni, who shook his head in response. Why would anyone send a gang of thugs after him?

"Thanks all the same, but I have business to attend to, and no time to visit with the likes of you boys," Akoni said. "Move along now, out of my way."

The stevedores did not move, although Thomas saw more than a little concern in their eyes as they took the measure of Akoni and contemplated how many of their heads would be broken by the giant before they were able to subdue him. They'd jumped at the opportunity to make a quick $20, but it was clear that a lot of second thoughts were being mulled.

He raised his revolver up to the sky and cocked it slowly. "You heard my friend," he said in a military command voice, "move away. Now."

Then a pistol shot rang out, and a .45 caliber ball lodged in a post just a few inches from Thomas's head, showering him with splinters. He whirled around and saw the sandy-haired man from the Pearl standing in the open door. It had to be Donegan. Thomas fired a return shot and jumped back behind the post. His aim was high and flew over Donegan's shoulder, shattering the entry door glass. Donegan leapt behind the door and fired twice through the broken window. Thomas felt one bullet streak past his face and the other tear through the side of his jacket.

He dropped to one knee and fired again, missing the assassin for a second time. He had four bullets left to Donegan's three. Out of the corner of his right eye Thomas saw the stevedores surge up the steps and throw themselves on Akoni. The King's nephew disappeared for an instant inside a swirling mass of kicking, swinging, shouting bodies, and then one of the stevedores flew through the air into the street, followed by a second man who was tossed like a piece of kindling through the Pearl's front window.

Thomas crouched lower and took aim, but Donegan was gone. A moment later he saw a blur at the corner of the front window, and another shot ripped past him. He heard a cry and turned his head to see a man in a bowler hat fall to the ground in the center of the street. He took a deep breath, focused on the window, and prepared to squeeze the trigger the instant he saw movement. The three men battling Akoni had other plans, however. They pushed the giant several feet down the porch until they were directly in front of Thomas, blocking his view inside the Pearl. He watched Akoni wrap his massive arms around two of the men's necks and smash their faces together with such brute force that he heard cartilage and bone crunch and was spattered with blood. The last of the stevedores still standing pulled back from the mêlée and took a quick look around. One of his comrades lay in a heap in the middle of the street, another was groaning and bleeding out on the floor of the Pearl after being tossed through the plate glass window, and the other two were trying to get to their knees after having their noses and jaws shattered. $20 wasn't enough to risk his hide, the man decided. He jumped down the steps and raced across the street to safety.

Akoni was leaning against the front of the building struggling to catch his breath, and Thomas motioned for him to stay flat against the siding so that he would not get caught in the crossfire. It was time to end this. He readied himself to rush through the door and confront Donegan head on when whistles began to sound up and down the street.

"Constables," Akoni shouted. "We've got to get out of here."

Thomas was conflicted; he wanted to get to Donegan, but he could not afford to be arrested and held for the inevitable arrest warrant that would be coming from San Francisco courtesy of Stafford's bought-and-paid-for-judges.

Donegan heard the whistles, too, and decided it was time to cover his own ass. "Scoundrel!" he yelled out the door. "Hold off now, or this little whore is dead."

Thomas and Akoni looked towards the door, where Donegan stood behind the young woman who had waited on them. The assassin's arm was wrapped tightly around her waist, and his pistol was pressed against her temple. Her face was white with fear, and she began to sob.

"Quiet, you bitch," Donegan growled before he pulled back his pistol and then slammed it against the side of her face.

He didn't need to do that to make his point, Thomas thought. He wanted to do it.

The girl slumped back against Donegan as a line of blood formed on her broken cheekbone and rolled down her neck. Outside the Pearl, traffic had come to a halt, and a crowd was gathering to watch the donnybrook.

"Neither of us wants to deal with the coppers," Donegan said, "given our mutual issues and all. You know what I mean."

Thomas did know. He looked at Akoni and understood his friend would also prefer to avoid an encounter with the law.

"What do you propose, Donegan?" Thomas asked.

"We go our separate ways. For today, at least. We will meet again soon enough and settle our business."

Akoni nodded at Thomas and motioned down the street where three uniformed constables were trotting towards them.

Thomas holstered his revolver and watched as Donegan released the girl and slipped his pistol into his waistband.

Thomas stood up straight and stared into Donegan's eyes. "Soon enough," he said, and then he and Akoni turned and walked at a measured pace down the boardwalk. A moment later the constables rushed past them, blowing their whistles, and waving their billy clubs in the air.

~ TWENTY-SIX ~

Onboard the Schooner Kai Douglas Starlight
June 1872

homas was leaning against the railing amidships when the whale breached, flinging half of its 60-foot body completely out of the water, and splashing down just a few yards from the stern of the gaff-rigged schooner. Its knobby head and white-tipped fins gleamed in the twilight before disappearing below the surface and then exploding out of the water a second time a moment later.

"It's dying," a voice said. Thomas turned to see that Timothy Boswell had come up beside him. The English botanist had a pipe in his mouth and a bottle of brandy and two glasses in his hands. He handed a full glass to Thomas and braced himself against the rail to counter the light swell.

"What do you mean?" Thomas asked. "A creature who can do that should live forever."

"It should be in the Bering Sea by this time of year," said Boswell. "They mate and calve here in the South Pacific, then migrate thousands of miles to the north to their ancient feeding grounds." He tapped his pipe against the rail. "This one didn't make the journey, which means it couldn't. We don't know all that much about any of the *Order Cetacea*—the whales—but I promise you there isn't another humpback within 1,000 miles of this poor fellow. He will not see their return this winter."

Thomas watched the great fan tail of the whale slap the water two times, and then its massive form slipped into the depths. He stood

178

quietly for a moment, listening to the snapping of the canvas sails and the rush of water breaking around the bow. They were six days into the 17-day voyage from Honolulu to Tahiti, and every minute of every day had been a learning experience. The 96'-foot, two-masted Kai Douglas carried a captain, a cook, three crew members and 250 tons of cargo in its hold, as well as three paying passengers: Thomas, Boswell, and an American-educated Tahitian missionary named Edward Kahale. Their destination was Matavai Bay on the island of Tahiti, the largest of the Polynesian Windward islands.

The day after the fight with Fitch Donegan at the Pearl, Akoni introduced him to Captain Winston McNab, who he sailed with when collecting specimens for the British Museum. "You've got to leave the island for a couple of months," Akoni told him as they made their way from the Pearl to the home of the fisherman, Henry Kakaako. "It looks like Donegan has purchased the Pearl; he isn't going anywhere, at least not until he settles the business with you. You can't return to the mainland, and you cannot remain here."

"So, I just keep running and wait for that bastard to show up one night and shove a knife in my back?" asked Thomas. "I won't do that."

"No, you will let me work through my uncle's contacts in California to see what pressure we can bring to bear on Stafford. He is a much bigger problem than Donegan. We will find a way to persuade him to call Donegan off."

He hated to admit it, but Akoni was right. The cat and mouse game with Donegan could go on for a long time. One way or another, Stafford was the key to resolving this business and letting him get on with his life.

He and Akoni met with Taiana that night and learned that Princess Noelani had arranged a domestic position for her with missionary Grimthorpe and his family. She would be fine until he returned. Then they met McNab at the Palace Hotel and arranged for Thomas to board the Kai Douglas when it sailed in three days. That gave him time to collect the four months of Army pension that the Office of the American Counsel had finally been authorized to pay, to purchase clothing and supplies, and to borrow two books about Tahiti from the

King's Principal Secretary. He desperately wanted to see Noelani, but caution got the better of him and he spent most of his time waiting at Kakaako's house. He would come face to face with Donegan soon enough.

Captain McNab stepped out of the gathering darkness and joined Thomas and Boswell at the railing. "This a private conversation?" he asked.

Boswell lifted the bottle of brandy. "Not if you brought your own glass," he said.

McNab held out a tin cup for the botanist to fill. "Bembé has got the helm and we're making six knots under a following wind," he said. "The sky is clear; we've got a whale leading the way and in three or four days we'll cross the equator. We'll pick up the southeasterly trade winds around 5° south of the line, and from there to Nuka Hiva and on to Tahiti will be a downwind sail." He lifted his cup. "Here's to a sweet passage, boyos."

Thomas liked the scrappy Maine-bred sailing master. He was a born storyteller who put the lie to the notion that New Englanders were a thin- skinned, taciturn lot. On their first morning at sea, McNab took Thomas and Edward Kahale aside and presented them with a choice: "Seventeen days at sea will seem like an eternity if ye choose to do nothing more than eat, sleep, and wander the deck. You're paying for your passage, and you can do nothing if you wish. Mr. Boswell will be sketching and cataloging what he hauls in with his dredge net, and more's the better for him. But if you'd like to make your days pass quickly, we can help with that. We can introduce you to the noble art of rigging, and teach you how to tie knots, work with a needle, and manage the canvas. Might even have a lesson or two in practical navigation. You won't qualify for a First Mate's rating before we make landfall, but ye'll pick up a few things that will stand you in good stead for the rest of your lives. And boys," he continued, "even though the cyclone season is mostly passed in the Southern hemisphere by June, truth is we could still hit a squall, and I wouldn't mind if you knew how to lend a hand if a blow hits."

McNab's proposition presented an easy choice for Thomas and the young missionary and by that first afternoon they were seated on the deck for a lesson in knot tying with Heron, one of the Kai's four crewmen. Heron began his lesson with a description of his crewmates.

"Now, Bembé is a yar shipmate to have at your back when a cyclone drops," said the thin, bearded sailor as he laid a dozen short lengths of manila rope on the deck. "Jamaican fellow, superstitious about everything and everybody, and the best sail rigger I ever met– next to my own self, of course. A gaff-rig only needs one man per mast, see. And ye've met Willy, our ship's boy. Fourteen and sharp as a sea wolf's saber. McNab's the perfect master for a boy like him; there ain't no buggering allowed on his watch, that's the saint's truth. I seen far too much of that in my 15 years in the navy. Cap'n believes the proper port for a storm brewing in a man's trousers is under the petticoats of a proper bit of jam. No sir, a boy's backside is safe on the Kai Douglas."

Thomas shook his head with a bemused smile and looked over at Kahale to see if the missionary was blushing, but Heron's remarks seem to have blown over his head.

The old sailor handed them each two lengths of manila rope and lit his pipe, signaling it was time for the lesson to begin.

"And what about the ship's cook?" asked Kahale as two chickens raced past them on the deck, followed by the captain's dog in hot pursuit. Heron reached out one hand and grabbed the mutt before it could take out the ship's fresh egg suppliers.

"Jacob? Aye, I forgot to mention him. Fine cook, minds his stores and keeps the galley spotless. Serves up the tastiest bags o'mystery I ever et, too."

"Bags of what…?" Thomas began.

"Mystery, boy. Mystery. Also known as sausages. Nobody knows what the hell they pack into the gut they use for them torpedoes," he said with a wink, "and that's probably a good thing, don't you think?"

The sailor picked up a coil of manila line from the deck. "Now, this here's called rope, lads," Heron began.

Kahale chuckled. "Perhaps we can bypass the obvious and get on to knots?"

Heron scowled. "Obvious? To understand knots and hitches ye need to understand rope." He held a length of rope up high. "There are three strands in this line, and they are right laid, which means they spiral around the rope in a clockwise fashion. Each strand is made of seven individual threads that are left-laid, meaning they go counterclockwise. That there—the clockwise and counterclockwise construction—is why rope holds its form and does not unlay. Now watch…"

Heron quickly tied a knot in his rope and dipped it into a bucket of seawater that Willy was using to wash the deck. "Rope gets stronger when it gets wet because the water makes the fibers soft and fairs up the lay. So, bends, hitches, and knots tighten up when they get wet, so much so that there are some we can't use at sea because they get so damn tight that you can't untie them, and that can condemn a poor soul to a nasty death in the wrong circumstances. I once seen a boy about Willy's age get his throat crushed when he couldn't loosen the knot around his neck that held him to a mast to keep him from washing overboard in a storm."

Heron pulled the soaked rope from the bucket and handed it to Kahale. "Untie that," he instructed.

The missionary tugged and struggled but he could not undo Heron's knot. He grinned sheepishly and handed it back.

"Two masts and dozens of knots, bends and hitches," said Heron. "We check every one of 'em every day, sometimes twice. Look there…"

He pointed to Bembé, who was wrapping a length of rope around the base of the mainmast. "Ye must master knots and hitches before you can learn how to rig, and boys, solid rigging is the soul of every ship that raises sail. By the time I was 12 I knew how to fully rig a ship, from the bowsprit to the lower masts, top masts, jib-boom, and whiskers—every part of every sail. Most important thing I ever learned, well, maybe 'sept how to properly stroke the withers of a pink-cheeked lassie so's she'd happily unloose the doors to her sweet little treasure chest."

Heron laughed at his own joke and ignored the flushed expression on Kahale's face. "Let's to it, now," Heron said. "First the reef knot, then the bowline, the figure eight and then the constrictor. I'll show ye the proper way of tying each and then you'll practice till your hands are blistered and your knots are perfect."

Heron took them through the paces for their first four knots and then left to tend to his sail. McNab was at the tiller and Jacob, the cook, came up on deck to peel potatoes in the fresh air while Boswell jotted notes in his journal in the shade of a stack of barrels lashed to the deck. An hour later Bembé stepped away from his sail and joined Thomas and Edward to check on their progress. The tropical sun was high overhead, and when the Jamaican peeled off his linen shirt to get some relief, Thomas gasped. The black man's back was a mass of thick burn scars from the base of his neck to his waistline. Thomas had witnessed the effects of burns many times during the war, but Bembé's wounds were the worst he had seen.

Bembé felt his stare, but only smiled. "Burned by water," he said in a thick accent as he tied a constrictor knot and handed it to Kahale to try again.

"Water?" the missionary asked. "How's that possible?"

"I worked two kinds of cargo out of Maine before I tossed my seabag on Cap'n McNab's deck. The first was river ice out of the Kennebec, above Bath. We hauled ice to Baltimore and all over the Caribbean and South America. Hell, our ice was so pure and beautiful that some schooners carried it all the way to Calcutta, India. I came out here in '70, and the year before over half a million tons of ice were transported around the world by schooner."

"So, you were burned by ice?" Thomas asked.

"No," laughed Bembé. "By slack lime. That was the other cargo I worked. Lime has to be burned in giant kilns for days before it takes on a form that can be mixed into mortar or plaster, and the burning causes it to change chemically. Problem is, when slack lime comes into contact with sea water it ignites."

Kahale and Thomas shook their heads in disbelief, and Thomas spoke for them both when he said, "Then why the hell did they transport it on schooners?

"The sea is the only road that circles the world," replied Bembé with a shrug. "Shipbuilders used extra thick planking in the hulls of ships that carry slack lime, and we did everything to keep it dry when we were at sea, but in a storm sometimes it just wasn't possible. One way or another some water would leak through the seams and a burn would begin. Sometimes the fires burned so hot the schooner had to be scuttled. My fire happened off the coast of Georgia. I was lucky; five of my shipmates were roasted alive below decks."

Thomas grimaced inwardly at the thought of such a fire, but before he could reply, Willy raced over from the starboard side, ducked under a sail, and plopped a wooden bucket on the deck between him and Kahale. There were six or seven brightly colored fish in the bucket, each about a foot long.

"A whole school of them," gushed the boy. "Best fishing day for me ever."

Boswell set down his sketch pad and pencil and joined the group gathered around the bucket. He lifted out one of the iridescent fish and inspected it carefully. "Parrotfish, or *Cetoscarus bicolor*," he said. "First described by Rüppell in 1829, I believe. They are extraordinary creatures, sequential hermaphrodites, actually. They begin life as females and then change to males. Their coloring changes, too." He turned the fish over several times and then asked Willy if he could keep it to sketch and dissect.

That's when Jacob appeared with a basket in hand. "Male or female is no concern to me, Mr. Boswell," said the cook. "Parrotfish are prime eating, and as long as there are enough for dinner ye are welcome to keep one for a pet."

The leathery old man wiped his hands on his apron, winked at Thomas and then turned to Willy. "They taste best raw, laddie. Did ye know that?"

The boy blanched at the thought.

"Marinated in lime juice and coconut milk," the ship's cook continued. It's called *poisson cru à la Tahitienne*."

"And it's damn tasty," said Captain McNab, who had just handed the helm over to Heron. "But, like Willy, I believe we should prepare this batch with a little lemon and butter and break out some of that dry Chablis Jacob has been hoarding."

Jacob waved his hand in the air at the mild reproach and shuffled off to prepare the feast. McNab sat down with Edward and Thomas and watched as they tied each of the four knots they had been working on all day, while Boswell pulled his colored charcoal from a canvas pouch and began to sketch the parrotfish.

When Thomas tied the final bowline knot to the captain's satisfaction, his hands were a bit blistered and his fingers ached, but he felt a sense of achievement that he had not experienced in months. He looked up into the full sails, felt the sweet sea mist on his face and listened to the music of the bow slicing through the turquoise sea. Tonight, he and his shipmates would have a fine dinner with an excellent French Chablis, followed by cigars, brandy, and storytelling on deck under a glittering carpet of equatorial stars.

He smiled and thought, *'I could get used to this.'*

~ TWENTY-SEVEN ~

Matavai Bay, Tahiti
July 1872

Captain McNab's two story clapboard house sat on a bluff overlooking Matavai Bay on the north shore peninsula of Tahiti. It was built with lumber carried from San Francisco in the hold of the Kai Douglas and looked down on a curving black sand beach that wrapped around for a half mile to the foot of One Tree Hill. Just beyond the beach a stream emptied the floodwaters of the Vaipopo'o River into the sea from its source in the foothills of the Tua'uru Valley under the mountains of Aora'i and Orohena. A giant tamarind tree—believed to have been planted by Captain Cook–kept watch at the end of the peninsula where his men set up their tents in 1769. Captain Bligh built a house along the stream during his second visit to the island in 1792, which the first British missionaries converted into a storeroom and shelter when they arrived on the island in 1797. Seventy years later McNab built his green-roofed, whitewashed home atop the ruins of the old missionary structure.

The shape of Teauroa Peninsula offered good shelter for schooners when the easterlies blew, and wood, water, and provisions were plentiful for vessels at anchor inside the banks of coral reef. In recent years the preferred anchorage on the island had shifted seven miles west to Pape'ete where the Kai Douglas now lay, but McNab had both emotional and historic ties to Matavai and no intention of moving.

"I can see why you picked this spot," Thomas said as a cool breeze lifted off the bay and washed through the two sets of open French doors leading out to a wide porch. He and Kahale and Boswell had just finished an excellent dinner of pork tenderloin and roasted sweet potatoes accompanied by a fine Bordeaux. The housekeeper cleared the table and brewed fresh coffee to go along with brandy and bread pudding, which McNab and his guests would enjoy outside above the lush gardens that spilled down to the edge of the bluff. Masses of fragrant Tiaré gardenia bushes planted in the rich coral soil lined the perimeter of the property, filling the air with floral perfume.

"Good lord, yes," answered Boswell as he lit his pipe. "I could spend a month cataloguing the flowers and trees on your property alone."

"And you are welcome to do that," said McNab as he led the men out onto the deck to settle into comfortable wooden chairs. "However, I think you will find that most of the plant species here along the coast have been studied to some degree, at least. If you want to be the first to examine Tahiti's real botanical treasures, you will have to hike inland."

"No scientists have done that?" asked Kahale. "The island really isn't all that big."

"The interior of both Tahiti Nui where we are now, and that of the smaller Tahiti Iti to which we are joined by a narrow isthmus, are rugged and mountainous, and more suited for the mountain goat than for a man. There are hundreds of streams and waterfalls, few—if any—passable trails, and even fewer inhabitants."

Boswell grinned. "A challenge, then."

"When I built this place four years ago, I determined to explore some of the interior," said McNab. "I even hired a local who claimed to have hunted all across the island to guide me. It took just one day of hacking through vines as thick as your arm and progressing only a few feet per hour to dissuade me of that romantic notion."

The housekeeper came out onto the porch with coffee and bowls of bread pudding topped with crème anglaise as the orange sun slipped below the western horizon.

"How much time do you spend here?" asked Thomas. "I don't think that I could ever leave."

McNab chuckled. "And someday I will watch another master sail off on the Kai Douglas and spend the rest of my days here. For now, I am content to spend about three months per year on the island."

"When do you sail for San Francisco?" asked Kahale.

McNab set his pipe down and sipped at his brandy. "Two weeks," he said. "I'll take on baled cotton, copra, vanilla, coffee, and oranges." He looked across at Thomas. "And I will take your letters to your editor at the *Chronicle* and to your friend Mr. Kwan."

Thomas nodded. He had described his odyssey to his friends during the voyage. From his fateful dinner with the Kwans in San Francisco after his story about Stafford was published to the fight with Donegan at the Pearl three weeks ago, he detailed the twists and turns his life had taken for the past five months. In return, his shipmates pledged to do whatever they could to stop Donegan and get Thomas back to the mainland.

"You will not want to miss dinner at the Kwan's *La Rue de Paris*, I promise you," Thomas told McNab as the captain poured a shot of brandy into his coffee. "I dream about that place almost every night."

Boswell set down his glass and laughed. "If food is all you dream about after weeks at sea, Thomas my lad, I'd venture that you have bigger worries than being chased by an Irish assassin."

Thomas grinned and raised his glass to the botanist.

"Tomorrow after breakfast I have something to show you gentlemen," said McNab. "Then we'll ride down to Pape'ete and introduce Timothy to the British counsel and get Edward squared away with Reverend Simons. Thomas can get acquainted with the town while I do a little business, and then we'll come back for a grand dinner and a fresh batch of tall tales."

The men lingered quietly over their coffee and dessert as the sun was swallowed up by the purple sea and the heavens began to glitter gold and silver. Then McNab topped off their glasses and the four men settled back to watch the velvety tropical darkness fold the island into its arms.

After a breakfast of eggs scrambled with ham and peppers, fresh fruit, and biscuits the next morning, McNab invited his guests to take their coffee and follow him across the expansive, wood-floored living room and through a set of double doors leading into his library. The east wall of the 16-foot-high room was lined from floor to ceiling with books, while a bank of tall windows spanned the width of the west wall, cranked open to catch the morning breeze. But it was the wall directly across the room from the entry doors that brought Thomas, Boswell, and Kahale to a halt.

The sea-blue wall was bare, except for an oil painting positioned at dead center. But what a painting, Thomas thought. He looked over at McNab and his friends and knew each one was thinking the same thing.

The framed oil was six feet wide and four feet high. It was a landscape, with tree covered cliffs and rocky outcroppings that spilled down to a wind-whipped sea. Other than those discernable features, however, the style, color, lighting, paint application and shadowing were completely foreign to Thomas and his friends. He had seen countless paintings in homes, museums, libraries, and in his visits to the War Department and the White House. His entire experience of art, however, was of paintings that portrayed heroic people and events realistically, using sober colors, geometric—almost stiff—composition, and gray and black shadowing. The focus of those classical paintings was the central subject matter, but the focus of the painting in front of him was more about light and color. The brush strokes looked to have been applied quickly and loosely, an effect that was enhanced the closer he stood. The vivid colors appeared to have been laid on the canvas in chunks alongside one another, not blended on a palette before applying as was done with all the other paintings he had seen. In fact, the reflection of the colors from object to object in the painting almost created the illusion of motion.

Thomas took several steps back and looked at the painting again. Distance increased the clarity of the work and magnified the interplay of light and color. He could only shake his head and stare.

"Did you paint this?" Boswell finally asked McNab.

"By the saints, no!" answered the captain. "But I am blessed to know the artist. His name is Émile Jean-Baptiste Aubert, a bit of a wild man, especially for a Frenchy."

"Was it painted locally?" asked Kahale.

"Not fifteen minutes from here," said McNab. "Aubert is my friend and frequent houseguest. I brought a chest of supplies for him from San Francisco, and I am taking them to the village a day and a half's ride south of Pape'ete, where he has been painting. I know that you and Boswell will be on your own journeys tomorrow, but I thought that Thomas might like to accompany me."

"What's that?" Thomas mumbled, uncertain about the invitation he had just received.

"Come with me to Chief Varua's village," said McNab. "You're going to be in Tahiti for some time after I sail, and it would be good for you to make some new friends."

Thomas blinked; Aubert's painting was having the same effect on him that the works of his favorite author, Jules Verne, had each time he sat down with the French author's *Journey to the Center of the Earth,* or *Twenty Thousand Leagues Under the Seas*. It was a feeling of light-headed unreality, a dreamlike sensation in which he hovered between wakefulness and slumber.

"What say you, Colonel?"

Thomas shook off the trance. "What? Sorry, yes, of course," he finally answered, "I can't think of anything I would rather do."

McNab smiled, and then called for the housekeeper to go out to the stable and have the grounds man saddle four horses for the seven mile ride to Pape'ete. Then he turned and followed Boswell and Kahale out of the library, leaving Thomas rooted to the floor in front of Aubert's painting.

~ TWENTY-EIGHT ~

Western Coast, Tahiti

Thomas woke at dawn to the sounds of a fluorescent plumed bird screeching from its perch in the open window of the thatch-roofed church on the bank of the Vaipoe River. He swung his legs off the hard wooden pew that had served as his bed and stretched to loosen the kinks in his back. Edward Kahale was still asleep on the pew closest to the seashell covered alter, and through the open window he could see Captain McNab and Boswell talking in the vegetable garden with mugs of coffee in their hands.

He ran his hand through his hair and exited through the side door nearest the river. The air was heavy with moisture, though there wasn't a cloud to be seen in the July sky. He made his way to the water, and as he unbuttoned his fly, he looked upriver into the dark recesses of the Tefaaiti Valley through which the river coursed. Like everywhere they had traveled yesterday in their journey south along the coast from Pape'ete, the topography of Tahiti was the same: a narrow strip of black sand at the water's edge, an even narrower band of rough dirt road that followed the coastal contour, and to the east, a few dozen yards of relatively flat, tree-and-shrub- covered land over which hung the great, furrowed mountains that until this morning had been enshrouded in masses of thick grey clouds.

The absence of cloud cover did not provide much more of a view of the island's interior, however. In all his travels, Thomas had never seen such dense, deep green vegetation like the foliage that seemed to cover every square inch of this volcanic island. He could only see about 100 yards up the placid waterway before low-hanging branches obscured the view beyond. To look up into the hills and mountains was to be overwhelmed by massed formations of trees, ferns, bushes, and shrubs grown together so tightly that they formed an impenetrable dark green wall that any self-respecting medieval lord would have been proud to use to protect his castle.

He rinsed his hands in the cool water and climbed up the bank. In a small cookhouse behind the church, a woman was preparing breakfast, and when Thomas approached, she handed him a steaming tin cup of coffee without being asked.

"*Bonjour et merci,*" he said to her as she turned to pour a cup for Kahale, who had just made his own trip to the river.

"My French could use some practice," said the missionary as they walked towards the garden to join their friends. "But you will be in welcome company."

"You could always learn Tahitian," replied Thomas with a grin. "I understand that a handful of Europeans have mastered the tongue with just eight or ten years of study."

"*Je resterai avec le français, alor,*" mused Kahale.

"Yes, it would be good for you to stick with French," Thomas agreed. "After all, they say there are no words for promiscuity or gambling or theft in Tahitian. How would your sermons convey the proper wrath of God if you weren't able to condemn those fundamental human vices?"

Now it was Kahale's turn to smile. "And do they have a word for heathen?" he asked with a wry expression.

"They didn't until your kind arrived and set about wringing out the last drops of carnal pleasure from their lives," laughed Thomas.

They went to the garden and joined Captain McNab and Boswell on wicker chairs around a stone-topped table. The pastor of the little church was already off making sick calls around the village, leaving his guests in the care of his housekeeper. She carried a tray to the table and set down bowls of oatmeal with fruit, a plate piled high with bacon, a loaf of fresh-baked bread and more coffee.

"This is excellent," said Thomas as he held up a piece of bacon.

"Though it does seem more an American breakfast than Polynesian."

"The Tahitians raise pigs for themselves and for export," said McNab between spoonfuls of thick oatmeal. "I take them regularly to New Zealand, though God knows it isn't my preferred cargo."

"Do they raise pigs where we are going?" asked Boswell.

"For export?" replied McNab. "Not in Papara. They raise just enough to eat. No, Chief Varua's people mostly fish and raise vegetables, some of the women produce decorated bark cloth to sell to off-island traders, and the Chief himself buys pearls and pearl shell from Tuamotu and Mangareva that he peddles to schooner owners like me."

"Is the schooner business profitable?" asked Thomas.

"Most years, yes," replied the captain, "though the truth is that my life here is an endless search around the islands and atolls for cargo to carry back to San Francisco. Pearl shell prices are the best they have ever been, but the best shell banks and lagoons have been picked over thoroughly and shells are getting harder to find. Good divers can work down to 50 or 60 feet and haul up 40 or so six-inch shells in a day, but the last load I purchased was mostly filled with four-inch shells. Not much profit in those, and that's why I'm going to see Chief Varua; I need better shell, and lots of it."

The men finished their breakfasts and Kahale helped Thomas and McNab hitch the horses to the wagon of supplies they were taking to Papara. Kahale would stay at the church for the next six months to accustom himself to the people and routines he would need to master before he could build a church of his own on the northeast shore, while Boswell would travel on with the others to study plants and flowers in areas of the island that had not been visited by scientists.

Thomas tightened the canvas lashings that secured their cargo and then climbed up onto the seat next to McNab. The captain released the brake, snapped the reins, and eased the horses forward as Boswell mounted his horse and swung out onto the red dirt road beside them for the eight-mile journey to Chief Varua's village.

The captain liked to talk, and as Thomas settled back onto the hard plank seat, he figured that was just fine, especially today. He'd spent much of the previous night staring up at the church ceiling, wondering what his life would be like if he hadn't been on the run for six months. He missed writing for the *Chronicle*, he missed his friends, and he missed Mr. Kwan's extraordinary cuisine. Perhaps McNab's tales could help tamp down his growing sense of futility, if only for a while.

The breeze that blew across the choppy waters and up into the canopied forest as they pulled away from the church at Paea smelled of salt and rotting seaweed. They would follow the line of great green cliffs south along the shoreline, crossing innumerable streams, swinging around waterfalls that sprayed cool mist across the road, and navigating the rocks, jagged fissures, and fallen logs that loomed before them at every turn.

The wagon settled into a steady rhythm, and Thomas looked out beyond the surf line to the great expanse of lazuline ocean that stretched across the horizon. McNab was prattling on about a tribe of headhunters he once encountered in New Guinea, but Thomas only had ears for the crashing surf and whirling gulls. He was struggling against the darkness that came when he felt becalmed, unable to move forward or even to make sense of where he had just been, and he was certain of only one thing; he had to make something happen before he slipped into the seductive pool of melancholy so completely that this time, he might not be able to climb out.

He turned his head from the sea and stared steadfastly at the road ahead.

~ TWENTY-NINE ~

Papara, Tahiti

Aata drew himself up to his full height and brought his spear hand back behind his head. The tattoos on his heavily muscled shoulders and back danced in the bonfire's shadowy orange light, and the crowd of villagers seated on logs and rocks in a semi-circle behind the warrior held their collective breath in anticipation of his next move.

His left leg was planted a few feet behind his right leg, his left arm was crooked and raised to chin height, and his torso was turned slightly to the right. At the instant his arm began to propel the spear forward, he would whip his torso back to the left and use the additional momentum to send the spear hurtling towards the target with astonishing speed. Many of the villagers had seen Aata split small trees in half with a single throw, and his bravery, taking on huge wild boars whose razor-sharp tusks could open a man's leg to the bone with one slashing motion of its bristled head, was legendary around the island.

But his target tonight wasn't a tree, or a boar. Forty feet from where he stood ready to loose his spear was a gnarled tree with a 'Y' shaped trunk. A man was planted upside down against the tree, his head resting on the dirt and his legs splayed wide and tied to branches with braided cord. Nestled in his crotch was Aata's target: a large, unhusked coconut.

The upside-down man was in his 20s, shirtless and wearing only loose linen trousers. His arms were stretched out on the ground, and Thomas could see that he was gouging his fingers into the soft dirt. Not surprisingly, rivulets of sweat were pouring off his chest and face and dripping onto the soil. If Aata's aim was off by only an inch up, down, or to either side, the man would either lose one of his legs, have his abdomen pierced, or feel his manhood nailed to the bark by the razor-sharp spear tip.

Thomas turned and made eye contact with Captain McNab, who was seated on a stump a few feet away beside Chief Varua and the chief's sister, Keani. In reply, McNab shrugged and shook his head. None of the 100 villagers gathered around the fire showed any concern about what was happening—why should he or Thomas raise an objection? The damn fool tied to the tree had apparently offended the spear-wielding warrior while fishing earlier that day, and Aata's honor could only be restored in the eyes of his people with a very public display of humiliation and penance. If that meant some poor fool's balls could end up being pinned to the tree like a butterfly in a schoolchild's science display, so be it. This was the Polynesian way.

It had been a day of contrasts and extremes. Thomas and McNab wheeled their horse-drawn cart into the center of the scattering of thatched huts and wood shacks that made up the seaside village of Papara just after noon. Boswell rode in an hour later after being sidelined by the sight of an unfamiliar flowering bush that smelt of burnt sulphur and peppermint.

Chief Varua had just completed his midday meal and came out from under a covering woven with reeds and palms where several women were working over low, domed ovens. McNab and the chief embraced, and when the captain introduced Thomas, he was struck by how the darkness of Varua's eyes contrasted with his wide, snow-white smile. Like most Tahitian men, Varua wore a baggy, buttonless cotton shirt over lightweight trousers that were chopped off just below the knee. His long jet-black hair was held against the back of his neck with a blue ribbon, and a ten-inch pearl shell knife dangled from his belt.

"Welcome home, old friend," said the chief as McNab leaned up over the wall of the wagon to retrieve a wooden box. Varua's eyebrows went up and his smile widened further when he saw the word 'Cognac' stenciled on the side.

"A dozen bottles of *Cognac Frapin*," said McNab with a smile. "Just enough for us to conduct our pearl shell negotiations."

Varua pried the lid off the box with his knife and pulled out a single dark- brown bottle. He unwrapped the cork, pulled it out, and took a deep smell. "Heaven," he said. "And to think you were able to get a full case even as the grape phylloxera is ravaging the vineyards in France where it is produced."

He held up the bottle for Thomas to see and added, "This is *Frapin's* 600th year producing the nectar of the gods, colonel. I am truly a lucky man."

Thomas cast a sidelong glance at McNab as if to say, "We are 10,000 miles and several centuries of civilization from Paris, and yet this tribal chieftain of an isolated village miles from anywhere is a connoisseur of fine cognacs?"

McNab grinned. He knew what Thomas was thinking. "Chief Varua is a man of many talents, colonel. I highly recommend against engaging him in cards."

The chief laughed and led them to a stone bench at the edge of a creek that spilled into the lagoon. He waved to the open-air kitchen, and two women brought plates of fruit, fresh-baked bread, and several empty glasses.

"I am sorry that Aubert is not here to enjoy this moment," said Varua as he filled three glasses and motioned for the men to sit. "His heart will be broken, but he chooses to paint on the other side of the mountain, while I choose to attend to my duties." He raised his glass, and they drank deeply of the aromatic liquid that tasted of dried fruit, dark chocolate, and caramel.

"Extraordinary," was all that Thomas could say.

McNab nodded his head in agreement. "But have no worries for Aubert," he said to Varua, "I brought a case for him as well, and also a box of paints and brushes and a roll of fine canvas."

"Tell me, colonel," said Varua as he topped off their glasses. "What has brought you to Tahiti, and more importantly, out here to the edge of nowhere? You don't appear to be a businessman, and unless France and the United States have declared war, you are not here to do battle."

Thomas started to speak, but McNab laid a hand on his forearm and answered for him.

"Colonel Scoundrel is sitting out a dangerous situation," said the captain. "I would like for him to stay here for week or so while I tend to some business, and then he will come with me back to Matavai Bay until…"

"…until those who are pursuing him give up the chase and turn back for America?" the chief interrupted.

How, and why, Thomas wondered? How could Varua know about Donnegan and Stafford and their quest to have him killed?

The chief's eyes sparkled. "No mystery, colonel," he said. "Men only come here for a few reasons; to sell and buy, to paint and study…" he lowered his voice, "…or to hide. McNab is a buyer, Aubert is an artist, and Boswell is a scientist. You strike me as being none of those. And so, if you are one who needs to hide, there must be someone you are hiding from. A simple deduction."

"But you have left out a category of visitors, friend Varua," said McNab. "The missionary. Surely you don't think they come here to hide from the authorities?"

"Ah, but captain, I have included the missionary. He is here to sell."

McNab looked perplexed.

"Salvation comes at a cost, does it not? There is an exchange of value between sinner and savior, and the missionary is the middleman in the transaction." The chief smiled at his own cleverness.

"Fill my glass, Varua," grumbled McNab, "and let's talk about the next pearl shell delivery."

❖

That evening Thomas, McNab, and Boswell joined dozens of villagers under a balmy, star-swept sky for a dinner of whole roast pig.

The animal had been salted before its carcass was filled with hot stones and placed on hardwood coals. Then more hot stones were placed on top of the pig beneath layers of flattened banana tree brush, *ti* leaves, and several inches of soil. Slow cooking in an imu oven was a Polynesian tradition that went back centuries, Boswell explained when they were handed ceramic plates piled high with the succulent shredded pork alongside local fruit that had been liberally marinated in sweetened rum punch.

"Food of the gods," said Boswell as he watched the expression on Thomas' face when he took his first bite.

"I have to agree," Thomas replied. Then he turned to Chief Varua and nodded his appreciation.

McNab leaned over and whispered something into the Chief's ear.

"Is it true, Colonel, that you are an authority on fine wine?" asked Varua.

"I am becoming one, at least as my pocketbook permits," Thomas answered with a smile.

"And what wine would you serve with roasted pork?" continued the chief.

"Something with a bit of fruit and good acidity, I would think."

"A Beaujolais, perhaps?"

Thomas nodded agreement between bites and Varua turned to his sister and said something that Thomas could not hear. She rose from her seat and walked swiftly away from the fire in the direction of the Chief's residence.

"You say Keani is mute?" Thomas asked Boswell.

"Since birth, though it does not seem to have held her back in any way. I understand she was educated by the missionaries and is something of a famous reader. McNab regularly brings cases of books for her library, and I dare say she has read each of them at least twice. A priest also trained her in the French Gallaudet hand language, and she has taught several of her friends how to speak with their hands, as well."

"She seems so young; do I understand that she was married?"

"At 14," Boswell answered. "Varua wanted to build an alliance with a neighboring chief to lobby for a better yearly stipend payment from the Queen for all the chiefs. Three months after the wedding her husband was killed when his fishing boat overturned on a coral reef. Nasty death, I was told.' He held up a forkful of pork. "Apparently his body was shredded on the razor-sharp coral spines just like this exceptional pork."

Thomas grimaced. "And now she is…"

"Twenty, and happily single," said the botanist. "Dedicated to her brother, and shows no interest in remarrying, though I am told that Aata has been an unrelenting suitor."

"She's not interested?" Thomas asked.

"He can't read, and he is unwilling to learn," said Boswell. "She requires literacy as a condition for even considering matrimony, though I suspect that Chief Varua is growing tired of her refusing every man who asks him for her hand. He has no heirs, and so he expects Keani to marry and produce a healthy male child so that his seed will continue to rule Papara for generations."

Before Thomas could reply, Keani returned with a small burlap sack and a tray with five wine glasses. She handed glasses to her brother, McNab, Thomas, and Boswell, and then withdrew two bottles and a wine opener from the bag and gave them to her brother.

Varua held up a bottle in the firelight for Thomas to see. "*Beaujolais Nouveau*, made from the *Gamay noir à Jus blanc* grape. A gift from my friend Louis Henry Denis Jadot, who first visited Tahiti five years ago and carried with him two dozen cases of the nectar. Sadly, Beaujolais has a rather short cellar life, and so I must rely upon my purchasing agent in Pape'ete and the services of good men like Captain McNab to keep it flowing from France on a regular basis."

Varua opened both bottles and filled their glasses, which Keani handed to the guests before filling her own glass. At the instant she handed Thomas his wine, a shower of sparks from the great fire in the center of the village common area shot up into the clear night sky. He was so startled that he pulled back and put his open hand on her elbow to steady himself on his wooden chair, without spilling a drop of wine, he was proud to note.

Keani smiled and rested her hand briefly on his shoulder before returning to her brother's side. Thomas took note of two things in that instant; first, he had not realized how beautiful Keani was, and second, he felt the heat of Aata's intense stare even before he saw the warrior glaring at him through the flames for sharing so intimate—though harmless—a moment with the woman Aata claimed as his own.

Boswell saw it, too. He took a sip of his wine and said, "I suggest you keep your ship tied tightly to the dock, my friend. This is one storm you do not want to sail into."

Thomas shrugged, and inhaled the bright, fruit-filled aroma of the Beaujolais before taking a deep drink. McNab and Varua were deep in conversation, and Boswell's attention was suddenly diverted by a young boy who brought him a basket of unusual flowers that bloomed for only a day or two each year.

Thomas looked past Varua to where Keani was gazing into the heart of the fire. In the orange light of the flames, her forest green eyes seemed to glow. Encircling her head was a simple wreath of fern mixed with leaves that were dotted with small white flowers. Her olive complexioned skin was unblemished, and her nose turned up slightly at the tip, giving the suggestion of a mischievous personality. Her dark brown hair was naturally parted in the middle and spilled in soft curling waves down below her breasts, but the loose, sleeveless white linen dress that went down to her bare feet gave no hint about the contours of the body that it covered.

Keani felt his gaze and turned her head to look directly into his eyes. Her expression was a mix of curiosity and welcome, but before Thomas could rouse himself enough to even think of saying something to her, a shout went up on the far side of the bonfire. Everyone stood as three men marched the hapless victim of Aata's anger over to the 'Y' shaped tree, turned him upside down, and spreadeagled and lashed his legs to the trunks. When an elderly woman walked saucily over to the man and gently lay a coconut on his upended crotch the crowd realized what was going on and began to cheer.

THIRTY

A young man carried Aata's spear across the compound with a reverence that reminded Thomas of the way he had been instructed to carry and place candles on the altar during Mass when he was a boy. The warrior took the spear and held it high above his head, and as the firelight played upon the gleaming steel tip, he made eye contact with Thomas and then stretched the spear out in Thomas' direction. The message was clear to everyone in the village.

Captain McNab looked at Thomas and shook his head, and Boswell raised a toast to him with a wry smile. Only Chief Varua was smiling. He approved of the match between Aata and his sister, and if this evening's events were a sign that Aata was about finished with being a doormat for Keani's indecision, so be it. For her part, Thomas noticed, Keani seemed oblivious to the drama playing out around her. At the same time, she did not return his gaze.

Aata gripped the spear tightly, pulled it behind his head, and without hesitating hurled it forward with astonishing speed. The man tied to the tree who was serving as the repository for Aata's target closed his eyes and dug his fingers deeper into the dirt as the spear flew towards his crotch. Thomas was surprised to see the shaft of the spear wobble as it sped along its path in the warm night air, but the knife-edged tip stayed straight and true as it flew across the compound.

Then there was a cracking sound, and cheers rang out around the bonfire as Aata's spear cleaved the coconut in half, spilling milk down the front of the victim's pants, which Thomas thought, would probably hide the evidence of the urine he had surely been passing in fright in the moments before the spear took flight.

Aata walked to the tree and retrieved his spear as two men cut down the sobbing fellow who had nearly lost his manhood. Then, to the shouts and backslaps of the villagers, Aata walked to the edge of the fire and sat down beside Chief Varua, who handed the warrior a tankard of rum punch. Aata downed the sweet potion in one gulp and raised the cup high in celebration of his own magnificence. And why not, thought Thomas. He was skilled in the art of war, calm under pressure, and over-flowing with confidence. The men of the village respected and feared him, and from the glow on the faces of the women showering Aata with praise, it was clear that more than a few of them were imagining what it would be like to be splayed against the tree in anticipation of being pierced by Aata's other spear.

But not Keani, Thomas noticed. As Aata continued to bask in the adulation of his people, she turned towards Thomas, her eyes twinkling. But she was not joining the others in celebrating the hero. Instead, she clapped her hand over her mouth to prevent herself from giggling.

Thomas woke just after dawn in one of the soft cots that had been prepared for him and McNab in a newer thatched hut at the edge of the stream that flowed into the sea. He stepped outside into a hazy sunrise, and, as he walked to the edge of the water, three chickens and a pregnant sow pig skittered across the path.

He nodded to two women who were carrying baskets of fruit they had just harvested and stood in the shadow of a tree and watched as a group of fisherman—including Aata—loaded nets into two outrigger canoes and pushed then out into the surf before hopping in and paddling towards the fishing grounds to the east. Several of the men greeted him, but Aata piled into his canoe without acknowledging he existed.

"You always make friends this way?" asked McNab, who had come up behind him with two mugs of coffee.

Thomas grinned sheepishly and accepted the drink. "It seems to be my fate, though I can't recall ever having made an enemy for just smiling at a woman."

"In this culture a smile is all it takes, my lad," answered McNab with a laugh. "Had you winked at her, we might be burying your sorry carcass this morning."

Thomas sighed. "She doesn't want to marry him, you know."

"And you do, Thomas? Keani must live here among her people, and that includes marrying one of them. A dalliance with a dashing young colonel just isn't in the cards. Not for her, and sure as hell not for you."

They stood quietly as the outriggers raised their sails and slipped over the reef and into the open sea. Thomas was about to reply when a woman appeared and asked them to join Varua for breakfast.

"We'll speak more on this later, my friend," said McNab as they walked up towards the commons, where villagers were gathering at three large tables piled high with platters of fresh-baked bread, eggs scrambled with ham, and plates of fruit, coal-roasted fish drizzled with lime, and mounds of bacon.

A lovely young woman wearing only a bright smile and a flowered print skirt handed Thomas a plate filled with the delicious food. The sight of her perfectly shaped naked breasts just inches above the plate she was handing him made him beam.

"And you wondered why this place is called paradise?" asked McNab. "Let's join Varua."

With a sidelong glance at his server's perfectly proportioned bosom, Thomas joined Varua, Boswell, and McNab at a table.

"You seem to have discovered a species worthy of your study," said the botanist with a grin.

"There was a time, good friends, when all of our women dressed this way," said the chief. "You can thank your missionaries for disrupting that delightful tradition, among others."

McNab and Boswell laughed, but Thomas did not respond. Then Varua saw that the young American was scanning the compound.

"My sister is taking her breakfast alone this morning, colonel," said the chief. "I thought that best given last night's fireworks."

'Fireworks?' thought Thomas. *'A few simple glances?'* McNab had been right about the culture. Almost without thinking he found himself saying, "My apologies, Chief Varua. I certainly intended no harm or disrespect with anything that I said or did with your sister."

"Our ways are different, Colonel," the chief replied in a thoughtful tone. "And even though a half-naked woman just served you breakfast, we actually have quite rigid protocols when it comes to who may be familiar with an unmarried woman. Aata is Keani's intended, and as you saw with the speared coconut, he is not a man to cross."

"I second the colonel's comment, Varua," said McNab. "He was simply being polite, and frankly, even I have had some difficulty thinking about how to communicate with your sister, given that she is mute, after all."

Varua accepted another serving of roasted fish from a woman before replying. "I have no doubt as to the propriety of the colonel's behavior," he said, "and yet, since you and I are leaving today to travel to Pape'ete to arrange our new pearl shell contract, I think it best that we do not leave Thomas here in our absence. Aata's honor would be sullied, and his spear might find its way into the colonel's gut if there was a repeat of last night's flirtation."

Boswell interrupted the conversation before Thomas could speak. "Gentlemen, I may have a solution to this dilemma. I am leaving shortly for the trek over the mountain to Aubert's encampment, where I will spend the next several weeks studying the flora in the hills and canyons surrounding the little bay. I propose that Thomas accompany me. He is, ahem, seeking to keep a low profile for the time being, and that is something he can do more successfully with Aubert than he can here, wouldn't you agree?"

McNab shared a questioning glance with Chief Varua. "Why not?" asked the captain. "Thomas can assist Boswell with his specimen collecting, and I daresay Aubert will be grateful for the company. And they can deliver the art supplies I brought, too, and save me the trip over that damn mountain."

Varua banged his coffee mug on the tabletop. "It is decided then," he said with a satisfied smile. "Sand fly season is almost upon us, Colonel," he continued. "If those tiny demons don't do you in, Aubert's stories should finish the job. If not, we will see you back here in a few weeks."

With that Chief Varua and Captain McNab left the table to prepare for their trip up Tahiti's eastern coast to Pape'ete.

Thomas had always been uncomfortable with anyone else charting his course, no matter how small the circumstance. Still, Boswell's suggestion made sense. He could use the time on the isolated bay to write letters to the editor of the *Chronicle*, and to Mr. Kwan, who he still hadn't thanked for alerting him to the assassin who was on his trail. It was also time for him to develop a plan to deal with Colin Stafford. He might not be able to return to San Francisco, but he was not going to spend the rest of his life in hiding, either.

A moment later the young lady with the magnificently perched breasts approached the table and asked if she could bring him anything else. Thomas fought the urge to reply to her welcoming smile with a ribald invitation and instead looked down, sighed, and shook his head.

As she turned and walked away, Boswell sputtered with laughter into his coffee mug.

<h1 style="text-align:center">~ THIRTY-ONE ~</h1>

Océane scurried along the curved path at the base of the green-shrouded volcanic hills that sheltered the small cove where she lived with Émile Jean-Baptiste Aubert. The artist had constructed their raised two-room house with local timber and palm thatch under the overhang of a protective basalt cliff six months ago. It sat on the western side of the cove, 20 yards from the surf line, and a short walk from where the fresh waters of the Haamaea stream tumbled out of the hills and into the ocean.

It was a fine home as shacks go, with an open-air kitchen and stone baking oven on one side, and a well-maintained privy just off the back steps. Aubert picked the site for its natural privacy and protection, easy access to drinking water, and especially for the presence of a large natural cave in the cliff wall behind them. He discovered that the house-size space with its 20-foot vaulted ceiling stayed completely dry no matter how hard the tropical downpours pelted the island. It took a little digging to open the entrance up high and wide enough to comfortably walk through, but once he was sure that the cave would remain dry and free from any kind of moisture, he set lanterns against the walls and built three cabinets and a dozen wooden racks in which to store his paints and canvasses.

Only then, after three months of hard labor, did Aubert mix his colors and pick up his brushes. And once that began, mused Océane as she neared the spot where Aubert had set up his easel to capture the best of the early morning light, the 26-year-old Frenchman had painted like a man possessed. He left each morning before dawn with a freshly stretched canvas mounted on a portable easel strapped to his back, along with a bag full of paints, brushes, rags, and turpentine, which he used to thin his oils. He liked the way turpentine evaporated and dried quickly when he wanted a matte appearance to the work. If he was painting close to the cove, Océane would bring him a midday meal of onion, apple, cheese, and bread. If he was hiking into the hills or making his way along the coast, she filled a bag with food, a bottle of red wine, and several cigars.

While he had no trouble covering two or even three canvases with paint each day, Aubert had disciplined himself to do just one. A good one. He had a small income from family properties in Paris, and every two months he made the two-day journey up the coast to Pape'ete with a pack horse to deposit the latest letter of credit that had arrived by schooner from France. He paid his bills, purchased supplies, and shopped for a bolt of cloth or ready-made dress for his wife.

When he collected the most recent package from his family, the letter inside from his father reminded Aubert that his 'holiday' wasn't going to be supported forever. "Paint if you must," his father the chemist groused, "but paint work that you can sell. A true artist must have his work displayed at the annual *Salon* of the *Académie des Beaux-Art*s. Only then can you earn your way as an artist."

That damn Salon. Like his great friend Camille Pissarro, Aubert had had enough of the stiff, dark, formal architecture of classical painting. He worshipped light and air and the interplay of elements in motion. He painted with colors that one could almost taste and feel, hues that leapt off the canvas and shimmered like a bright spring morning in the garden.

And yet, he understood that at some level his father's exhortations were true; he could not dabble or play the lifelong student forever. He was passionate, talented, and ambitious. He wanted to sell his work, but on his terms, not according to the rules of the hoary old dinosaurs in frock coats and tails who had not so much as contemplated a new variable in artistic composition or style in 200 years. One day he would take his work to London, New York, or even Paris. He would engage an agent, mount a gallery exhibition, and charm the critics and art patrons. His work would sell. One day.

Océane neared the stream bank where her husband was putting the final touches on a painting of an outcropping of rocks and flowered bushes surrounded by drift logs that had washed along the eastern coast of Tahiti until they were pushed into the cove and up the beach by the tide and the winds.

She paused and sat on a flat boulder until he applied the last dabs of paint and turned to acknowledge her. As he did, she pointed 100 yards up the hill to where a trail had been cut through the rocks and trees.

"Nous avons des visiteurs," she said in a soft voice.

Aubert raised his palm to shield against the sunlight, and looked to where his wife was pointing. Two men on horseback, each leading a heavily laden packhorse, were making their way along the narrow trail.

"They are a half hour away," he said. "Plenty of time to get a meal started."

Thomas and Boswell stopped their horses where the trail widened enough to sit side by side. A tree-and-bush-covered hill swept down below them to an azure cove, where gentle waves lapped onto the broad sandy beach. The entrance to the cove from the ocean was just wide enough for a small boat to pass through, but there was no dock on the shore, just a skiff pulled up out of the water near a plank cabin raised on stilts.

Their journey from Varua's village at Papara to this isolated cove was only six miles, but they had been riding since an hour before dawn. That was almost eight hours ago, Thomas thought as he shifted in his saddle to relieve some of the numbness in his back. Eight hours of steep climbs along paths that were barely three feet wide in most places, and equally steep descents into narrow gulches cut by dozens of streams and waterfalls.

Boswell was taking delight in Thomas's discomfort. "I thought you were an American cowboy," he said. "Aren't you used to long rides?"

"This isn't a ride," Thomas replied. "It's torture. Perhaps next time we could load a boat and sail down here?"

The botanist laughed and snapped his reins to move ahead. "My sailing skills are about like yours, my friend. I doubt we would have made it across the reef."

They followed the trail for another 100 yards as it curved down towards the cove, passed through a stand of palms and spilled out onto the beach just a few yards from Aubert's house. The bearded artist was standing on his covered porch, pipe in hand, wine glass on the rail. A moment later his wife joined him, and they climbed down the steps to welcome their guests.

An hour later the smells of savory baked chicken and fresh bread drifted out from the cookhouse to the small corral where the men had just offloaded the packhorses. They hung the smoked hams and wrapped cheeses on pegs in the cave, and stacked canned milk, flour, coffee, rice, beans, sugar, cases of wine, and especially, the prized vintage cognac on the storage shelves along one wall.

Thomas took an immediate liking to the shaggy artist. As Boswell had promised, the Frenchman was a bubbling cauldron of exuberant energy. When he noticed that Thomas wore a Colt revolver, Aubert exclaimed. "Ah, but this is wonderful. We will hunt wild boar and make their tusks into a necklace for you that will make men tremble and women faint with desire." And at the sight of the razor-sharp cutlass McNab gave to Thomas being unwrapped from its canvas sheath and laid upon a shelf in the cave, the artist declared that the two of them should steal a double-hulled pahi outrigger from Varua and pirate their way to Australia. "Legends, *mon héros*, that is what we shall become," gushed

Aubert as he raised the sword and twirled it above his head, "The Frenchman and the Yankee, corsairs extraordinaire, making ship captains soil their trousers and lovely maidens wet their…."

"Oh, do give your fevered dreams a rest," chuckled Océane as she entered the cave with a basket of sliced fruit she had dried in the sun and smoked over a low fire.

"Do not encourage him, Colonel," she said to Thomas. "He spends too much time with his head in the clouds and his feet in the hammock."

"And my arms around you, my sweet," Aubert replied, "To say nothing of how I engage you with my own sword."

He laughed at his own crude joke as Océane rolled her eyes and placed the dried fruit in a sealed jar alongside a dozen more. "We have cots to set up for our guests, *mon amour*," she said with her hands on her hips, "kindling to chop for the oven, and perhaps a bottle or two of wine to decant for dinner."

Aubert grasped the cutlass with two hands and feigned a smack on Océane's bottom. "Only two bottles?" he roared as he chased her out of the cave. "For my friends? That is *blasphéme*! Away miscreant!"

Océane did not try to suppress her laughter. She turned and skittered out of the cave towards the stairs leading to the back door of the cabin, patting the ancient dog who slept all day at the foot of the stairs as she passed by. Beyond the small house the beach sloped to the water's edge, where deep green wavelets lapped on shore across the length of the half-moon shaped cove. From the rugged tree-covered hills rising sharply behind them to the rocky promontory at the cove's inlet and out into the sea, everywhere around them was bursting with life. Thomas saw movement around the reef outside the cove, and watched as a trio of dolphins exploded above the surface and spun several times in the air before slipping back into the clear emerald deep.

He turned to watch Aubert inspect one of the rolls of canvas McNab had sent and he smiled to himself at the expression of expectant delight on the face of the artist who was imagining the glorious splashes of colors he would soon apply to the fabric.

Thomas stepped outside the cave and felt a cool breeze wash across his face. He breathed deeply of the rich, earthy air tinged with hints of gardenia, and he heard waves breaking on rocks and water tumbling over smooth stones in the creek.

Then he heard Océane singing, and she waved at him from the front porch, where she was shaking out a small rug. Thomas had never envied any man's material possessions or romantic relationships. He was content to make his own life and accept the outcomes he himself created.

But this was something different. The life that Aubert and Océane had fashioned for themselves on this tiny Tahitian cove thousands of miles from the cold and chaos of Western civilization stirred emotions he had never experienced.

He stooped and picked up a pebble and tossed it far out into the cove. The small ripples the stone made as it splashed into the water were quickly washed smooth by the incoming tide.

'And that is my life,' he thought.

At midday three days later, Thomas and Aubert were huddled at a small wooden table the artist set up just off his porch. Boswell was on a trek to gather specimens, and Océane was napping in the hammock under the warming July sky.

"This is lapis lazuli," Aubert was saying as he held up a handful of strikingly blue rocks flecked with particles of gold. "It is rare and expensive, and since ancient times it has been used to make the most exquisite blue paint the human eye can behold."

The artist began cracking the stones on the table with a small hammer. "When I was 14, I was apprenticed to a porcelain works on the *Rue de Rivoli* in Paris, where I painted flowers and leaves on the rims of the most beautiful plates and dishes you can imagine, many of which were made for the court of Napoleon III, who had a particular affection for the spectacular blue tints that are locked within the lapis."

He brushed the crushed lapis into a large stone pestle and ground it to a fine powder before mixing in a paste made with wax, pine resin and linseed oil. Thomas watched transfixed as the paste took on a glorious hue of deep cobalt blue.

"In the old days artists mixed all of their paints by hand and stored them in pig's bladders," Aubert continued. "Today we can get any color we desire in small metal tubes like the ones you delivered from Captain McNab. But this one, this transcendent blue, I still prefer to mix myself."

He dipped a small brush into the fresh paint and made several lightning-fast strokes on a piece of scrap canvas on which he had painted two crimson-red flowers only minutes earlier. The effect was astonishing; the deep cobalt blue against a background of glorious red could be seen from across the cove.

Before Thomas could say anything, Aubert's dog began a series of whispery barks. Both men turned their heads to the sea, where an outrigger canoe fitted with a crab claw sail was catching the crest of a small wave through the opening into the cove. The two young men aboard swept their single-side paddles just below the surface of the water in time with the breaking wave until the wave caught the little boat and carried it right up onshore.

The young men jumped out onto the sand and pulled the canoe up away from the water line as Thomas and Aubert walked down to greet them. It was clear to Thomas that the artist recognized the sailors, and he kept his hand from the handle of his Colt.

"*Salutations, mes amis,*" said the taller of the two lads as they all shook hands.

The other young man tossed down a piece of bark cloth covered in writing, pulled a pearl knife from his waistband, and pinned the cloth to the ground with a flick of his wrist.

"You are being invited to something special, Thomas," said Océane, who had come up behind them with the watchdog. "This is how it was done in ancient times."

Thomas grinned, bent down, and pulled the knife out of the sand. He returned the blade to its owner and stared hard at the cloth. "I'm sorry," he finally said. "I can't read Tahitian."

"Few of us can," said the tall sailor with a laugh. "It is a summons from Chief Varua. You are commanded to attend the annual festival and games to be held beginning tomorrow in Papara. We have come to collect you."

"Commanded?" said Thomas.

"It's a formality of language, Colonel," said Aubert. "Nothing more. You can go or not—there is no penalty for not attending."

"Other than the shame, you mean," added Océane.

"Shame?" asked Thomas. "For what?"

"It seems you were familiar with another man's intended bride, and he did not get the satisfaction of publicly reprimanding you on the spot. Tahitian warriors do not forget or forgive such a slight."

Thomas shook his head. "Aata," he simply said.

The sailors who had come to fetch him nodded their heads in unison.

"It won't be a bow-and-arrow competition, or swimming or climbing. Aata will want to defeat you at something far more personal. Something everyone in the village will be able to see close up," said Aubert in a thoughtful tone. It was quiet on the beach.

"A wrestling match," Océane finally murmured.

Aubert looked into her eyes, then turned his head to Thomas. "In traditional Polynesian matches, the combatants often grappled until one of them died. That was especially true when a matter of honor was at stake."

"Surely we have moved past such barbarity," said Océane. "This is 1872, after all."

Thomas' face darkened. He had locked eyes with Aata after the warrior pierced the coconut wedged between the upside-down man's legs. Aata's expression—and his intentions—were clear.

"Then this would be a match to…" he began, and his words trailed off.

Aubert took a long draw on his cigar. "Yes," he said. "To the death."

~ THIRTY-TWO ~

Papara

McNab and Chief Varua walked down to the water's edge as the outrigger carrying Thomas swept over the coral reef and slid up onto the beach. Thomas stepped out onto dry land and turned to thank the two young men who had whisked him up the coast to Papara in under an hour. He'd been impressed by the speed and stability of the single-outrigger canoe with its canted mast and crab claw sail that could be easily tilted and rotated to best work the wind. Compared to the eight hour horseback ride through mountainous terrain he and Boswell had made several days ago the canoe trip had been an exercise in pure luxury.

Two small children raced down the beach and ducked beneath the Chief's legs before scooting off towards the cook shack, where a dozen women were working over coal fire ovens and bubbling copper pots.

"Welcome, Colonel," said Varua with an expansive smile. "To be honest, few of my people thought that you would accept our invitation to the games."

"The knife through the printed fabric routine had more the feel of a royal summons than an invitation, Chief Varua," Thomas responded. "Regardless, I am happy to be here, and I am looking forward to watching the competitions. Monsieur Aubert says there is nothing quite like them in the entire world."

"Ah, but you shall do much more than observe, my dear colonel," said Varua. "Captain McNab has extolled the courage and skill you displayed during your War of Rebellion, and we are anxious to see you engage our warriors in Tahitian sport." Before Thomas could reply, Varua turned to speak to a woman who was carrying a basket of smoked fish.

Thomas raised his eyebrows and looked at McNab, but the captain merely shrugged his shoulders and motioned towards the village's central compound, where preparations for opening of the games that evening were well underway; young women and children were wrapping posts with colored bunting and fresh leaf garlands, others were chalking lines around palms that would be used for javelin throwing, and two boys were hammering a line of sharp-tipped steel poles into the ground for the coconut husking competition. Down the beach a group of men were checking the sails and paddles on a dozen outrigger canoes that would slip into the ocean just after dawn for the grueling 36-mile race up the coast to Pape'ete and back.

The smell of savory pork roasting in underground clay ovens mixed with the aroma of fresh baked bread under the cloudy sky as they took seats at a small stone table. A young boy and girl brought them a tray of fruit and a small loaf of bread still hot from the oven, along with a bowl of honey butter and two mugs of coffee.

Thomas sipped his coffee thoughtfully. "We need to talk about these games," he said, "especially about the wrestling. I have no intention of going into the ring with Atta, or anyone else, for that matter….and as for a fight to the death, that's a damn fool idea."

McNab lowered his cup and smiled. "A lot of assumptions are rolled up in that statement, my friend. No doubt Aubert suggested that you and Atta would play the role of warring Titans for the amusement of one and all?"

Thomas was about to respond when Keani and a friend rounded a hut and walked in his direction. Keani made direct eye contact with him, smiled, and tilted her head slightly to one side as she passed. She slipped by so close that he caught scents of lilac and ripe strawberry.

He realized he was holding his breath when McNab poked him in the ribs and said, "And that, Colonel, is exactly the kind of thing that is going to get you crippled or killed. Take your pick."

"It was just a smile."

"No, it was an invitation, and lord knows how many people just saw what happened." McNab leaned back and dug a pipe and tobacco pouch from his pocket. When it was lit, he said, "I'm no gambler, but I'd bet that within the hour you will be receiving an emissary from the great Atta. The gauntlet is about to be thrown down on you, Thomas, and it will not be an invitation to play a game of cricket."

"I can refuse to accept," said Thomas.

"And do what? Go where? This island isn't that big, lad. Atta was already humiliated by Keani's refusal to marry him before you arrived, and now she is practically throwing herself at the first American soldier she meets. He is going to have his honor restored whether you choose to willingly participate in the games or not."

Thomas set down his coffee and watched the gentle waves roll onshore. In his mind's eye, he saw his desk in the *Chronicle* newspaper office, and the candle-lit dining room of Kwan's restaurant. He felt himself flying off the deck of the *König Wilhelm* and splashing in the iridescent lagoon with Princess Noelani. He galloped on horseback across his sugar plantation, saw the face of the leper who cared for him on Moloka'i, and watched as Akoni slipped beneath the crashing surf when their little boat was smashed on the rocks. Fitch Donegan fired at him through the door of the Pearl, and a great whale breached the surface of the water beside his schooner.

So much had happened since he stole the tiny dinghy and rowed out into the freezing waters of San Francisco Bay six months ago. And at every step along the way he was running from someone or something, perhaps even from himself.

He took a deep breath, pushed away from the table, and stood up. "I have done no wrong to Atta, or to any man here," he said to McNab. "But if he comes for me, I will meet him head on."

McNab looked into Thomas's eyes and saw that he was completely at ease with his decision. *"I'm sure you will,"* the captain thought to himself, *"And God help Aata should it come to that."*

McNab's prediction was only off by a few minutes. Boswell and Aubert arrived in their skiff, and the artist had just kissed Thomas on both cheeks. "From Océane," he laughed, "a reminder to come back to the cove in one piece."

Thomas clapped a hand on Aubert's shoulder, and then turned at the sound of someone coming up from behind. It was one of Aata's warriors, a tall, shirtless fellow wearing not much more than a somber expression and a leaf-garland headpiece. Thomas sighed when he saw that the young man was holding a pearl knife and a piece of fabric in one hand.

Boswell raised his eyebrows. "Another invitation?"

McNab grunted as the warrior dropped the fabric and then flicked the knife to the ground, pinning the printed cloth into the red dirt.

"You will meet Aata on the field after the midday meal tomorrow," said the warrior, "where you will compete in a wrestling match in the manner of our ancestors. Until then I shall stay by your side to assure you do not run away."

Thomas was about to answer when Chief Varua stepped up. "Your presence will not be necessary," he said to the young man in a stern tone. "Colonel Scoundrel is a great warrior in his nation; he will do the honorable thing. Now, return to Aata and tell him what I have said and also tell him that his actions bring shame upon our village."

"But…" began the warrior.

Varua's eyes flashed. "Go now or take your canoe and leave our village!"

The rebuked warrior left the group and walked quickly down the beach.

"I do not wish to cause strife among your people, Chief Varua," said Thomas.

"And yet that is exactly what you have done, Colonel," Varua replied. "Aata sees himself as my successor, and he is probably right. My people respect him, and he is the natural choice to take on my duties when I die. After he thrashes you tomorrow his succession will be guaranteed."

"With respect, Chief Varua, you should not dismiss Thomas's chances against Aata," said Aubert. "The match may not go the way you think."

"That is the only way it can go," chuckled Varua. "No man has ever come close to besting Aata in the games, especially at wrestling. God willing Colonel Scoundrel's neck will not yet be broken when I call an end to the combat just before Aata sends him to meet his ancestors."

Varua nodded to the men and walked away. A cooling afternoon breeze drifted down from the craggy volcanic peaks that ringed the village, and a group of children playing with hoops and sticks raced past and disappeared down the sandy beach.

Boswell and McNab took seats at the stone table and were joined a moment later by Aubert and Thomas.

The artist raised one arm and waved to the women in the cookshack, who knew Aubert and had no doubt what he was asking for.

"Am I the only one who thinks it is time to uncork a few bottles?" he asked with a grin.

The feast began just as the sun was dipping below the western horizon. The sky was clear, the air balmy, and a soft breeze rustled the palms around the village common area. Thomas estimated there were over 200 people scattered around, some seated at tables, others on logs or stones. Children carted platters of savory roast pork, broiled fish, breads, fruits, and cheeses from group to group, while young men and women poured wine, rum punch, and fresh creek water from clay pitchers.

Where most of the villagers had been dressed in some version of Western clothing earlier in the day, tonight the village was a sea of traditional costumes; men wore woven reed waist belts above loin cloths with grass skirts front and back that left most of their legs bare. They fashioned leafy garters around their knees and above their elbows, and many wore elaborate head gear of tightly woven plant materials and dried flowers that swept up above shoulder capes fashioned with reeds and trimmed with seashells and red seaweed. Varua wore a woven hat shaped like a chimney that towered three feet above his head. It was festooned with dried flowers and featured intricate triangular shaped designs.

Most of the women wore *pareu* skirts made with a rectangular piece of cotton fabric. The fabric was wrapped around their waists and tied securely, with the excess fabric draped to one side or at the front, sometimes with intricate knots or pleats. All the women and girls, including toddlers, wore flowers and greenery crowns on their heads, and many also wore flowered strands around their necks.

A half dozen bonfires blazed around the compound, and together with the light from dozens of pitch torches, the area was bathed in flickering shades of rich ocher and gold.

Aubert, who had been deep in his cups for hours, was exhilarated by the sights and smells of the festivities. "Who among you would not wish to be an artist tonight, to capture these colors, these…." He paused as a stunning young woman danced past him with her hips swiveling left and right and up and down to the rhythm of the drum music. "…these magnificent human forms," he finally finished. "God help me, but I must paint now." He stood unsteadily, tried to begin walking to where his paints and easel were waiting, and then collapsed back down on his seat.

"Tomorrow, my friend," said Boswell as he helped the artist settle back before turning to McNab and Thomas. "He is right about painting this extraordinary scene. I will sketch what I can from memory in the morning, but nothing can compare to being here in the middle of all of this as it is happening." He swept his arm around the compound, where dancers, musicians, servers, and tumblers whirled and children laughed as they chased chickens and dogs in, around, and under the tables.

Thomas heard what his friend was saying, but he wasn't paying attention. His gaze was fixed across the compound and though the flames of a bonfire to the table where Keani sat with several friends.

Her *pareu* and woven top were dyed fuchsia and purple and decorated with gold stars. Atop her head she wore a crown of red, purple, yellow, and green flowers and leaves, which flowed into a double strand that encircled her neck and trailed down below her partially visible breasts.

Like Thomas, Keani was ignoring the conversation around her. She, too, was staring through the flames, directly into his eyes.

Boswell watched as the famous American soldier and the sister of a powerful Tahitian chieftain locked eyes in a lover's firelit embrace.

McNab was right, the naturalist thought. Tragedy was bubbling up from deep inside the volcano, and the coming eruption could only unleash a river of death and loss.

<h1 style="text-align:center">~ THIRTY-THREE ~</h1>

At dawn Thomas joined the villagers who weren't too hung over from the previous night's festivities for the launch of the outrigger race to Pape'ete and back. Each of the twelve 18-foot boats would be launched into the surf and paddled by two men; one on the left side where the *ama* float was located, and one on the right. In ancient times the construction of a canoe was a religious event shared by boat builders, laborers, priests, and chiefs. Most boats were carved from a single tree and fitted with sails woven from pandanus leaves. Such outriggers were regarded as living entities, with their own spiritual mana.

Today's canoes had sails made from canvas, and only a few of the oldest men still held a spiritual regard for them. But each canoe was still fashioned from a single tree, and they were the lifeblood of Tahitian transportation, fishing, pearl shell diving, and *Va'a*, the race. To win a race was a great honor, and every young man longed to have a victory *lei* draped over his head at least once in his lifetime.

"Eight hours of paddling with no rest," said Aubert as he came up alongside Thomas. The artist seemed remarkably fresh-eyed and robust for someone who had consumed at least three bottles of wine by himself only hours earlier. He looked out across the line of young men waiting for the order to push their canoes into the water and paddle across the reef and into the open sea and said, "I could be wrong, Thomas, but I don't believe that any of those boys were with us at the celebration last night."

"Of course they weren't, *Monsieur artiste*," cackled a toothless old woman as she passed behind them and slapped Aubert on his rear. "A drunken sailor can't raise his mast any more than a drunk painter can unfurl his canvas!"

Aubert feigned a shocked look, made an exaggerated bow and replied, "My wife would beg to differ, dear mother, but then, such is the superiority of the French constitution."

The old woman and her friends howled with laughter as they walked past, and Thomas watched as the woman raised one hand in the air and mimicked the words 'French lover' before letting her forefinger droop slowly until it was pointing to the sand.

Thomas managed a half-smile at the antics, but his mind was focused on the match against Aata to be held this afternoon, and on Keani. They hadn't exchanged a word, of course, nor would they, but it was not the fact that she was mute that kept him from speaking to her. It was the suffocating presence of her friends, family, and especially of Aata and his very watchful warriors.

He had not been alone with her, written to her, or done so much as walk with her along the beach. And yet, the stirring he felt inside each time he thought of her or caught a glimpse of her going about her business in the small village was something he had never experienced. He had known women, desired them, pursued them, and bedded more than a few willing partners since his first bedroom experience six years earlier with Titia Freisch, the buxom Ohio farmer he encountered on his way home from the War. He could not deny his physical desire for Keani; the way her simple linen dress clung to her hips, breasts, and buttocks when she walked was mesmerizing.

But there was more rumbling around inside his head than primitive lust. Much more. The way she held her head with an almost regal serenity, the softness of her smile, the mischievous glint in her eyes, the cascade of thick hair that flowed in waves nearly to her waist. As for her being mute, he had experienced more communication in the few simple glances they had exchanged than he had known with any woman.

When McNab waved him over to where a crowd was gathering to

watch one of the events, he knew he was going to have to find a way to steal even just a minute with her.

"I'm sorry," Thomas said to McNab, who was standing next to a post from which a bright blue ribbon stretched ten feet to another post across the path. "But did you say this was a fruit carrier race, as in fruit?"

The captain lit a fresh bowl of tobacco and chuckled. "Exactly. And you are going to be impressed."

"By a coconut racing a pineapple along a foot path?"

"Be patient, lad, you'll understand soon…"

The sound of a gunshot in the distance cut McNab off, and the villagers lining both sides of the path began to cheer and yell out the names of their favorite runners.

"For fruit," Thomas thought to himself. *"I don't think I will ever understand these people."*

A few moments later McNab tapped his shoulder and pointed off to the north, where the path emerged from a thick wall of greenery. Thomas strained to see what was happening, and to hear over the din of the crowd, who were growing more animated by the second.

Then there was a flash of movement at the tree line 200 yards distant, then another and another, until Thomas could make out the forms of several men running full speed towards the village, and the outline of the thick five-foot pole each was holding on his shoulders behind his neck.

More runners poured out of the woods, until at least a dozen men were racing towards the compound. That's when Thomas could finally see the tightly bound bundle of coconuts and bunches of green bananas dangling from each end of their poles.

He turned to McNab and raised his eyebrows, his expression a combination of disbelief and amazement.

"Each man is carrying upwards of 100 pounds of fruit," said the captain, "and the race is just over a mile long."

"It's…" Thomas began.

"Ain't it though."

As the runners drew closer, Thomas saw that they had leaf garlands on their heads, wore only loincloths and were barefoot. From the way their bodies shone in the sun it also appeared that each man had been liberally coated with coconut oil on his chest, arms, back, and legs.

Two stocky young men pulled away from the pack as they neared the village, and they crossed the finish line together, tossing their fruit-laden poles on the ground and acknowledging the cheers and applause of the crowd, and Thomas noticed the openly inviting stares of the young maidens. The rest of the runners quickly followed until there was a huge mound of poles and fruit covering the ground in front of the cook shack.

Aubert and Boswell joined them, and the four men went down near the water's edge where sharpened metal stakes had been jammed upright into the sand for the coconut husking competition. One woman stood beside each stake, where ten unhusked coconuts had been piled. Thomas noted that at least three of the eleven women were quite elderly.

When Varua clapped his hands, each woman picked up a single coconut and began jamming it down on the tip of the pole, turning the nut in their hands rapidly, pulling it back up, and then striking again and again. Thomas estimated that the fastest women took less than four seconds to completely husk each of their coconuts. In less than a minute one of the elderly competitors–the same toothless grandmother who had teased Aubert earlier– finished her tenth coconut and stepped away from her pole to the cheers of the crowd.

"It would appear, gentlemen, that the winner has husked a nut or two in her time," said Aubert with a chuckle and a wave to the winner.

Now the crowd moved up from the beach to where three 60-foot palm trees grew in a straight line. At the foot of each tree a husky young man was tying a piece of cloth around his ankles and securing it tightly. When Varua shouted a command, the men hopped forward, wrapped their arms around their tree in a tight hug, pulled their feet up level with their midsections, and then began to shimmy in small frog hops up the tree. Thomas was amazed to see the winner reach the top of his tree in six seconds.

The games swirled on around then for the next several hours; teams of three men each hacked open and split as many as 100 coconuts in four minutes; children did foot races and acrobatics, men of all ages tossed long, reed-thin javelins at coconuts suspended thirty feet in the air, and, in a contest Thomas deeply wished Akoni could have been present for, the strongest men in the village lifted great stones weighing nearly 300 pounds up to chest height.

"The swimming events will take place after lunch," McNab told his friends as the crowd began moving towards the cook shacks and the tables laden with fish, pork, roast chicken, cheeses, fruits, and breads. "And so will wrestling," he added as he placed a hand on Thomas's shoulder. "I'm sure you will want to prepare."

The captain was surprised by Thomas's wordless reply—a simple smile and nod of the head.

Boswell, McNab, and Aubert piled their plates high with the village's bounty, while Thomas settled for a spoonful of fruit and a small portion of roast pork.

"I suppose you don't want to wrestle on a full stomach?" Boswell asked.

"Something like that," said Thomas.

McNab slapped his hand on the edge of the table. "Damn your hide, colonel, but you don't seem to appreciate the seriousness of the situation! Aata nearly killed the last man who faced off with him; he choked off the flow of oxygen to the poor fool's brain for so long that he still drools uncontrollably."

Thomas seemed bemused. "And what was Aata's style in this competition," he asked calmly.

"His style?" sputtered the captain. "What does that mean?"

"I mean how did he fight, what technique did he employ,

what strategy?"

McNab was clearly agitated, and so Aubert cut in. "Thomas we are your friends; you are about to come up against the strongest warrior and best athlete, probably in all of Tahiti. We do not wish to see you maimed or killed. And so, forgive Captain McNab, and me, for that matter. We simply do not understand your lack of concern."

And as for his 'style' as you put it, Thomas," McNab finally said, "he stood straight, grabbed his opponent in a bear-hug, swung him to the ground and dropped onto his back and began choking him."

"With his hands or his arms?" Thomas asked.

McNab swept his pewter mug of wine aside and stood to go. His face was red, and his lips were pursed.

Boswell shot Thomas a questioning glance.

"Please, captain, sit down," Thomas said in a quiet voice. "Please."

McNab took his seat as the crowd around them began clearing their tables and preparing for the next round of the games.

"Well?" asked the captain.

"I am concerned, of course," said Thomas, "but not for myself."

His friends looked at him as if he had just gone mad.

"Aata will not defeat me," Thomas went on in a serious tone, "in fact, the only concern I have is whether I should hurt him more or humiliate him more. Either way, he will lose face with the villagers, and Varua will quite probably lose a brother-in-law.'

Aubert lit another cigar and leaned forward. "Thomas, I think it is time to explain yourself."

Thomas pushed his plate away. "When I was a boy in Ohio my father taught me just three things; how to ride a horse, how to play cards, and how to fight. And by fighting I don't mean just fist-a-cuffs."

His friends were silent, hanging on his every word.

"My father was raised outside Paris, on his grandfather's estate. The grounds included several acres of manicured gardens, and the old man in charge had been born and raised on the island of Okinawa, which is near Japan."

"I know it well," said McNab, "I have sheltered the Kai Douglas there many times."

Thomas nodded. "The old man was called Taishi, and from childhood he had been trained in the fighting arts known as *Shuri-Te*, which originated on the island over 1,000 years ago."

"I have heard of these Oriental methods," said Aubert," but I have never met anyone with any knowledge of them. In fact, I thought they were only legends."

"Many people thought that right up until the first time they confronted a *Shuri-Te* master in one-on-one combat."

"And you are trained in this technique?" asked Boswell.

"My father studied with the old gardener for his entire childhood, until he left France for America when he was 19. He trained me until he died when I was 15. For what it's worth, I am quite good."

"Good enough to beat a highly skilled Tahitian warrior," mused McNab.

"I would not dare to compete with him with spears," said Thomas. "But I have never been bested in a fight. I was the champion wrestler in the 109th Ohio Regiment, too."

Most of the villagers had made their way over to an open patch of grass on which a chalk circle about 20 feet across had been drawn.

"This *Shuri-Te* is a boxing technique?" asked Aubert.

"It relies on speed and agility and combines Western and Eastern punching, grappling, kicking, and throwing."

"Kicking?" asked McNab.

"From a standing position I can kick a six-foot-tall man hard enough to break his jaw," Thomas answered.

Aubert noticed that there was no braggadocio in his friend's voice. He was simply stating a fact.

Thomas stood and looked at his friends with a smile. "Shall we go?"

Two hundred villagers sat in a ring around the grassy circle where the wrestling match was to take place. They all knew of the great insult that the American colonel had delivered to their beloved Aata, and they longed for justice, especially the old people who still chaffed under French rule on the island, benign as it was. Varua was seated on a high-back chair, close to the chalk line that marked the combatant's arena. Next to him, on a much smaller chair, Keani sat silently, staring straight ahead, dreading the events that were about to unfold. Her brother had been clear: when the dust from the match settled and Colonel Scoundrel was carried broken and bleeding from the field, she was going to accept Aata's suit, and consent to being married within the week. Now, in defiance of her brother's commandment, she looked across at Thomas and briefly locked eyes with him. He seems so calm, she thought.

Aata emerged from his hut like a demigod arising from the sea. His oiled, jet-black hair was swept back into a ponytail that trailed down his heavily muscled back, and his miniscule loincloth did little to hide his manhood from the villagers.

Every inch of the warrior bulged with muscle and taut sinew; his biceps were the diameter of a coconut, the thighs with which he routinely crushed wrestling opponents looked sculpted from marble, and his abdomen was as solid and tight as battle armor.

He soaked in the adulation of the crowd for a minute before throwing back his shoulders and striding slowly over to the grass ring where he was going to slam this peacock of an American soldier to the ground over and over until he heard the man's spine snap and his voice cry for mercy.

On the other side of the ring, Thomas slipped off the sandals he had taken to wearing since he came to Tahiti and loosened two buttons on his long-sleeved linen shirt. That was all the preparation he needed. He had stretched as they walked from event to event, and he had spent the last two minutes in meditative thought.

Boswell and Aubert sat on rocks beside him, while McNab stood close for a final word before the combat began.

"Given the choice between public humiliation or death, I can tell you that Aata would choose to die," said the captain.

Thomas looked into his friend's face. "Then humiliation it shall be," he said with a grin before stepping across the chalk line and walking to the center of the circle in front of Aata.

There would be no formalities, no instructions, or rulings from Chief Varua. When the chief signaled it was time, the men would go at it, and they would continue until one man was no longer able to continue, either because of exhaustion, injury, or death.

Thomas scanned the crowd of onlookers who were there to witness his total defeat at their champion's hand. If that meant the American colonel must die, so be it. He had been so arrogant as to think he could steal Keani away from her intended, and he had disobeyed the chief's warnings. These insults could not stand.

He turned his head to Varua and nodded that he was ready. Then he glanced at Keani and felt a deep sorrow in her gaze.

Varua raised his hand for quiet. "This is your fight, Aata," he said. "You will choose when to begin, and when to end. My part is done." He lowered his hand, the crowd began to cheer, and the fight was on.

Aata took two steps back and smiled to the crowd. Then he turned to Thomas with a look of disdain and pity. The idiot didn't even know how to stand properly to fight, he thought, a sentiment shared by the crowd who were mystified by the way that Thomas had spread his legs two feet apart, with his left foot forward and his knees bent at almost 90 degrees. His shoulders, knees, and even his toes were perfectly aligned, and his hands were thrust forward, bent at the elbow and tight against his sides. His head was erect, motionless, his eyes boring into Aata's.

Then, as McNab had promised, Aata made his move. He stood straight and tall, threw his head back, roared, and rushed towards Thomas with his arms spread wide.

"He wants to engage me in a bear-hug contest," thought Thomas. *"Not today."*

He lowered his body and shot forward towards Aata's frontmost leg, wrapping both his arms around the warrior's leg as he pulled Aata closer. He pushed on his opponent's hip with his shoulder, lifted his leg higher, and began to dance in a counterclockwise motion.

To the people watching the match, the colonel's lightning-fast move was a blur of motion. One second, he was standing stalk still in front of their champion, the next he was stooping and exploding forward, holding Aata's leg high in the air, and making him spin around like a child.

Aata's arms flailed to help him stay upright, but there was really nothing he could do. Gravity and inertia were on the American's side.

Thomas spun around in a complete circle with Aata twice, and then lifted Aata's leg high over his head and pushed him back several feet. When Aata tried to stop the backwards motion by putting all his weight on the one leg that had contact with the ground, Thomas slid his hands down the leg he was holding in the air and took hold of Aata's ankle. The next time Aata tried to hop forward, Thomas simply twisted the ankle and shoved the foot back. Then he let go and watched Aata fall back into the crowd on his backside.

The crowd roared, as much in surprise as in anger that the mighty Aata had been thrown to the ground in the first five seconds of the match. Aubert looked over to Varua, who had a Cheshire cat grin on his face. For her part, Keani was fighting to hide her emotions, but the artist saw that her cheeks were flushed, and her breathing was fast. He shared a quick smile with Boswell and McNab and decided against lighting a new cigar. The match wasn't going to last that long.

Thomas returned to his side of the ring and went back into his fighting stance. Now that Aata had some sense of what he was up against, he was going to be far more cautious, and that meant more dangerous, too. The warrior flew up off the ground and advanced slowly towards Thomas, his arms down and close to his sides. He wasn't going to give the American another easy opening.

Thomas didn't wait. He advanced straight towards Aata until he was almost touching his chest, and just as quickly put his right hand behind Aata's neck and his left hand on Aata's right bicep. He snapped down on Aata's neck just as the warrior responded the way that all untrained fighters did: he pulled back, and at the same time tried to raise the arm on which Thomas had the bicep grip.

The instant Aata's right arm began to move away from his body Thomas released his grip on Aata's neck, lowered his body, ducked his head under the arm and swung around behind the warrior and onto his knees. He grabbed each of Aata's ankles from behind, pushed hard with his chest against the warrior's legs, and controlled his fall to the ground. When Aata tried to push himself up, Thomas waited for him to put his palms flat on the ground and start to bend his elbows. That was the signal for Thomas to throw himself on the warrior's back, thrust his hands and forearms under Aata's armpits and interlace his fingers behind the Tahitian's neck. He applied heavy pressure and brought his elbows back, causing Aata to drop his face back into the dirt, gasping for air.

This was the tricky part, Thomas knew. At this point he could continue increasing the pressure until he broke his opponent's neck, or he could ask the warrior to yield the match. Neither choice was a good one.

So, he picked a third way. He pulled his hands off Aata's neck, stood up and walked over in front of Varua's chair. The warrior coughed several times, turned on his side, and stood up, weaving slightly from side-to-side as he regained blood flow in his upper body. All around him the crowd chanted and jeered. This was not the fight they had come to see.

"You wish to end the combat?" Varua asked Thomas.

"I'd say that he does," Thomas replied. "We can stay here all day, Chief Varua, but the outcome of this match is not going to change. He cannot defeat me, and I will not take his life."

"Aata may have other ideas."

Thomas turned and saw Aata walking towards him with a look of cold fury in his eyes. "It's time to end this," Thomas said.

Varua shrugged and waved his hand in the air as if to say, not yet—Aata deserves one more chance to recoup his honor.

Aata raised his fists and increased his speed. His strategy was to simply power his body against Thomas and pummel him to death, suffering whatever blows may come his way in the process. Thomas waited for the warrior to get within a few feet of him. Then he twisted his body perpendicular to Aata, grabbed the warrior's left wrist, and in a great sweeping motion used Aata's own momentum to hurl him into the air, do a somersault, and land flat on his back, coughing with pain. It was a classic *Shuri-Te* move, one that he had used to great effect when wrestling for the 109th regiment during the War.

Aata tried to push himself up on his elbows and catch his breath. Thomas walked over to him and pressed his foot down hard on the warrior's throat. Aata tried to dislodge Thomas's foot, but he was too tired and in too much pain.

"I did not come here to fight," Thomas said in a voice loud enough for all the crowd to here. "I bear this man no ill will, and I choose not to do him any further harm." He looked directly at Varua when he spoke his next words.

"I came here as a guest, and I will leave the same way."

He removed his foot from Aata's throat. "To those who would pursue this fight, know that I will not show them the mercy I have shared with this man."

He looked down at Aata, who was struggling to sit up. "Let this be the end of it," he said. Then he turned and walked past Keani and Varua without turning his head towards them. He did not notice Boswell, Aubert, and McNab fall into line behind him, or the crowd begin to disperse, and he did not see Aata being helped to his feet by his friends.

He walked to the edge of the water and looked out across the cloud-shrouded sea. Despite what he had just said, his fight with Aata would not be over until one of them was dead. One more burden to bear, he thought, and I am losing count.

THIRTY-FOUR

Thomas's defeat of Aata an hour earlier should have been a cause for celebration, but he turned down McNab's invitation to have a drink and instead found himself wandering aimlessly along the beach, where he sat on a rock at the surf line a hundred yards up shore from the village. The air was soft, and the full moon set beams of yellow light rippling across the calm water of the bay.

The villagers went silent when he walked away from the grassy patch where he had humiliated their champion. Varua sat stone-faced on his chair, and Keani slipped away without him seeing. There would be no celebrating in Papara tonight.

Aubert recommended that they take the skiff back to the artist's cove at first light. "You will no longer be welcome here, my friend," Aubert said. "Best to leave before you are set upon by a few young warriors eager to avenge the honor of their people."

"I simply beat him in a contest that he insisted on having," Thomas replied. "I meant nothing more."

Aubert smiled and took a deep drink of wine. "Most of the things we do are never meant, Thomas, and so they find their own meaning, our intentions be damned."

"You are a philosopher now, Émile?"

"One need not philosophize to understand that you have stepped into a very deep pile of *merde*, from which the safe escape is to flee."

Flee. Once again, the solution to the problems piling up on his doorstep required that he turn tail and run. That is exactly what he had determined not to do when he faced off against Aata, and yet, despite his resounding victory in the match, it was he who must leave Papara. And Keani? Had she, too, felt humiliated when Thomas threw Aata to the ground and placed his boot upon the warrior's neck? Is that why she had rushed off without so much as a sidelong glance?

"I am beyond weary of running," he thought. "And yet, that is all I seem to be able to do these past months."

He slid down off the rock and walked along the sand towards McNab's hut at the outer edge of the village. Rum would not solve his predicament, of course, but in his present frame of mind, it sounded like the best medicine.

As he passed a grove of thickly massed trees that formed the northeast boundary of the village, he caught the scent of tiaré flower. Then he heard a rustling in the underbrush and Keani stepped out from between two palms. She had changed into a simple white linen dress with an embroidered front piece. Her hair spilled in waves down off her shoulders, and she wore a fresh crown of white and red flowers. Her sea-green eyes glowed in the moonlight, and her flawless skin seemed lit more from within than from the moon high above them.

Thomas froze, his hands clenched at his sides, his eyes questioning. How did you communicate with a mute? He knew she could hear, and that she spoke with her people with hand signs, but the emotions flooding over him as he was finally standing close by her were unlike any he had experienced. He was speechless.

Keani solved his dilemma. She stepped close and took his right hand in both of hers. She lifted it, opened his closed fist, and tenderly kissed his palm before raising her head to look into his eyes. At that moment a wind swept out of the north and gusted through the palms, lifting their fronds against the glittering, blue-black sky. Thomas felt the night air suddenly chill and saw Keani begin to shiver. He instinctively wrapped both arms around her waist and pulled her close. Her hair smelled of gardenia, her skin was softer than the finest silk. Keani returned his embrace, lowered her head, and rested her cheek on his chest. Thomas sighed and looked up into the heavens. He could stay like this forever.

A moment later the errant wind dwindled away, a wave splashed against a rock, and a shower of orange sparks from the village bonfire drifted over their heads and out to sea. Thomas felt an unfamiliar sense of peace, and when he gently raised her chin, her eyes spoke and told him that she felt the same way.

Then Keani let her head go back and parted her lips. Thomas lowered his head and brushed his lips against hers. In that instant he lost track of time and place and, unfortunately, also of circumstance.

A great roar thundered from out of the darkness, causing the startled lovers to pull away from one another. Thomas whirled to see Chief Varua rushing towards them, his wooden war club raised high above his head. Varua was upon them before Thomas could react, but the chief had come too close to hit Thomas with the heavy end of the four-foot club. Instead, the shaft smashed across the bridge of his nose, breaking it with a snapping sound and sending hot blood spewing from both of Thomas's nostrils onto the sand.

He fell to one knee, bright lights flashing before his eyes. He shook his head and struggled to stand, fighting the loss of consciousness he knew was near and preparing himself for the next blow, which he feared would be better aimed than the first.

He raised both arms defensively to ward off the next assault and tried to focus his blurred vision. He could just make out Varua raising the club for a second time, and what looked like several men surrounding the chief and wrestling the club from his hands.

Thomas made it to his feet and tried to raise his fist for whatever lay ahead. Then his vision cleared, and he saw Boswell and McNab half-dragging Varua back towards the village. The club lay at Thomas's feet, but Keani was nowhere to be seen.

A cloud passed by the moon, and for a moment it was almost pitch black. Then the cloud slipped away, and Thomas saw that he was alone on the beach. He went back down on one knee and buried his head in his hands, mindless of the blood that continued to flow down his face and onto his chest.

A form came out of the darkness and squatted down in front of him.

Thomas almost didn't recognize Aubert; he had never seen the artist wear such a serious expression.

"Cette bataille est terminée, mon bon ami," said the artist in a grim tone.

"My battle is over?" thought Thomas. *"Keani lost, my life uprooted once again, a new crop of enemies to add to the growing list?"*

His friend helped him to stand and gave him a handkerchief to staunch the blood and a flask of brandy to clear his head. He took a long drink and wiped his hand across his mouth, tasting salt tears mixed with warm blood. Thomas shook his head. *"Mais ça ne fait que commencer…"* he replied. "But it has only just begun…"

~ THIRTY-FIVE ~

Honolulu

Fitch Donegan waited at the bottom of the dockside ramp for the steamship California to secure its mooring lines. He saw Colin P. Stafford among the passengers waiting to disembark, but he thought better of waving. Stafford was not someone with whom you took familiarities, and in any event, the wealthy businessman would know Donegan would be there to collect him even if he couldn't see him from the crowded deck.

Donegan had only a one-week warning that his boss would be arriving. A letter had been hand delivered to him at the Pearl, with instructions to meet the California. That was all. No names, no itinerary. Just an order from master to servant.

He wasn't worried that he had yet to deal with Colonel Scoundrel as Stafford had commanded. Even though the Polynesian islands were spread across a vast swath of ocean, Donegan knew the bastard was out there somewhere and would turn up in due time. When he did, Fitch would finish the job. It was that simple. In any event he knew that Stafford came to Hawaii once a year to check on the business interests his brother managed on his behalf, and, if the rumors Donegan had heard were true, to also take care of business of a much more personal nature.

A few minutes later passengers began to stream down the ramp and climb into waiting carriages. Stafford was one of the last to get off. He was accompanied by a single servant, a young Chinese woman Donegan recognized from the household staff at the Stafford mansion. A curious choice for a traveling assistant, Donegan thought, unless his boss wanted to be assured of absolute discretion in whatever circumstance he might find himself.

He set aside his idle curiosity and turned to instruct the porter he had brought along to manage Stafford's luggage.

"My brother is not here?" Stafford asked when he approached Donegan. He felt no need for greetings or small talk.

"He is waiting for us at the Palace Hotel," replied Donegan. "He has had a recurrence of the infection in his eye socket and is limiting his time out in the bright sun. The porter will see to your things. Would you like your servant to ride in the wagon with him?"

Stafford managed a half smile. "We're not meeting at your establishment? I have heard that the Pearl is a true jewel among swine here in Hawaii."

Donegan shook his head. He had fully intended to tell Stafford about the Pearl, but he wasn't surprised that he already knew about the place. It seemed he was not the only spy on Stafford's payroll.

Stafford did not wait for a reply. "Jing Kwan will ride with us. You have arranged a room for her?" Donegan nodded and stood back as Stafford and Miss Kwan mounted the step and settled into the open carriage. Then he mounted his horse and trotted behind them to the hotel.

"An exceptional year," said a cheery Wallace Stafford as their waiter set three plates of salad on the table. "Sugar is up, pineapple is steady, and pearl shell looks poised to make a comeback."

"Is activity in and out of the port increasing?" asked his brother.

"Slowly, but it is improving. The demise of the whaling fleet during the War certainly reduced the number of ships visiting, but we are seeing a healthy rise in traffic."

"Which is good for your business, eh, Mr. Donegan?" asked Colin. "Lonely sailors and all that."

Donegan smiled and stirred his salad around on the plate. He did not know why he had been invited to join the Stafford brothers for lunch, and he was equal parts bored and uncomfortable with their business talk. What was interesting was the stark contrast between the Staffords; Wallace was tall, fair, and soft, while Colin was short, dark, and wiry. Wallace's conversation wandered, Colin was blunt and to the point. What they did share in common, Donegan knew, was extreme avarice and boundless ambition, which was clearly the only pillar of their familial ties.

The waiter delivered their soup, and Colin directed the conversation to a topic that Donegan was interested in.

"Tell me about this priest, this Pa'ao," Colin began. "The one who took your eye."

Wallace instinctively raised a hand to the eyepatch that covered the festering wound. Red, swollen skin surrounded the eye socket, and an occasional drip of liquid oozed down his cheek.

"He lives on the proceeds of his family's trading fortune on the island of Kaua'i," Wallace said in a soft voice, his eye fixed on the tablecloth. "He is consumed with the fantastic notion that he can expel all foreigners from the islands and restore the old kingdom."

"And that is why he kidnapped you and ripped out your eye?" asked Colin.

"It was a warning to others, including you. He and his followers are coming."

"Coming? For what? And are there many?"

"No more than a few dozen, I expect," answered Wallace as he dabbed his cheek with a handkerchief. Donegan could tell that the banker wanted this conversation to come to an end.

"A few dozen," said Colin in a schoolmaster's scolding tone. "And yet you did not report what they did to you to the authorities, or hire someone like Mr. Donegan here, who has expertise dealing with fanatics."

"His family is wealthy and powerful, with a trading empire that stretches across the Pacific," Wallace replied. "They do business with firms we do business with, and if it was known that I had, ah, dealt with the man, it would be hell for our bottom line."

"And so, are we to dance to any tune the man plays? Have you no pride, brother? No desire for vengeance?"

Wallace fiddled with his fork and knife for a moment before replying. Without raising his head, he whispered, "I fear for my life, Colin. As long as I do not retaliate, I know I am safe."

Colin reached across the table and placed his hand gently on his brother's forearm.

"As long as you are my brother, Wallace, you are safe."

Late that afternoon Colin Stafford stepped into the Pearl and asked for Donegan. The bartender shuffled off to the back and Stafford eased into a private booth in the far corner. Only a handful of customers were there at this hour, but by the time night fell the bar would be crowded and there would be a line waiting for the upstairs entertainment.

Donegan appeared with a brandy bottle and two glasses. He sat down across from his boss and waited. He had an idea what Stafford wanted, but he was not going to make any suggestions and risk being wrong. Too much was at stake.

"It's going well?" asked Stafford.

Donegan nodded. "Word gets around quick in the islands. And it ain't just the quim that's bringing in the dollars; the food's pretty good and we serve a fair pour at the bar. I'm thinking of making an offer on the warehouse space next door and putting in some gaming tables."

Stafford was uncharacteristically subdued. "My brother is doing his part?"

"He has offered me a line of credit, though I don't need it quite yet."

Stafford downed his brandy, cleared his throat, and slid the glass over for another. *'It's coming any second now,'* Donegan thought.

"I thought I might arrange for a little company while I'm on the island," Stafford finally said in a matter-of-fact tone. "Makes sense to do that while I'm away."

"I have a very fine selection of companions," Donegan replied. "Something to suit just about anybody's taste."

Stafford had been staring at the tabletop, and, as he slowly raised his head, Donegan was struck by how hollow and dark his eyes suddenly seemed. Stafford cleared his throat again. "And might you also have a more special menu, one that might satisfy, let's say, a taste that does not fit within your typical range of average?" By the tone and tenor of Stafford's question, Donegan was now certain what his employer was fishing for.

"I am confident that I can fulfill any preference Mr. Stafford, including those who might be looking to spend time with a young girl or an even younger…" he let his sentence trail off, and then whispered, "boy."

The great captain of industry and finance squeezed his glass with both hands, and Donegan observed that when he had said 'boy,' a spark flickered in Stafford's reptilian eyes.

Donegan stood up. "It will take an hour or so for me to make the arrangement. Why don't you go upstairs to Room 17, third door on the left. I'll have our girl draw a bath for you, and I'll have some food and wine sent up."

Stafford nodded his head and began to reach for his wallet.

"That won't be necessary," said Donegan with a faint smile. "Tonight, you are the guest of the Pearl."

Two nights later, under the light of a brilliant full moon, Fitch Donegan came ashore from a small boat on the southeastern coast of Kaua'i. He instructed the man he had hired to sail him here from Honolulu to wait near the sugar loading dock and began to hike inland.

The route he had been given was easy to follow; straight up along the stream that emptied into Waimea Bay until he reached a settlement of four houses. The largest house, which sat on a low rise and faced the ocean, was his destination.

He was dressed in black from his watch cap to his boots. On his back he carried a small pack containing three razor-sharp carving knives, a flask of brandy, and a handwritten note in an envelope. That is all he would need to complete tonight's business.

The trail was clear and smooth, and the light from the moon made travel easy. He reached the first house in about 20 minutes and passed by quietly without being heard by the dog or the people inside. A few minutes later, he saw the house on the rise. It was far bigger than the others and was aglow with lamp light. The main room featured folding exterior walls, a common feature in this tropical climate to catch breezes off the ocean. The walls were open tonight, and as he stole up the rise, he saw a man and woman seated at a table drinking tea. Beside them was a toddler playing with a doll, and nearby was a crib that he knew contained the couple's twin daughters.

His heart began to beat faster as he neared the house, not out of fear, but from excitement. He lived for moments like this, for the thrill of the hunt and the sheer exhilaration of the kill. Make an example of them, Colin Stafford said when he gave Donegan his orders. The entire family. I want the gruesome details of their murders to reverberate from here to Australia. I want people to lie awake in their beds and tremble at the thought of such a thing happening to them and their families. I want everyone to know, and no one to forget.

He knelt in the grass a few feet from the open partition where the family was enjoying their last moments on this earth. He slipped off his pack, opened it, and selected his favorite blade. He was breathing harder now, and he felt a familiar and welcome warmth begin to spread across his groin. He knew he would not be able to prevent himself from exploding down there during the butchery he was about to inflict on this family. That was fine. The blood and gore would clean off, too.

He took a deep breath, stood up, and strode calmly into Pa'ao's home. The priest looked up from his tea, a surprised expression on his face. His wife let out a soft cry, and the toddler looked confused.

"Perfect," the assassin thought.

~ THIRTY-SIX ~

~ THIRTY-SIX ~

Tahiti

Océane dipped a clean cloth into a pitcher of cold water and laid it gently on Thomas's shattered, swollen nose. It had been two days since Varua's attack, and the skin under the colonel's eyes was turning bluish purple and black. She knew the discoloration would get much worse before it began to improve.

He hadn't left the comfortable woven chair on the porch of the Aubert's cabin except to go to the privy since they returned from Papara. The physical pain was receding, and in a moment of honest reflection that morning, he realized that the combination of frustration and melancholy that he was feeling was the real cause of his misery, not his fractured nose.

It rained hard the previous night, unusual for July. Now, as the late afternoon sun began its drift towards the horizon it was hot and sticky and there was no breeze off the ocean. Boswell was excited about the weather because it meant he would be able to net even more butterflies for his growing collection. Each day at dusk, he returned to the cabin with a bag containing jars in which he stored his day's catch, and today he had been excited to share a brand-new species of lepidoptera.

"*Ocaria ocrisia* I shall name him," said Boswell as he held up the clear jar for Thomas's inspection. "It means the black hairstreak. Do you know that this makes the tenth new butterfly I have discovered? I am convinced that there are hundreds of species present on these islands. A man could spend his life catching and cataloguing them."

It was painful to talk, but Thomas couldn't resist. "And is fame and fortune awaiting that man, Timothy?"

Boswell grunted and snatched the jar away. "Science is an end and reward unto itself, my dear colonel. Suffice it to say that two centuries from now lepidopterists will still be reading about my work. And your legacy will be.....?"

"Hundreds of great-great grandchildren spread around every corner of the earth...if the lad doesn't change his mating habits," chuckled Óceane as she walked behind Thomas and tousled his hair. She retrieved a jug of wine and poured a glass for the three of them, and then another one for Aubert, who was walking up the beach with his easel and the day's painting.

Émile's return marked the end of the workday. Óceane laid out a tray of cheese, bread, and fruit to go with their wine and her husband stirred the coals under the iron grate in the cook shack to grill a mahi-mahi that two fishermen had brought them earlier in the day. He seasoned the fillets with salt and pepper and cooked them over hot coals for five minutes on each side before drizzling them with lemon juice and serving the fish with hot bread.

"Can you taste?" Aubert asked Thomas as he handed him a plate.

"Taste, yes, smell, no," Thomas replied. The light flaky white meat was naturally sweet, and his only regret was that there was no white wine to accompany the tuna. A sacrilege, Mr. Kwan would say.

Dusk came on, and a cool breeze picked up off the water. Boswell made coffee, and Óceane picked up her violin and began to play a lovely piece by Bach. Aubert lit a fresh cigar, and splashed brandy into everyone's coffee.

Thomas was drifting off when he heard Boswell ask, "Is that a sail?"

He looked out to sea and made out a swatch of sun washed canvas bobbing in the light chop outside the entrance to their cove. Óceane set down her instrument and went into the cabin to fetch the Dolland 4-draw bronze telescope from the bureau. She raised the glass, adjusted the sight, and then whispered, "Dear God......it's Keani."

❂

Thomas bolted up from his chair, which set his nose bleeding again. Aubert nudged him back. "We will take care of this, Thomas," he said.

Thomas watched his friends go down to the water's edge and help Keani pull the canoe up off the beach. Then they hauled three canvas bags from the little boat and came up on the porch.

Thomas was astonished, excited, and embarrassed. Whatever the purpose of her visit, he was ashamed to be seen by her in this condition; a disheveled, unwashed, racoon-eyed invalid.

Keani felt differently. She dropped to her knees in front of Thomas's chair and took his hands in hers. Her face was aglow, and his discomfort melted away in the warmth of her smile. She lifted the damp cloth he had been using and dabbed at the blood seeping from his nose. Then she turned to Óceane and made a series of hand signs.

"I am not completely fluent in sign language," Óceane said, "but I believe she is telling us that she has left her brother and Papara forever." She pointed to the bags they had carried from the canoe. "Everything she owns in the world is in those bags."

Aubert folded his arms across his chest. "Thomas," he said in a soft voice, "Do you understand what this means?"

"Yes, I do."

"And is it what you truly want?" Óceane added. "There can be no turning back. If Keani stays, she is your responsibility. Not just for a night, Thomas. Those days would have to be over. She would be with you forever."

"You mean she would be my wife," Thomas replied in a thoughtful voice.

Aubert, Óceane, and Boswell nodded as one.

Thomas stretched out one arm and folded Keani against his side. "Yes," he said. "That is what I want."

Keani and Óceane disappeared into the house a few minutes later. Aubert filled three glasses with brandy and pulled a chair over beside Thomas.

"Varua will not allow this situation to stand, Thomas. Nor will Aata. You have done much more than defeat their champion; now you have defiled their customs. A price must be paid."

"You and Keani cannot remain here, that is for certain," Boswell said. "As soon as you are able to travel, you will have to seek another refuge."

Thomas sat up. He felt strangely energized and filled with new purpose. "I can travel right now," he replied. "It is just a matter of where and when."

"As to that matter, I have some thoughts," said Aubert. "Varua will look for Keani in Pape'ete first, since they have family there. The idea that she would go immediately to you would simply be unbearable for him to contemplate. And so, I believe that we have at least three days to prepare before Varua's warriors come here."

"Warriors," Thomas repeated in a quiet voice.

"Oh, yes," Aubert replied, *"Les chiens de guerre."*

"Sorry, what was that?" asked Boswell.

"The hounds of war," Thomas said somberly. There really was no turning back.

"And where do you think they should go?" asked Boswell.

Aubert looked out to sea, and turned his gaze to the northeast where the sky was pitch black and clouds hid the waning moon and evening stars.

"I must speak to Óceane before I commit to any plan," he said. "Tomorrow we will decide."

He turned and went into the house. Boswell searched Thomas's face and slowly shook his head from side to side before finishing his brandy and joining the others inside.

Lamplight from the cabin spilled down the beach, almost to the water's edge. Thomas could hear waves rolling onto the black sand, the rustle of tree branches swaying in the breeze and the gentle rush of water flowing over rocks in the stream where it spilled into the cove.

Married. To a woman he barely knew and with whom he would

never have a normal conversation. A woman he had only briefly kissed and never shared a bed. He touched his throbbing nose. The bleeding had stopped, but it was still swollen and painfully tender.

It had been seven years since Robert E. Lee surrendered to General Grant at Appomattox Court House and ended the Civil War. When Thomas swung up on Cornwall for the long ride home from the military hospital a few weeks later he believed that his fighting days were over. Now, he stood at the railing on Aubert's porch and looked out to the wine-dark sea, deep and black, foreboding and unforgiving, and realized his hope was a fool's dream.

"Walk out with me toward the unknown region," the poet Walt Whitman had read to him as he tended to Thomas's wounds at Mt. Pleasant hospital. *"Where neither ground is for feet nor any path to follow, no map there, nor guide, nor voice sounding, nor touch of human hand…."*

Whitman was describing the inevitability of war and death. That was a poor choice of memories to reignite on the very night Keani had come to him, he mused. And yet, war and death continued to haunt his every step and nothing he did had been able to turn them back.

He turned to join the others, anxious to shake off his fatigue and despair. Through the windowpane he saw Keani laughing at some remark Aubert had just made. What manner of man could carry such heaviness in his heart in her presence, he thought.

Then she saw him through the glass and invited him in with her eyes.

~ THIRTY-SEVEN ~

The waning moon was shrouded in clouds when the canoe slipped silently over the reef and into the cove. Tihoti and Manatea beached the outrigger and ran into the brush behind Aubert's cabin.

The warriors had pulled their canoe onto the sand a mile north of the cove earlier that day and hacked their way through the foliage until they came within 50 yards of the cabin under the cliff. They spent the afternoon observing the man they had been charged with killing, watching him come and go from the cabin, walk along the beach with Keani, and dine with the others on the front porch. Then they returned to their camp to wait until nightfall.

Aata had been very clear when they visited him in Papeete, where he fled after his humiliating defeat at the hands of the American. Take only the American colonel, spare the others, and bring no harm whatsoever to Keani. Kill him, haul his body out to sea, and dump his corpse for the sharks. Then return to me with the news and prepare to sail to Hawai'i.

Now, as the moon dipped behind a screen of wispy clouds, Tihoti motioned that it was time to make their way past the cabin and into the cave where they had seen Keani and the American enter two hours earlier.

The *putain* had wasted no time falling on her back for the soldier, Manatea thought. But Aata was mistaken; we should avenge him and the honor of our village with her death, as well.

He checked his short spear and watched Tihoti withdraw his striking club with its razor-sharp volcanic rock tip from his belt.

Then they trotted along the tree line until they were only feet from the darkened cabin. The only sound Manatea could hear as they brushed past the side of the cabin and neared the cook shack in front of the cave entrance was the pounding of blood in his ears. He gripped his spear tightly with both hands and held it in front of him at chest height. He had taken on wild boar from this stance; it should be no different with a man. And if the colonel was soundly sleeping after his roll with Keani, so much the better. Manatea had no qualms about jamming his spear into the back of a sleeping man.

It wasn't going to get any darker or any quieter. Tihoti patted Manatea on the shoulder and motioned him forward. They were only a few feet from the cave entrance now.

Then, a sound broke the stillness. Not quite a real bark, Manatea thought, more like the hoarse cough of someone who was dying. Then another cough, followed by a growl. The warriors froze in place. They hadn't seen a dog while watching the cabin that day, but something was there, and it continued its low growl and short, sputtering cough.

Tihoti felt something brush against his leg and looked down to see that an ancient, crippled dog had hobbled up and was trying to take hold of the hem of his black cotton trousers.

The warrior knocked the dog back with his fist and then raised his club and struck it squarely in the center of its head. The dog uttered a feeble cry, buckled to the ground, and died.

Manatea looked over at Tihoti. That was not much of a watch dog, but they were sure no one had heard.

Thomas heard something. He had been unable to sleep since he and Keani had gone to bed hours ago. He stared at the roof of the cave for some time, then turned on his side and softly brushed the hair back from her angelic face. They had only been together for two days, but he had never been happier or more content. A half smile creased his face at the thought that this was the second night in bed, but they had yet to make love. It wasn't for lack of desire on either of their parts, but rather a sense from deep inside that there were more important things to do, starting with learning how to communicate. Keani had already taught him several words and expressions in sign language, and he was eager to learn more.

Then, another sound, like a large animal stepping on a pile of dried leaves. Thomas rolled off the bed and made his way to the shelves against the cave wall. It took a moment in the dim lamplight to find the cutlass on the top shelf, and with a last glance back at Keani, he slipped through the woven covering that shielded the cave from the outside. There was only a sliver of light from the moon and an oil lamp in the cabin, so it took a moment to make out the two men moving swiftly towards him with weapons drawn.

"And so, they have come," Thomas thought to himself. To his right was the cook shack, to his left a jumble of boulders. He could only charge headlong into the two, or retreat to the cave, which would expose Keani to more danger.

"Émile, Timothy!" he shouted as he rushed forward with both hands gripping the cutlass handle tightly. Whether his friends heard his cry or not, he was going to have to engage the warriors by himself.

Manatea heard the shout and saw a dark form barreling at him with a cutlass raised in the air. He motioned to Tihoti to make a half circle around their opponent, which would allow them to attack the fool from two sides.

He raised his spear, wrapping one hand around the shaft near the tip, and the other at the butt. His plan was simple: he would surge forward and impale the American before the man could begin to swing his cutlass.

Tihoti raised his club, stepped to the right, and nearly stumbled over a fallen log. In the instant it took to right himself, he saw the dark shadows of Manatea and the American merge together.

Thomas had no time to formulate a plan. He took a quick measure of the size of the man in front of him and saw that the warrior had chosen to come towards him with this spear thrust straight out at abdomen height. A crude strategy, but effective if the warrior had the strength and speed to carry it off.

An image of him practicing with the cutlass against McNab on the deck of the *Kai Douglas* flashed before him; unlike a long sword, the captain had said, the shorter cutlass could slash side to side and up and down to equal effect.

The cutlass was pressed hard against his shoulder, and he estimated he had only a second before the warrior was on him. He made a half turn to the right and swung the sword down towards the ground and then straight up into the air in one lightning-fast slashing motion.

The cutlass caught Manatea's sword mid-shaft and sent it flying into the air. The Tahitian dove to the ground to recover his weapon, but as he leapt back up, Thomas swung again and cut deep into Manatea's gut. The warrior fell to his knees, a look of surprise on his face. He raised his eyes towards the American but saw no pity in the man's expression. As it should be, Manatea thought. He closed his eyes. The final blow would be to his neck.

Tihoti was only a few steps behind Manatea, and he watched in disbelief as his friend was quickly dispatched by the American colonel. He uttered an ancient war cry and rushed forwardwith his club raised above his head, the thirst for vengeance blurring his vision.

Then the crack of a Spencer rifle shattered the tableau, and Tihoti dropped his club, went to his knees, and toppled dead on the ground.

Aubert stepped out of the darkness and lowered his rifle. Boswell was at his side, carrying a hatchet, and Océane was behind him with an old musket in her arms.

Thomas let the cutlass fall to the ground and wiped the sweat from his face with the hem of his nightshirt. The little group turned at the sound of someone else approaching, and a moment later Keani rushed into Thomas' arms.

A wind blew through the palms, and the clouds slipped away from the face of the moon, illuminating the battlefield.

"War has been declared, lad," Aubert said in a solemn tone. "We will leave on the first tide tomorrow."

Thomas held Keani tightly against his side. "For where?"

Aubert glanced at Océane, who nodded in agreement.

"Moorea," said the artist.

~ THIRTY-EIGHT ~

Moorea

Aubert's outrigger canoe sliced through the glassy sea in the arms of a following northwesterly wind. The artist was a masterful sailor who took every advantage of wind, wave, and tide as he charted a course around the southern tip of Tahiti, up the western coast to Pape'ete and across the 11-mile strait to the volcanic island of Moorea.

Océane and Boswell had helped them pack before dawn, but Thomas and Keani's meager possessions barely filled the space between the canoe's two center seats. They weren't beginning their new life with much other than themselves, which, Océane observed to her husband, seemed like more than enough as far as the young couple were concerned.

"L'amour est vraiment tout, n'est-ce pas," she had whispered to Aubert as Keani and Thomas walked hand in hand from the cabin down to the waiting canoe at the water's edge.

"Oui, my love, you are right; love really is everything," he replied.

"But what chance will they have on Moorea? Varua will learn they have gone there, and Aata is not going to give up his quest for vengeance. Shouldn't they leave for Hawaii as soon as possible?"

Aubert set down his travel easel and supply pack and took his wife's hands in his. "Chief Varua will not pursue them. Aata's attack last night will be a source of shame for him, and by taking Keani off Tahiti we are giving him the perfect excuse to simply pretend that she does not exist."

"And Aata," asked Océane. "Will he also be willing to forget?"

Aubert looked up behind the cook shack, where the bodies of Aata's assassins lay on the ground under a canvas tarp. Boswell would load them on a packhorse shortly and carry them up the mountain to a spot where he could simply roll them off the horse and into a deep gorge. A grisly job, to be sure, but the attackers deserved no more respect in death than they had commanded in life.

He picked up his bag and easel and kissed his wife on the cheek. "When he learns that his warriors have failed, his fear of Varua's anger will be greater than his desire to see Thomas dead. Thomas and Keani are free of him."

Thomas and Aubert pushed the outrigger off the beach and into three feet of water. Keani and Océane embraced as Aubert rigged the sail, and then Keani joined Thomas and climbed into the canoe just as the wind picked up and the sail began to billow. Océane watched the outrigger pick up speed, slip out of the cove and across the reef, and disappear into the turquoise sea.

❈

The voyage took six hours, just as Aubert had promised. A pod of spinner dolphins accompanied them for a half hour, a lone humpback whale glided beside them for a few minutes and the jagged volcanic peaks of Moorea were in view for most of the way. The ocean was calm, and the opalescent sky was free of clouds.

Thomas liked the way Aubert stood tall and reveled in the warmth of the sun, the feel of the wind and the sprays of salt water as he stood at the rudder and guided the little vessel across the channel towards their new home. The French artist's exuberant embrace of every aspect of life showed as much in how he lived as in how he painted.

Keani broke out some bread, cheese, and a jug of water when they turned away from the Tahiti coast and began their transit across the narrow channel.

"You will like the village at Ha'apiti," Aubert said between bites. "It is on the southwestern coast, in the shadow of Mt. Mouaroa. Fewer than 100 souls call it home, but my friends, if there is such a thing as paradise on this earth it is called Moorea, and as a painter, I can tell you that

Ha'apiti is the island's crown jewel."

"And yet you choose not to live there," said Thomas.

Aubert smiled and adjusted the sail to hold the changing wind. "I paint in Moorea from time to time, but there is a probvlem with perfection, my friend: it can get a little monotonous. Within an hour's ride from my home on Tahiti I can paint in eight entirely differentlandscapes. Different plants, different light, different geological features. There..." he pointed towards Moorea looming close ahead, "there is perfection, but it is a singularly harmonious and unchanging composition, and for a painter that is akin to painting with only two colors."

"And you want to paint with ten."

"I want to paint with hundreds," laughed Aubert as he brought the craft around to ride the early swells that led to Moorea's shore.

Thomas wrapped his arm around Keani. "I could never have survived these past days without your help, my friend," he said to Aubert. "I am forever in your debt."

"And I have given that matter some serious thought, Thomas," replied the artist. "I think I have the perfect solution."

Keani looked at Thomas with questioning eyes, and he gently kissed the top of her head.

"Yes," Aubert continued, "there is a way forward that will be of great benefit to us all. You and Keani will rest on Moorea for a few months, get to know one another. And while you rest, you can think about a way to get Colin Stafford off your trail for good. With him gone there is no limit to where you can go and what you can do. My God, man, aren't you a friend of the President of the United States? I am sure he could persuade Stafford to do the right thing."

"I know him, yes," chuckled Thomas," and if I could sit down with him at the White House perhaps I could prevail upon him to intervene. But he is 5,000 miles over there," he pointed to the northeast, "and we are here."

Aubert looked at Thomas like a schoolmaster whose best pupil just failed an exam. "The White House is actually there," said

Aubert, pointing to the east. "Sailing lessons should be part of your new routine."

"So that is your plan, that I should contact President Grant and ask him for help?" Thomas asked.

"It couldn't hurt. Meanwhile, there are many other things you should prepare for."

"Like?"

"First, you need to get properly married," said Aubert.

Thomas felt Keani squeeze his arm.

"I will contact Edward Kahale and tell him to pay a visit to Ha'apiti. There is a small chapel in the village, and he can marry you there. Then, focus on bringing Stafford's crusade to an end. When that is done you and Keani can return to Lana'i, have lots of fat, happy babies, and build up your sugar plantation until you become very rich. That is important to my plan, as well."

"And why is that?" asked Thomas with a smile.

Aubert moved the tiller to begin the final approach over the reef and up to the beach at Ha'apiti. "Ah," he said, "because then you can become my patron and introduce my work to the world!"

Thomas looked up into the lush, ragged mountains that cut across the island of Moorea. The water around the reef was a milky blue color, and the bottom of the outrigger cut through the water only inches above the sharp-edged coral outcroppings.

"There is nothing I would rather do, Émile, whether I am rich or not," he said. "You are a remarkable painter, and the world needs to see your genius."

Aubert smiled, and pointed to the shore where they could make out a sprinkling of thatched roofs in a clearing that had been carved out of trees and brush. "Ha'apiti," he said.

Keani turned to Thomas and made the signs for two of the words she had taught him.

"Welcome…home."

❈

~ THIRTY-NINE ~

The village fires had been banked for the night when a young girl led Thomas and Keani to the guest hut they would share until they built a place of their own at the edge of the village clearing. Aubert wandered off towards his hut with a half jug of wine and a puppy who had adopted him earlier in the evening.

The artist was a well-known and welcome guest in the village since he had painted a portrait of Queen Pomare IV for them two years ago. The painting occupied an honored place in the tiny chapel built by a priest from Papeete at the request of Terii Nui, the village elder.

"I am told you are a friend of the king of your country," she had said to Thomas during the elaborate meal the villagers had prepared for them. "I myself am first cousin to her majesty Pomare, but as you can see, I realize no special benefit from that relationship."

"Except, perhaps, the benefit of the respect and admiration of your people," Thomas replied. "That is no small gift."

"He is a wise one, is he not?" Terii Nui said to Keani, adding, "for a barbarian of course," with a laugh.

Keani smiled. Like Thomas, she had felt at home the minute they climbed out of the canoe and walked up into the village. They had been greeted like old friends, and offered food, baths, fresh clothing, and the local rum punch. Now, after a feast of broiled tuna, skewered pork marinated in sweet sauce and cooked over coals, fruit salads, and hot bread, they said good evening to all and followed their respective guides to their huts under a soft, starry sky.

Thomas and Keani parted the reed and branch door and stepped into the small, one room hut where the villagers had already deposited their bags. There were two chairs made with bamboo and rushes, a wood table with a mirror and a single drawer, two oil lamps, and on the floor in the center of the room sat a large woven bed topped with handmade blankets and pillows. Thomas smiled when he saw that someone had scattered aromatic gardenia petals across the bedspread.

Keani excused herself and ducked out of the hut while Thomas sat on a chair and removed his boots and socks. This would be his third night with Keani, but he had yet to remove his clothing in her presence or seen her remove hers. At Aubert's he had stepped outside the cave to slip on his nightshirt while Keani did the same inside. He wasn't going to overthink the reasons he had refrained from letting her know he wanted to make love; what it came down to was simple: it just hadn't felt right.

Tonight, was different. The battle at Aubert's cabin the previous evening had brought them even closer. When she rushed into his arms after the fight was over, he had been overwhelmed with a sense of protectiveness towards her. He understood in that moment that caring for her and keeping her from harm would be his life's purpose from that day forward.

The door was pulled aside, and Keani stepped into the hut. He was surprised to see that she had not changed into her nightgown, and from the expression on her face, she was surprised he wasn't ready for bed, either. She closed the door and walked across to the small table, where her hairbrush lay in front of the mirror. She sat down, picked up the brush, and began running it through her long, auburn tresses.

Thomas came up behind her, and gently took the brush from her hand. He saw a questioning look in her expression in the mirror as he began to run the brush softly through her hair, and he replied by kissing her on the top of her head. After two more brush strokes, Keani stayed his hand and set down the brush. She stood up, wrapped her arms around him, and kissed him, softly at first, and then with a fierce urgency that caught him off guard.

He responded by holding her even tighter for a moment until she pulled his hands away and stepped back. She went over to the bed, and, with her back towards him, lifted her cotton dress over her head, dropped it lightly onto the floor and then stood still with her hands at her side.

Thomas almost forgot to breathe. The creaminess of her skin, the symphony of her curves and the arch of her back flowed together in an ethereal harmony that he knew not even the greatest master painter could capture on canvas.

He went to her and pressed himself against her back, taking her hands in his and showering kisses on her shoulders and neck. Keani turned, wrapped her arms around his neck and pulled his head down to her breasts, but only for a moment. Then she leaned back and began to unbutton his shirt. She tossed it on the floor beside her dress, and then lowered herself to her knees and undid his trouser buttons. She motioned for him to lay down on the bed on his back before slipping his trousers off and adding them to the heap of clothing on the floor.

Keani straddled his waist and pulled her hair back, and then, with a smile that was as tender as it was mischievous, she bent down and kissed him on the lips.

Aubert was up at dawn to capture the first blush of morning light splashing across the lagoon. He set up his easel, patted the little dog, and unpacked his paint tubes and brushes. For the sky today he chose a light cerulean blue. Cobalt was his favorite color in the blue spectrum, but he found cerulean to be more opaque, and he liked the way it formed a soft layer and resisted changing appearance, even in harsh light. Like his friend Claude Monet, he chose not to use black in his paintings because the color was almost non-existent in nature, and because the effects he could create with changes in hue were so much richer than those caused by changes in shade. Black dulled the look of a painting, and so to create contrast Aubert picked a color's complement when darkening an area. To darken his cerulean sky this morning, for example, he would add some red or orange.

With his canvas set up and his paints around him, Aubert visualized the completed piece and began to quickly lay down short, quick strokes of paint with his palette knife. The composition was simple: an outrigger beached under a palm at the edge of the lagoon which was bordered in flowering bushes and trees. His greatest ally was also his greatest enemy: the changing light. He worked swiftly to capture the motion of the waves and the sparkle of sunlight on the water. To depict the colors of the sea and the sky he used a multitude of blues, from deep blues to shimmering turquoises, with dabs of purples, pinks, and yellows in the sky.

Today he would paint *alla prima*, all at once, attempting to finish the work in a single two-hour session. Sometimes he painted for under an hour and then returned another day at the same time and under the same weather conditions to complete a piece. He seldom took more than two hours to complete a painting, and since he chose not to apply a coat of varnish to his canvases, other than adding his signature, the work was done.

The light was cooperative this morning, and the puppy was content to nap at his feet. Océane would be pleased when he brought the dog home; she had been devastated by the death of their old and faithful companion at the hands of Aata's warriors.

A few moments after he made the last adjustments of shadow on the outrigger's furled sail, the painting was complete. He stepped back for a final look and declared today's work done. As he began packing his supplies, he saw Thomas and Keani walking towards him along the beach, hand in hand. It was good to have a new friend like the young American colonel, Aubert thought. And who knew, perhaps one day Thomas would assist him in getting his work to the art markets of the world.

Keani approached the painting on the easel and made a show of putting a hand under her chin and shaking her head as if she were saying. "Tut-tut, and what kind of abomination is this?" Aubert felt a momentary sting, and then Keani smiled, laughed, and put her arms around his neck and kissed him on the cheek.

"It is beautiful," she signed, "so very beautiful."

"And that is a good thing," replied Aubert with a broad smile, "because that is your wedding present, and you will at least have to hang it up any time I visit you."

Keani giggled, and then held her arms high at her sides and did a twirl around the easel, stopping again to kiss Aubert on the cheek.

"That could well be the most positive critique I have ever received," he said to Thomas.

Thomas did not hear a word his friend was saying. He was enchanted into silence by Keani's spontaneous outburst of joy when she danced around Aubert's painting.

The artist gave the back of Thomas' head a playful slap; "Are you with us, my friend? Or have you been completely bewitched?"

"A little of both," Thomas finally replied with a sheepish grin. "Between last night and this…" he pointed at the painting, "I suppose I am a bit overwhelmed."

"Ah, last night," said Aubert as he looked into Thomas' eyes and then Keani's. "From the expressions on your faces I think we had better get Edward Kahale here to marry you. A French painter cannot afford to be seen in the company of such a scandalous pair as you two, you know. Whatever would people think?"

Keani blushed and took Thomas' arm. But her eyes were shining, and she stood straight and tall, Aubert noted. '*What a lucky man you are Thomas,*' he thought to himself. '*I hope you realize that.*'

She dropped to the ground and began playing with the puppy, and Aubert and Thomas walked to the water's edge.

"What now?" asked Thomas in a wistful tone. "We can't just remain here and do nothing."

"You disappoint me, Brother Scoundrel," Aubert replied. "Do nothing? There is much to do, starting with building your cabin."

"I have never built anything."

"It's time you learned." Aubert picked a stick up off the sand and sent it sailing into the lagoon. "I will return to Océane tomorrow. We will pack supplies and food for a month and have a villager stay in our home. She loves it here, and she and Keani will have much to do to get your new house ready."

"So you and I will build this house?"

"And Boswell, and…do you have any money, Thomas?"

"I have some from the profits of my plantation."

"Good, then we will hire a dozen local men, more if we can afford it. I saw a pile of beams and milled lumber covered in vines behind the chapel. We will make a deal to buy them from Terii Nui and start on your cabin as soon as I return. That will be in four or five days. While I am gone, you will have time to write letters—no doubt there are many people who would like to know where you are and what you are doing."

Thomas nodded. From his editor at the *Chronicle* to Akoni in Honolulu and Kukane on his plantation, he did need to share his story with a lot of people. He looked over at Keani, who was tickling the puppy's stomach underneath Aubert's painting. Behind her a sea of green swept up the slopes of Mt. Mouaroa under one of Aubert's perfect cerulean skies. She caught his glance and smiled.

Yes, he thought. They would build a home.

It took Aubert six days to return to Moorea. While he was gone, Thomas spent his time writing more than a dozen long letters to a host of people, including his partner on the plantation, banker Stafford, and the Grimthorpes, who were caring for Taiana. He did not share his whereabouts with any of them for fear Colin Safford or his hired assassin Fitch Donegan should come into possession of one of the letters. He did drop a hint to Akoni, who had visited Moorea and Tahiti on one of his specimen collection voyages. "I saw a painting in a private home of the Tiaré Apetahi," he wrote, referring to an extremely rare flower that Boswell told him was only found in Tahiti, "and it reminded me of the collections that you have gathered for the British Museum."

In fact, Boswell had prepared several dried specimens of the flower and one sat atop Thomas' nightstand in the cave behind Aubert's cabin.

Thomas and Keani had just finished breakfast when two children raced up from the beach to tell them that Aubert had returned. They went down to the lagoon to see three outriggers piled high with bags, chests, and large wooden crates. Aubert helmed one outrigger while the other two were sailed by islanders from Papara.

"Your first two hires," grinned the Frenchman as he embraced Thomas and Keani. "They are experienced builders and will help lead the crew. Have you marked out your site?"

A swarm of villagers offloaded the outriggers and hauled everything up into the common area at the center of the village. Terii Nui took command of the process until Océane pointed to one of the chests and said it contained gifts for the village leader. Inside were bolts of bright colored cloth to make clothing, bags of candy for the children, a fiddle to replace the one Terii Nui had broken while playing a jig a bit too enthusiastically, and assorted canned goods, pencils and paper, wine, cognac, smoked hams, and several large, dried cheeses. Terii Nui lost no time tuning the fiddle and striking up a jaunty tune to accompany the distribution of the bounty.

Keani and Océane walked arm in arm to a table near the village cook shack while Aubert and Thomas walked a hundred yards along the beach to the northwest to the spot Thomas had picked for their cabin. The beach curved inward at that point, and a natural rock jetty diverted the larger waves to the south, creating a perfect place to swim or fish, no matter the weather. Thomas had staked out an area 50 yards back from the shoreline, not far from a small creek that spilled from the mountains into the lagoon. Ten-foot-high walls of ancient volcanic rock formed a half circle around the site, and a thick, nearly impenetrable mass of thorny brush completed the barrier on the other sides.

"You may be no builder, my friend, but you do know something about selecting a defensible position," said Aubert after appraising the layout.

"I did learn a few things in the Army," Thomas replied.

Aubert walked the area to see where Thomas had marked locations for the privy and cook shack. "Other than suggesting you move the privy a few yards to the north, I can't see why we don't begin building tomorrow morning," he said.

At dawn the next day, Aubert assembled the 11 men who had agreed to help build Thomas and Keani's cabin. They would be paid wages comparable to what workers were paid in Pape'ete, and they would get both breakfast and lunch, which Keani and several women from the village would prepare.

Aubert arranged to purchase the beams and milled lumber that had been piled behind the chapel for more than five years, and he had three chests of nails, saws, hammers, wood planes, chisels and other tools carried to the site. More supplies, plus glass for real windows, would arrive in the next week from Pape'ete.

Everyone gathered around Aubert at the lagoon waterline as he took a stick and drew the cabin design in the sand. "I will do a charcoal drawing later today," he announced, "but I want everyone to understand what we are building. Today we start with the pier and beam foundation." Eleven faces looked at him with questions in their eyes.

Aubert pointed to a pile of shovels. "We dig!"

It took three weeks to complete the cabin, which Terii Niu called, *'A house on stilts.'* It was almost identical to Aubert's house, with a spacious living room and separate bedroom, attic storage space, and a covered wrap around porch with a railing and stairs. The house had wooden doors front and back, and three glass-paned windows.

Keani and Océane made several trips with a horse and carriage up the coast to the northern village of Papetoai, where the London Missionary Society was headquartered. The offices and church were built next to Temple Protestant, located on the site of an ancient temple dedicated to Oro, son of the supreme Taaroa and the god of war. The missionaries maintained a supply warehouse from which Keani purchased a dresser, table and chairs, material to make curtains, dishes and glassware, a claw foot bathtub, linens, cooking pots and utensils, and other household goods.

When the cabin was complete and the crew turned to constructing the privy and cookshack, Keani and Océane set about turning the place into a real home. One of the villagers fashioned a cane and wicker rocking chair ("For when you have babies," she told Keani) and Océane quickly determined that the single painting Aubert had given Thomas and Keani wasn't enough to decorate a house. "But we insist on paying you for these," Keani signed to Océane when the artist delivered four small paintings of the landscapes around their home. Océane translated Keani's wish to Aubert, and with a laugh he said, "Name your first boy after me, and I will call us even!"

Three nights later under a balmy sky, a procession of villagers carrying torches wound down along the beach to Keani and Thomas' new home. They carried baskets of dried fish, fruit, and breads, and as they came closer their voices rose to the moonlit sky in harmonious song. Terii Nui led her people, followed in order by Aubert and Océane, the men who built the cabin, and then the rest of the men, women, and children with whom Thomas and Keani were going to share their lives. At the end of the procession came the botanist, Timothy Boswell, and the minister, Edward Kahale, who was to officiate at the wedding the next day.

Thomas wrapped his arm around Keani's shoulder and held her tight as the line of villagers snaked towards them, the light from their torches spilling up the beach and into the lagoon where it melted into the golden rays of the moon as they skipped across the peaceful water.

When the villagers arrived at the cabin they assembled in a half-circle at the foot of the stairs. When their song of welcome died out the only sound was the crackling of pitch in the torches, and the palms rustling in the soft night breeze.

Terii Nui raised her arm to the sky and shouted, *"Mavea!"* Welcome.

Then the villagers also raised their arms to the sky and in one voice shouted, *"Manuia!"* May you enjoy good health.

Thomas looked down across the crowd at the faces of friends old and new and was overcome by the moment. He turned to Keani and said, "I will love you always."

"And I will love you, my darling Thomas," she replied with her eyes.

~ FORTY ~

In keeping with Polynesian custom, the ceremony began one hour before sunset. The gently curving beach in front of the village was a sea of flowers, leaf garlands, ceremonial headdresses, and vividly dyed garments. Minister Edward Kahale stood at the water line in his coat and tie, next to a *Tahua*, a Tahitian priest garbed in a splendid robe of shimmering red and yellow, topped with an elaborate red feather headdress.

When the *Tahua* raised his hand to the sky, a village elder held up a conch shell and blew a single deep, haunting note that drifted across the assembly and out to the deep-blue ocean. The sound called upon the air, land, sea, and fire to be witnesses to the ceremony and was the signal for Keani and Thomas to walk through the crowd and take their places in front of Kahale and the *Tahua*.

Thomas wore a crisp new cotton shirt that McNab brought from Pape'ete, along with a crown of green leaves. Keani wore a simple, ankle-length white linen dress embroidered with crème-colored blossoms on the bosom and at her wrists. On her head was a crown of fragrant, pure white tiare mā'ohi flowers. Bride and groom, like their guests, were barefoot.

As the disc of the sun melted into deep orange and sank towards the purpling horizon, Kahale asked the couple to face one another. Then he pulled a piece of paper from his jacket pocket and read an Irish blessing that Thomas had requested in remembrance of his mother:

"May your mornings bring joy, and your evenings bring peace. May your troubles grow few as your blessings increase. May the saddest day of your future be no worse than the happiest day of your past. May your hands be forever clasped in friendship and your hearts joined forever in love. Your lives are very special, and God has touched you in many ways. May his blessings rest upon you and fill all your coming days."

Now the *Tahua* tied a split leaf of the sacred *Auti* plant on Thomas and Keani's wrists to call in good and banish evil. That was followed by the approach of a young girl carrying a water basin made of iridescent shell. Keani and Thomas held out their hands and the girl poured water over them to signify the purification of the union.

Kahale motioned for the couple to turn and face their guests as two young women from Keani's village came forward carrying flower leis. They'll feel the wrath of Chief Varua for defying his order to blot Keani from memory, Thomas thought, but then he began to recognize face after face in the crowd as villagers from Papara. Dozens had made the trip across the channel from Tahiti for the wedding. He grinned. Varua couldn't banish his entire village.

Each girl carried two red and white leis, which they draped around Thomas' and Keani's necks. They melted back into the crowd, and, as the edge of the sun dipped below the western horizon, Kahale and the Tahuna wrapped a red and white *tifaifai* quilt around the newlywed couple before stepping back several feet to proclaim the final wedding blessing.

"You are now man and wife," said Kahale. "Blessings upon you both."

"Tané and vahiné," added the *Tahua*. "May you live forever in happiness and peace."

Six months ago, Thomas could not have believed that he would be here on this distant island, crowned in flowers and wrapped tightly in a colorful quilt with an astonishingly beautiful Polynesian woman—now his wife—on a tropical beach at sunset as warm lagoon water lapped at their bare feet. It was beyond comprehension.

Then a chorus of voices lifted a song to the sky. Thomas recognized the tune as a Christian hymn, but he did not understand the Tahitian words. It didn't matter. Keani was pressed close with her head resting on his shoulder and they were surrounded by friends who had come to celebrate their new life. For the first time since he met her, he understood that her muteness took nothing away from the life they were going to build. He gazed deep into her sea green eyes and then lifted his head and looked out to the setting sun.

"She doesn't need words," he thought.

As the wedding feast whirled around them, Thomas and Timothy Boswell joined Aubert, Captain McNab, and Edward Kahale on a stone bench near one of the fires that illuminated the central village compound and its revelers. Terii Nui held forth on her fiddle as people danced and sang and piled their plates high with the leaf-wrapped roast pork that had been baking all day in an underground pit at the edge of the village. Children darted in and out among the adults, and young men and women—no doubt inspired by the day's events—carried on the kind of flirtatious rituals that pre-dated recorded history.

McNab pulled a bottle from a canvas sack and filled two hand-cut crystal glasses for Thomas and the artist.

"Where did you find these?" asked Thomas as he held up the glass and inspected the deep-ruby wine.

"Best save your inquiry for what's in 'em," chuckled the artist, who had clearly been enjoying the bounty from the bottle.

Thomas inhaled the wine's perfume, swirled it in the glass, and took a sip.

"Good lord," he said to McNab. "Where on earth did you get this? It is extraordinary!"

"As I said," Aubert added. "No need to worry about the glass. You could pour this elixir through a trollop's soiled knickers and drink it out of a sweaty boot, and it would still be good enough to make Zeus himself blush with joy."

The men laughed, but Aubert had a point. "Don't know as how I'd go that far, but it is something special, and I'm glad you all agree," said McNab.

"France?" asked Kahale.

"Château Gruaud Larose, a winery in the *Saint-Julien* appellation of the Bordeaux region of France," replied McNab. "It's a blend of Cabernet Sauvignon and Merlot, pretty young, really, '71, or so the bottle says."

Thomas could not help but finish off the rest of his glass in a single gulp.

"Hand it over," the captain said with a smile," we have plenty more."

Thomas and Boswell both held out their glasses. "And you just pick it up from a local purveyor in Pape'ete?" asked Boswell.

"Not exactly," said McNab. "I have told you about my brother who lives in St. Louis. Made his fortune in the war and now spends his time collecting art and…" he held his glass high, "fine wine. He had five cases sent to me, and you, Thomas, are getting a full case as my wedding present to you and Keani."

Before Thomas could reply, Aubert growled, "And are we going to have to crack open the groom's private stash tonight?"

McNab threw back a blanket that had been covering a small box and lifted out another bottle of the red Bordeaux. "Knowing you lads and your propensity for the grape, I brought six bottles for our celebration tonight. We just finished the first, so worry not. There's plenty for all."

He uncorked the new bottle and filled their glasses. "A toast," said the captain, "to Thomas and his bride."

The men raised their glasses and downed the wine. As McNab filled them again, Aubert said, "Seems to me that we should manage Brother Thomas's intake of this magic potion. After all, the boy has a performance to present at home tonight, and more than a few men have fallen victim to the malady of vintner's droop when imbibing a bit too much on their wedding night."

The normally austere Boswell exploded with laughter, and even Kahale could not hold back a belly laugh.

Aubert lifted his glass to the light from the bonfire. As the fiddle played, dancers spun and villagers launched into spontaneous song, Aubert raised his glass higher and said, "May the saints preserve

Thomas and protect him this sacred 'eve against the ravages of vintner's droop, lest she who deserves his complete upright attention boots him outside to sleep with the dogs!"

"As she should," Kahale answered in a dead serious tone, which set the men to laughing again.

Thomas looked across the compound to the table where Keani was sitting with her friends. Under the stars, in the light from the village fires, she was positively aglow. He had never seen her look more beautiful. She caught his glance and smiled, and he raised his glass to her.

Shortly after the fourth bottle of the excellent Bordeaux was opened and McNab finished detailing how he was going to send some of Aubert's work to his brother in St. Louis, one of Keani's friends from Papara came over to Thomas. "Keani would like you to meet her at your home in one hour," she said, barely able to suppress a giggle. "Not before. One hour exactly."

Thomas nodded and the girl scooted back across the compound.

"And so it begins," said McNab in a fatherly tone.

"Begins?" asked Thomas.

"Your first new husband training session," the captain answered with a sigh. "I can tell you from experience that it will be the first of many."

It must have been the expression on his face, Thomas thought a moment later, when his friends exchanged knowing glances and began to laugh.

One hour later—exactly—Thomas made his goodbyes to everyone and walked down the moonlit beach with Aubert. The Frenchman had grabbed a half bottle of the Bordeaux and was sipping straight from the neck as they walked along.

"I envy you, my friend," the artist said. "Oh, not in your choice of wife, which was perfect by the way." He lifted the bottle to his lips, wiped his sleeve across his mouth and continued. "I envy what you are going to experience for the next few months, what Océane and I experienced. Love in its most pure and unblemished state. The excitement of getting to know one another, the passion, the discoveries that only a newly united man and woman can make."

Thomas heard Aubert sniffle. "It's nothing," said the artist, "merely a stray cinder from the fires."

Thomas smiled and the two friends walked in silence down the beach until they were a few yards from the cabin, which was glowing with light. Then he saw movement, and a moment later Keani's four friends rushed down the cabin steps and raced past him and Aubert, trying unsuccessfully to suppress their giggles.

Thomas neared the bottom of the steps, where an elderly woman was sitting beside the porch on a rocker with a pipe in her mouth. She stood, gave Thomas a peck on the cheek, and then hurried down the beach back towards the village.

Thomas and Aubert looked up the stairs into the living room, where dozens of candles were burning. "That would explain the old woman," said Aubert. "Fire protection."

Thomas was mystified by Keani's giggling friends and the fire warden, and the artist was too much the gentleman to venture a guess. He simply embraced Thomas, kissed his cheek, and without saying a word slipped into the darkness. Thomas watched for a moment as Aubert weaved along the beach, and smiled when the artist held his wine bottle up high in a parting gesture.

He walked to the top stair and looked back at the village, alight with bonfires and music drifting down the beach.

He ran his hands through his hair and straightened his shirt collar. Married. The word felt as if it weighed a hundred tons, and yet he could not remember being happier or more excited about the future. He was 23, Keani was 20. They would have years and years together, they would build a family, and one day, when the business with Stafford was straightened out, he would take her to San Francisco to dinner at

Kwan's *Rue de Paris* restaurant, where Mrs. Kwan would have to keep her promise and finally put fresh flowers on his table.

He paused at the door and took a deep breath. Keani was not in the room. Inside there were candles everywhere, and scents of plumeria and gardenia permeated the air. A bottle of wine and two glasses sat on the table next to a basket of fresh fruit and cheeses. Then he noticed that a trail of bright red blossoms had been laid on the floor from the porch to the bedroom.

He went to the door and slowly pulled it open. More candlelight spilled out into the living room from the dozen candles that had been affixed to the back wall. The flickering golden light reflected off the dresser mirror, creating a magical, otherworldly feeling.

In the center of the room, facing him, stood Keani. She had replaced her crown of white flowers with red ones, and her eyes glowed with love and anticipation. She was completely nude, her head high and proud, her shoulders back, her feet pressed together. As extraordinary as that vision was, something else caused Thomas to hold his breath.

Starting at her left shoulder, a soft rope of pure white flowers wound completely around her body. It started at her left shoulder, went around behind her back, across her breasts, down to her abdomen, and around her waist. The garland continued around her body, encircling her hips, the soft triangle of hair between her legs, and on down to her thighs, her calves and finally, her ankles.

Thomas could not imagine a painting more beautiful, a portrait more perfect, a woman at once more desirable and yet innocent. He felt a momentary regret that he was not a painter like Aubert, but not even the titans of classical art could adequately capture the vision that was standing in front of him at this moment.

The candles and the floral rope explained the giggling girls who raced out of the cabin upon his arrival, and he shook his head thinking about what that scene must have looked like as the girls wrapped Keani from head to toe in flowers, laughing all the while as they thought about how he would react.

Then Keani parted her lips, tilted her head, and met his gaze.

He hadn't been aware until that instant that he had been frozen in place for a full minute.

"Aren't you going to unwrap me?"asked her eyes.

~ FORTY-ONE ~

San Francisco, August 9

Colonel Thomas Scoundrel loomed large in the hearts and minds of people from San Francisco to Hawai'i, though nearly as many wished him dead as hoped he was well.

In the offices of the *San Francisco Chronicle*, Andrew Whitton paced back and forth across the room until his assistant couldn't take it any longer and pleaded with him to stop. Whitton finally relented. He sat at his desk, added brandy to his coffee and unfolded Thomas' letter for the third time this evening. The 11-page, handwritten missive detailed his former reporter's adventures from the day the brick had been tossed through the *Chronicle's* window by Colin Stafford's henchmen, until Thomas departed from Honolulu for parts unknown aboard the schooner Kai Douglas.

Whitton shook his head at Thomas' experience aboard the German warship and grimaced at the description of his friend being tossed 30 feet from the deck of the ship into the waters off Honolulu. He was not surprised that the journalist San Francisco knew as 'TES Bayside' had walked away from a poker game owning half of a sugar plantation, and as for the way Thomas hinted at the moonlight swim with Princess Noelani and his conflict turned friendship with her brother, Akoni, it was vintage Scoundrel, the editor mused.

Thomas' detail about Fitch Donegan was another matter. The fact that Colin Stafford had hired an experienced assassin to track Thomas down was exactly the kind of thing Whitton expected the wealthy businessman would do. And, like Thomas, Whitton had no doubt that Donegan would stay on the trail, despite his temporary dalliance with the Honolulu brothel he had just opened.

Thomas' trip to the leper colony on Molokai and his rescue of the girl, Taiana, cemented the editor's conviction that Scoundrel was a man of genuine character, and the description of the 17-day voyage aboard Captain McNab's schooner to a destination that Thomas felt best keeping secret was the stuff of a grand adventure novel. If Scoundrel didn't write the book one day, Whitton decided, he would do it himself.

What stopped the editor in his tracks more than anything else Thomas wrote about was his description of the painting that hung above the mantel in McNab's island home. Whitton was something of an art collector, and he had been hearing rumors about a new form of painting that rejected the rigid boundaries of classical art and instead focused on the interplay of light and color and the way the viewer interacted with the work. He was going to have to look into that.

He pulled several sheets of paper from his desk, dipped his pen into the inkwell, and began to compose a reply, which Thomas asked to be sent in care of Akoni at Iolani Palace in Honolulu. God help the lad, Whitton thought as his pen began to move across the paper. On the other hand, how much more trouble could Colonel Scoundrel possibly find himself in?

Three other people were thinking about Thomas in San Francisco that night. In his newly completed mansion on Nob Hill, Colin P. Stafford was also penning a letter, this one to Fitch Donegan in Honolulu. Stafford agreed with Donegan's assessment that Thomas would have to return to Honolulu at some point if he wished to make his way back to the U.S., but his patience was wearing thin. The articles Scoundrel wrote about him in the *Chronicle* had not been forgotten, despite his best efforts to rebut every slander the paper had made against him. Stafford would have his revenge—his justice—no matter how long it took. As for Donegan, he had contemplated having the man killed when the business with Scoundrel was concluded. On the other hand, the amusement Donegan had arranged for him on that evening at the Pearl had been the most delicious and satisfying sexual experience he had ever known.

He would be returning to Hawai'i on occasion to check on his business interests in any event. Why not let Donegan continue to procure perfect diversions for his rather exceptional tastes?

When he finished the letter, he slid the jar containing his brother's eyeball in embalming fluid across the desk and under the light of his oil lamp. *"You had better be keeping your one good eye open, brother,"* he thought. *"We have much at stake, but more to gain."*

At that same hour Kam Sung Kwan and his wife Bo sat at a table in their Rue de Paris restaurant, which had closed only minutes earlier. It was their custom to share a meal after closing and talk about the day's events. Tonight, however, they had a letter to read.

Kwan opened the envelope and sipped tea as he read Thomas Scoundrel's letter aloud. It did not contain all the detail that Andrew Whitton received, but it was enough for the Kwans to get a sense of where their friend and loyal customer had gone after the fight in their kitchen with Stafford's men. Thomas thanked them for the information their niece had overheard at Stafford's mansion and passed along to alert him that Fitch Donegan was on his way to Hawai'i, and Mrs. Kwan teared up when Thomas told her to be ready with a flower for his table the next time he came to their restaurant. "I won't be coming alone," he wrote.

She took her husband's hand when he read that sentence. "It will be a bouquet," she said.

It was late afternoon Honolulu time when the Kwans were reading

Thomas' letter. Akoni was about to leave his rooms inside the Iolani Palace for a carriage ride to the Merchant Hotel for an early dinner when a messenger arrived from the U.S. Counsel's Office carrying a letter. He slipped the envelope into his jacket pocket and went outside for the carriage.

He was guided to a discrete corner table overlooking the Merchant's expansive gardens, where he ordered a salad and a bottle of the California Zinfandel that Thomas had introduced to him. Only then did he open the letter from his friend.

The letter began with Akoni seeing Thomas off with Captain McNab for the journey to Tahiti and the islands beyond, and, while Thomas did not specify where he was writing from, the clue he dropped about a rare flower Akoni had collected that only existed on Moorea told him all he needed to know. Also in the envelope was a separate page over Thomas' signature authorizing Akoni to collect his Army pension at the Counsel's Office. "When I am able to get to Honolulu it may have to be a very quick visit," Thomas wrote. "I wouldn't mind if you held onto the cash so I can grab it on the run!"

Thomas ended the letter by asking his friend to visit the Grimthorpes, who were caring for Taiana. "Please thank them," he wrote, "and let Taiana know that I will find a way to get there to honor her parent's wish that she finds a real home."

Akoni raised his wine glass to the setting sun. "To honor," he said quietly.

At the same hour on Lana'i, Kukane was walking a two-acre cane field that had been harvested earlier in the day. Thomas' plantation manager watched the last of the Third Gang members deposit their cane knives in woven baskets and shuffle off to their cottages for the evening meal. It was a good harvest, and more than 20 carts laden with cane had been sent to the coast for the trip to the boiling houses on Oah'u.

Since Thomas left, his partner, William Fortnite, had been barely visible around the plantation. The only times Kukane could be sure of seeing the man was at their weekly accounting meetings each Saturday afternoon. Fortnite was almost always drunk, or well on his way. Despite that, the man was keeping meticulous records, and as long as he kept out of Kukane's way the plantation operated smoothly. New fields were being cleared and planted, they continued testing new varieties of cane per Thomas' instructions, and it even seemed like the endless war against the ravenous cane rats was turning in his favor. As for Fortnite's gloomy disposition, Kukane attributed at least some of his dark mood to the fact that he knew that if he ever touched another child like he had done with the Chinese girl in the line shack, a .45 caliber bullet was going to plow a path through his brain pan.

He was enjoying a quiet smile at that thought when a boy raced across the stubbled cane field carrying an envelope. Kukane handed the lad a peppermint candy from the supply he kept in his pocket and sat on a stump in the waning light to read the letter.

Fitch Donegan did not receive a letter from Thomas, but he had no doubt that the colonel was in touch with his friends. From his corner table at the Pearl, Donegan kept track of the network of snitches he had in place from the Hawaiian Islands to Brisbane, Australia, where most of the ships out of San Francisco and Honolulu made port.

He had considered finding watchers on Tahiti in the port city of Pape'ete but finally decided against it as an unnecessary expense. Scoundrel was a cosmopolitan man who thrived on the kind of hotels, food, gaming, and exotic women that could only be found in larger cities. Tahiti was a flea-bitten backwater that offered none of those luxuries.

Donegan signaled to the barman to bring another drink. Then he motioned to the new girl who had just arrived from the Big Island to join him. She was young, fresh, doe-eyed, and he had been told that her family was in dire financial straits. That was the perfect recipe for a compliant whore. The girl sat down beside him and did her best to look confident.

His lap and legs were covered from view by the table, so he didn't hesitate when he unbuttoned his fly and forced her hand beneath his underwear. The flicker of fear and disgust in her eyes when he showed her how to move her hand back and forth between his legs only excited him further. *"She has never done this before,"* he thought with a smile. When he was done, he would make her clean him up, and then see to it that she was all his for the next few days. By the time he was done instructing her she would be the finest, most expensive filly in his stable.

Donegan leaned back and closed his eyes as the girl continued massaging his groin, unconcerned about the people in the bar around him. *"This is a god damn whorehouse,"* he thought, *"and I know everything there is to know about every person who steps through my door."*

A moment later the girl brought him to climax, and he allowed himself one more self-congratulatory reflection. *"And that includes Thomas Scoundrel."*

~ FORTY-TWO ~

Moorea, September

Tomas stepped out of the brush near their cabin with an eight-foot timber balanced on his shoulder. He wiped the sweat from his brow with his sleeve and looked over at Keani, who was weeding a row of vegetables in the rich volcanic soil of their garden.

They had been married for almost five weeks, and, in that brief time, his life had been completely transformed. He had been a wanderer for seven years after the end of the Civil War, drifting from town to town across the continent in search of something he couldn't even define. He'd been a soldier, gambler, newspaperman, trail hand and land speculator. He lost count of the women with whom he dallied, the saloon doors he had pushed through, the men he had fought, and the dry, dusty main streets he had walked. It was an existence neither hot nor cold; just one day piling up on the one before without leaving behind any sign that he had been there.

Keani smiled and waved for him to join her in the garden. He set down the timber and went up on the porch to fill a gourd with water from a bucket and pour over his head. Married. If anything, he supposed his vision of the institution when he was a younger man was of living a life of routine bordering on tedium; a solid, dependable mate, a stable job, a neat clapboard house, children, church membership, and perhaps a gold watch upon his retirement.

With that thought in mind he stepped off the porch and walked towards the garden. Truth is a strange land, his poet friend, Walt

Whitman, used to say. To say that his life today was a perfect reflection of that sentiment was an understatement. Their home on stilts sat just off the beach of a tranquil, deep blue cove teeming with exotic tropical fish and gloriously colorful birds. One hundred yards beyond the cove was a snow-white coral reef that encircled the entire island of Moorea, and, on the other side of the reef, humpback whales glided silently past, corkscrew dolphins spun and whirled six feet above the ocean surface, and great sea birds swooped low to scoop small fish into their beaks.

Behind their home was a nearly impenetrable barrier of trees, bushes and flowers that swept up the slope of Mt. Mouaroa, part of a chain of ancient volcanoes that towered high above the island. Eleven miles to the southwest, the island of Tahiti thrust its own volcanic mountains into the cobalt sky, and 100 yards down the beach the tiny village of Ha'apiti dotted the cove's southern rim.

Aubert and Océane had just departed for Tahiti after a four-day visit, and Boswell would be arriving tomorrow to continue his work cataloguing the teeming flora around the village. Keani was expanding the vegetable garden and looking after their sow pig and chickens, and each evening after dinner she worked with Thomas on reading sign language. He was a quick study, and he loved being able to understand her more completely, but the truth was that he was equally satisfied just to look into her eyes. Somehow, they were even more expressive than her signs.

Each morning at dawn, they paddled out to the reef where Keani demonstrated the technique and strategy of spear fishing from inside an outrigger canoe, a skill that required balance, timing, and speed. Thomas sat in the stern of the canoe and used a paddle to hold the outrigger in place while she stood tall and graceful in the bow, her spear held in both hands at shoulder height. Her eyes were fixed on any movement below the surface, and she held her breath just before she let the spear fly. From the arch of her neck to the smoothness of her bare shoulders and the wild tumble of her hair down her back, Thomas was mesmerized by the vision.

Keani almost always speared one of the dozens of fish darting in and out of the fan-shaped coral branches after three or four attempts, but Thomas had no such luck at his first attempts. It took 41 tosses—many of them accompanied by Keani's barely perceptible giggles—before he impaled his first catch, a fat, multi-colored parrotfish that she insisted on gutting immediately before the flesh was fouled.

His labors did not go unrewarded; that evening they enjoyed the day's catch drizzled in fruit juice and garlic, wrapped in *ti* leaves, and baked in a clay pot over hot coals. Keani explained that the leaves did more than enhance the flavor of the fish; they were sacred to Lono, God of fertility, and Laka, the Goddess of hula, and they were used by Kahuna priests to ward off evil and bring in good spirits.

After dinner, as the stars began to pop across the horizon and an offshore breeze cooled the land, Keani placed candles on the railing of their covered front porch and pulled a thick reed mat out onto the wood deck. Thomas looked at her with raised eyebrows, uncertain what was happening. In reply she flashed an impish smile and signed for him to remove his clothing and lie face down on the mat.

When he was in position, she pulled off her linen dress and straddled his lower back. Then, slowly, gently, and lovingly she ladled a small amount of coconut oil onto her palms and began massaging his back and shoulders, first with her hands, and later with her breasts. The only sounds in the night air were of waves breaking on the coral reef outside the cove, the rustling of palms in the soft night wind, and the crackling of coals in the cook fire.

"How did she know how sore I was after today's spearfishing?" he wondered. Then he sighed, let his mind rest, and gave in to the magic.

September rolled into October, and with each sunrise Thomas awoke, looked at Keani sleeping quietly beside him on her side, and marveled at his good fortune. Life flowed through her calm and strong as the current around Moorea, even when she was sleeping. Sometimes he would lift the light sheet under which they slept so that he could take in the spectacular contours of her body the way he would examine a classical painting in a great museum. He loved the way her back curved down to the top of her buttocks, and how, from the back of her neck to the top of her ankles, her body flowed in perfect harmony.

One morning she turned her head on the pillow while he was drinking her in, and immediately understood what he was doing. But she only smiled softly and turned her head to go back to sleep. Despite her clear invitation to continue, Thomas lowered the sheet, and when his head went back down on his pillow, he felt his eyes moisten.

How could any woman love a man this much?

~ FORTY-THREE ~

Moorea, November

A boy from the village was waiting on the shore when Thomas pulled the canoe up onto the sand in a warm rain and unloaded the fish he had speared. Keani stepped out of the cabin with a piece of peppermint candy for the messenger, who popped it into his mouth and skipped happily along the surf line back towards Ha'apiti.

Thomas settled into a wicker chair on the porch and opened the sealed oilskin pouch the boy had delivered. Inside were several letters, the first he had received in months. They were addressed to Akoni at the Iolani Palace in Honolulu and took three weeks to arrive by schooner in Papeete, where they were delivered to Aubert before being handed off to a trusted friend to deliver to Thomas on Moorea.

He opened the first letter, which his editor Andrew Whitton at the *San Francisco Chronicle* had penned in early October. *"I'm well,"* Whitton wrote, *"but you won't be surprised to know that Colin Stafford has the long knives out for the paper. He has threatened, bribed, and cajoled most of the hotels, shops, and restaurants in town to stop advertising with us, and our delivery wagons have been vandalized a dozen or more times, but we're not giving up. Enough good people continue to buy the daily paper to keep us in ink and newsprint. Be well lad and come back to us as soon as you are able."*

The next letter was from Kam Sung Kwon, the owner of the *Rue de Paris* restaurant, whose niece had overheard Stafford's instructions to Fitch Donegan to go to Hawai'i and kill Thomas. Business was booming, said his diminutive friend, and we all look forward to your return to our tables, especially Mrs. Kwan.

The last–and most important— letter in the watertight pouch–was dated three weeks earlier. It came from the missionary leader Edward Grimthorpe, in whose care Thomas had left Taiana after he spirited her away from the leper colony on Moloka'i.

"The child is well, and often visits Princess Noelani at the palace," Grimthorpe wrote. *"She is being tutored in several subjects and shows a real head for learning."*

Thomas smiled and hoped that the news had made it to Taiana's parents at Kalawao. Leprosy would inevitably claim their lives, but knowing their daughter was safe and doing well might ease their suffering.

"The other information I must share will be, I am afraid, quite distressing for you, Thomas," continued the missionary. *"I have it on good authority from the prefect of police here in Honolulu that your plantation on Lana'i is to be seized by order of the court and its assets handed over to Wallace Stafford's bank."*

Thomas was so visibly startled that Keani sensed something awful had happened. She came over and sat on the arm of his chair and put her hand on his shoulder. In reply he simply handed her the first page of Grimthorpe's letter before turning to the next page. *"According to my police friend,"* the letter went on, *"your partner, William Fortnite, came to Honolulu just weeks after you left the islands and withdrew the entire $50,000 line of credit you secured for plantation operations. He also emptied the business accounts and then just vanished. Stafford sent people to Lana'i when Fortnite missed the first repayment that was due. They found that operations had come to a halt, and that only your foreman Kukane, and a handful of workers remained on the land. Hawaiian law allows the bank to begin foreclosure proceedings the day the second payment is late, which means that by the time you receive this letter your plantation will be in the hands of the courts. I am so very sorry to have to tell you this."*

Thomas took a drink of water and handed the second page of Grimthorpe's letter to Keani. Theft, foreclosure, ruin, he thought. If only he had known of this earlier; it would have been worth risking discovery by Donegan to return and fight for his plantation, and to deal with Fortnite.

Keani shared a worried glance with him, and it took all his inner strength to muster a half-reassuring smile before he returned to the final page of the letter.

"Sadly, there is more to report. Hawaiian courts are notoriously slow, and Akoni tells me that he is using all his personal influence to slow their hearings on your plantation even more. He believes that it will take at least five to six months for the foreclosure to wind its way to conclusion. If you can reconcile the account before then by paying the bank, ownership of the plantation will revert to you, though, unfortunately, to Fortnite, as well."

That was a serious load of trouble, Thomas thought, but perhaps not as grim as the missionary was suggesting. When he read on, he realized how wrong that optimistic assessment was.

"Stafford is not waiting for the courts, however," Grimthorpe wrote. *"My police friend tells me that he has assembled a group of toughs to come after you and collect the $50,000 by whatever means necessary."*

The next line sent a chill up Thomas' back. *"They know you fled to Tahiti, Thomas. Apparently, the leader of the men coming after you is some kind of Tahitian warrior with a personal vendetta against you. Do you know of such a person, and would he know how to find you?"*

Thomas cursed under his breath, *"Aata,"* he thought. It could be no one else. He looked across at Keani, who had just finished the second page of the missionary's letter and was waiting for the final page with worry etched across her face. "Damn, why did I share this with her before reading it all myself?" he thought. But having allowed her to read the first two pages there was no way he could hold back the last one.

"I love you," he signed to her as he handed the page over. "And I promise, everything is going to be alright."

Tears formed in her eyes as she read the last of Grimthorpe's letter. She dropped it to the ground and looked into Thomas' eyes with an expression of sadness and fear.

He stared down at the paper. *"I don't know how,"* he thought to himself. *"I just don't know."*

Then he raised his head and placed his hands gently on either side of his wife's face. "I promise," he said.

He went into the cabin and sat at the small desk beneath the painting Aubert had given them. He took out a piece of paper, an inkwell and pen, and quickly scribbled a note to the artist. Then he walked along the beach to the village and sought out two of the young men who had helped build his house and offered them the equivalent of two days good wages in Pape'ete to leave immediately for Papara, a three-hour sail across the channel.

"Wait for him, and bring him back with you," Thomas told the men as they climbed into the outrigger and pulled up the sail.

"And if he can't come with us?" one of the men asked.

"He will come," Thomas replied in a quiet voice.

An hour after sunset the outrigger dropped sail and slid up to the beach in front of Thomas and Keani's cabin. It was starting to rain as Aubert climbed the steps and joined Thomas, Keani, and Timothy Boswell on the covered porch. The artist grinned when he saw Keani was holding a bottle of wine and a glass for him.

"Thank you for coming, Émile," Thomas said. "I am sorry to break into your day like this."

The Frenchman downed the glass of red wine in a single gulp before taking a chair alongside his friends. Keani refilled his glass and hugged him before sitting down.

"Your note simply said you were in trouble," said Aubert. "What can I do?"

Thomas was pleased that his friend asked how he could help before he asked what kind of trouble he was in. He filled his own glass and told Aubert about the letter from Grimthorpe.

When he was done, Aubert nodded and looked across at Boswell. "Thomas somehow manages to step into more piles of steaming *merde* than any man I know," he began. He waited for the group to laugh and added, "I think we are going to have busy times ahead, my friends."

"Thomas and I have come up with an idea, a bit wild, but we believe it could work," Boswell said.

Aubert's eyes twinkled in the lamp light. "Wild? But your timing is perfect; I was telling Océane only this morning that our existence was becoming a bit mundane. Your wild plan may be just the antidote we need to escape our increasingly monotonous daily routine."

Thomas shook his head and smiled. No one who knew Aubert would describe the artist's life as dull. "You may have a change of heart when you hear us out, Émile, and I'm afraid Timothy may have chosen too mild a word to describe what we have in mind."

Aubert lit a cigar and looked out into the stormy night. "Whatever your plan may be, *mes bon amis*, I assure you they cannot be so extreme as to frighten me away."

Thomas looked across at Boswell, and then Keani. They both nodded for him to continue, and he pulled his chair a little closer to Aubert and began to speak.

"I am not the only one tonight who is in some degree of peril, Émile."

The artist looked puzzled.

"The bank wants my money and my hide, my partner has cheated me, and somewhere out there an Irish assassin bides his time until he can get me in his gun sight again."

Thomas saw Keani shiver at those words.

"But you also are in danger, my friend. As things are now, you risk seeing your life's work rot away in that cave without the world having the great opportunity–the great blessing–of seeing your work in person."

For the first time that evening Aubert's expression took on a serious cast. Thomas was right. He was at the peak of his artistic skill, and yet every work he completed ended up rolled up in tubes and stored away. That was not the life he wished for himself and Océane.

"And your proposal, your plan, will somehow remedy both of our dire situations?" Aubert finally asked. " 'Twould be *merveille* beyond my poor ability to describe if such a plan could be pulled off."

"How long would it take you to prepare a dozen of your finest paintings for shipping?" Boswell suddenly blurted out.

Aubert raised his hands in a questioning gesture. "My paintings are the plan?"

"Not exactly," Thomas answered. "But they are a very important part."

"I am all ears," said the artist.

Keani filled their glasses, and Thomas laid out the plan he and Boswell had concocted only a few hours earlier.

"I need to pay the bank if I am to save my plantation, my reputation, and quite possibly, my life. You need to have representation for your work, and to sell enough of them to justify your remaining here in the islands."

Aubert sat in silence for a moment. "And who do you propose would represent my work," he finally said. "Are there knowledgeable art professionals hereabouts that I have somehow not run into in the course of day-to-day living?"

Keani stood up and moved behind Thomas. She placed her hands on his shoulders and smiled.

"You?" Aubert thundered. "God's wounds, my friend, but you wouldn't even know which end of a hog's hairbrush to dip into the paint."

Thomas and Boswell laughed, but Keani appeared to have been stung by the artists' rebuke. Aubert took note of her discomfort. He stood and took her hand. "It's alright, my child. I am simply a bit dumbfounded by the idea."

Thomas set down his wine glass. "You are right that I don't know the first thing about selling art. But I can learn. It will take me nearly six weeks to travel to New York City, and…"

At the mention of New York, Aubert's face lit up. "New York! By the stars, my friends, New York. A gallery on every street corner, most of them hungry for new work. And better yet, the new Metropolitan Museum of Art is scheduled to open sometime late this year. It would be the perfect venue for my canvasses." He leaned over and slapped Thomas on the back. "The planets are aligned, good friends, I can feel it!" He threw back his head and laughed.

"Package my best canvasses for travel you say? Consider it done."

"There is more, Émile," Thomas said. "About the money…"

"I have a little set aside I can give you for travel," Aubert volunteered.

"No, I can manage those expenses myself," Thomas replied. "I mean the money we make from sales of your work."

"Ah," said Aubert. "What is your thinking?"

"My best hope would be to sell enough of your work to make a sizeable income for you, and, with my fees, for me to be able to pay enough to the bank that I will not lose my property on Lana'i."

Aubert took a moment to think it over. He was not concerned about sharing the money with Thomas, but he wanted to make sure he was sending enough paintings to be able to help his friend out.

"Two dozen," he finally said. "I will need to send two dozen paintings with you."

"Will I be able to carry that many?" Thomas asked.

Aubert chuckled. "Rolled tightly and wrapped in waterproofing we will end up with two rolls, each weighing less than 15 pounds. A child could carry them."

Boswell stood and raised his glass. When the others joined him, he said, "A toast, my friends, to a safe and profitable excursion into the world of fine art."

They tapped their glasses together under thickening clouds that heralded the arrival of a new storm.

Aubert felt exhilarated. After four years of complete isolation from the international art scene, he was going to have his work shopped around to the most important galleries in the Americas. He was about to burst into song when he saw that Keani's stoic façade was crumbling, and she was fighting to hold back tears. And why wouldn't she want to cry, he realized. Her idyllic existence had been shattered in a matter of a few hours by people and events she had no connection to; her future was being scattered to the four winds with each passing minute. He set down his wine and soberly contemplated the dangers the young colonel would face on his 6,000-mile journey to New York, and the obstacles that would confront him as he attempted to get the ossified snobs of the art world to give his work so much as a glance. *"At best, a profitable excursion,"* he thought. *"At worst, a descent into the fetid art world of confidence men, scalawags, and posers."* But when he caught Thomas' eye a moment later, he flashed a broad grin and lifted his glass to the sky.

"Que Dieu nous aide tous," he said cheerfully.

"May God help us, indeed," Thomas whispered as he looked into Keani's eyes.

~ FORTY-FOUR ~

It was just after first light when Captain McNab maneuvered the skiff across the reef and into the cove in front of Thomas and Keani's home. He and Océane pulled it onto dry sand and were greeted a moment later by Thomas, Aubert, and Boswell. Keani saw the boat arrive from her front window. Her eyes were puffy from crying, and she had not slept, but she knew how much her husband was going to need her strength today. She ran a brush through her hair and splashed cold water on her face before joining her friends on the beach, where she immediately pulled Océane aside for a private conversation.

"This is a bad business," McNab said to Thomas. "Awful."

Thomas nodded somberly in reply. "I am glad you have come; it seems I am in need of transportation to Honolulu, and beyond that, San Francisco."

The men walked up to the porch as they talked. "And for that, Thomas, I may have good news for you."

"The *Kai Douglas* is scheduled to sail soon?"

"Even better," replied McNab as he accepted a mug of coffee from Timothy Boswell, who had been scrounging up breakfast for everyone in the kitchen behind the cabin.

"The Chalmers Steamship Company has begun monthly passage from Australia to Hawaii and on to San Francisco, by way of Tahiti. Their *Island Maid* departs Papeete for Honolulu in three days."

The men took chairs on the porch and were soon joined by Keani and Océane.

"You're not returning to Hawai'i any time soon?" Thomas asked.

"Next week at the earliest," replied the captain, "though I don't know how much longer the *Kai* will be in business."

"And why would that be?" asked Aubert. "Are there not enough goods to transport to make your voyages profitable?"

"Aye, there be no lack of merchants with goods to fill the Kai's hold," said McNab. "It isn't for lack of cargo…it's all about time."

"I don't understand," said Boswell.

"The sail to Honolulu from here is 17 days, figuring, of course, fair winds and smooth seas," said McNab. "With her compound steam engine and auxiliary sails, *The Island Maid* will run at 15 knots and make the trip in just six days. She's 400 foot long, iron hulled, weighs 5,000 tons, and can carry 1,400 passengers and ten times the cargo of the *Kai.* The days of the wooden paddle-wheeler steamships are over, boys, and that goes for schooners, too…"

McNab's voice trailed off, and he looked out to sea. Then he pulled his shoulders back and shook his head. "But that is what they call progress, my friends, and damned if an old mariner like me can hold that juggernaut back."

Thomas leaned over and patted McNab on the back. "Thank you for coming."

"We best be getting ready to leave," said McNab. "The storm last night was just the tip of a bigger blow, and we don't want to be caught in the channel in the middle of a real squall."

"Can you take us to Papara so that I can wrap my canvasses for Thomas to take with him?" asked Aubert.

"Of course," McNab replied, "and I'll stay the night. In the morning I'll coast Thomas up to Pape'ete to buy his passage to Hawai'i and on to San Francisco. The Chalmers agent says the *Maid* will berth in Honolulu for two days; plenty of time for our boy to meet with Akoni to sort things out."

Boswell and Keani appeared from the kitchen with platters of eggs, ham, fresh bread, and fruit and ladled food onto plates for everyone. They ate silently, each deep in their own thoughts. Thomas waited for everyone to finish and Boswell and Océane to collect the breakfast dishes before he spoke again.

"This is all happening so fast," he said to the group, "and I can't thank you all for everything you are doing. I will be in your debts forever."

"Hah!" exclaimed Aubert. "Sell my paintings in New York and we'll never need to speak of debt again!"

Boswell handed Thomas a sheet of paper. "Bring back the natural history books on this list, and I, too, shall scrub the word 'debt' from my vocabulary."

"I will ask you to visit my brother in St. Louis with a letter from me," said McNab. "That's all the thanks I require."

Thomas was overwhelmed. When he turned his head to Keani, she smiled softly and made a series of short signs. "Come home to me, and I will never ask anything of you again."

An hour later the group assembled at the water's edge. Aubert loaded Thomas' bags into the skiff and clambered in beside McNab and Océane. Thomas pushed the little boat out until it sat in three feet of water, and then sloshed back up to the beach to Keani.

"I don't know what to say," he began. "But I promise I will come back to you."

She put her hand on his mouth and shook her head. "There are just two things you need to know," she signed.

"Yes?"

"The first is that I have loved you since the day you appeared in my brother's village."

"And the second?"

She kissed him deeply and held him tight. Then she took three steps back and lifted her hands to sign again.

"I am going to have your baby."

With that she clapped her hand over her mouth, turned, and raced up to the porch.

Thomas was dumbstruck. His feet became lead weights, and he did not hear McNab calling for him to get into the boat. A moment later Océane left the skiff and came up beside him. She took his hand and said, "There is no time, Thomas."

Above them, thunderclaps echoed from the base of the thick grey clouds, and the wind picked up and grew chilly.

"But she is pregnant. We are going to have a child," he whispered.

Océane tugged at his hand. "I know, Thomas. All the more reason to get this business settled quickly."

Thomas felt numb as he climbed into the skiff and took his seat beside Aubert. McNab raised the sail, and they began to move slowly towards the mouth of the cove and the roiling waves beyond the reef.

Thomas fixed his gaze on the cabin until it was just a speck on the horizon. The last thing he was able to make out before the sea swallowed them up was Keani clasping her hands protectively across her belly.

That was her promise to him.

~ FORTY-FIVE ~

At the equator

The *Island Maid* was the largest iron structure Thomas had ever set eyes on, so big that it took nearly ten minutes to navigate the ship from bow to stern. He walked her length three times a day, carefully weaving around steam funnels, auxiliary masts, capstans, deck cabins, and the assorted crates and machine parts that were lashed to the deck. Sharing the passenger freighter with him were 85 first class passengers, 200 second class travelers, and 800 steerage class passengers, most hailing from China or Japan and on their way to Hawai'i or California to seek work. According to the First Officer with whom he had struck up an acquaintance, many of the workers had their $150 tickets paid for by their future employers.

The ship made easy business of the waves and currents, and Thomas was amused to learn that while all the officers were either American or European, all the crew were Chinese. Of course, none of the sailors spoke English, and none of the officers was conversant in Chinese. They communicated with a crude style of sign language that Thomas was sure missed the mark in nearly every exchange between officers and crew.

On the voyages from San Francisco to China and Australia the holds were filled with staple foods and grains along with molasses, guns, leather goods, furniture, whiskey, and all manner of hardware. On the return trip to the States, he had been told, the ship was packed with tea, silk, sugar, rice, hemp, spices, and several tons of raw opium sap.

"Don't be surprised about the opium," said Thomas'

portly dinner companion on the second night of the voyage. "I am a representative of the Merck Pharmaceutical company, founded in Germany in 1688, and I am personally overseeing the delivery of this syrup to our warehouse. In a month it will be transformed into a host of miraculous patent medicines designed to ease the burdens of every member of today's busy household."

"Every member?" asked Thomas as he reached for another pour of the indifferent burgundy the steward had placed before him. "Even children?"

"Yes, of course," said the opium drummer. "Do you have children, sir?"

Thomas shook his head, and a wave of loneliness engulfed him when he thought of Keani standing on the porch with her hands resting on her belly.

"Then let me tell you that should the blessed day come that you have a child, you will forever be grateful to my company. One of our most popular products is *Mrs. Winslow's Soothing Syrup*. It is a remarkable elixir that calms the little rascals, freshens their breath, cleans their teeth, and even relieves constipation. As for its benefits to the mistress of the house, well sir, three tablespoons of *Mrs. Winslow* per day and your wife will be the very model of a meek and submissive spouse. Your every wish will be her command, and you will seldom find a need to apply a leather backstrap to her petticoated backside!" The salesman slurped at his wine and laughed at his own joke.

Thomas could not repress his own laugh as he envisioned Keani standing tall and strong and commanding in the bow of their outrigger preparing to spear a 20-pound reef fish. As for flogging her backside for disobedience, the idea of anyone—especially someone like the rotund drug representative—trying to take a strap to Keani made him laugh even harder. God pity the man who tried.

The food was bland and the wine second-rate, but conversation with most of his fellow first-class passengers was lively, and by the second evening a group of men had organized a poker game that proved to be a pleasant distraction from Thomas' growing list of worries.

Stored in the small cupboard in his stateroom were Aubert's two dozen paintings, rolled, wrapped and double-sealed against moisture. The artist had shown him each step in the wrapping process, and more importantly, walked him though exactly how to unseal and unroll the paintings. Each was rolled with the painted side out, which surprised Thomas, but which Aubert assured him was the only way to maintain the integrity of the paint. Aubert also spent half a day showing him how to fashion and apply stretcher bars to each canvas. The corner joints on the artist's stretchers were not glued or fastened in any permanent way, which Thomas found fascinating. This would allow the canvas to be re-tensioned later, the artist explained, as it has a natural tendency to stretch and sag over time "You won't be doing this part, of course," said Aubert, "it is the gallery's responsibility to stretch and frame each canvas. However, you do need to know how it should be done to ensure the galleries do not cut corners."

For his part in Thomas' whirlwind education about the art world, McNab explained that the letter for his brother in St. Louis would let him know why Thomas needed a more in-depth understanding of everything about the business of fine art, from selecting works to currying favor with important newspaper critics. "My brother is a serious art collector," said McNab, "and he knows the major dealers and critics in New York City. Despite the money and power and influence they wield; he will tell you that the typical wealthy dealer or pompous critic is little more than a pile of shit in a silk stocking."

Aubert chuckled. "And now you understand why I have chosen to remain here in paradise, Thomas, where no one I have met wears silk stockings."

On the night before their arrival in Honolulu, Thomas spent several hours writing a long letter to Keani. "In the event I am unable to return to you," the letter began. He went on to thank her for opening a new world to him and assured her that she and their child would never lack for people to care for them; from Aubert and Océane to Boswell,

McNab, and even Akoni—whom she had yet to meet—good people would stand beside her no matter what path she chose to travel.

As of his departure from Tahiti five days earlier, Donegan had not set foot on the island. Whatever the reason for his delay, Thomas had to make sure that the assassin stayed in Hawai'i until this business with Colin Stafford was settled. One of his first orders of business when he got to Honolulu, then, would be to see that Akoni got word to Fitch Donegan at the Pearl that Thomas had left Tahiti, perhaps for Australia. The source would have to be persuasive and credible. If Donegan believed he was being misled, it would only increase his fury and quite possibly endanger Keani.

Thomas knew that Aubert and McNab's counsel to lie low while he waited for the *Island Maid* to depart for San Francisco was the best course of action, and yet he longed to pay visits to both banker Stafford and Donegan. He was certain he could work out a financial arrangement with the banker, and equally certain that the only way to finally stop Donegan would be to kill the man. Thomas felt neither troubled nor morally compromised by that decision. In any event, he knew that Donegan was thinking the same thing.

He glanced in the mirror above his stateroom dresser and wondered what kind of man he was becoming. Then he shrugged inwardly, adjusted his tie, and left his cabin to have a drink before his last shipboard dinner on the Tahiti to Hawai'i leg of the journey.

Constables and courts from Hawaii to California were already looking for him, he reminded himself as he walked along the open-air corridor and breathed in the salt spray splashing off the *Maid's* bow as she sliced through the deep blue water. Killing Donegan before the business with the bank was cleared up would only put more searchers on his trail and complicate his return to Keani on Moorea.

As he stepped through the double French doors and into the brightly lit first-class dining room, he made up his mind; he would let Fitch Donegan live a little while longer.

❋

~ FORTY-SIX ~

Honolulu, November

The *Island Maid* dropped anchor a half mile outside Honolulu Harbor because there were no docks large enough to accommodate her massive length, and, in any event, the harbor had not been dredged to a depth sufficient to handle her keel. Two flat barges steamed out to offload cargo, and the captain of the Maid ordered the ship's two launches to be winched over the side to begin ferrying passengers to shore. First and second-class passengers who would be going on to San Francisco were allowed to debark to relax in town, but the only steerage passengers who were allowed to leave were those who would be staying in the islands to work. The rest would have to wait onboard for two days while the Maid took on additional cargo, provisions, and coal.

The night before the ship docked, Thomas paid a visit to the second officer's cabin. He carried a bottle of McNab's Cognac *Frapin* and a crisp $50 bill to give the man to see that Thomas' luggage and Aubert's rolled up paintings would be delivered to the home of his friend, the fisherman Henry Kakaakao, and that every record of Thomas' presence on the *Maid* would be erased. The officer happily accepted the gifts, and assured Thomas that his wishes would be followed.

The next morning, an hour before they reached O'ahu Thomas climbed down three flights of metal stairs to the crowded steerage deck. It was packed with Chinese and Japanese laborers and their families anxious to reach their destinations and begin their new lives.

He wandered through several huge compartments that held 100 or more people until he found a man about his height and build. Using crude sign language, Thomas offered the astonished man $20 to trade clothing with him, from his floppy hat to his open-toed sandals. Given that Thomas' clothing was finely tailored quality and the Chinese laborer's were tattered and threadbare, his offer was accepted without hesitation. Thomas put on the man's clothing and pulled the stained, loose-fitting hat low on his brow. Then he crouched in a corner of the compartment and waited an hour until the crew announced they were ready to deboard passengers who had jobs in Hawaii'. His fellow steerage travelers paid the American eccentric no mind; where they were from it was never a good idea to pry into the affairs of anyone with more money or status than you. Whatever the American's game was, they wanted no part of it.

As he melted into the throng heading up the stairs to board the waiting launch, Thomas kept the hat pulled down below his eyes. He carefully watched the feet of the people around him to avoid tripping, and he had to grab the hem of the passenger's shirt in front of him several times to avoid falling.

The ocean swells were light, and he easily climbed down the narrow stairs affixed to the side of the ship to the launch platform. When the next boat arrived, he and 40 other passengers stepped over the gunwales and dropped onto the hard wooden benches for the ten-minute ride into the harbor. The boat passed the rock jetty, pulled alongside a floating dock, and the passengers climbed out. Just like that, he was back in Honolulu. No immigration officials, no harbor agents, and, as far as he could tell, no watchers sent by Donegan to report on who was coming and going from the island. Even so, he kept his hat pulled low and walked with a stoop until he was off the dock and onto the hard-packed red dirt road that wound up to Henry's home.

"Good lord, is that you, Thomas?" said Henry when he answered the door. Thomas grinned and embraced the giant fisherman.

"Your luggage arrived a half hour ago, no note, no message from the man who delivered it." Henry took a step back and examined his friend. "I must say that you could do with a wardrobe upgrade."

Thomas gave Henry's son a pat on the back before replying. "You are the only person who knows I am on the island. I will be here for two days and then leave on the *Island Maid* for San Francisco. I hope you don't mind me bunking with you until then."

Henry pulled a bottle of rum from the shelf and poured two glasses. He toasted Thomas, and said, "You are always a welcome guest in my home. Now sit, tell me why you have come, and what I can do for you."

"Let me first ask a favor, and then I will tell you everything. Could you go to the palace and tell Akoni that I am here?"

"Just that?"

"Just that. My story will take a while, and it would be best for the two of you to hear it at the same time."

Henry stood and walked to the door. Before he stepped out, he turned and said, "It is good to see you, my friend. Some were saying that you were dead."

Thomas smiled. "I have heard the same thing more than a few times these past few months."

"Keep an eye on my boy," said Henry with a wave. Thomas watched the fisherman disappear up the road towards Iolani Palace before he went over to his luggage for a clean change of clothes. He could be wrong, but since he put the Chinese clothing on a few hours ago he had the distinct feeling that he was sharing them with a few small, itchy friends.

An hour later Henry returned. Akoni was with him, and to Thomas' surprise, so was Taiana. They crowded into Henry's small living room and took chairs around the table.

Akoni could not stop grinning. "Had you arrived two days from now I would be off island onboard an Australian frigate. They are carrying a scientific team looking at plants that are reputed to possess strong healing qualities and were kind enough to invite me along."

"Your sister is well?" asked Thomas.

"She is, and she sends her respects, and her personal emissary."

"That would be you?" Thomas asked Taiana.

"I am almost 15," the girl answered with a touch of indignation. "Old enough to be an emissary or anything else I want to be."

The men laughed. "How about we don't go down that path," said Thomas, remembering the emotionally charged conversations he and Akoni had with Taiana when they took her away from the leper colony on Moloka'i.

Taiana allowed herself a smile and reached across the table to squeeze Thomas' hand. "I'm sorry. I really am glad you have come back. Please tell me that you will be staying this time."

He shook his head. "That I cannot do. But, let me tell you where I have been these past five months, and why it is so important to each of you that my presence here not be shared outside this room."

Henry poured the men a glass of rum and set his boy on the floor with a piece of hard candy and a toy. Taiana went to the kitchen and prepared a cup of tea, and, when she returned, Thomas began his story.

He detailed his voyage to Tahiti, the friends he made, and the enemies. The table went quiet when he described meeting and later marrying Keani, building their house, and fighting both Aata and the warriors he sent to kill Thomas. At the mention of Donegan's name, Akoni slammed his glass on the table. "I should have dealt with that bastard long ago, Thomas. Damn me for a fool."

"It would have done no good," Thomas answered. "Colin Stafford would only have sent more men to finish the job. No, the only way to end this is for me to resolve the issue directly with him in San Francisco."

"And that's why you are going there in two days?" asked Henry.

Taiana gasped and covered her mouth; tears welled in her eyes. Thomas was leaving. Again.

Thomas took note of her sorrow but continued with his story. "That is only part of the reason I am going." He went on to describe the plan he had come up with to take Aubert's paintings to New York City, sell them, and pay off the Hawaiian bank that was chasing him. Then he could deal with Stafford.

Akoni nodded. The plan made sense.

Now Thomas turned to Taiana. "I promised your parents I would look after you. It was never my intention that you should remain forever here in Hawai'i, however. So, I want you to come to California with me. While I travel to New York, you will stay at the home of my friend, John Hayden, who I served with in the war. He is a good man, with a prosperous business and a good family. When I return, we will work out a more permanent situation for you, including school."

Taiana lit up. California! She had never dreamed that big. She turned to Akoni. "Is that even possible?" she asked.

"Are you certain you wish to invite that kind of trouble, my friend?" Akoni said to Thomas with feigned shock. "In case you don't remember, she can be a rather troublesome young thing."

Taiana reached across the table and pretended to slap Akoni on the cheek.

"I think I can manage," Thomas said, "though I do want Noelani's blessing. Would you present my idea to her tonight? I will need to purchase one more ticket on the *Island Maid*, and Taiana would have to meet me on the docks an hour before sailing."

Akoni seemed deep in thought, and it took a minute for him to reply. "Yes, I will speak with my sister, and I will purchase the girl's ticket so that you don't have to risk being seen by Donegan or your banker."

"We're agreed then," said Thomas. "Taiana will come with me to California."

It was nearly dark when Akoni and Taiana left Henry's house to return to the palace.

"A married man," said Akoni as he shook Thomas' hand goodbye. "I never thought the world would see the day that Colonel Thomas Scoundrel settled down. Many's the young lass who will be crying in her champagne, and many's the father who will be thanking the saints that he can breathe easy because you won't be crawling through his daughter's bedroom window."

"To be clear, I never actually crawled through," said Thomas with a chuckle. "I almost always came through the door."

Henry and Akoni laughed, and Taiana pretended not to hear, though she could not suppress a smile at the picture forming in her mind's eye.

Thomas hugged her. "Until Wednesday morning," he said. "And do try to pack only what you need."

Taiana kissed him on the cheek and walked out into the yard.

"I can never thank you for everything you have done for me," Thomas said to Akoni, "and that goes for your sister, as well. I promise I will come back to the islands one day, my friend."

"Na ke Akua e hoʻopōmaikaʻi iā ʻoe a mālama iā ʻoe," replied Akoni. "As your Hawaiian isn't all that good, it means, may God bless you and keep you safe."

Thomas felt his eyes mist. He started to take Akoni's hand, and then changed his mind and hugged him instead. The giant Hawaiian grinned, and he and Taiana stepped over Henry's low fence and onto the road that led to the palace.

Thomas arrived at the dock on a cool and overcast morning an hour after sunrise. Henry and his son pulled his luggage along on a hand-drawn cart, and when Thomas said goodbye to the fisherman, he pressed a sealed envelope into the man's hands.

"You should know better by now than to turn down my gift, Henry," Thomas said. "Use it for your son."

Henry tapped the envelope against his forehead. "I won't be saying goodbye, my friend. Only, *a hui hou kakou*…until we meet again."

Thomas shook Henry's hand, gave his son a hug, and watched them disappear into the crowd of people coming to re-board the ship.

A few minutes later Akoni and Taiana appeared with a worker from the palace who was pulling two oversized steamer trunks on a cart. '*She does not travel lightly,*' Thomas thought.

Both of the *Island Maid's* launches were nearing the dock as they joined Thomas. Akoni greeted Thomas and handed him a small leather pouch.

"What's this?"

"Open it," replied Akoni.

Thomas unfastened the pouch and gazed at the thick wad of bills inside.

"Money?" he asked. "From where-from whom?"

Akoni grinned. "Yesterday the King's Principal Personal Secretary paid a visit to the office of the United States Counsel. He carried with him a letter that he typed and upon which I forged your signature."

Thomas' eyebrows shot up.

"The letter-from you-asked that your unpaid Army pension for the past six months be handed over to the Secretary to satisfy certain debts you owe to the Kingdom. A lie of course, but a counselor official does not turn down a request that appeared to have come from the King himself, especially when the Secretary suggested the money was to repay a gambling debt to His Highness. I can tell you from personal experience that on more than one occasion the American Counsel has found himself owing a little money to his Majesty after a high stakes card game."

Thomas was overwhelmed. His funds were getting low, and he hoped to be able to collect his overdue pension at some point, but he did not expect to be able to do that in the two short days he had on O'ahu.

"I'm running out of ways to say thank you," he said to Akoni. "And, I think I've had enough surprises these past few months to last a lifetime."

The sun was burning through the thick gray clouds, and Taiana opened her parasol. "You may want to reconsider those words, Thomas," she said with an impish smile. "I'm afraid the surprises have just begun."

"And how is that?" he asked.

Taiana laughed and pointed to Akoni, who was directing a ship's crew member in loading the steamer trunks onto the launch. "He'll tell you," she said.

"I'll tell you what?" asked Akoni as he rejoined them. "Ah, I see, you haven't told him, have you."

Taiana shook her head.

"Well, here's the thing, my friend, "Akoni said. "You have a way of getting yourself buried under more stinking piles of manure than any man we have ever met. Isn't that right, girl?"

Taiana put her hand over her mouth to suppress a laugh.

"Not saying it's always your fault, of course," continued Akoni. "I know that your life gets complicated. That being the case, and me having some business to take care of at the Natural History Museum in Washington D.C., I decided that I would come along with you. Keep a weather eye out, knock down the odd troublemaker, that sort of thing."

Thomas was dumbfounded. The idea that anyone, let alone the nephew of the monarch of Hawai'i, would step away from his personal and public duties to accompany him on what could end up being a complete fool's errand, was beyond his comprehension. He didn't know what to say.

Akoni solved his friend's dilemma. "The launch is ready. What say we go to California this morning?"

Taiana stepped between Thomas and Akoni and took their arms. "I think that's a perfect idea," she said, and they walked towards the deep green water under the warming sky.

Honolulu

Two days after the *Island Maid* departed for San Francisco, Fitch Donegan was seated in his regular evening booth at the Pearl. Across from him sat a small cross-eyed weasel of a man, an informant who, until today, had proven to be a reliable snitch.

The weasel was squirming in his seat, not an unreasonable behavior for one who fully expected his throat to be cut before sunset. Donegan, however, was in an unusually magnanimous mood, perhaps due to the exhilarating romp he'd just enjoyed with the dark-skinned Māori twin sisters who had recently joined his stable. He sat back in his seat, his elbows on the table and his fingers open and pressed together.

"You assured me that he wasn't on the Tahiti steamer," Donegan said in a matter-of-fact voice.

"Our people in Tahiti watched every passenger go aboard," the weasel said. "And I was on the dock as each of the first and second-class launches came in. Colonel Scoundrel was not on them. I am sure of that."

"And the launches that brought the coolie laborers ashore, did you also inspect them?"

"The coolies? No, but why would I? He would not have been traveling in steerage. The man is famous for his expensive tastes."

"No, of course not. What sense would that make, unless he wanted to use the cover of those ragged peasants to sneak in right under your nose."

The weasel had no answer. He stared at the table, trying to

prepare himself for the razor-sharp blade that would soon sever his carotid artery and send blood spewing around the alley behind the building.

Donegan poured a shot of whiskey into the informant's glass. "Perhaps you can redeem yourself, a little. At least tell me what you have learned about the girl."

The weasel's head perked up. Redeem? That was a good thing, wasn't it? He gulped down his drink and wiped a hand across his mouth.

"The Grimthorpe woman is telling friends that the girl went back to her family on Lana'i the same morning the *Island Maid* left for California. Problem is, she ain't got family on Lana'i, and there were no coasters or schooners out of Honolulu for the island that morning."

"You're certain of that?"

"Damn straight," replied the weasel. "The Grimthorpe's cook has a daughter who is addicted to opium. Spends all her time in one of them little cubbies in the back of the Chinese laundry smoking the stuff, when she can get the money, that is. She's uglier than a sea monkey's pustule-covered arse, so she can't make any money renting out her twat. So, she does what she can, including listening in on the kinds of conversations that poor folks should keep their noses out of, and selling anything juicy she hears."

"And that's how she learned about the girl?"

The weasel nodded and slid his glass across the table. Hell, it didn't hurt to ask.

Donegan filled up the glass and motioned for the man to go on.

"I knew you was keeping an eye on the girl since you learned that Colonel Scoundrel had dropped her off there to work as a housemaid. I have been paying the cook's daughter a buck here and a buck there to give me any news she heard about the kid. This morning she looked me up at my, uh, my home and said she had important news."

"Yes, your home," Donegan thought, *"a rented room behind a livery stable. Quite the abode."*

"So, she shows up this morning and says she's got the goods now, only it'll cost me two dollars. The bitch wouldn't so much as give me a hint, so I agreed, if'n that was, she included a little tug job in the deal."

"You said she was ugly as a what?" Donegan asked with a smile.

"In my world it's any port in a storm, Mr. Donegan," answered the informant. "Anyway, I paid her, and she tugged me, and then she spilled."

"Well?"

The weasel bit his lip and prepared for the worst. "The girl packed up everything she owned and met two men on the docks the morning the *Island Maid* pulled out for San Francisco. I talked to a stevedore who remembers seeing them get into a launch."

"But you yourself were not at the dock? Wasn't that your job?"

"I saw the *Maid's* 2nd officer in the bar at the Palace Hotel the night before they sailed," said the informant. "Bought him a drink, even offered to get him a deal on a whore here in exchange for a little information. He said there weren't no one by Scoundrel's name or matching his description coming out of Tahiti, and not on the manifest for San Francisco, neither. There was no point in me going to the docks."

Donegan sighed and leaned back in the booth. "The colonel got to the 2nd officer ahead of you. Putting that aside for now, what did the two men with the girl look like?"

"One was a big Hawaiian, mountain of a man. The other..." the weasel hesitated. The next words he spoke would likely be his last on earth. "The other was a tall American, lean fellow with sandy hair who looked like he spends a lot of time outdoors."

"Colonel...Thomas... Scoundrel," Donegan said.

The weasel said nothing. He had failed, and in Donegan's world there was only one penalty for failure. To his surprise—and relief—Donegan continued the conversation.

"When does the next steamer leave for San Francisco?"

"Two weeks, end of the first week of December."

"And the transit time?"

"Nine to ten days, depending on the weather."

"So, Scoundrel has a nearly three-week lead on me," Donegan said. "And I have no idea about his ultimate destination."

"It ain't San Francisco?" asked the weasel.

Donegan thought about Colin Stafford's network of watchers and laughed.

"Someone must know where he is going," Donegan finally said.

"His people in Tahiti?"

"Perhaps, but if I have to travel there first, he will be a good two months ahead of me. No, someone here on the island knows."

The informant was silent. It was a longshot, but he had to suggest something that would save his neck.

"I know someone who would be able to give you that information, Mr. Donegan."

Donegan raised his glass and took a long sip. "Yes?" His eyes bored into the weasel's head.

The informant gulped and took the chance. "That gal from the opium den? She told me that the girl who is with Scoundrel shared everything with the Grimthorpes. She had no secrets."

Fitch Donegan did not normally approve of floral pattern wallpaper. When he redecorated the Pearl he used solid patterns, sometimes with flocked or brushed surfaces. He thought they added a bit of class to the place.

But, as he sat in the parlor of the Grimthorpe's three-story home in the center of Honolulu, he had to admit that the mistress of the household had chosen well. The color and style worked well with the dark walnut furniture, and even played off the fresh flowers in the vase on the small table in the center of the room.

He would have complimented Mrs. Grimthorpe on her decorating abilities, but he doubted she would be able to reply. She and her husband were tied, bound, and gagged on two hard backed dining chairs, facing one another about five feet apart. Mr. Grimthorpe's left eye was swollen almost shut, and a trickle of blood from the nostril that had been sliced open flowed down his upper lip and onto his chin before dribbling onto his shirt. His wife's right cheek was bright red from being repeatedly slapped, and her dress and undergarments had been ripped from her throat to her waist, exposing her breasts, one of which bore a burn mark from Donegan's cigar. Fitch had to acknowledge that for a woman in her 40s she was pretty well put together, or had been before tonight. Even with her bruises and burns she still looked good enough to diddle, and Donegan allowed as to how he might have to dip in a bit before the night was over.

He stood and walked to the sideboard, where he refilled his glass with the excellent port the Grimthorpes kept in a large crystal decanter.

"I am always impressed by how well you professional Christians live, no matter where in the uncivilized world you may be," he said. "Good to see how lucrative it can be to do the Lord's business."

Mr. Grimthorpe grunted and shifted in his chair. His wife lowered her head to her chest and began to sob until her gag started to fill with spit and made her fear she was going to choke.

"Let's get down to business," Donegan said. "I'm sure you wonder why I am here, and why I gave you a little taste of what's ahead for you both if you don't cooperate fully with my requests. Do you understand?"

Mrs. Grimthorpe nodded, but her husband remained stoic and did not so much as blink an eye.

Donegan lifted his knife from the corner of the table and walked over behind Grimthorpe. He grabbed the missionary leader's left ear firmly with one hand, and, with a single slashing motion, cut most of it off and tossed the bloody flesh on the floor in front of Mrs. Grimthorpe, who recoiled at the sight and nearly toppled over.

Her husband groaned and struggled harder against the rope that bound him to the chair.

"Now that's what I'm talking about," Donegan said in a friendly tone. "When I say something or ask a question you will respond without hesitation. Is that understood?"

Mrs. Grimthorpe nodded immediately, and her husband did the same.

"Good, then we understand one another," said Donegan. He went to the sideboard and refilled his glass. Then he pulled a chair next to Mrs. Grimthorpe and began to caress her exposed breasts. She threw her head back and held her breath, and Donegan was amused to see the anger flashing in her husband's eyes.

"Them's some nice titties your wife's sportin," Donegan said. "When's the last time you paid them proper attention?"

Without waiting for Grimthorpe to grunt or shake his head, Donegan lowered his head to Mrs. Grimthorpe's chest and began to slurp at each breast. When he was finished, he raised his head and kissed her on the cheek.

"It's been fun," he said, "but now it's time for you to tell me everything about, what was her name? Oh, yes, Taiana. I want to know where she is going, who she is with, and what their plans are. Everything. Tell it all to me and we can call it a night and I will leave you to your own business."

Grimthorpe's eyes told Donegan that the missionary wasn't buying the part about leaving them alone. Of course, the pink-skinned, fleshy preacher was right, but Donegan had to give them some hope that they would still be alive when the sun rose over the mountains that encircled Honolulu.

He leaned forward and ripped the gag from Mrs. Grimthorpe's mouth. She coughed once and spit out a mouthful of blood mixed with mucous.

"You ready, darlin?" asked Donegan. "Let's have it."

"You are an evil man, and God will strike you down," she said in a trembling voice.

"And on both counts you are correct," said Donegan. "But my eternal fate wasn't the question, was it. And there is a penalty for not answering."

He went over to Grimthorpe and used his knife to cut the man's dress shirt down to his lower belly. Then he stuck his knife a half inch into the missionary's flesh just above the sternum and slowly pulled the blade down to his navel. Grimthorpe arched his back and shrieked into his gag. Tears flowed down his face, and he began to shake.

"That, little lady," Donegan said to Mrs. Grimthorpe, "was because you defied me. His blood is on you. Pull that shit again and I'll take out both his eyes. Any part of that you don't understand?"

She replied with a look of hatred and fear. Good, Donegan thought. She understands.

"Now before I ask one more time, I think I'll get me a look-see under them petticoats," he said. He finished his port, pulled his chair close in front of her and thrust her legs apart. Then he reached up under her dress to the top of her petticoat and ripped it down to her ankles before pulling her dress up around her waist.

"Now ain't that just the prettiest little quim," Donegan whispered as he held her legs apart with his hands on her knees. "Just about perfect." He reached one hand forward and thrust his fingers inside her. "Oh, yes, I'll be paying you a visit pretty soon."

Then he went over to her husband and grabbed the hair on the back of his head. "Steady, boy," said Donegan as he ran the fingers that had violated the missionary's wife back and forth under the man's nose. "Smell familiar?"

Donegan laughed and went for a refill of the port. "I expect you're ready to sing," he said to Mrs. Grimthorpe. "Let's have it all."

She felt a glimmer of hope, tiny but still a glimmer, that this beast would let them go if she complied. "She is going to San Francisco with Colonel Scoundrel, and from there to stay with a friend of his in a place near Los Angeles called San Pedro. I do not know the friend's name."

Donegan searched her face. She was telling the truth—so far. "And who is the man traveling with them? The big fellow."

She had to take a deep breathe to control her sobbing before she continued. "That I do not know. Taiana did not tell me. I'm not sure she knew."

Again, the woman was being truthful.

"And what about Scoundrel. Where is he going after he leaves the girl in San Pedro?"

Mrs. Grimthorpe looked across at her husband. "Please, please, let me tend to my husband first and then I will tell you everything else I know."

Donegan leaned over and held the point of his knife against Grimthorpe's throat. "That ain't part of the deal. Now talk."

She lowered her head, and said, "Taiana says he is going to New York City. Something about taking some paintings to a new museum that is opening in late December."

Mrs. Grimthorpe raised her head and said, "That is everything I know. As God is my witness, that is everything."

Donegan regarded her general countenance and thought about what he had just been told. San Pedro. New York City. Artwork. The woman could not have been making any of it up.

He reached out and gently caressed her cheek. "You know what, darlin? I believe you. Don't you feel unburdened now for telling the truth?"

"So, you are going to leave us alone now?" she asked hopefully.

"I am going to unburden you both, that's what I'm going to do," he replied as he re-tied her gag. Then he stepped behind her husband, cupped the missionary's chin in his palm, and ran his blade across the man's throat.

The seam of bright red blood that appeared along the knife's path became a gushing torrent when Donegan released Grimthorpe's head and let it fall to his chest.

Mrs. Grimthorpe tried to scream through her gag as blood streamed down her husband's chest and poured onto the carpet. Donegan didn't care. He had everything he needed to find Scoundrel. He would have to leave his beloved Pearl for a few months, but his barman had proven to be a competent manager and would be able to handle things until he returned. Right now, he was surrounded by everything he desired most in life; blood, death, and the promise of a level of pleasure he only experienced when he took a woman by force.

He turned Mrs. Grimthorpe's chair around so she would not have to look at her dying husband. He wasn't an animal, after all, he thought as he stood in front of her and unbuttoned his trousers. Then he pulled her gag out and said, "Do this properly, and everything else I ask you to do, or you will be joining your husband. Do you understand?"

He watched the terror flash in her eyes as he thrust his hardness between her lips and into her mouth.

Fitch Donegan could not imagine having a more perfect day.

~ FORTY-EIGHT ~

San Pedro, California, November 1872

Thomas and John Hayden walked along the mud flats below Timm's Point, where Hayden had built a fine two-story clapboard house overlooking the natural harbor. Thomas was hard-pressed to understand how San Pedro had become the most important port on the Pacific Coast. Because of shallow water and extensive tracts of mud, ships had to drop anchor a mile offshore and transfer passengers and cargo on barges and small boats. And yet, he counted at least six ships at anchor outside the breakwater, just past Dead Man's Island and Rattlesnake Island.

"It actually makes sense," Hayden was saying as they walked along the shore. "Congress has authorized the construction of a larger breakwater, and they're going to dredge the harbor so ships can tie up along the wharfs you can see are now being built. But the most important part of the picture is that the Southern Pacific Railroad just completed their line to Los Angeles, and they purchased the little Los Angeles and San Pedro railroads last month. We are now connected to every part of the nation."

"Doesn't Los Angeles have only about 5,000 inhabitants?" asked Thomas. "New York City has nearly one and a half million….so why are investors throwing money into this little pueblo?"

Hayden chuckled and threw a pebble into the muddy saltwater. "For one thing, this is a perfect place to build a large port. The weather is spectacular, we are only a few hours from the most fertile soil in the world, there are all manner of valuable minerals for the taking, a large pool of workers is available, and new people still arrive from around the world every day to seek their fortune in the gold fields."

"So, what does this all mean for your import-export business?"

"I'll be honest," Hayden replied. "Until the announcement of the railroad coming, I was struggling, and not sure I was going to survive. I was paying freight wagon companies $13 a ton to haul dry freight down here to barge out to ships headed west, and that was killing me. As of last November, and the completion of the railroad spur right over there," he pointed to where a locomotive and six freight cars were parked just a quarter mile away, "I pay just $6 per ton."

"So, things are better?"

"Better than better," said Hayden with a wide smile. "I'm expanding operations, building a new warehouse, and I have hired seven more people. As of today, I am the largest operation on the harbor."

Thomas patted Hayden on the back. "You've earned it, John. And thank you for taking us in on such short notice. When I telegraphed from Stearns Landing in Santa Barbara that we were headed your way I had no idea what kind of situation you might be in."

Hayden pointed to a trail from the flats that wound up a low hill to a cluster of buildings. "There's one decent saloon in these parts," he said. "Let's get a beer and something to eat."

When they settled into the wood frame, high-ceilinged saloon Thomas was finally able to pull off his jacket. The weather here was at least 30 degrees colder than what he had grown used to in Tahiti. That plus the fog and the incessant sounds of bells clanging, stevedores shouting, teamsters calling out to their horses, and the general clatter of a busy port made him lonesome for his cabin on the beach with Keani.

When the Italian barmaid carried a tray of sandwiches and another pitcher of beer to their table, Hayden asked Thomas to share his story. "Last I heard from you was a letter you sent when you started work at the *Chronicle*," Hayden said. "Somehow I suspect a few things have been going on in your life since then."

Thomas smiled wryly. "A few," he began.

It was nearly dark when they left the saloon for the short walk to Hayden's home, where his wife and three young sons would be preparing dinner, with Taiana's help. Akoni had left at dawn with one of Hayden's employees, a Japanese man who knew the local coves and tidepools well and had offered to be the Hawaiian naturalist's guide for the day.

The lamps were burning as they approached the house, and through the windows they could see Taiana playing with Hayden's three-year-old.

"She is a fine girl," Hayden said. "We're happy to have her stay with us until you return from New York."

"She'll earn her keep," Thomas replied.

Before they stepped up to the door, Hayden turned. "I don't have enough cash to help you pay off the bank in full, Thomas. I wish I did. But I can help fill in the gap. When you return, we'll sort it out. I have no qualms about making a loan to you."

"Thank you, John. I hope not to have to ask, but I will keep that in mind. The most important thing you can do right now is to make sure no one knows I visited, and make sure no one knows about Taiana. In fact, I'd go so far as to suggest you and your wife give her a different name to use while she is here."

Hayden put his hand on the doorknob. "Donegan is that ruthless? He would kill a child?"

Thomas nodded. "He has, and he will again with no hesitation. And the banker in Honolulu who wants my money or my hide isn't much better. Be careful John. These aren't like the people you deal with every day."

Hayden pulled his jacket open, and Thomas saw that he was wearing a revolver in a shoulder holster. "You'd be surprised who I deal with every day," his friend said as he closed his jacket and stepped into the house.

Hayden's children were fascinated by Akoni. Between his enormous size, the sheer exuberance that radiated from him like heat from a bed of campfire coals, and the way he got down to their level when talking with them, he immediately became their favorite uncle.

As he was finishing his third helping of Mrs. Hayden's exceptional *coq au vin* with mashed potatoes, sautéed mushrooms, cooked carrots, and glazed pears, he turned to Hayden's six-year-old son. "I spent the day in the tidepools, lad," Akoni began, "sketching all manner of creatures, from mussels and anemones to sea stars, crabs, and even an octopus."

The boy's eyes grew large. "Really? A real, live octopus?"

"Aye. And do you know how many hands that creature has?"

The boy wasn't sure, so his nine-year-old sibling chimed in, "Eight. He has eight hands!"

"That's right, boy. Eight hands." Akoni raised his own hands into the air and shook them around. "Now, most of us would like to have a few more hands, wouldn't we. Imagine being able to hold eight pieces of candy at once. What a treat that would be."

Then his face became serious. "Of course, having eight hands wouldn't be all fun and games. It would also present some real difficulties."

"How, Mr. Akoni," asked the six-year-old.

"Well, now, imagine what it was like when your father asked for your mother's hand in marriage. Pretty simple, right? A wedding ring goes on one finger on one hand. Easy. But how does a boy octopus ask a girl octopus to marry him?"

The children were on the edge of their seats. "How?" asked the youngest.

Akoni grinned at having the punch line set up for him. "Why, he just says, 'I would like to ask for your hand, hand, hand, hand, hand, hand, hand, hand in marriage.'"

The children squealed in delight, and the adults at the table groaned inwardly at the silly joke. Thomas watched the happy mayhem spilling out around the table and sipped his Bourdeaux. *"This is what I will have with Keani someday,"* he thought.

They stayed with Hayden for three days. Each morning Akoni rode off on one of Hayden's horses to explore the tidepools and shoals from San Pedro to the peninsula that jutted a mile out to sea just north of the harbor. Thomas accompanied Hayden to his warehouse, and even ventured out on a skiff with his friend to meet with the captain of one of the steam freighters who carried his goods to Japan and Australia. Taiana spent her time helping with the children and household chores, but it was clear to Thomas that she was not happy with the larger plan.

"I would rather come to New York with you and Akoni," she told him one morning after breakfast. "You will need my help more than the Haydens do."

"That's probably true," Thomas replied, "but it's not just about where you can be of the most use. It's about where you will be the safest. In any event it will only be for four or five weeks."

"And then?" she said with a pout. "Do I get left with another stranger?"

"No," said Thomas. "Then we sort out what you want to do with the rest of your life, and we make it happen."

His response was clearly not what she wanted to hear, but he knew she would make the most of it. He encouraged her to send a letter to her parents in care of Father Damien on Moloka'i, making sure that she understood she was not to talk about where she was, or who she was staying with.

Hayden sent an employee to the train station to purchase tickets to St. Louis for Akoni and Thomas, where they would meet with Captain McNab's brother to learn about the business of fine art.

The night before their train left, they sat around a blazing fire in a brick pit beside Hayden's home. They had a fine view of the harbor, and as the sun went down, they could make out the contours of Catalina

Island 26 miles off the coast. When Mrs. Hayden and the boys grew chilly and went back inside, Akoni asked Hayden to relate the story of the battle of Pebble Creek Ridge at the close of the war.

"I've heard Thomas' view of the events of that morning," said Akoni, "but I have often wondered what it must have looked like from your perspective when you looked up on that ridge and saw him being swarmed by a couple dozen Confederate riders."

Hayden sipped at his brandy before replying. "It was pretty much as chaotic as you can imagine," he began. "When Thomas—who at the time I believed to be a full Colonel—ordered my men and me to wait at the bottom of the ridge while he rode up to take the measure of the situation, I thought he was chock-a-block crazy. When we saw him reach the top of the ridge and realized the Rebs were attacking, we cut loose up that hill as fast as we could go. Two dozen of us were on horseback, about 70 were on foot.

As we swept up towards the top, we saw the damn fool suddenly whip his horse around and charge at a line of a dozen or more Reb cavalry. He rode right through them so fast they didn't have time to get any shots off. One of the most amazing things I witnessed in the war."

Thomas looked over at Taiana, who appeared to be regarding him in an entirely new light. He raised his glass to her, and she lofted the little glass of port they had permitted her to have on this special occasion.

"Back and forth they went, the Rebs closing in time and again and Thomas finding a way to evade them. We knew he had been hit at least once or twice by Rebel fire and when we breached the top of the ridge and saw how many graybacks were boiling up from the valley below we thought we were all done for. We were outnumbered at least ten to one."

"And yet here you are," Akoni said in a quiet voice.

"My men were equipped with the new Spencer repeating carbines. Short barrel, .55-56 rimfire cartridge, seven cartridges per load. That meant each one of our men were worth seven of theirs. And we held."

"Watching Thomas on that beast of a warhorse, Cornwall, when they were both hit multiple times was one of the worst moments of my life. Then when that damn horse reared back and Thomas lifted

Old Glory high into the morning sky in the face the enemy, it was one of the proudest moments of my life."

"You thought he was dead?" asked Akoni.

"Oh, I was certain he was dead, and Cornwall, too. But when the Reb line broke and they retreated down into the valley we discovered they were both alive—barely. We patched them up, and got them to a field hospital and them to Mt. Pleasant Hospital in D.C."

"Where they somehow kept Thomas alive," said Taiana.

"And my horse, too. There were some remarkable people taking care of me," said Thomas, holding back the tear that was forming in his eye.

"That poet, Walt Whitman, who was working as a volunteer nurse was one," said Hayden. "I'll never forget his hair and beard, or the way his eyes seemed to glow in the dark."

"And Angela, my other nurse," Thomas whispered into the fire. "She saved me in every way a man can be saved."

"That would be a tale worth hearing someday," said Akoni.

Thomas shook off his melancholy and forced a smile. "Someday," he replied.

The Hayden family and Taiana gathered in the gravel road across from the house the next morning to wish Thomas and Akoni goodbye. The driver of the rig Hayden rented to take them to the train station in Los Angeles piled their luggage in the back and waited for the hugs and backslaps to wind down.

The boys cried when Akoni climbed up onto his seat, and then laughed when they saw how much the carriage springs sagged under the giant Hawaiian's weight.

Thomas shook each of the boy's hands, and hugged Mrs. Hayden and then Taiana. "Stay well," he said," "I will be back for you." She sniffled and kissed his cheek.

Hayden stepped over to Thomas with a cardboard folder. "There are timetables for every train from Los Angeles to New York in here," he said. "And an envelope with $700 in it. That's a gift, not a loan."

Thomas started to object but thought better of it. "I will be back as soon as I can," he said to his friend. Then he climbed up onto the seat beside Akoni and waved as the carriage trotted up the hill, rounded a curve, and disappeared.

~ FORTY-NINE ~

San Frncisco, November

Colin Stafford found it amusing that the first business meeting he was holding in his new four-story sandstone-and-brick office building at the corner of California and Sansome Streets was with an assassin. What he did not find amusing was the paid killer's attitude.

"I have done my best, Mr. Stafford," Donegan was saying, "and I ain't saying I'm quitting, but sweet Jesus, how far do you expect me to go to find the bastard?"

Stafford leaned forward and tapped the blotter in the center of his desk with his middle finger. "I expect you to go to the gates of hell if that's where the chase leads you, Mr. Donegan. You have been well paid, and you've even found the time to open a whorehouse in Honolulu, the services of which, by the way, I have appreciated greatly. The chase ends when Colonel Scoundrel is dead. No sooner."

Donegan drummed his fingers atop the hat in his lap. "And them three island boys sitting out in the lobby? I work alone, Mr. Stafford, you know that. I don't want their help—I don't need their help. I mean, can you imagine them trying to look inconspicuous in a crowd? Hell, they look like the drawings you see of Polynesian warriors in old books."

Stafford smiled and rang for his assistant to bring more tea. "That's because they are warriors, Mr. Donegan, just like the ones in the old books. They happen to be in the employ of my brother, who you know well. He has his own reasons for finding Scoundrel, which is why you are having this conversation with me this morning instead of getting on the next train east."

A young Chinese woman opened the door and set a silver tea service on the desk. She poured a cup for Stafford, and, without asking Donegan if he wanted any, left the room.

Stafford wrapped his hands around the warm cup. It was cold in the building and the fireplace in the corner of the office was not putting out much heat. One more thing to take up with the builder, he thought.

"So, you want me to let them three tag along all the way to New York?" Donegan asked.

"First, there are actually six Tahitians, not three," replied Stafford. "The others, as I understand it, are at the haberdashers getting outfitted with civilized clothing, courtesy of my brother."

Donegan muttered a curse under his breath, which brought a thin smile to Stafford's lips. He sipped at the tea and said, "The group's leader is named Aata, and, according to my brother, he is a warrior of some renown."

Donegan looked puzzled. "I know that name. Is he the same one who popped up in the islands a few months ago and began to run a small-time gambling and prostitution operation for the sugar cane workers and wharf labor?"

"Competition?" asked Stafford.

"Not a bit. His customers can't afford my menus."

"And you know nothing else about this Aata."

Donegan shook his head.

"It seems our Colonel Scoundrel stole Aata's woman right from under his nose," Stafford added. "Ran off to a remote island with her after beating Aata in some kind of wrestling match."

Donegan had to laugh. He knew nothing about the intricacies of finance and politics at which Stafford excelled, but he knew a damn sight more than his employer about sex and revenge. "And Aata is here to even the score?"

"He is here for two reasons. The first is to collect the $50,000 that Scoundrel owes my brother's bank. The Colonel's business partner absconded after withdrawing the full credit line available to their sugar-cane business, and my brother has decided to wring the money out of our boy."

"And the second reason?"

"As you suggested, Aata is also here to restore his honor by killing Scoundrel…"

"Which is my job," Donegan interrupted, "not his."

Stafford nodded. It was time to thread the needle. "And therein lies our conundrum, Mr. Donegan. I want Scoundrel dead for my own reasons. My brother wants the bank's money back, after which he has no reservations about Aata slitting the colonel's throat."

"And then just how in the hell am I supposed to do my job?" asked Donegan. "You want me to stand aside with my dick in my hand until Aata and his boys get their money, and then help him finish Scoundrel? Christ, can you imagine what that would look like?"

"Actually, I can't. And as for working with the Tahitians, no, I don't expect you to hold their hands until they get the money. But my brother is my brother after all, and…."

Donegan pointed to the jar in a corner cabinet that he knew contained Wallace Stafford's embalmed eyeball and said, "Even though you don't see eye to eye…"

"Exactly," said Stafford with a smile. "I am willing to compromise somewhat in this matter for the sake of family unity. The end game does not change; I want you to be the one to kill Scoundrel. Personally."

"And if the Tahitians get in my way?"

"I suggest you don't let that happen. Allow Aata a reasonable amount of time to collect the money. I am certain the colonel himself does not have that kind of money, but he is well-connected, and he may get some help raising the funds. Use your own discretion, but I must be able to tell my brother honestly that Aata made the attempt to get the cash before you stepped in to end the chase."

"Must I travel with them to New York?"

"Of course not. But you must stay close enough to them to know what they are doing."

Stafford opened a desk drawer and withdrew a thick envelope.

"Travel money, a ticket on tonight's train east, a list of hotels my secretary drew up, and a letter to my banking associate in New York authorizing you to draw more funding. I have watchers in the better city hotels, and they will telegraph when Scoundrel arrives."

"You're convinced that is where he is going?"

"When I received the information you extracted–or rather, that is, you obtained–from the missionary in Honolulu, I made inquiries through my corresponding bank in New York City. It seems a new art venue called the Metropolitan Museum of Art is opening at the end of December. In addition to the items they will have on permanent display, the museum is inviting the leading galleries in the city to display their best paintings. If Colonel Scoundrel is taking paintings to the city that can be his only logical destination. He will attend the grand opening. I am certain of that."

Donegan nodded. A clear path had been laid for him. He took the envelope from Stafford and stood to leave.

"One last thing, Mr. Donegan," his employer added. "I read the Honolulu newspaper account of the deaths of the missionary and his wife. Did you really need to be that, ahem, how shall we say, thorough?"

Donegan felt a familiar wave of heat surge through his loins. "Oh, yes," he replied in a quiet, almost reverent voice, "I did." Then he stepped out into the lobby and walked past Aata and the other two Tahitians without making eye contact.

~ FIFTY ~

Southern Pacific Rail Car New Mexico Territory
December 1,1872

The man approaching Thomas was in his mid 40s, tall, with shaggy hair, mutton chop whiskers and an unruly moustache. Akoni leaned forward in his seat at their formally set table in the walnut-paneled dining car. The man didn't look like trouble, but the Hawaiian was taking no chances, and his hand drifted down to the revolver in his waistband.

"Colonel Thomas Scoundrel, I believe?" said the man as he extended his hand. "My name is Bret Harte. I met with your editor, Andrew Whitton, not five days ago in San Francisco, and I recognized you from his description."

Harte. Thomas knew of his work as a short story writer and poet who specialized in tales set in California's gold rush country.

"Forgive my reticence, Mr. Harte," Thomas said as he shook the writer's hand. "I had not thought my travels had been shared by anyone."

The waiter appeared and Thomas motioned for Harte to join them. "With your permission, sir?" the writer asked Akoni, who begrudgingly nodded. "You, I am sure I know," said Harte to Akoni. "Whitton said that Thomas would be traveling with the largest man in the Pacific Islands. He did not exaggerate, sir."

Harte sat down and accepted Akoni's outstretched hand.

"You're traveling alone?" Akoni asked.

"Alas, yes," Harte replied. "My wife will join me in New York but not until after the winter snows clear in the mountains."

Thomas poured Harte a taste of the excellent zinfandel the waiter had recommended and waited for him to approve before he filled the glass.

"A wonderful choice," said Harte with a smile. "And have you both ordered dinner?"

"Brook trout, seared antelope steaks and salad," Thomas replied, "to be followed by a berry compote and coffee." The men steadied their wine glasses as the train swung around a curved grade and clattered across a trestle bridge. Outside the dining car, stars carpeted the sky above an expanse of land that their porter said was Mescalero Apache territory. "Best be stayin' away from these parts if you value your scalp," he had warned them in the same ominous tone he had used the previous two days when describing the homelands of a half dozen other tribes they crossed while passing through Arizona territory.

"May I ask why you sought me out?" Thomas asked. "If you know I was on my way to New York you also know that the purpose of my travel is known only to a handful."

"As your editor made clear, Colonel. He is an old and trusted friend and I assure you he would not have made mention of your journey had he not thought I might be of some service to you."

Thomas appreciated the writer's sincerity, and he could tell by Akoni's expression that he felt the same way. A moment later the waiter uncorked a second bottle of zinfandel—without having to be asked, Thomas noted. That was the sign of a true professional.

"We share something in common, Colonel," Harte began.

"Yes?"

"We each fled northern California to save our hides; me 12 years ago, you only a few months past."

"And what forced you to leave?" asked Akoni between bites of bread and butter.

"I was an editor at the Northern Californian newspaper at the time," said Harte, "and I made the fateful decision to report on the massacre of over 150 Wiyot Indians in Humboldt County, mostly elderly people, women, and children. Their men were away at a celebration the night the townspeople rowed out to the village and used axes, hatchets, and clubs to murder the defenseless people."

"Had the Wiyot attacked the locals?" Thomas asked.

"No, they were the most peaceful of peaceful peoples. The sheriff later claimed the Wiyot has been rustling cattle, but no charges were ever made."

"Was anyone arrested?" Akoni asked.

Harte responded with a bitter chuckle. "The Humboldt Volunteers, as the murderers called themselves, were pretty much hailed as heroes. The army did a sham investigation, the upshot of which is that they forced the remaining Wiyot to move north to the Klamath Indian Reservations."

"And so, you became the villain," Thomas said.

"I did," replied Harte as the waiter placed a bowl of soup in front of each man. "I quit my job and fled south to San Francisco, but the powers that be hounded me about the Wiyot story for years. You might say they never gave up."

"And that is why you are moving to New York?" Akoni asked.

"In part, yes. Opportunities for my short stories and poems have pretty much dried up in California, thanks in no small part to those I angered with the massacre story. The other reason is that the literary world is centered in New York City, and I have been offered a job writing for the *Atlantic Monthly*."

After the waiter served the trout and antelope steaks from a silver chafing dish Thomas turned to Harte. "Why did Whitton think you might be able to help me?"

Harte raised his glass. "Because, my dear Colonel Scoundrel, I know everyone in literature and the arts in New York who is worth knowing." Then he smiled and tossed back the last of the deep red wine.

The locomotive swung south into northwestern Texas at El Paso just after dawn and began the journey across the vast Texas landscape of brushy canyons, small, snow-dusted mountain ranges, and sparse vegetation. Harte was a peerless storyteller with a deep reservoir of tales about life in the gold camps of California and Thomas and Akoni sat in the First-Class Club Car for hours as he spun one raucous adventure after another. From the Pecos River to Fort Worth, where the train turned due north into Indian Territory, Harte regaled them with stories of grub stakes gone wrong, thievery and sophisticated cons, and even an occasional account of real-life whores with hearts of gold who committed acts of such genuine kindness and generosity that they became legends in the boomtowns that sprung up anywhere a motherlode was uncovered.

Not to be overshadowed, their diligent porter sought the men out several times a day to tell them which tribe of savages lurked in the rolling hills and sagebrush the train was passing through now. "Choctaw Nation out there gents, keep your irons handy," he said at lunch, and, "Creek Country boys, and it's dangerous, but not as bad as the Arapaho and Osage lands we are about to cross," was his warning at dinner. The irony of a nattily dressed railroad employee delivering dire warnings of impending doom while Akoni, Harte, and Thomas were sipping an 1870 *Dom Perignon Reserve de L'Abbaye* champagne and enjoying caviar on toast and fresh oysters was lost on the porter. The Indian wars weren't over, Thomas reminded himself as he looked out the window and watched the sun setting over the Arkansas River, and he had no doubt that he would be recalled to Army duty one day to do his part. But it was hard to reconcile that reality with the experience he was enjoying in the plush dining car hurtling through the darkening emptiness of the American West.

On their fourth night out of Los Angeles, Bret Harte dined with Akoni and Thomas for the last time. He would be leaving the train in

Wichita in the morning to tend to some family business.

"I will look forward to seeing you gentlemen at the grand opening gala for the new Museum of Art," he said over their meal of grilled rib-eye steak with mushrooms and asparagus. "And you have told me enough about your circumstance that I feel honor-bound to do whatever I can to be of assistance."

"You know about the world I am about to jump into," Thomas replied. "I know almost nothing about art, and even less about the art market. We are traveling on to St. Louis where we will meet a gentleman who is a noted collector, and I hope to learn a great deal from him."

Harte nodded. "I will leave the instruction in painting and painters to your associate," he said. "But you must understand that there would be no art market were it not for collectors, and, by definition, collectors are wealthy individuals. In New York City those individuals are among the richest people on earth, and they live a highly cloistered life."

"Meaning they don't take to outsiders like us?" Akoni asked.

Harte refilled his wine glass and chuckled. "Think of New York society as a harem in the court of a Turkish sultan. It is filled with maidens so beautiful, so alluring, so exquisitely proportioned that no ordinary man would hesitate to risk his life to enter the gates of paradise and prostate himself at the feet of such beauty."

Thomas grinned, filled Akoni's glass and his own, and gestured for the waiter to bring another bottle of the fine Bordeaux.

"When can we book passage?" asked Akoni. "I can think of no greater sacrifice that I would be willing to make."

"Ah, but your joy would be short-lived, my friend," continued Harte. "Within the walls of the harem the maids are protected by castrated eunuchs, who, despite living *sans testicules*, are none the less highly proficient with swords, daggers, and all manner of poisons they would slip into your wine even as they smiled at you. But you wouldn't have to worry about the *castrati*, because you would not survive the climb over the garden wall. The harem is guarded by a full regiment of highly trained Janissaries whose only loyalty is to the Sultan. Should any of them fail at their job they would face immediate execution, and it is rumored that the current ruler, Abdulaziz, has reinstated the marvelously gruesome torture of slowly lowering unfortunate bastards into a vat of boiling oil. The process, they say, involves dipping the screaming individual into the burning liquid a few inches at a time, then pulling him out to watch pieces of his own burning flesh fall from his bones… before dipping him right back in."

Harte paused a moment and then said, "Thomas, could you pass the mashed potatoes, please?"

Akoni downed the last of his wine. "And you liken New York Society to those barbarians?" he asked.

"I assure you the Ottomans are not barbarians," Harte answered. "Their empire has ruled over much of the world for seven centuries. But what they share in common with New York elite is a propensity for ruthlessness, backstabbing, toadying, incest, unquenchable avarice, and every conceivable kind of old-fashioned chicanery."

Thomas shook his head. "And these are the gatekeepers of the world of fine art?" he asked.

"In truth, my friends," Harte said with a smile, "they are the gatekeepers and rule-makers regarding any encroachment that any person outside their class attempts to make into their territory. It has been thus for all human history, and the rules have not changed since the days of ancient Rome."

"The virgins of the harem must be protected," mused Akoni.

"Yes," Harte answered, "and that harem includes the best jobs, the mechanisms of political influence, the ability to raise capital to start a business, even the approval of one's intended marriage partners."

"I always thought Henry IV had it wrong," Thomas said in a thoughtful voice.

Akoni and Harte raised their eyebrows. What did a French king have to do with the New York social world?

Thomas gestured for the waiter to bring a third bottle of wine and said, "My Catholic mother told me the story; Henry was a Protestant king of an overwhelmingly Catholic nation. He was unsuccessful at uniting the warring factions in his country and so he finally abandoned his personal religious beliefs and became a Catholic only to achieve his political goals. *'Paris is worth a mass'*, is the way he put it."

Harte thought for a moment about what Thomas had said. "And you fear you will have to give up something important of yourself in order to pull off the sale of Aubert's paintings?" he asked.

A half smile creased Thomas' face. "Perhaps not. If it is as simple as getting past the Janissaries, climbing the wall, dodging the eunuch's daggers and poisons, and then persuading one of the untouched maidens to open the gates of her heavenly paradise for the first time, how can I fail?"

~ FIFTY-ONE ~

25 Vandeventer Place, St. Louis

Phineas McNab was tall, thin, and dapper, with a waxed handlebar moustache and mischievous air that belied his 60 years. Even his home, built in the Second Empire style with elaborate brick and stonework, heavily detailed porches with extensive woodwork, a large gabled roof in front, and decorative fretwork above its dormers, spoke to the retired businessman's impeccable taste.

The proprietor of the livery stable next to the St. Louis train station had raised his eyebrows the day before when Thomas asked for directions to Vandeventer Place. "Ah," said the compact Swede, "Our own little Madison Avenue for the swells. I'd best be rentin' you a couple of our finest…"

He broke off mid-sentence when Akoni stepped through the stable door and set down their bags. The Swede took one look at the colossal Hawaiian and shook his head. "I can't be rentin' no horse to a man that big, no sir, not unless I want a crippled nag on my hands. No sir, it's a buggy you'll have to rent."

Thomas was amused, but Akoni did not share his lighthearted reaction. The nephew of the King of Hawai'i had been the butt of over-sized jokes since he was a boy. Before he could reply to the livery owner, however, Thomas cut in:

"I was planning on having our luggage delivered by carriage in any event. Looks like we won't need to do that now."

Akoni shrugged and placed their luggage and Aubert's rolled canvasses into the back of the buggy the Swede was hitching to a handsome Morgan. Thomas climbed up onto the seat, took the whip into his hands and gave it a light flick. They trotted out of the stable and onto the city's main street under cold, thickening gray clouds.

"I didn't expect it to be this big," said Akoni as they passed block after block of commercial buildings before emerging out onto a limestone bluff overlooking the western shore of the Mississippi River.

"I'm told that over 180,000 people live here," replied Thomas. "St. Louis is bigger than New Orleans, and it looks to be growing even more." He pointed towards the river, where construction crews were ferrying stone blocks out to three enormous caisson structures that held back the river so they could build the stone foundations for a new bridge inside dry enclosures.

Thomas drove the buggy a half mile north to where a row of handsome three-story houses dotted what until recently had been a corn field. "And our Mr. McNab made his fortune in the war?" asked Akoni.

Thomas nodded. "Supplying pretty much everything but weapons to the Union Army. He sold them horse tack, uniforms, blankets, food, and a whole host of sundries. According to his brother, he made a fortune by supplying quality merchandise where so many others became rich selling rotted food, spoiled molasses, and uniforms that fell apart after a single wearing."

"Meh, profiteers," said Akoni. "I have dealt with their kind in making procurements for our government. May maggots and worms infest their infernal bowels."

Thomas laughed and swung the buggy off the dirt road and onto a hardpacked lot next to McNab's home at #25. "I had more than a few camp meals made with their foul provisions," he said. "Soldiers joked that rancid meat had three lives; it wiggled while it was being cooked, wiggled when you ate it, and it was still wiggling when you crapped the remains into the latrine."

Akoni shook his head in disgust. "It's a wonder you are alive to tell the story."

Phineas instructed his grounds man to stable the buggy and carry his guests' luggage to their rooms on the second floor. Then he led them into an airy, high-ceilinged library with stained glass windows, floor to ceiling bookcases and an ornate marble fireplace in which a low fire burned. Akoni could not hold back a low whistle of astonishment at the sight of dozens of museum quality *objets d'art* that filled the room. Some were in glass display cases, others were on tabletops, bookshelves, windowsills or mounted on the walls. There were small, brightly colored porcelain and vitreous enamel boxes and decorative eggs from Europe and Asia, engraved gems and netsuke ivory carvings, jewel-encrusted cigarette cases, portrait miniatures, gold and enamel clocks, tabletop sculptures, tapestries, fragments of Greek temple friezes, and elaborately bound leather books. As amazing as the quantity of treasure in the room was, what Thomas found more impressive was that the library did not look a bit crowded. Each object was placed in such a way that the eye could linger on it without being distracted by the surrounding pieces. The arrangement of the collection was itself a masterwork of art.

He allowed himself a moment to try and calculate the value of the artwork in this one room, only to be stopped short by McNab's fatherly expression of disapproval. *"A great deal,"* it said. Thomas smiled softly, knowing that Akoni was wondering the same thing, and realizing that McNab had probably been asked the question a hundred times.

"My brother's letter arrived only yesterday," Phineas said as he motioned for them to sit. A servant appeared and he asked her to bring coffee and sandwiches to the conservatory. "Extraordinary circumstances you fellows have become wrapped up in, simply remarkable," he said. "And as I understand it, you are carrying paintings by an unknown French artist living in Tahiti to New York for the opening of the new museum of art? And you want to learn about the art business?"

"That's pretty much the picture," Thomas replied.

"Well, it is if you leave out the parts about the assassin on our trail, the bank looking to squeeze Thomas for $50,000, assorted lepers, whorehouse proprietors, German warship commanders with a penchant for tossing stowaways overboard, and a Tahitian warrior looking to avenge himself against Thomas in a matter of love," Akoni added.

"Is that all?" said McNab with a smile.

"Oh, there's much more, Mr. McNab, but we'll need to get to know you better before we slip under those sheets with you."

Phineas slapped his knee and laughed. "By God, I understood from my brother's letter that you were not a man to hold back his feelings, sir. May I call you Akoni, or is it Your Highness? I don't know the protocol of the Hawaiian court."

Akoni shared a glance with Thomas. They had both taken an instant liking to their host. "Akoni will do fine. Only my uncle and sister are addressed by their titles."

"Very well, then, Akoni and Thomas it is." He stood and said, "Let's join my wife in the conservatory. We'll take our lunch there."

He led the way through the oak-paneled entry, down a hall lined with gilt-framed landscape paintings and into a large room made mostly of glass, from the walls to the ceiling. The conservatory was attached to the south side of the house and featured a bay front and ornate ridge details. It was packed with plants and flowers of all kinds, and despite the winter chill outside, the greenhouse was almost tropically humid, to his guests delight, McNab noted.

"Remind you of the weather at home?" he asked.

Akoni removed his jacket and hung it on the corner of a chair. "It's perfect," he said with a smile.

After lunch the men walked out behind McNab's home, where a large red barn had been recently built. "Do you also farm?" Akoni asked as McNab slid open the main door.

"Not exactly," Phineas replied with a smile.

That was an understatement, thought Thomas when he took in the interior of the building. More than a dozen windows brought in natural light from every side of the structure, and a second floor was accessible by a wide staircase. A free-standing 8-foot wall ran down the center of the first floor, and woven carpets helped the wood stove to warm the cold wooden floor.

"This isn't a barn…" Akoni said in a hushed tone.

"It's an art gallery…" Thomas finished.

"Gentlemen" said McNab with a flourish of his arm, "welcome to my collection."

Three walls of the barn were covered with framed paintings, as were both sides of the interior wall. A half dozen comfortable armchairs were scattered around the expanse, no doubt so McNab could sit to contemplate any of his works, Thomas thought.

"Upstairs, too?" asked Akoni.

Phineas nodded. "There are just over 300 paintings, engravings, and sketches in here representing over 25 years of collecting."

Thomas walked over to the first painting on the left wall. The brass plate beneath it said, *Nocturne: Blue & Gold-Old Battersea Bridge, by James McNeill Whistler.* The 26" x 20" work of the old bridge on the Thames River was done in muted tones of blue and gray. Next to that was a larger oil of a Greek man and woman in classical dress examining themselves in a hand mirror. This realistic painting, in rustic blues, oranges, and browns was by Laurens Alma Tadema, a painter whose work Thomas had seen in Washington. As he walked the length of the building he saw works by Ingres, Delacroix, Manet, and many others whose names he did not recognize. Most of the paintings were in the classical tradition still favored by the English and French academies and art dealers, but a few contained hints of the style that Aubert was perfecting, where color and light reigned supreme, and where lines and forms were not rigid and structured.

On the other side of the barn, Akoni was having an experience like Thomas.' McNab's tastes were wide-ranging, and the only thing most of his collection had in common were that each had been done with extraordinary skill.

For the next hour neither Thomas nor Akoni spoke. They wandered both floors, lingered in front of favorite works, and came back several times to those they liked the most. When a servant came into the barn with a bottle of vintage port and a tray of cheeses and crackers, the men gathered in armchairs around the warmth of the wood stove.

"Your brother's description of your collection did you little justice," Thomas said to Phineas. "It is simply remarkable."

His host raised his glass in reply.

"Do you collect for your personal enjoyment, or do you also sell your paintings?" asked Akoni.

"I collect what I like, and hang what the critics say, is my philosophy," Phineas replied. "But as to your question, no, nothing here is for sale. When my time is done, they shall become the initial collection for a new St. Louis art museum, which my estate shall also help to fund."

Thomas accepted a glass of port and shook his head. "And all this culture out here in the wilderness of Missouri. It's hard to imagine, my friend, but good on you for your vision."

"As to our own business and your education in the world-wide art market, I think we should outline a plan," said Phineas.

Thomas nodded.

"First, how much time do you have? I understand from my brother's letter and from Akoni's comments this morning, that you are in something of a race against time."

Akoni chuckled. "That is a mild way to put it."

"This evening I will tell you the complete story in detail," Thomas said. "But, yes, the short of it is that we are in a race against enemies who have been sent to kill me and who will stop at nothing until they succeed."

The art collector's expression turned serious. "Then let's get to work right away."

"Phineas," Thomas replied, "you need to know that in helping me you may be exposing yourself and your wife to grave danger."

McNab's tone was incredulous. "For teaching you about the art business? It seems preposterous."

"I assure you it is real," Akoni added. "The people chasing us have committed all manner of crimes along the way, from arson to rape and even murder."

Phineas looked into the faces of his new friends and refilled their glasses. "Let's get to it, then."

Over the next two hours the men worked out a plan designed to educate Thomas in at least the rudiments of the operation of the art business. A friend who was both a fine painter and an expert framer and canvas stretcher would come the following day and unroll Aubert's paintings so that Phineas could provide his honest assessment of their marketability.

"As for you, Akoni," said Phineas when he noticed that the Hawaiian was nodding off, "I think we had best find a more productive use for your time. How does joining a paleontology dig sound to you?"

Akoni rocketed up from his chair. "Would that be possible?"

"There is small team under the direction of Professor Woodson Holt working a few miles north of the city in some ancient clay beds close to the river. They've found fossilized remains of giant sloths, mastodons, and a number of other creatures. Normally they would have closed the camp for the season, but we've had a very mild winter and they have continued the excavations."

"And you think they would permit me to join them?" Akoni asked.

Phineas grinned. "I am the sole patron of the project, my friend. You will be welcomed with open arms, especially when they recognize you as a fellow scientist."

"I'll need gear," mused Akoni as he began to pace back and forth.

"I have a tent, sketch pads and all of the field gear you will need," Phineas said. "Early tomorrow my man will load the buckboard and take you to the site. He'll return to gather you up in …shall we say four days?"

Akoni looked at Thomas, who could only grin at his friend's good fortune.

The McNab household employed a staff that included a cook and housekeeper, but Martha McNab insisted on preparing tonight's dinner of lamb stew, roasted brussel sprouts in garlic butter, twice-baked potatoes, fresh-baked sourdough bread, and winter asparagus by herself. She gave Thomas a lantern and the key to their wine cellar where he found himself overwhelmed by hundreds of bottles of the finest wines in the world. He held the lantern close to labels for Sangioveses from Tuscany, *Château d'Yquem* sauternes from France, and a host of offerings from the finest Bordeaux cellars. He was pleased to see that the McNabs had included his favorite California zinfandel in their collection. After what seemed like an hour of uncertainty, he selected three bottles of an 1868 *Château Pape Clément Bordeaux* that he was certain would pair perfectly with the lamb. He also tucked a bottle of the sweet *Château d'Yquem* under his arm for dessert.

Akoni had to be pulled away from the stable where he had been arranging his field gear. When they were all seated at the candle-lit table, Phineas filled their glasses with the *Château Pape Clément*, and each took a first taste.

Thomas was impressed by the deep ruby color, and the hints of plum, black fruit and orange citrus. Then the housekeeper brought the feast to the table and Mrs. McNab ladled the savory lamb stew into their bowls. When Thomas dipped a piece of fresh sourdough bread into the broth and tasted the subtle herb and spice seasoning his hostess had used to create a perfect balance of flavors, he lifted his glass and offered a toast.

"To friendship and the bounty of the land," he said as the others joined in enthusiastically.

Then he thought of Keani alone in their cabin, 7,000 miles away on a remote Polynesian island, and his smile faded. Akoni searched his friend's eyes and knew what he was thinking.

"And to Keani," Akoni softly added. The McNabs and Thomas raised their glasses for a second time and toasted Thomas' wife.

"May she and the baby be well."

~ FIFTY-TWO ~

A light snow was falling, and soft winter light streamed through the upper windows of the barn as Thomas sipped coffee in an armchair beneath the Whistler painting. He was watching Preston Winters carefully unroll Aubert's canvasses before arranging them individually on the wooden 8' x 10' table McNab's people had set up. The artist was compact, with dark features, an unruly beard, and quick, intelligent eyes. Thomas was impressed by how deftly the man had separated the paintings, but Winters' silence and his absence of any facial expression of either approval or dismay was concerning.

Phineas, too, was silent. He stood across the table from Winters, his arms crossed, his face impassive. One by one Aubert's color-splashed paintings of landscapes and people around Tahiti and Moorea took their place on the table, until all 23 canvasses had been laid out for display.

Phineas held a sheet of paper on which Aubert had given a title to each work that corresponded to a number penciled on a back corner of the canvas. As Winters unrolled each piece, Phineas stepped forward, checked the number, scanned the list, and then gazed intently at the work, but only for a moment. Then he stood back and waited for the next painting to be laid down.

When all the canvasses had been opened, Phineas and Winters began to pace around the table, pausing a little extra time at one painting and then another. When they circled the table for the fourth time, Thomas was ready to leap out his chair in frustration. Had he been wrong about Aubert's work? Was the interplay of light and color that radiated from each piece too overwhelming? Did the softness of forms and the near total absence of gray and black colors mark too radical a shift from the academic structure of the landscapes and portraits that dealers and collectors had favored for more than a century? Was it possible that they were simply no good?

He struggled to hold back an overwhelming sense of discouragement. So much hinged on the success of Aubert's paintings, from the artist's career to repaying the bank and settling with Colin Stafford so he could return to Keani. And what of the others he had enlisted to help with the scheme? Akoni had walked away from his official position at the royal court in Hawai'i, and he had taken Taiana thousands of miles from the only life she had known. Captain McNab, John Hayden, and even Princess Noelani had also stepped up to aid in what increasingly seemed to be a fool's errand, a fantasy. Even worse, by bringing so many good people into his quest he had now marked them as possible targets of Fitch Donegan's murderous pursuit.

In his mind's eye, he saw Keani standing alone on the beach as he and Aubert and Océane sailed over the reef and into the open water. He suddenly felt very tired and slumped forward in his chair.

"Thomas? Thomas!"

He was jolted from his deepening despair by the sound of McNab's voice.

"Are you sleeping lad? At a time like this?"

Until that moment he hadn't realized that his eyes were closed. He opened them to find McNab and Winters standing in front of his chair, with wide grins on their faces.

"Yes, of course, no, I wasn't sleeping," he finally said. "It's just…"

As the words spilled out of his mouth, he knew how foolish he must look.

"Just what, Colonel?" asked Winters.

"I saw no reaction on your faces to Aubert's paintings," Thomas said, "and I feared you did not think much of them."

Phineas and the artist shared a knowing glance. Then, in a stern voice Phineas said, "As a matter of fact we didn't think much of them."

Thomas's heart sank. His worst fears realized, months of planning, thousands of miles of travel, lives lost or disrupted, and all for what? Pure tomfoolery. He began to stand, only to have Phineas place a hand on his shoulder.

"My boy," said Phineas, "please forgive two old art snobs for reverting to our lifelong habits of never allowing our faces to betray how we feel about a painting. When we are looking at a new piece, we are deep into the negotiating mindset, and that requires that we maintain the most severe kind of poker face until we are ready to commit to an offer to buy."

Winters nodded in assent. "Exactly so," he added.

"Come with me, Thomas," said Phineas. He led the way back to the table on which Aubert's canvasses lay almost gleaming in the pure white December light.

"I have had the privilege of being present at the birth of the careers of more than a few remarkable artists, Thomas, each of whom is represented in my collection. But this…" he waved his hand above the canvasses on the table, "this is beyond remarkable painting. This is genius, my boy, complete, original, unfiltered genius. The work is simply exquisite…"

Thomas saw that Phineas was overcome with emotion. Winters touched the corner of a painting that was done right outside the front door of Thomas and Kean's cabin on the beach. "This work, all of them in fact, are the product of a revolutionary. A master of his craft and a singular brilliance. I am simply in awe of his talent."

"Feel better?" asked Phineas with a sly smile.

Thomas hadn't breathed for the past minute. Now he inhaled deeply, and then began to laugh. Phineas and Winters joined in, much to the amusement of Mrs. McNab, who had arrived to let them know luncheon was ready. Her mission was forgotten, however, the moment she saw the overflowing cornucopia of art lying on the table.

She ignored the men and began her own tour of the paintings.

Phineas poked Thomas in the side. "See what I mean, boy? That's the reaction you are going to get in New York."

Winters went over to a sideboard and filled four glasses with port. He handed them around and proposed a toast. "To an artist whose fame will only grow with each canvas, and whose name shall live forever."

"And to his worthy representative, Colonel Thomas Scoundrel," Phineas added.

Thomas took a drink and said, "So, you believe they will sell?"

"Let's sit," answered Phineas.

The men pulled chairs close to the potbelly stove while Mrs. McNab continued her examination of the paintings, cooing softly over her favorites.

"Oh, yes, they will sell, Thomas, genius cannot be kept hidden under a rock. However..." his voice slowed.

"You will be faced with a well-financed, deeply entrenched and implacable enemy who will do everything in their power to see that these paintings never see the light of day," Winters added. "Art dealers will throw you out of their shops, the newspaper critics will not give you so much as a single line in their columns, and the wealthy collectors who would be the most likely to purchase Aubert's paintings will never get the chance to see them."

Phineas nodded in agreement, but Thomas was perplexed. "How is that possible? If the work is as good as you both say it is, won't the art world welcome Aubert with open arms?"

Winters and Phineas laughed as one. "They won't," said Phineas "it's as simple as that. Aubert isn't an asset in their minds—he is a threat to their very way of life. He represents not just the slow and natural progression in style and technique we would expect to see in art, but an explosive revolution."

Mrs. McNab finished her viewing and brought the port when she joined them beside the wood stove.

"The art world is dominated by ideas and practices that are older than the fossils our friend Akoni is even now pulling out of the limestone cliffs above the Mississippi," said Phineas. "In fact, 'fossilized' is the perfect moniker to hang around the necks of the French and English Academies, the leading dealers in Paris, London, and New York, and even the artists who deny their own impulses and desires to continue turning out the same dreary works by the cartload."

"Landscapes," Winters said dryly.

"And more landscapes," Phineas added. "Albert Bierstadt, to note an example, is a fine painter who I include in my collection. He specializes in landscapes of epic, even heroic proportions. They are romanticized to the point of being unreal, but my friends, how they sell. One of his paintings, *The Rocky Mountains Lander's Peak*, sold recently for $25,000."

"After he took it on tour to galleries, hotels and salons," added Winters. "The man is a master at selling. It seems he is even copyrighting his works with the Library of Congress so he can control the production and sale of the reproductions that are now priced within the reach of average working people."

"Reproduction rights are that valuable?" asked Thomas.

"You of all people should know the answer to that, lad," said Phineas. "A reproduction of that god-awful painting of you at the Battle of Pebble Creek hangs in every saloon from Boston to Portland, Oregon. There's one in a tavern not a half-mile from here. Not that I would have seen it in person, of course, my dear," he added for his wife.

Thomas and Winters laughed, and even Mrs. McNab joined in.

"Have you seen so much as a penny for that painting and its hundreds of offshoots?" asked Winters.

Thomas shook his head. The syndicate that was producing the chromolithographic reproductions of the original work—for which he had also not been consulted or paid—had never asked his permission or offered any kind of royalty. But, since he detested the painting and its false depiction of what he considered to be, at best, accidental heroics, he had never pursued the matter.

When Mrs. McNab remembered why she had originally come from the house and escorted the men in for lunch, Thomas took the opportunity to ask the obvious question about Aubert's work of Phineas and Winters.

"What the hell do I do then?"

"I know a few of the more open-minded dealers to whom I can provide you with letters of introduction," said McNab.

"And there is at least one art critic in the city, a young man fresh out of college, who might be willing to risk his reputation and actually review the work," Winters added. "I can also recommend the finest framer in New York. You'll want modest frames and quality stretchers."

"But how do I get the new museum to consider putting them on display?" Thomas asked. "If every influential person in the business is determined to stop me, how can I hope to get approved for a dedicated wall to hang the paintings on?"

"The grand opening is at the end of the month?" asked Winters.

"Yes."

"We have much to do, Preston," said Phineas as he helped himself to another slice of roast pork. "Letters, telegrams... all of the personal persuasion we have at our command. And I will travel to the city myself and do some old-fashioned arm twisting. I dare say Preston will accompany me, too."

Winters nodded, and Phineas beamed. "I have waited a lifetime to be the mid-wife at a birth of this significance," he said. Then he slapped his thigh and added, "You shall have your wall in the museum, Thomas, and Aubert's paintings will take the city by storm!"

They raised their glasses in unison and, for the first time in weeks, Thomas allowed himself to feel hopeful.

The sun was setting on a landscape of powdery snow and ice-covered tree branches when the telegram arrived at McNab's home. Thomas and Phineas were going over the plan to descend on the offices of a dozen New York City art dealers at the same time Winters would work on getting at least one newspaper art critic to agree to look at

Aubert's work.

The messenger waited in the entryway with a mug of Mrs. McNab's hot apple cider to see if Colonel Scoundrel wished to send a reply.

Thomas unfolded the yellow paper and read it aloud. It was from John Hayden and had been wired from San Pedro that morning.

'Donegan and 6 others 1 week behind you. Special delivery letter to follow. Taiana well, take care. John H.'

Thomas crumpled the telegram and tossed it into the fireplace. How Donegan had figured out where he was going was a mystery, but the man had proven to be a relentless tracker, so he wasn't completely surprised. What was confounding was the identity–and purpose–of the other six men. Donegan worked alone.

"How long will a special delivery letter take to get here from Los Angeles?" he asked Phineas.

"It's an expensive proposition, about $100 to keep it moving around the clock on every available train and coach, but in general I'd say three days."

"So, it should arrive the same day Akoni returns from the dig," Thomas said. "We'll leave as soon as he gets here, maybe rent a rig and take it to the next railroad stop and spend the night."

"Why the hurry?" asked Phineas. "You will still be at least four days ahead of the bastard if you leave from St. Louis."

Thomas looked grim. "I cannot risk Donegan learning that I came to your home, Phineas. Believe me when I say that his boss has watchers everywhere, and those who help me may be in serious peril."

Phineas walked to the fireplace and opened a brass and rosewood box on the mantel. He withdrew a pistol and slipped it through his belt. "Both of the men who work for me here saw plenty of battle in the War, Thomas. On the side of the South, I'm sorry to tell you. I'll speak with them; they'll know what to do if your friends arrive uninvited. When I leave for New York a couple of days after you, I will send my wife to her sister's place in Terre Haute. We'll be fine."

Thomas nodded. "Who knows Akoni and I are here?"

"Preston Winters. No one else."

'Let's hope that is true, for the McNab's sake,' Thomas thought as he grabbed a pencil and paper from a desk and scribbled a reply to Hayden's telegram.

A moment later he handed the paper to the messenger.

'Will be ready,' is all it said.

~ FIFTY-THREE ~

Aata often dreamed about the greatest day of his life, when he killed three attacking boars in a matter of minutes with just his spear and a long knife.

It was early January, and the rains had pelted southwestern Tahiti for weeks, even burying one small village under a mountain of mud that slid down off the mountain that had sheltered the people for generations. When the skies cleared, Aata chose two young men to accompany him into the hills to search for boar. They had been eating only fish and bread for weeks, and the village's storehouse of dried meat had long been empty. A warrior required smoked meat for energy and strength, and even the children seemed thinner and sicklier since wild pig meat disappeared from their plates.

Aata was an experienced hunter who had brought many boars to the cooking pits, but his two companions were new to the hunt and required instruction.

"*Te puaa* is strong and he is smart," he said as they hiked up the trail that wound up into the thickly forested hills that surrounded the village. "He can run as fast as a horse, jump the height of a man, and his tusks are as long as your hand. He weighs more than you, and he can smell you from across the mountain."

He looked into the eyes of the two men and was pleased to see an appropriate mix of fear and respect.

"This time of year, you must thrust your spear into his side, not into his chest as you would do most of the time. You will not pierce his chest."

"Why?" asked the men in unison as they rounded a bend in the trail and began to navigate a field of boulders that been loosened in the rains and rolled down the mountain.

"This is the mating season," Aata answered. "It lasts for three months, and in preparation the male *puaa* develops a thick coat of armor under the skin of his breast. He needs the protection because when he comes upon a group of sows, he will probably have to fight one or more rivals for their affection."

"Males do not live among sows and young ones?" one of the hunters asked.

"They live alone most of the year. When their testicles swell to three times their normal size and begin to secrete a thick, foamy liquid that smells like the gates of hell, they know it is time to find a female."

"Just one, after all that time alone?" asked the other hunter with a chuckle.

Aata slowed and turned on the narrow trail. "He will mount as many as ten sows, and at least half of them will bear his offspring."

The two young men looked at each other and laughed. "So perhaps living a few months alone isn't such a bad thing," said one. "He must go back to his den with quite a smile on his face."

"And his body shredded from the tusks of the other males he has fought, and with deep bite marks on his *ule* from some of the sows he has taken."

Both men looked down at their crotches and grimaced at the thought of such an encounter.

Aata stopped beside a fallen tree that had dried out after the rains and motioned for the others to join him. "Do you see the muddy markings here?" he said, pointing to a wide smear of mud that ran the length of the trunk. "Touch them."

His companions ran their fingers along the muddy streaks.

"Well?" asked Aata.

"They are damp, but the rest of the tree is dry," said one of the men.

"A boar has been here in the last hour," Aata replied. "They wallow in mud and then rub the mud off against trees. The wind is blowing up trail, so he knows we are here."

The young hunters shared worried looks. Talking about the chase for the mighty boar around the village fire was one thing; coming face to face with the razor-tusked monster—especially one in full romantic rut—was quite another.

Aata smiled. A healthy fear was the beginning of wisdom. "Stay 50 paces behind me and walk side-by-side on opposite sides of the trail. If I do not kill him with the first thrust, he might run down the trail in your direction. Be patient and wait for him to be almost on you before you strike. His head will be swinging from side to side; it's their way of making sure they get you with at least one tusk."

The younger men waited for Aata to take the lead and followed well behind him. It was midday, and the sky was completely clear for the first time in over a month. Small streams cut across the path in many places, and they had to hack through fallen brush several times. Then they stepped around a rock-strewn bend and saw Aata about 100 feet up the trail, walking stealthily towards a rock outcropping on which a massive male boar was taking his rest. When Aata was 50 feet from the rock the boar's head snapped up and turned towards his attacker. The great pig uttered a piercing, high-pitched cry, scrambled down the rock, and charged Aata, it's head down and shoulders hunched, ready to engage.

The young hunters froze in place, marveling at how calm Aata seemed. He stepped to the center of the trail, raised his spear to waist height, and waited. The boar was on him in less than five seconds. Just before the pig's slashing tusks ripped into his leg Aata leapt to the side of the trail and thrust his spear into the pig's gut, pulled it out, and readied for a second stab. The boar squealed, pulled to the side, and then righted himself and charged past Aata down the path towards the two inexperienced hunters, huffing in loud bursts with each step he took on his short legs.

The men did as Aata had told them and jumped to separate sides of the path, their spears at the ready, but they did not move quickly enough. In an instant, the 200-pound beast slammed into the first of the young men just as his bristly head was swinging upwards and caught the unfortunate hunter in the center of his belly. The man lurched backwards, but not before the pig swung his thickly muscled neck to the left and ripped across the hunter's abdomen.

The other hunter stabbed at the boar's side, but he did not aim straight, and the spear only creased the animal's thick skin. The boar kept slashing left and right, and the hunter trying to stab the pig in the side watched in horror as his friend's intestines spilled out of his belly and onto the ground. When the dying man collapsed in a pool of his own blood and slippery guts, the pig pulled back and turned his attention on the other hunter.

The young man willed his hands to stop trembling and steeled himself for the final battle with the infuriated boar, but when the pig was no more than a foot away, a spear flashed from out of nowhere and the pig fell to its side, flailing, kicking, and screaming. Aata stepped forward, pulled his spear from the pig's side, and stabbed it again and again until he felt the spear go through muscle and sinew and penetrate the animal's heart.

The young hunter collapsed to one knee, trying unsuccessfully to suppress the sob welling up from deep inside. He was about to thank Aata when the older warrior suddenly whipped around and went into his fighting stance, spear at the ready.

The young hunter's heart sank; two large boars appeared from out of the bright morning sun and were hurtling down the path towards he and Aata.

'But I thought they were solitary creatures who did not travel in packs,' the hunter thought as he tried to stop the shivers that were racking his body.

Somehow, he managed to raise his spear and begin trotting up the path, just as Aata leapt into the air over the back of the first boar and shoved his spear into the back of the second boar's neck. The young hunter watched in amazement as Aata pivoted on the end of his spear around behind the boar before falling to the ground with the spear still in the boar's neck.

The second pig turned and rushed towards Aata, it's head almost on the ground so that its tusks could tear Aata's legs to shreds. Aata pulled his knife and shot to his knees in the face of the charging boar. When the animal was close enough that he could see the dull yellow luster in its eyes and smell its fetid breath, he gripped the handle of the knife with both hands and thrust it upwards with every ounce of his strength. He felt the knife start to penetrate the pig's lower jaw just as the animal's momentum knocked him off his knees and onto the ground.

Aata was half buried beneath the animal, which was wriggling ferociously to pull its head off the knife, but Aata kept pushing until he felt the blade pass through the mouth cavity and break through the roof. Now on his side, Aata summoned his last reservoir of strength and thrust the knife through the top of the boar's mouth and into the animal's brain. He felt the pig shudder, followed by a sickening warmth when its bowels and bladder lost muscle and nerve control and spewed a bucket of foul-smelling waste over the warrior who had vanquished him.

Aata pulled himself out from under the dead animal and struggled to his feet. He saw the other boar circling the young hunter, looking for an opportunity to rush past the lowered spear and tear the man apart.

Aata gave a great shout, and when the boar turned his head in the direction of the sound he rushed forward, stepped to the side, and ran his spear all the way through the boar's chest. When the pig crumpled to his front legs the young hunter shook off his fear and dealt the boar a death blow to the heart.

Aata smiled and walked over to a fallen tree trunk, where he rested his spear and took a seat. A moment later the younger man joined him, and they sat in silence as the sun rose directly overhead.

There was mourning and celebration around the village fire that night. The young man killed by the great boar was eulogized by friends and family, and then when the other young hunter stood in front of the assembled villagers and told the story of how the mighty Aata had killed not one but three giant, deadly boars, the crowd roared its approval.

As for the story of Aata leaping over one boar and coming down in mid-air on the next animal with his spear stabbing deep into the beast's neck, and then swinging on the end of the spear over to the side of the trail before letting go and rejoining the battle, the villagers were beside themselves with pride and admiration. The tale of the epic fight quickly spread all the way to Hawai'i and beyond. Aata was the greatest hero since the days of the ancient demi-gods who once ruled the islands.

When the locomotive swung around a grove of oak trees outside Springfield faster than it should have been traveling, the passengers who had been sleeping were jolted awake by the pitching of the cars from left to right and the sounds of dishes falling off tables in the dining car.

Aata was shaken out of his dream and found himself wishing again that he had not accepted Wallace Stafford's offer to pursue Colonel Scoundrel to recover the bank's $50,000. The money Stafford was paying him fully funded the travel expenses for Aata and the five warriors who accompanied him from Tahiti, and it would have been difficult to find another way to pay for the trip, but he had become so filled with rage in the days and weeks following his humiliating loss in the wrestling match with Scoundrel that he grasped at the first opportunity to take his revenge, without thinking through the longer term consequences of that fateful decision.

He supposed he should have been grateful that Stafford only shrugged when Aata told him the real reason he wanted to catch up to Scoundrel.

"Kill the man or do not kill him." the banker said in a matter-of-fact tone. "I really do not care what becomes of him. But first you must collect my money. Either he has it, or he knows who does."

"And what of your brother's man?" Aata asked in a slow, measured voice. He was fluent in his native Tahitian language and in French, but he had only been studying English seriously for a few months.

"Donegan? He should not be a problem for you. My brother and

I both want the Colonel dead; I simply want a little something extra before the deed is done. Your job is to see to it that no one kills Scoundrel until you collect my cash. After that the devil may kill him for all I care."

"Donegan may have other plans," Aata replied.

Wallace blotted at the patch that covered his empty eye socket.

"And you, my well-paid friend, will see that those plans are never put into motion."

Aata stared to the back of the Pullman car, past his sleeping men and to the last brushed red velvet seat, where Fitch Donegan sat alone, smoking a cigar, and sipping a brandy while he read a Chicago newspaper.

Donegan felt Aata's stare and looked up from the paper. There was no fear or concern in the Irish assassin's eyes, thought Aata. No worry, no uncertainty. Only curiosity.

Aata held his competitor's gaze for a minute and then took a deep drink of whiskey from his hip flask, lowered his head, and went back to sleep.

~ FIFTY-FOUR ~

Moorea, December

Océane walked to the water's edge with Keani. It was just after sunrise, and the cool, cloudy world around them was completely grey, as if all the vibrant greens and blues and oranges that normally colored the island had been wiped from nature's palette.

They could see Aubert ambling up the beach with his easel and pack, but no one from the village was heading out to fish and they could not smell the cook fires or hear the sounds of children playing.

Keani lay her spear and a jug of water on the floor of the canoe and Océane helped push the little outrigger into waist deep water before Keani clambered over the side and took up a paddle. She giggled, and signed to Océane that, even at just four months, the child growing within her was making it a bit more difficult to perform the tasks that she had always taken for granted, like balancing on the prow of the canoe as she scanned the reef for fish.

"The fishermen in the village would be happy to share their catch with you," Océane said. "Perhaps you should stay on shore today. There is so much to do to get ready for Thomas' return, and for the baby's arrival."

"You are probably right," Keani signed. "I do love going out to the reef, but it won't be long until I won't be able to see over my belly to find the fish among the corals."

They laughed, and Keani added, "Today shall be my last hunt for parrot fish, then…at least until after the little one is here with us."

Océane squeezed Keani's hand and gave the outrigger a push. Then she watched her friend paddle out past the cove entrance and navigate the shallows above the reef until she found a spot that was teeming with the rainbow-colored fish favored by her people.

When she reached shore, Océane turned to wave to Keani, but her friend was already standing in the bow of the canoe, her spear raised above her shoulder, ready to pierce the surface of the water when streaks of color began to flash below her.

Océane felt a sudden chill and hurried up to the cabin for a wrap to warm her shoulders. It would be days before the grey cloak that enveloped the island would give way to the sun. For some reason, that thought made her shiver.

FIFTY-FIVE

East of Pittsburgh, PA

The freezing rain that swept down off Lake Erie had been pelting the side of the Pullman Silver Palace car all day. Thomas and Akoni holed up in their small walnut paneled staterooms until dinner time. Thomas spent his time reading a book on art given to him by McNab, while Akoni tried to stay warm as he fleshed out the journal notes from the three-day fossil dig on the banks of the Mississippi. The small pot-bellied wood stove in his room did not put out enough heat to warm his Hawaiian constitution, and he could not for the life of him understand why anyone would want to live in such a frigid climate.

They met in the ornate first-class dining car at seven, and Thomas sighed when the waiter told them that their only choice for dinner was roast beef with potatoes, glazed winter carrots, bread, and barley soup. If they cared for dessert, it would be rice pudding.

"December is the cruelest month for a gastronome," he complained to Akoni. "No seafood or fresh pork, few vegetables, no fruit, dry beef… at $4.25 per day one would think the railroad could put out a better spread."

Akoni smiled. "At home right now, they are feasting on roast suckling pig, grilled ahi tuna, savory rice, pineapple, and greens fresh from the garden. And we're the uncivilized ones?"

Their waiter heard the conversation and approached the starched linen and crystal-goblet topped table. They had learned in the past three days that Louis had an irreverent sense of humor and was unafraid to take familiarities with the first-class passengers.

"More's the pity for that, colonel," said their waiter, "but I think you will find this will ease the pain considerably." He lay a bottle of deep red wine across his forearm and lowered it beside the candle in the center of the table.

"*Chateau Lafite Rothschild,* 1871," he said with a flourish.

"Is it good?" asked Akoni.

"It's $20, if that means anything," the waiter replied.

Thomas' eyebrows raised. An average bottle of wine cost $1. A very good bottle might fetch $5. How could a bottle of wine possibly cost as much as a new revolver?

Louis read his mind. "When our wine purveyor recommends a new purchase for the railroad, he is required to open a bottle for the first-class stewards and waiters to taste. The beauty and balance of this wine are phenomenal, my friends. Seamless tannins and fruit. Full body yet so balanced and refined. You will note hints of sweet tobacco and berries and minerals and cedar. It is a beautiful wine with superb depth. But if you choose not to purchase this wine, gentlemen, I will have to sit in on the poker game that is warming up next door in the smoking car and do my best to earn enough to buy it for myself."

Akoni looked at Thomas with an expression that said, "Why not!"

Thomas smiled and shook his head. This waiter would be fired for such impertinence at Delmonico's, but somehow out here in the frigid darkness of Pennsylvania his attitude lifted Thomas' spirits.

"Did I mention that the magic of this wine will also hide the taste of what is about to come out of the kitchen?" said Louis.

"Uncork it," said Thomas. "Let us see…"

A moment later Louis had Akoni's and Thomas' glasses filled halfway.

"You didn't do that quite right, "said Thomas as he inhaled the complex aromas of the deep red wine.

A worried look crept across the waiter's face. "Sir?"

Thomas slid an empty glass across the table. "I want you to join us."

The very surprised waiter looked around the car to see if anyone was paying attention, but the other diners were engrossed in their own conversations and so he happily poured a glass for himself. The three men tapped their stemware together in a quiet toast and took their first tastes.

Thomas was a relatively new oenophile, but he was a fast learner who took every opportunity to explore new wine varieties and vintages wherever he traveled. The instant the *Lafite* made contact with his taste buds he looked into Akoni's eyes and saw that his friend, while admittedly no wine connoisseur, was experiencing the same emotions that were overwhelming his own sense of smell and taste.

The waiter set down his empty glass. "Well?" he asked.

Akoni spoke first. "I have no idea what you were talking about with all that tannin and tobacco chatter. But I am pretty sure this is the finest wine I have ever tasted."

"Extraordinary," Thomas said in a hushed voice.

Akoni gave him a perplexed look; Thomas was not given to hushed tones about any topic he was passionate about. Especially not great food or wine. Then the Hawaiian realized his friend was not thinking about the wine at all; the real effect of the remarkable vintage on Thomas had been to make him equate the perfection he was experiencing with the wife he was longing for. In fact, what Akoni saw in Thomas' eyes was pure guilt.

The waiter was also taken aback by the colonel's change in temperament. He started to turn to go to another table when Akoni said, "Do you have more?"

"Of the wine, sir?"

"Yes. We'd like another bottle."

Thomas managed a strained smile. He knew what Akoni was doing.

"We have more, sir, a full case, I believe," the waiter said. "I did mention that it is…"

"$20. Yes, you did," Akoni replied. He pulled his wallet from his breast pocket and withdrew two crisp $20 bills. "In case the meal you are about to serve kills us before we settle up," he said.

The waiter grinned and left to fetch another bottle of the *Lafite Rothschild.*

"And so now drink is the solution for melancholy?" Thomas asked. "And here I had always believed that it only deepened the condition."

"Melancholy you may become, *ho aloha*, but after two bottles of this wine it will be a quite satisfactory kind of unhappiness. You'll see."

Thomas couldn't help but smile. Akoni's use of the affectionate variation of the Hawaiian word for friend touched him. He raised his goblet. "To a pleasant melancholy," he said, and they drained their glasses.

The eastbound train cut through the rain and sleet sheeting across the Allegheny Plateau, slowing a bit as they reached the foothills of the Appalachian Mountains west of Johnstown, where the locomotive would make an early morning fueling stop and allow passengers who wished to disembark for a couple of hours to stretch their legs and perhaps enjoy a meal at a nearby hotel. The last leg of the journey to New York City was just over 300 miles, which would see the train arriving late tomorrow evening.

Thomas and Akoni pushed away from the table and walked down the narrow aisle of the lamp-lit dining room towards the rear door of the car. It was fortunate that the first-class car was only about a third full because Akoni had to turn sideways and shuffle down the aisle, apologizing to the people at each table he squeezed past. They slid open the connecting door to the smoking car and walked into a haze of cigar smoke and animated conversation. This car was full, and Thomas felt the familiar tug of the game tables, but there was still a lot of work to do before he retired for the night.

They reached the back of the smoking car and opened the door to the next cabin, which turned out to be a completely empty standard fare coach. The porters were keeping the wood stove going, but without the usual 40 or 50 bodies inside to help contribute to the heat the space was so cold that they could see their breath. Thomas was about to make a joke about the freezing morning in Ohio when he was a child and had been told to milk their cow only to discover that her teat was covered in ice, when the compartment door at the end of the car slid open and he found himself just 20 feet from Aata, who was surging into the car with five Tahitian warriors in ill-fitting suits behind him.

Thomas froze, and then felt Akoni's hand on his shoulder.

"What is this," the Hawaiian whispered.

Thomas reached inside his jacket for his pocket revolver, and he knew without checking that Akoni was drawing his weapon.

Aata came to a halt five feet in front of Thomas, raising his hand for his men to also stop. "I have traveled a long distance to find you," Aata began in halting English.

"And now that you have," replied Thomas in French.

The Tahitian seemed relieved that he did not have to continue in an unfamiliar language. His eyes bored into Thomas,' and his hand gripped the handle of the knife in his waistband. The warriors bunched up behind him looked tense, ready to spring.

After a moment of silence, Akoni spoke. "What do you want, brother?"

Aata ignored the fact that he had just been addressed as a kinsman by this great oaf simply because they both came from the same far distant corner of the globe.

"You should ask *me* that question," said a familiar voice from behind the crush of Tahitians. Thomas and Akoni were astonished to see Fitch Donegan push his way through the warriors and stand beside Aata. The look of triumph in the assassin's eyes told Thomas that his sudden appearance had had exactly the reaction he had hoped for.

Aata began to take a step forward, but Donegan placed a hand on the warrior's forearm. "I'm giving you two minutes," Donegan said to Aata, "and then I will do the job I have come here for."

"You both work for Colin Stafford?" Thomas asked. This was beyond belief.

Donegan chuckled. "Relatively speaking, colonel, and I must

emphasize the 'relative' part."

"What is your game, Donegan?" asked Akoni.

"No game," Donegan replied, "just a quiet pow-wow between two men who work for a pair of, let's say, unusual brothers."

Thomas kept his hand on his revolver butt. "Brothers? What the hell does that mean?"

"It means, my dear Colonel Scoundrel, that the entire Stafford clan is out for your hide, though my friend, Aata, has been also charged with a little extra work on the side before that particular job gets done."

The entire clan? Brothers? A light of realization began to spark in Thomas' eyes. "Colin Stafford is Wallace's brother," he said in a tone devoid of emotion.

"Bravo, colonel," said Donegan with a smile. "The Hawaiian banker and the San Francisco businessman. As unlike in physical appearance as any two men could be. All they share in common is a ruthless appreciation for money and the desire and ability to get rid of anyone who stands in their way."

"Brothers," mumbled Akoni. No one had ever breathed a word of this possibility at the court of the Hawaiian king, or in social gatherings or business meetings. It was a staggering thought.

"One dark, one fair, both committed to turning out the good colonel's lights forever," Donegan continued. The train clattered onto a long trestle, and the gas lamps on the walls flickered off and on for a moment. One of the warriors behind Aata said something in Tahitian, and Aata snapped his fingers for silence.

"I'll ask you once more, Donegan. What do you want?" said Akoni.

"My wants are few," Donegan replied. "I have been paid to find Colonel Scoundrel and deliver justice for the unwarranted attacks he made on Colin Stafford in that piss-ant newspaper he works for. His slander caused pain and humiliation and loss of revenue, and Stafford will have his revenge. Tonight."

Akoni had pulled his revolver completely out of his waistband now. Shoot Donegan and Aata first, he calculated, and the other five will scatter.

Donegan extracted a toothpick from his vest pocket and picked at a front tooth. "Terrible roast beef tonight, wouldn't you agree?"

Neither Thomas nor Akoni answered.

"And now, Aata, get to your business," Donegan said. "Two minutes, no more."

Aata put one hand on the corner of a bench seat to steady himself as the train went into a long curve.

"You owe Wallace Stafford's bank $50,000," he said to Thomas. "Pay it tonight and I will leave you."

Thomas turned to look at Akoni. "But he won't," said the Hawaiian, nodding towards Donegan.

"Donegan's business with you is of no concern to me, or to Wallace Stafford. I am instructed to collect the money and return to Honolulu. What happens afterwards," he spat on the floor, "I do not care. If it were my choice, I would kill the bastard this minute and be done with it."

"Didn't care for the army boy marching between your girl's legs, eh?" laughed Donegan.

Aata did not take the bait. He kept his gaze fixed on Thomas' face and pistol hand. "Pay now," he said, "and we are through."

Thomas looked around the car. The warriors with Aata were itching to fight, and Donegan was holding a long knife flat against his leg. Even with their pistols, he and Akoni would be lucky to kill two or three of the men before they were overwhelmed.

"I don't have the money, Aata," said Thomas. "In fact, I am on my way to get it in New York City. From there I will take it directly to your boss, and, as you say, we will be done."

Aata sensed that the colonel was telling the truth. "Then I will come with you to New York, and I will wait while you gather the money. Then I will travel at your side to Hawaii and watch you pay your debt in full."

Donegan chuckled. "That's your plan?" The hand holding the knife began to raise up from his side. "I have another…"

Thomas stepped back and prepared to shoot. Then Akoni let out a great cry, leaned over to the wall of the compartment, and ripped a heavy brass lamp from its mooring. He flung it at Aata, striking him in the chest and knocking him backwards into his men. All six Tahitians were shoved back in the narrow corridor between the seat rows by the momentum of the lamp and Aata, and Donegan got caught up in the avalanche of bodies and was briefly knocked off his feet.

The respite was brief. Aata and the rest of his men leapt to their feet and rushed forward in single file between the seats. Just as he pulled the trigger on his revolver, Thomas was momentarily surprised to see Donegan slink to the back of the car, only to realize that the assassin was making a strategic retreat. He would let Thomas and Akoni tire themselves fighting Aata and his men, and only come to the fight if the Tahitians could not get the job done themselves. His contract called for Scoundrel dead. At that moment he didn't care how the job got done.

The sound from Thomas' pistol was deafening in the enclosed space. His shot missed Aata, caught the man directly behind him in the shoulder and sent him reeling to the floor. Before he could fire again, Aata and another man were on him, punching and clawing and hammering with their fists. Out of the corner of his eye, Thomas saw three of Aata's warriors climbing over seat backs to get to Akoni, and a moment later his friend was smothered beneath a pile of thrashing bodies.

Thomas kept his elbows close to his body and began to punch methodically at Aata and the man behind him. He caught Aata once on the chin and landed a solid blow to the other man's jaw, but the Tahitians got their blows in, too. Thomas felt the air escape from his stomach, and a pain like a bee stinging slash across his forehead.

He grabbed the front of Aata's shirt with both hands and smashed his head into Aata's with all his strength. Aata fell back against a seat, which knocked down the man fighting alongside him.

Thomas looked quickly behind him where Akoni was punching and wrestling three of the warriors. The giant Hawaiian tossed one of the men like a rag doll across the compartment, only to be swarmed again and pushed to the floor. Thomas aimed and fired into the coil of arms and legs flailing around on the floor, hitting one of the Tahitians right behind his knee. The man rolled to the side, shrieking in pain. Now it was just two against one, odds that Thomas knew would be in his friend's favor.

Aata and the warrior fighting beside him had gotten back up, and they came towards Thomas and then suddenly stopped. Aata wiped blood from his mouth with his sleeve and fought to catch his breath.

"Enough!" he yelled to his men. "We must remember why we came here."

Thomas kept his pistol aimed at Aata's chest until Akoni threw off the two men he had been grappling with and got to his feet. The Hawaiian was bleeding from a cut above his eyebrow, but other than that he appeared to be in one piece.

"We will return to our cabin," said Aata between gasps for breath. "I will follow you to the city tomorrow and you will give me the bank's money as soon as you collect it. After that…" His voice trailed off.

After that, what? Thomas wondered as he re-holstered his gun.

The car smelled of gunpowder and sweat, and a deep cold seeped in from the Pennsylvania countryside and enveloped the exhausted combatants. Aata and his men took seats on the velvet cushioned benches, not sure what to do now.

Thomas was getting ready to reply to Aata when Fitch Donegan walked swiftly towards them from the back of the car with a revolver pointed at Thomas' head.

"Put it down," Donegan barked at Akoni, who had pulled his own revolver. "I will not miss his head from this distance."

Akoni slipped his gun back into his waistband and stood still with his arms at his side.

"What about Wallace Stafford's orders for Aata to collect the money?" asked Thomas. "I assume Colin was going along with them to mollify his brother, and you agreed?"

Donegan grinned. "Now ain't you the funny one, colonel. From the rumors I have heard, you disobeyed a direct command from a superior officer during the war and charged up some damn fool hill and took on a swarm of Confederates all by yourself. Got lucky that day, by God, but you did. So don't preach to me about following orders." He drew back the hammer of his revolver with his thumb. "I was ordered to kill you, colonel and that's…"

Two things happened in the blink of an eye. Thomas felt rather than saw Akoni leap forward towards Donegan, and at the same instant he caught a blur of motion coming up behind the Irishman. Then a brass tube flashed in the candlelight, arced downwards and smashed Donegan's skull. He dropped his revolver, toppled forward, and lay still.

Akoni rammed into the corner of a seat, and he, Aata, the warriors and Thomas craned their necks to see who had wielded the fire hydrant with such deadly precision.

Thomas and Akoni were too stunned to speak. They could only stare, their mouths agape.

Standing over Donegan's prostate form, wearing a man's trousers, cap, and jacket was 14-year-old Taiana, whom they had left for safekeeping with John Hayden in San Pedro ten days earlier.

~ FIFTY-SIX ~

Johnstown, PA

The locomotive was firing up as Thomas sipped coffee in the first-class Pullman car and watched the rotund county sheriff talking with Donegan and Aata on the station platform under a clear, cold December sky. A moment after Taiana had decked the Irishman with the brass fire hydrant last night, the connecting door from the smoking car slid open and the conductor and four armed attendants raced into the battle ground. They gathered up everyone's guns and had them take seats while the conductor tried to sort things out.

Thomas tried never to trade on his fame in the course of day-to-day life, but this was one of those times when being a recognized hero was in his favor. He explained the situation to the conductor, who nodded gravely and then ordered everyone—including Aata and the slowly recovering Donegan—to separate to opposite ends of the car and remain there until they arrived in Johnstown at sunrise. The sheriff would take things from there. The conductor left three armed porters in the car to make sure everyone behaved, and the combatants settled into an uneasy truce until the sun rose above the eastern hills and they pulled into the station.

When the sheriff and six deputies arrived, Thomas knew immediately that Donegan and Aata would not be spending much time behind bars. The corpulent lawman in the poorly fitting three-piece suit and bowler hat had the look of a civil servant who took maximum advantage of the benefits his station allowed. From free food—much of it greasy judging from the smears on his coat—to the smell of gin from too many drinks on the house, the sheriff wore his corruption on his sleeve.

The dining car door opened and Akoni and Taiana made their way down the aisle. The giant Hawaiian was sporting two black eyes, but judging from the way the warriors he battled last night had hobbled off the car under guard a few minutes ago, Thomas knew who had the best of the fight. Taiana handed Thomas a plate with toast and jam and sat down beside him.

"I sent a porter to telegram John Hayden in San Pedro," he said to her. "I'm sure he and his wife are worried about you."

Unlike Akoni and Thomas, Taiana seemed none the worse after last night's donnybrook. One of the benefits of youth, Thomas mused.

"I'm not going back, you know," Taiana volunteered in a defiant tone.

"They mistreated you?" asked Akoni.

"Oh, no, they were wonderful. The nicest people I have ever met."

Thomas was perplexed. "And so, you left because…?"

Taiana held her head high and stared directly into Thomas' eyes. "Because you need me." Then she looked over at Akoni. "You both do."

Akoni laughed. "You think we need a nanny?"

"You needed one last night," Taiana answered.

Now Thomas laughed. "Hard to disagree with that. The problem is that we are headed into more trouble, and unless I am mistaken Donegan and Aata will telegraph Colin Stafford this morning and be out of jail by nightfall, if not sooner."

"This part of the journey is no place for you, *wahine 'opio*," Akoni said in a tender voice. "A young lady should be in school or working as an apprentice in a dress shop. We signed on for this, you didn't."

A porter passed by, and Taiana asked him to fetch a pencil and paper. When he returned a minute later, she scribbled something, signed it, and slid it over to Akoni.

"What's this?" he asked.

"A contract," she replied. "I am now signed up, the same as you two."

Thomas sighed. "We wish it were that simple, Taiana. Getting a dealer to show Aubert's paintings at the opening of the new Metropolitan Museum of Art will be difficult enough. But, with Donegan and the Tahitians on our trail, it will be more than difficult—it will be downright dangerous. You need to go home."

Taiana's eyes welled with tears. "Home? My home was on Oah'u before we were transported to the leper colony on Moloka'i. Which of those places do you plan to send me to?"

Akoni and Thomas were silent. Taiana stared at the tabletop for a moment and then said, "Here is my proposal: take me to New York City with you. I will run errands, shuttle messages, fetch meals, whatever you need. I can save you a great deal of time, and I will be an extra set of eyes when Donegan shows up."

"If he shows up," Thomas added. "He knows we are going to the city, that's all. We'll be swallowed up among more than a million people and dozens of hotels. Needles in a haystack, that sort of thing."

"And yet he will come," Taiana insisted. "You know he will."

"Yes, he will come," Thomas said in a thoughtful voice.

"Was there more to your proposal?" asked Akoni.

She nodded. "Let me stay with you and be your assistant. I have a little money…"

"That I gave you," Thomas chimed in.

"Yes, that you gave me. But I can pay my own way with it. I don't have to stay at the kind of luxury hotel you will, and I don't eat much."

Akoni chuckled and exchanged a glance with Thomas. This girl was a warrior, and since they were outnumbered 7 to 2 by Donegan and the Tahitians, having another warrior—even a young one—beside them was not a bad idea.

"You will do as you are told?" Akoni asked her.

"I will."

"And when we have completed our business, you will get back on the train and return to San Pedro?" Thomas said.

Taiana could not hold back the note of triumph in her voice. "I promise."

The steam in the engine's dome had built up to pressure, and Thomas could feel the engineer opening the throttle valve. The familiar 'chuff-chuff' sound echoed outside the Pullman car's windows, and the pistons began to push the drive wheel rods forward.

As they began to inch away from the platform, Thomas locked eyes with Donegan, who was still talking with the sheriff. The assassin shot Thomas a smirking half-smile and a nod that said, 'see you soon.'

When the train cleared the station, Thomas turned and looked back. The last thing he saw before the train rounded a bend in a cloud of blue-white steam was the sheriff removing Donegan's handcuffs. The man wasn't even going to see the outside walls of the county jail, Thomas realized. He finished his coffee and wondered how much that little courtesy had cost the man who had been sent to kill him.

The iron locomotive built up speed and hurtled to the east. Thomas and Akoni spent the day mapping out plans for introducing Aubert's paintings to the New York City art world, and filling Taiana in on everything that had transpired since they left her in California.

"We will arrive in the city tonight," Thomas said when they took lunch, "and take a carriage from Grand Central Depot to the Gilsey House Hotel on Broadway at West 29th Street. I have been told that it is new, and rather elegant." He looked at Taiana and smiled. "And you will have a room there as well, young lady. Phineas McNab and Preston Winters will meet us in three days. They will have several of Aubert's paintings stretched and framed, and they will scout out the best art dealers for us to visit."

"And what are we going to do for three days?" Akoni asked.

"Explore the city and get our bearings. Learn how to use the elevated trains and streetcars and memorize the quickest routes between our hotel and the Metropolitan Museum and any other important places. We'll also update our wardrobes—you included, Taiana. I have letters to write, and you have business with the Museum of Natural History. Taiana can come with you and study the exhibits while you meet with your people."

"My suits will require tailoring, you know," said Akoni, "I am not an easy man to fit."

"And I simply refuse to wear anything with a bustle," added Taiana,"and as for the hats women are wearing these days, no monstrosity like those will ever touch this head."

Thomas shook his head. *"With everything we have to be worried about,"* he thought...

~ FIFTY-SEVEN ~

New York City, December 1872

Thomas was in fine spirits when he began his journey through the art district at 10 AM. The gallery owners along newly fashionable 57th Street were rolling up their protective wrought-iron window coverings and opening their doors to the public when the hansom cab dropped him off. A short five hours later he was sitting on a curb with his hat in his hands; depressed, exhausted, frustrated, and cold.

Inside the two canvas satchels leaning beside him were the paintings that Preston Winters had stretched and framed the night before in the small warehouse they rented. As soon as two more were framed, Phineas would take them to dealers he knew on 5th and Madison Avenues, with an invitation to anyone who was interested to visit the warehouse and see all the canvasses laid out on tables. Winters would continue stretching and framing Aubert's paintings while Thomas and Phineas made their rounds.

By 2:30 that afternoon, Thomas had presented the paintings to the owners of four of the district's most successful shops. Each had been eager to view the work of a promising new artist, and he was welcomed with sherry, coffee, and sweets. The warmth was short-lived, however; within minutes of pulling the paintings out of the satchels, Thomas was being ushered to the front door and propelled out onto the sidewalk. Now, after the fourth disastrous call in a row he huddled against the biting wind and planned his next move. He hoped that Phineas was having better luck.

Phineas had explained that the art business was extraordinarily competitive, which meant that a dealer who discovered the right sort of new artist could see both his sales and his prestige soar overnight. "You'll have that going for you when you step through the door," he promised. "It also won't hurt that the art dealers will probably recognize your name, which will make getting an invitation to display the paintings an even easier proposition."

Thomas quicky found that the shops—and the proprietors who ran them—were cut from the same cloth. The display windows fronting the street were filled with eye-catching bric-a-brac, and the store interiors were crammed with landscape and portrait paintings, sculptures, vases, rugs, tapestries, and the kinds of *objects d'art* that filled McNab's library in St. Louis. The dealers tended to be overdressed for daytime and a bit too well fed, with slicked down hair, waxed moustaches, and well-trimmed goatees. Each also employed at least one attractive female sales assistant in her early 30s, the better, Thomas assumed, to help close a sale when a gentleman was contemplating the purchase of a gift for his lady.

The sequence of events at each shop had played out the same way; Thomas introduced himself, he and the art dealer exchanged a few pleasantries, and when Thomas explained the purpose of his visit the dealer invited him into a private viewing room with several empty wooden easels upon which to place paintings. The dealer turned his back while Thomas set the paintings on the easel, a formality Phineas told him was a normal practice so the owner could see the work for the first time the same way a customer would.

And then—with only the tiniest variations of timing and emotional intensity separating one dealer from another—the eruption took place. The man would turn to view Aubert's paintings, place his hands on his hips, sputter a bit, and go scarlet-faced. Then he would let fly with some of his native language's most colorful expletives. Thomas couldn't count the number of times he had heard terms like 'vile, atrocious, childish, barbaric, unfinished, monstrous, and sloppy, along with what he was certain were the darkest curse words in Hebrew at one of the shops.

At first, he attempted to counter the protests; the world is changing, he argued, people's tastes are changing, and collectors are ready for radical new approaches to light and color and motion. The epic landscapes and serene portraits that had constituted most of the painting market for the last hundred years had become lifeless and repetitive. Change was inevitable; why not be in the vanguard of the most transformative movement the art world had ever witnessed? There was profit to be made, untapped markets to exploit, and brand new income streams waiting to be navigated.

His arguments went nowhere. The first two dealers to whom he presented Aubert's work stormed out of their viewing rooms, leaving their assistants to take Thomas' elbow and escort him to the front door, which they slammed home as a final critique of Aubert's work. He did not attempt to counter the objections of the third and fourth dealers; instead, by the time the inevitable tirades began, he was already packing up and heading for the door under his own power.

Their train had arrived at Cornelius Vanderbilt 's newly opened Grand Central Depot three days earlier. The city was growing at a furious pace and was in desperate need of a new central station for their three major railroad lines. The enormous, vaulted structure along 42nd street on the outskirts of town was the world's largest, and a marvel of Second Empire architecture. It was crisscrossed by 12 tracks and could handle 150 cars at once. The Depot was so big that it housed a half dozen restaurants, billiard parlors, retail stores, and even a police station.

When they stepped outside the station, however, they came face to face with a problem more suited to the Middle Ages than to a modern, bustling metropolis. New York City ran on horsepower, and two months earlier a plague swept down from Toronto and New England and infected nearly every one of the 15,000 work horses in the city. The sickness only killed a few, but most horses were unable to work for weeks, which meant that thousands of men had to take on the tasks of moving goods around the city, pulling trams, pushcarts, wheelbarrows, and even carriages. City health authorities had declared the plague over the week before, but there were only a dozen rental carriages outside the station when there would normally be 100 or more.

They waited two hours for a carriage to take them to the newly constructed Gilsey House Hotel on Broadway, and their driver kept up a running commentary on civic doings during the 15-minute ride. "Them damn corrupt Tammany politicians are finally getting run out," he said between chews of foul-smelling tobacco, "and that there," he said, pointing to a massive steel structure rising along the East River, "is the new Brooklyn Bridge that should be complete in a couple years."

The driver looked back at Taiana, who was shivering beneath a buffalo robe blanket. "Yes, it's cold, little lady, but let me tell you that you are better off traveling across the city when it's freezing. Most of the year the sidewalks and streets are covered with sewage, trash, and all kinds of dead animals. Makes for quite a sweet bouquet come about August, damned if it don't."

Taiana looked disgusted, which set the driver chuckling. "All that wonderful stew is still out there, by the way—it's just frozen solid, so watch where you step when you are out and about."

It was nearly dark when they pulled up in front of the eight-story Gilsey. Its white cast-iron façade was covered with a three-story mansard roof, and each of the street-facing windows was topped with a green striped awning.

Two boys in bright red jackets raced from the outside bell stand to carry their luggage into the lobby. Thomas paid the driver and the fellow let fly with another gooey mass of tobacco juice. "I'm told they have speaking tubes in every room that allow you to talk to the folks in the office," he said. "Imagine ordering room service while you're still in your underwear." He laughed at his own joke and started to flick the reins. Then he looked at Taiana and decided to share one more piece of advice. "There are plenty of places in the city where you will be safe, and where you can find first-class restaurants. The hotel concierge will know them. But I'm tellin' you to stay out of the Five Points, and probably the Bowery, too. Nothing but trouble and death in those places for people like you."

With that he gave his horse a light tap with his whip and swung out into a street clogged with traffic. Akoni wrapped an arm around Taiana's shoulder. "Welcome to civilization," he said with a grin.

They took three rooms on the hotel's fifth floor, which they reached by a steam-powered elevator. When the bell boy opened Taiana's door, she looked ready to faint. The room was decorated in rosewood and walnut, with a veined marble fireplace, a bronze-gilt chandelier and gas lighting. She skipped across the room as Thomas and Akoni watched and rushed back a moment later. "There is a tub and sink with hot water!" she exclaimed.

Thomas smiled. "Let's get settled in and then go to dinner."

"I'm not sure I have the right things to wear," Taiana replied.

"We'll take care of that tomorrow," said Akoni. "There are shops here in the hotel and all up and down the street. Don't worry about what to wear tonight."

When they had freshened up, the trio met in the lobby. Thomas led them to the concierge desk and asked for a restaurant recommendation.

"We have a world-class establishment right here, Colonel," the attendant said in a clipped British accent.

"I'm sure you do, and we will avail ourselves of your restaurant over the coming days. Tonight, though, we thought we would like an authentic Italian dinner. Can you recommend someplace?"

"Of course, sir, the finest Italian eatery in the city is only a few blocks from here; let me write down the name for you."

As the concierge reached under his desk for a pencil and paper, Akoni said, "If you don't mind, we would like something small, more authentic, and relaxed. A family kind of place."

Taiana smiled. She knew that Akoni was doing this for her; she would not have been comfortable at a first-class restaurant in her traveling ensemble.

"Of that, I am not certain," the concierge began.

Thomas stepped closer to the desk and slid a $5 bill across the counter. "I know you are compensated by restaurants for recommending them," he said in a quiet voice. "Please allow us to do that for you in this instance."

The concierge pocketed the money and looked around to make sure no other hotel employees were in hearing range. "Of course, sir. My personal favorite is five blocks away, tucked around a corner. It's called *La Villeta*, and it is run by the most extraordinary woman. Her name is Isabella, and if you would please tell her than Robert sent you it will assure me the best table in the house the next time I visit."

Thomas nodded his thanks and the concierge signaled for a bell boy to lead them to the hansom cab stand out front.

They arrived at *La Villeta* just before 8 PM. The small restaurant was sandwiched between two office buildings and featured a red and green metal awning. Two plate glass windows offered a good view of the interior, but Thomas was disheartened to see that there weren't any customers present.

The door was open, and they stepped inside a warm, softly lit space filled with tables topped with white-linen tablecloths, candles, and vases of dried flowers. Paintings with scenes of Italy decorated the red brick walls, and a candle chandelier cast delicate shadows across the dark wood floor.

"It's so beautiful," Taiana said.

Akoni started to reply when the door from the kitchen opened and a petite woman in her mid 30s swept into the foyer to greet her guests. She had startlingly blue eyes, a Mediterranean complexion, and her hair was piled on top of her head in a no-nonsense fashion that proclaimed she was all business.

"*Buonasera,*" said the woman, "and welcome to *La Villeta.*"

"And good evening to you," Thomas replied. "Robert at Gilsey House gave your restaurant his highest recommendation, but we weren't sure if you were open."

"We typically close at 8 during the week," she said, "But…"

"Then perhaps we can come back earlier tomorrow," Akoni answered before she finished her sentence.

The woman chuckled. "What I was about to say was that we are closed, but if you and your companions would care to join my staff and me in our evening meal, you are most welcome." Then she looked Akoni over and added, "In any event, I would not want to be the person responsible for causing your death by starvation."

Thomas grimaced inwardly, knowing how much Akoni despised jokes about his size. To his surprise, the giant Hawaiian only smiled and nodded his head. *'My God,'* Thomas thought, *'I think he is smitten with her.'* He exchanged a knowing glance with Taiana and saw that she was thinking the same thing.

Thomas stepped into the awkward silence. "We would be delighted to join you all," he said.

A waiter stuck his head out of the kitchen and the woman asked him to bring bread and wine. Then she led the three friends to a corner table and seated them.

"Now then," she said, "I am Isabella Antonori, and this is my restaurant. And who do I have the pleasure of dining with this evening?"

"These are my friends Akoni and Taiana," Thomas said. "My name is Thomas."

"Just Thomas?"

"Colonel Thomas E. Scoundrel," Taiana chimed in before clapping her hand over her mouth in embarrassment for the outburst.

"I know your name, Colonel," said Isabella. "It is an honor to have you in my establishment. And Akoni and Taiana; forgive me, but I don't believe I have heard those names before."

"We are from the Kingdom of Hawai'i," Akoni began, "where our names have long and noble histories."

The waiter appeared with a basket of warm bread and a dish of peppered olive oil in his hands and a bottle of red wine under one arm.

"I look forward to hearing those histories," Isabella said to Akoni as she opened the wine and poured a taste into their glasses. "My family are from Piedmont, at the foot of the Alps in northern Italy not far from France and Switzerland. This is *Barolo*, our most famous wine. It is produced from the *Nebbiolo* grape and should age for at least five years to bring out its flavor. This bottle has been cellared for ten years."

Thomas inhaled the scent of mountain berries, cherries, and roses, which accentuated a note of spice on the tongue. He swished his glass and took a second taste, "Excellent," he said with a satisfied smile. His companions nodded agreement and Isabella filled their glasses.

"So, how does this staff dinner work?" Thomas asked. "Do we prepare our own?"

Isabella laughed and set a hand on Akoni's shoulder. "Would you like to prepare your own meal?" she asked him.

"I think you would be surprised at the result," Thomas said. "Akoni is a master of Polynesian cuisine."

"I shall look forward to discovering just what that means," replied Isabella.

'She doesn't waste any time,' Thomas thought.

Isabella poured more wine. "As to your question, Colonel…"

"Thomas, please," he said.

"No, you don't have to cook, Thomas. Right now, the kitchen staff is working with the main ingredients we featured for our guests tonight; I believe they will serve fresh pasta with a light red sauce and shaved truffles, veal sautéed with lemon and butter, baked sea bass, pork tenderloin with rosemary and garlic, roasted red potatoes, and several salads. For dessert we will have coffee and *maritozzos*, which are small, sweet buns cut down the middle and filled with custard. And more wine, of course. Perhaps a *Barberesco* to follow the *Barolo*, and of course a *Vin Santo* with dessert."

Taiana's eyes widened. "We eat and drink all that?"

"No, my dear," Isabella answered with a laugh. "My staff fill platters and dishes and roll them out on carts. Each time a cart rolls by your table you choose what you wish. *Simplice*-simple. And now I must see to the kitchen."

As she turned to go, Thomas said "Isabella, we would very much like you to join us for dinner, if that is possible."

She looked into Akoni's eyes. His smile said everything.

"I would love that," she said.

Isabella was a born hostess and storyteller, charming, witty, and despite being a very successful businesswoman, quite humble, as well. As they dished up pasta, savory sliced tenderloin, and salads, she told the story of how her family had come to New York City when she was ten. Her father had been a moderately successful businessman in Italy, and he built on that success with an import business that thrived and prospered until the day he suddenly died at his desk from a heart attack. Isabella had no interest in the import business, and with her mother's approval she sold the family business and built *La Villeta*, which was now recognized as one of New York's premier dining establishments.

"My mother passed two years ago," she said, "and so I am alone."

"You're not married?" asked Akoni in disbelief.

"I tried," she answered with a wistful smile. "It didn't take."

Thomas remained quiet for most of the dinner; he was learning more about Akoni by listening to him answer Isabella's questions than he even knew. What his friend did not share with their hostess, however, was the most important fact of all: he was royalty, the nephew of the Monarch of Hawai'i, and a possible heir to the throne. Perhaps not the easiest thing to tell a woman as she was casting her spell on you, Thomas mused.

Over dessert Taiana peppered Isabella with questions about life in the city. "This place is magical," she said. "Could you ever see yourself living anywhere else?"

Akoni's eyebrows went up at that question.

"Yes, in many ways it is magical," Isabella said. "Of course, we just went through a terrible horse epidemic, and we deal with regular bouts of typhus, cholera, diphtheria, smallpox, meningitis, and tuberculosis, mostly concentrated in the tenement districts on the Lower East Side. Irish gangs are growing in influence, city hall and the police are corrupt, crime and prostitution have sunk their tentacles into every part of the city, the air is foul with the stench of human and animal waste and garbage in the summer, and we live in constant fear of fire sweeping the city, especially after last's year's terrible fire in Chicago." She smiled tenderly at Taiana. "Other than that, New York is a perfect place to live…"

Taiana looked contrite. "I am sorry for asking so many questions."

"Nonsense," Isabella replied, "It is I who have been doing the questioning. And yet, I have not asked the most important question of all: how and why did you come here?"

"That question takes hours to answer," Thomas replied, "and sadly, Taiana and I have early morning obligations. Perhaps we can get together again soon."

"I'd like that," Isabella said, "and if you don't mind…"

Akoni interrupted her. "Speaking for myself, my morning is open, and I do not need to rush off. If you would care to make another one of those wonderful coffees, I would be happy to stay behind and tell our story. From the beginning."

Isabella's eyes sparkled. "Offer accepted." She stood and walked Thomas and Taiana to the door.

When she shook Thomas' hand, Isabella said, "I sense that you are here on very important and perhaps even dangerous business. I know the city and many important people, Thomas. Do not hesitate to call on me."

Then she turned and embraced Taiana. "You are a lovely young woman. I insist on pulling you away from these two for an afternoon of shopping while you are here."

Taiana was aglow as she and Thomas waved to Akoni and stepped outside into the clear, cold night air. Thomas raised his hand to hail a passing hansom cab and Taiana took his arm.

"Do you think Akoni has any idea what is happening in there?" she asked.

He squeezed her arm in reply and chuckled. "Not a clue."

As they stepped up into the cab he added, "But I don't think he is going to mind one bit."

~ FIFTY-EIGHT ~

Someone was trying to batter down the door. Thomas shook off his sleep, swung his legs out over the floor and turned up the gas lamp on the wall beside his bed. Donegan and the Tahitians wouldn't announce themselves this way, he thought. He pulled his revolver from its holster on the chair just to be safe, and as the pounding continued, he went to the door and opened it a crack.

"Let us in, boy, let us in," laughed a thoroughly sotted Phineas. Behind the art collector an arm holding a bottle of brandy raised up and a muffled voice rang out, "Breach it, Phineas, dammit, this business cannot wait."

For a moment Thomas wasn't sure if he should slam the door in his friend's faces or wave them into his room. "Alright," he sighed, "but for God's sake, try to hold it down. This is a hotel, not a brothel."

"And more's the pity for that sad fact," said Winters as he stumbled through the door behind Phineas. "If ever there was a day a man deserved a little slap and tickle, this would be it."

Thomas closed the door and pointed his friends to the Chesterfield sofa against the far wall. "Do you have any idea of the time?" he asked.

Phineas took the brandy bottle from Winters and started to take a drink, but Thomas reached over and snatched it from his hand.

"Well, ain't he the high and mighty one," said Phineas in a slurred voice. "And us with such good news, you might say."

"You could say, and you should," added Winters. "But to be precise I believe the colonel asked for the time of day."

"Ah, the time," mused Phineas. "Let's see…we entered the hotel bar at eleven and drank two bottles of that very nice Portuguese Madeira. Would have had a third bottle but the louts who run the place drove us away. A pox on their houses…"

"And on their balls," exclaimed Winters. "No one would worry about a pox on their house, but a pox on one's todger is nothing to laugh at."

"And have you had the great misfortune of suffering such a pox, my dear Preston?" asked Phineas.

"There was once this dusky gal in Philadelphia," Winters began, but Thomas had had enough.

"Gentlemen," he said in his best command voice. "Let's set aside the pox and the madeira and the brandy. Why are you here in the middle of the night?"

"Not quite that late, Colonel," Phineas answered in a hurt tone. "If we started drinking at…"

"Eleven…" Wintered chimed in.

"Yes, at eleven, I was getting to that my dear fellow. Let's see now…" he looked down at his hand and began counting on his fingers. "Two bottles, eight glasses in all, four glasses each, ten minutes per glass…"

"Make that 15, Phineas, I am no drunk," Winters objected.

"Fifteen then," said Phineas. "That means we finished the wine in an hour, and therefore, it must be no later than midnight."

Thomas couldn't help but smile at the look of triumph on Phineas' face for having unraveled the mystery of the time of day.

"No, no, I am sorry my friend, but you have left out several important details," said Winters.

Phineas raised his eyebrows.

"I went off to the pissoir at least once, and so did you."

"True enough," said Phineas with a shake of his head.

"And then there was the search for this," said Winters as he retrieved the brandy from Thomas' hand and raised it to his lips. "We had to find the bell boy," he said, wiping his mouth on his sleeve, "who had to talk to the porter, who had to step outside and around the corner to the saloon to get a full bottle. A good half hour spent there, Phineas."

"All for a good cause, lads. There's no denying that." Phineas turned to Thomas and said, "I'll amend my previous estimate, and say that it could be as late as 1 AM—but no later."

Thomas went to the bedside table and picked up his pocket watch. "In fact, it's closer to 3 AM. Time to call it a day."

"Is he joking," asked Winters. "Doesn't he know yet?"

Phineas shrugged. He wasn't in charge of people finding things out.

"Know what?" Thomas asked. "Other than that the two of you are quite drunk."

Phineas turned to Winters, "Do you think it was difficult for the boy to figure that one out?"

"Took him a while, that's for sure," Winters replied.

Thomas took a seat on the upholstered chair at the foot of his bed. "For the love of God, won't somebody just tell…"

"Haven't we taken care of that little matter?" asked Winters. He winked at Phineas and said, "Illuminate the boy before he wets himself."

Phineas leaned forward and placed his hands on his knees. "Thomas, we have news: our friend, the enormously talented and soon-to-be famous artist Émile Jean-Baptiste Aubert, late of Moorea, is now officially represented by the New York City gallery of Isaac Mandleman, one of the true giants of the American art world."

"May his children and his children's children be blessed," said Winters as he raised the bottle to his lips again. *"L'chaim."*

"What…when…how did this happen?" asked Thomas. A gallery was representing Aubert! He would have to add to the letter he wrote to Keani earlier in the evening. He smiled and shook his head. His friends had every right to celebrate.

"Who is he?" Thomas asked.

"Who, indeed," Phineas answered. "He is 80, scion of a wealthy Jewish merchant family, and for over 50 years one of the leading art dealers on the East Coast. "

"He's respected?" Thomas asked.

"He's reviled," Winters shot back. "The art world is a hive of treachery and villainy, and Mandleman has earned their active and undying enmity because he is an honest man who has carved out his own path with no concerns about his competitor's politics or policies. He has been a thorn in their side for decades."

"More like a turd in the Sunday punchbowl if you care to ask them for their perspective," said Winters with a hiccup.

"Aye," Phineas answered, "and by taking on Aubert's paintings, he is going to face a blizzard of condemnation. I have no doubt it will hurt his reputation as much as his profit line."

"I don't understand," said Thomas as he went over to re-take the brandy. "Why would Mandleman do it, knowing the damage it would do him?"

"Two reasons," Phineas replied. "The first is that he genuinely loves Aubert's work. You should have seen him when he stepped into the warehouse and saw the paintings..."

"Half of 'em framed, by the way," said Winters.

Phineas smiled at his friend. "And beautifully so, good Preston."

"Mandleman has been watching this new breed of painters with real interest," Phineas continued. "He told us that his friend, the art dealer Paul Durand-Ruel, who I also know, feels the same way, so much so that he recently purchased 35 paintings from a young artist named Édouard Manet for the princely sum of 35,000 francs."

"Is that a lot? "Thomas asked.

"A pittance," Winters replied. "Durand-Ruel is convinced that this new style of painting will turn the art world on its head, but not overnight. In fact, he's convinced that it will be 15 to 20 years before this style comes into its own and is accepted by dealers and collectors."

Thomas took a drink from the bottle. "But Mandleman thinks differently? He believes Aubert's work will sell now?"

"That brings us to the second reason the old gentleman has agreed to show the work. He is not concerned if there is not huge demand immediately. But he believes that condition can change as quickly as the weather. In the meanwhile, by supporting the work that his colleagues have declared to be monstrous and intolerable, he will be poking them in the eye with a very sharp stick."

"More like in the ass," Winters chuckled.

"He is prepared to invest in advertising, and renting space for the Metropolitan's Grand opening?" Thomas asked.

"He has already secured an entire room, one of the largest in the building. Since the Metropolitan is barely large enough to display their own permanent collection, they have rented a new hotel next door that is just completing construction for the grand opening. The bottom floors will be used to show works from all the major galleries in the city."

"Including Aubert's," Thomas said in a quiet voice.

Phineas and Winters smiled and nodded their heads in unison.

"It's a grand day, boyo," said Winters. "Tomorrow we will meet at Mandleman's gallery and map out our strategy. Today is the 9th...we have 14 days to the opening on the 23rd.

Phineas ran a hand through his unruly silver hair. "And so, we'd better get along for some rest."

He and Winters stood, and Thomas walked them to the door. "I can't thank you enough," he said, "each of you."

"Give the young lady the news over breakfast and take a cab to Mandleman's on 5th Avenue," said Phineas. "We'll have coffee and figure out just how deeply we can shove that stick up the New York art world's arse."

As Thomas closed the door, he heard Winters say, "I'm thinking it should be all the way. After all, if a thing is worth doing..."

Then, to the sounds of his friend's raucous laughter echoing down the hotel hallway, Thomas turned out the lamp and lay his head on the pillow.

It really had been a grand day.

~ FIFTY-NINE ~

"**I**t is neither unethical nor illegal if even a single collector is willing to pay the price," Mandleman was saying. A dusting of snow was falling outside the 5th Avenue gallery, and Thomas, Akoni, Phineas, Winters and Taiana were all seated around a coal-burning stove in a corner of the cluttered shop.

"So that I have it clear," Thomas replied, "we can ask any price we wish for Aubert's works, but until someone actually buys one at our asking price, collectors will simply ignore our price sheet and feel free to make any offer, even for a fraction of our list price?"

"Yes," answered the elderly gallery owner, "which is why at least one—preferably two—of Aubert's paintings should be sold to respected buyers before the opening event."

"Why 'respected' buyers?" asked Taiana. "If a buyer has the cash, what does their character matter?"

The old man smiled. "Out of the mouth of babes," he said in a gentle tone. "It is a trick as old as time for a dealer to arrange for a sham purchase before an opening so that he can create the illusion that a given work is quite valuable. When a work is sold a red tag is placed on the frame, indicating the price paid, and most importantly, the name of the buyer. We dealers constitute a rather small and closed world. We know one another, and we know if anyone is trying to pull a pricing scam. No, the buyer must be real, he must have stature in the collector's community, and if needs be, he must present a copy of the bank draft and receipts involved in the transaction. No banker in the city would be

395

a willing party to art fraud, so if the purchase documents are authentic, we all know that a real sale has taken place."

"And that single sale establishes the market value of the rest of the paintings?" Akoni asked.

"Sadly, no," said Mandleman. "The true market value of an artist's work is a function of time, increasing demand, and critical approval. But the first sales have an emotional impact on everyon: dealers, collectors, and critics. Where the first pathfinder goes, the herd will often follow."

Phineas rose and walked around the stove, stopping for a moment to pick up a porcelain figurine from a display table. Last night's visite *du vin* with Preston Winters didn't seem to have any lingering effect, much to Thomas' surprise.

"May I assume that you regard me as a respected buyer?" Phineas asked.

"I do, and I believe that assessment is shared by my colleagues, as well. You would be the perfect choice, Phineas. You are known as a discerning collector of landscapes and classical scenes; no one knows of your recent affection for the style in which Auber paints. It will be a revelation to the arts community. They may not share your taste in that regard, but they cannot deny your business acumen. 'What does that fellow know that we don't' is what they will be asking themselves."

"This feels a bit…" Akoni started.

"Byzantine?" interrupted Mandleman with a smile. "And it is, my dear fellow. This will be the first shot of many that we will hurl across the bow of the art world, and if we are lucky, it will get their attention. With a bit of luck, what we are doing here this morning is going to turn my competitors' bowels to ice water." He paused for a moment to savor that thought, and then, his face flushed and his eyes aglow, he said, "That is almost too glorious an outcome for an old man to contemplate, but my friends, my friends, how dear that thought is to me after battling these living piles of *merde* for so many years!"

Phineas crossed his arms on his chest and lowered his head. When he looked up, he said, "Fair, enough, Isaac, I will be your buyer. I had fully intended to purchase at least three of the works in any event.

As to price: shall we say $5,000 each for two paintings? That should be enough to attract a bit of attention to Aubert."

Mandleman set down his teacup. "Would you be willing to go $7,500 each? That would garner a lot of attention."

Phineas was quiet. Then he extended his hand to Mandleman and shook on the deal.

Thomas realized he had been holding his breath. $15,000? Just like that? And there were still 21 paintings to be priced and sold. Maybe, just maybe, the plan he had hatched with Aubert back in Moorea was going to succeed. He could repay the bank in Honolulu, sort things out with Colin Stafford and build a life with Keani and their child, while Aubert would become famous and rich.

Taiana hugged Thomas, and Mandleman asked who would like a celebratory glass of sherry. Thomas smiled when Phineas and Winters grimaced at the thought.

The list of tasks that had to be completed before the grand opening of the new Museum of Art on the 23rd grew longer by the hour. Preston Winters was to complete the framing of Aubert's paintings, Phineas and Mandleman were responsible for finding at least one brave newspaper critic who would be willing to review the work, and Thomas and Taiana had two days to create a full-page ad promoting Aubert that Mandleman was going to run in all five major New York daily papers. "It will be nigh unto impossible for the editorial side of the papers not to at least do a short article about Aubert's work once we have padded their pockets with a little advertising revenue," Mandleman predicted.

Akoni had an entirely different set of responsibilities. After checking in with his associates at the New York Museum of Natural History to confirm that the specimens he had been sending from the waters around Hawai'i and Tahiti were catalogued and displayed properly, he would visit the office of the Counsel of the Kingdom of Hawai'i and ask for introductions to high-level officials in the city's police department. Fitch Donegan, Aata, and the Tahitian warriors could already be in the city. The more eyes looking out for them, the better.

Akoni found himself humming as he walked down Broadway towards the elevated train station in the light, powdery snow. Tonight, he would see Isabella, the restaurateur who had so enchanted him at *La Villeta*, to ask her to be his guest for the Museum of Art opening. She was taking Taiana shopping on 5th Avenue today and he and Thomas would meet them at the restaurant for dinner. For the first time since their skiff crashed on the rocks off the Moloka'i leper colony, Akoni felt hopeful for Thomas and himself.

When the letter arrived, Akoni was seated on a chair in Thomas' hotel room reading one of Mandleman's books on art collection. Thomas was putting on a tie in preparation for their dinner at *La Villeta*. He tipped the bellboy, sat on the edge of the bed, and opened the oilskin pouch with 'Special Delivery' stenciled on the front.

A moment later, Akoni heard Thomas moan the word 'No,' before sliding off the bed and going down on his knees.

"Thomas," Akoni said in an urgent voice. "My friend…what is it?"

Thomas did not reply. The color had drained from his face, his shoulders slumped forward, and he breathed out the most desolate sigh Akoni had ever heard.

"Thomas!" Akoni repeated. "Look at me…tell me…"

Thomas raised his head in Akoni's direction, but his eyes looked right through the giant Hawaiian, to somewhere off in the far distance. Tears rolled down his cheeks, and he began to breathe in short, racking sobs. Finally, he stood up and looked around as if he did not recognize his surroundings. Then he tossed the letter on the bed and went to the door.

"I…" was all he said before opening the door and disappearing into the hallway. Akoni followed and watched Thomas stagger down the hall toward the stairs like a drunken man.

Akoni had to read the letter before he went after his friend. He gathered up the scattered pages froom the floor and sat down.

There were two letters in the package, written in separate hands. The first had Andrew Whitton's name on the top and was dated eight days ago. Whitton was the editor of the San Francisco newspaper Thomas wrote for, Akoni recalled. He took a deep breath and began to read:

"My friend, it began. I received the sealed envelope in this pouch yesterday. It was sent to me by Océane Aubert via steamship from Tahiti on November 12th with instructions that I get it to you as quickly as possible. It went out from the train station this morning by special delivery. Hoping all is well, yours, Andrew."

Twenty-nine days, Akoni thought. He set Whitton's letter aside and unfolded Océane's.

"My dearest Thomas," she began in smooth, flowing script, *"nothing could have prepared me for what I must tell you now, just as nothing can prepare you for what you are about to hear. Keani has left us. Four days ago, she went out past the reef to spear parrotfish. I watched her paddle out, and we joked that it was time for her to give up these adventures until after the baby was born. Émile and I were watching her from our porch and saw her lose her balance and fall from the outrigger. We didn't know at that moment that she had fallen onto a razor-sharp coral branch that lay just below the surface and was badly cut from her knee up to her thigh.*

When we saw that she was struggling to get back into the canoe we raced to our outrigger and paddled out to her as quickly as we could. She lay unconscious in the bottom of the canoe, bleeding so terribly from her thigh, and fighting to breathe. Émile paddled back with her in her canoe and I made my way along the beach to the village to ask for help. He got her to shore and tied his shirt around her upper thigh as tightly as he could to stop the bleeding. But he could not staunch the flow. By the time I made it back to them ten minutes later, she was gone. I could not believe it.

Thomas, she had a look of absolute, perfect, angelic peace on her face. It all happened so quickly, and blessedly, she did not die in pain. In my heart I believe that her last thoughts were of you and the baby. Nothing else could explain the serenity of her expression."

Akoni dropped the letter on the bed and stared into nothingness.

Keani dead. His best friend's life torn to shreds in an instant. For a moment he couldn't think, couldn't breathe. He could only imagine the agony Thomas was experiencing.

One page remained. *"Thomas,"* Océane continued, *"the village gathered around us that afternoon, and the women washed and prepared Keani's body while the men fashioned a simple wooden coffin. We feasted and sang songs around the village fire that night, as is the Tahitian custom, and at dawn we carried her up the mountain behind your house to a spot where there is a clearing and a promontory that juts out above the cove she loved so dearly. We placed her in a grave, covered it in flowers and greenery, and erected a stone above her. One of the men will carve her name into it later.*

Come home to us when you can. We love you.

Océane
12 Novembre 1872
Ha'apiti, Moorea

Akoni willed himself to stand. He had to get to *La Villeta* and enlist Taiana and Isabella to help him find Thomas. He knew they would find him in due time, but when they did…what then?

~SIXTY ~

Five Points, New York City

He leaned into the wind and snow that was pelting the city, but he didn't feel the cold. He didn't feel anything. He might have been wandering south towards the river or north towards the Bowery, but he paid no attention to street signs, or to the way the handsome brownstone and marble palaces along Broadway and 5th Avenue gradually gave way to rows of sagging storefronts and dilapidated warehouses.

Pools of shadowy, snow-flecked light formed around the tops of the streetlamps, and carriage traffic on the cobblestone streets was light. The handful of people who passed him on the sidewalk kept their heads down, and their hands jammed deep into their coat pockets for warmth. When he rounded a corner and came upon a blue suited cop smacking a shabbily dressed man on the back of the head with a billy club, he paid no mind.

The streets got narrower and the buildings shorter and more squalid the farther he walked, and when the wind and snow finally subsided, people began to emerge from roosts and tenements that were packed together like splintery cargo boxes on a rusting freighter's deck.

He had no sense of the time, but from the looks of the men and women shuffling along the sidewalk it must have been very late. The men were rough, dark-eyed, and unshaven. They might have stared into his face as he passed them, he didn't notice. The women were equally unkempt, with tattered dresses, unwashed hair, and threadbare bonnets.

They were more aggressive about looking directly into his face than the men; whoring was a highly competitive profession and being shy about picking your mark and making your offer was a sure ticket to a beating from your pimp, or the likelihood of starving.

He wasn't surprised when a disheveled young woman stepped directly in his path and then moved to block him when he attempted to go around her.

"It's cold, lovey," she said in a scratchy voice. "Give a girl four bits and we'll step into that alley, and you can do me however you want. Front, back, I'll take it anywhere you like. I ain't got the pox, darlin… here, have a look-see."

With that she pulled up the front of her dress with one hand to give him a peek at her wares, while with the other hand she took his elbow.

Without saying a word, Thomas grabbed her by the throat with one hand, pulled his other arm free and grabbed hold of her side, and then tossed her into the street like a bag of old garbage. The woman hit the ground hard and lay still a moment. Then she pulled herself to her knees and spat in his direction as he walked away without looking back.

Two men materialized out of the darkness and held their hands up for him to stop.

" 'ere now," said one, "you can't treat our Lizzie that way."

"He's an uptown snob, Barty," said his companion. "Lizzie's kind ain't refined enough for the likes of him."

"And what's the difference between an uptown twat and our home-grown quim, tell me that now?" said the first man. "Don't they all work the same, whether their sweet little purse is sewn with silk or with burlap?"

"Oh, now, your John Thomas would certainly know the difference between them materials the moment you dipped in," replied the friend with a chuckle.

Thomas was having none of it. Somewhere in the back of his tortured mind he was aware that these two were probably planning on robbing him. Part of him didn't care. Then, almost without willing it, he felt his fist raise and ram forward, smashing the first man in the cartilage at the center of his throat. The man groaned and crumpled to his knees. His partner started towards Thomas, and then backed off when he saw the gentleman draw a pocket revolver from his coat and point it at his head.

"There, there, now friend," said the man as he bent to help his accomplice to his feet. "There ain't no call for that…"

Thomas holstered his revolver and stepped off the curb, and for the first time that night he took a moment to read a street sign. He was standing at the intersection of Centre and Pearl, next to a soot-stained two-story brick building featuring a colorful mural that proclaimed, *"Fatty Walsh's Saloon."* He did not know the streets or the saloon. Being neither thirsty nor hungry, he kept walking.

The sky soon cleared, and crystal stars dotted the heavens around a full winter moon that was brighter than the streetlights. No matter where he traveled after this day's terrible news, a moonlit sky would remind him of his wedding night, when a yellow moon wove strands of golden light across the surface of a turquoise lagoon.

He stopped and leaned against a building, fighting to not remember, and struggling to force his lungs to breathe against the giant hand pushing into the center of his chest with crushing force.

He did not want to remember; he could not stop remembering. Swimming with her in still mountain pools, walking the curving sand beach in front of their cabin, lying on their backs under the stars, preparing meals, making love, working their garden, building their home. He saw her laugh, he watched her brush her thick, lustrous hair, he reveled in the memory of unwrapping the flowers and garlands that spiraled around her perfect naked body, and of the deep, heartfelt conversations they had without speaking a word.

Keani, dear…dear Keani, he thought as he pushed away from the wall, why had the icy tendrils of death reached out for you, and not for me? I am the vagabond, I am the one who has taken lives, I am the one with no roots, no family, no homeland. How could the angel of death have passed by the one who was so deserving of his gift and taken an innocent in his place?

He passed another saloon, and then a gambling hall where the sound of a piano spilled out through the open doors. The tune made him think of his friend Walt Whitman, and the poetry the bearded part-time nurse read to him as he recovered from his battle wounds at Mt. Pleasant Hospital. What was it Whitman had written about death in his *Song of Myself?* Thomas strained to recall. The verses were jumbled in his head, as if they did not want to rise to the surface of his consciousness.

Two blocks later he passed a putrid-smelling slaughterhouse, and for some reason the scent of death illuminated his memory.

"They are alive and well somewhere, Whitman wrote,
The smallest sprout shows that there is really no death,
And if ever there was it led forward to life, and does not wait at the end to arrest it,
And ceas'd the moment life appear'd.
All goes onward and outward, nothing collapses,
And to die is different from what any one supposed, and luckier."

Thomas kicked at a small pile of rubbish, knocking it into the street. Whitman was a fool to speak of death in hopeful terms, he thought. There was nothing of hope in death, there was only the pain and sorrow and unrelenting suffering of those left behind.

He stumbled on in the clear, cold night air, squeezing his eyes open and shut in an effort to force his brain to close off the flood of memories that were overwhelming his senses. But it didn't work. Nothing would. When he crossed the next alley, he saw a painted sign on the side of a three-story building that read, *"Sweeney's Establishment: Drink & Food."* Perhaps he could find a brief respite here. He pushed through the double bat-wing doors and stepped into a brightly lit, high-ceilinged space packed with tables and a towering mirrored back bar that spanned the width of the building.

Several dozen men and a handful of ladies occupied the tables, and three bar maids threaded their ways in an out of the crowd with mugs of beer, bottles of whiskey, and plates of bread, sausages, and cheese, the standard fare for working men in every saloon he had visited.

He made his way around the tables and up to the bar, and for the first time he could recall, he did not grimace at the sight of the reproduction painting of the Battle of Pebble Creek Ridge in which he was the heroic centermost figure, single-handedly fighting off hordes of Confederate soldiers.

The bar was a stand-up, with a brass rail on which to rest one foot while leaning against the top. Spittoons lined the floor at four-foot intervals, the proper distance a man should be able to accurately spit his tobacco wad or juice without soiling his neighbor's trousers. On the floor above, the short-time rooms used by the working girls were in clear view of the bar manager. Each time a door swung open a ride was starting or ending, and a dollar would make its way into the manager's money belt.

The bartender finished wiping a beer mug with a dirty towel and turned his attention to Thomas. He was rotund, bald, and wore a grease-stained apron that might once have been white. As he approached, the bartender simply raised his eyebrows. Why bother asking the question? To his astonishment the tall, well-dressed man replied with four words he had never heard in all the fifteen years he had worked at Sweeny's:

"Your wine list, please."

The bartender spit out a short laugh and slapped his hand on the polished counter. "My what?" he asked incredulously.

Before Thomas could answer a huge fellow with shaggy red hair and a thick beard stepped up beside him. "Harold," he said to the bartender, "what did this lavender lad just ask you for?"

"No concern of yours, Tarl," replied the bartender. The custom-er asking for a wine list was clearly a gentleman, and as ridiculous as his request was in a place like this, that meant a tip and maybe even a ride on his most expensive filly. Either way, he stood to make a little money if he didn't insult the man by questioning his masculinity as Tarl had just done.

"You call me Tarl, but you call my brother 'Mr. Coutts," said the big man. "What the hell is that all about."

The bartender shrugged and ignored the question. "We have whiskey, and we have beer," he said to Thomas, "and I can tell you that we have at least one whiskey that won't kill you."

"Your best whiskey then," Thomas answered.

The bartender reached below the counter and retrieved a bottle and a clean glass, which he set in front of Thomas.

"Like to keep it?" he asked.

Thomas nodded.

The Irishman wasn't having the bartender's rudeness. "One last time, boyo," he said. "Why do you call my brother Mr., but me by my first name?"

Harold grabbed a smudged glass from a rack, poured a no-name whiskey into it, and slid it across to Tarl. Then he looked at Thomas and said, "Mr. Coutts is Coutts Sweeney. He owns the place, and he pays my salary. That earns him some respect." Then he looked at Tarl and said, "As far as I know you don't own a damn thing."

Tarl slammed his fist on the bar, but Harold simply looked at him calmly and said, "The whiskeys on me."

Thomas almost felt a smile cross his lips. The big Irishman, though, was feeling no such levity. As Thomas raised his glass, Tarl's hand went to his belt and withdrew a twelve-inch hunting knife with a deer horn handle. He raised the knife over his head and rammed it down onto the bar, penetrating the wood by at least an inch and causing the whiskey in Thomas' glass to slop over.

The barman leapt back, and the Irishman yanked the knife out of the wood and pointed it at him.

"A little more respect, if you please," said Tarl, "or just maybe I'll cut off your pathetic little wanker."

Thomas sighed and started to gather up the bottle and glass to take to a table. The Irishman wasn't done, however. He grabbed Thomas' shirt sleeve above the elbow and said, "Did you say something, lavender boy?"

Thomas shook off Tarl's hand, turned towards him and took his measure. He was a good head taller than Thomas, and at least 20 pounds heavier. It didn't matter. Not tonight.

"In fact, I didn't say anything," Thomas replied.

The bartender relaxed and turned to take care of another customer. A fight had been brewing, but it looked like the storm had passed.

Thomas chose not to let it go. "But if I had," he said to Tarl, "It would have been along the lines of you being a cowardly pus-sucker with a hard-on for little boys."

Tarl was stunned. That anyone would say something like that to him was hard enough to believe by itself, but for a wine-drinking dandy to do it, and in his brother's establishment, surrounded by a good dozen of Sweeney's personal troops, that was just too damn much.

The Irishman roared, took two steps back and gripped the handle of the knife with both hands, lifting the blade high in the air. Thomas knew what was going to happen next, and even though experience had taught him that a downward stabbing attack was the weakest of all knife strategies, Tarl was as big and strong as a bull and that blade was going to come down with enough force to split his skull in half.

There was no time to pull and cock his revolver. He swept his open hand across the bar and in a single motion launched his whiskey bottle up towards Tarl's face. The giant reacted by batting at the bottle with the knife, which gave Thomas the instant he needed to whip off his coat and wrap it around his left forearm. By the time he thrust his arm up and across at a 90-degree angle in front of the enraged Irishman the knife was back in position in the air and was arcing down towards him.

Out of the corner of his eye Thomas saw the bartender reaching beneath the counter, no doubt for a gun or club. But who was he going to shoot? He heard shouts and cries of, "Stop, stop," from customers, but he could only focus on the blade.

As the knife hurtled down, Thomas swung his right leg back and bent his torso at an angle while holding his bent left arm in a rigid position. He felt Tarl's forearm make contact with his, and then the Irishman realized his blow was being parried and jerked the blade back to make another pass. Thomas felt the tip of the blade bite through his jacket and slice into the top of his forearm, but he knew without looking that it was not a serious cut.

Before Tarl could strike a second time Thomas pulled back his right arm and smashed his open hand against Tarl's face. The instant he felt his open palm against the Irishman's cheek and nose he pulled his arm back a few inches, made a fist, and jammed his thumb into the Irishman's left eye socket with all his strength. He felt the gelatinous mass of the eyeball give way, but before the shriek that was forming in Tarl's throat could make it past his lips, Thomas withdrew his thumb and rammed it again and again into the eyeball until he felt it dissolve into thick liquid and run down the Irishman's cheek.

Tarl stumbled back, still holding his knife at chest height but clearly in shock at the loss of his eye. Thomas saw the bartender pointing the shotgun at him, and he felt the press of the crowd all around. In that moment, though, he didn't care what happened. Whether the bartender blasted him into oblivion, or the crowd tore him to pieces, it didn't matter. Whitman was wrong; life did not go on.

Tarl dropped the knife on the bar and raised both hands to his torn and bloodied eye socket. It only took a moment, though, for him to realize that he had given up his weapon. He dropped his hands and lunged forward to grab the knife and finish Thomas off. And then, for the second time that night, Thomas' instincts and will to survive took control. Some part of him did care.

He got to the knife a fraction of a second before Tarl, and, without hesitating, gripped the handle in an underhand hold and shoved it deep into the Irishman's gut, just below his sternum. Without passion or pity, he pulled it out and thrust it in a second time, and a third, until Tarl groaned, pressed his hands against the edge of the bar, and then dropped to his knees next to a grimy spittoon. A look of surprise flashed across the Irishman's one good eye as he buckled to the floor, grabbed at the spittoon to stop his fall, and died.

All sound and movement in the bar ceased, and everyone watched as the noxious brown liquid spilled from the spittoon and over the dead man's face.

Thomas set the knife on the bar and stood still with his arms at his side. He was not going to leave the bar alive, and that was fine with him. He raised his head and looked into the bartender's eyes, and then at the double-barrel shotgun pointed at his chest. But the blast did not come. Instead, something heavy slammed into the back of his head. He fell to the floor, blinking against the pain and fighting to hang onto consciousness.

A ghostly image of Keani falling from her canoe into a forest of coral spikes flickered through his mind and then everything went black.

SIXTY-ONE

The concierge of Gilsey House called out to Akoni and Taiana as they hurried across the marble lobby to meet Phineas McNab and Preston Winters for breakfast. They were going to map out a plan to find Thomas, who had not returned to his room after walking out into the snow late last night. Akoni considered ignoring the concierge; he probably just wanted to make another restaurant recommendation or help them find tickets to some popular theatre event. On the other hand, a good hotel concierge was a fountain of gossip and tidbits of news. Who knew…

When they neared his desk, the concierge stepped away and motioned for them to sit with him on an upholstered settee next to a huge indoor fern that blocked them from the view of other hotel guests.

"I am told that you have lost, that is, that you cannot find Colonel Scoundrel?" the concierge began.

Akoni's face brightened. "You have news of him?"

"Alas, of that I cannot be certain. But I heard something this morning that I believe may be worth your looking into."

"Anything you know will be of real help, I'm certain of that," said Taiana. She had paced her room all night, and by sunrise she was dressed and knocking at Akoni's door.

"I hope that may be the case," replied the concierge. "This morning I had coffee with a group of friends who, like me, concierge for several of the better hotels in the city. Our conversations are never dull,

I can tell you that. So much happens behind the closed doors of these establishments that only a concierge is privy to…honestly you would be astonished to hear what goes on upstairs." He raised his eyes as if looking to heaven.

Akoni was growing impatient. "The Colonel," he growled.

"Yes, of course, the Colonel. One of my friends works at the hotel where the crime editor of the New York News lives. They swap gossip every morning, which makes my friend the absolute first and finest source of titillating…"

Akoni glared, and the man sighed and continued. "This morning my friend learned of a murder that took place at Sweeney's Saloon in the Five Points last night."

Taiana clapped her hand across her mouth and Akoni wrapped an arm around her shoulder.

"No, the Colonel was not the victim," said the concierge. "I am certain of that."

"Then why would this crime be of interest to us?" Akoni asked.

"According to my friend, the murdered man was Tarl Sweeney, twin brother of Coutts Sweeney, who both owns the establishment and controls the largest Irish gang in the city. They call themselves the Sundowners."

"And?" asked Akoni.

"Tarl was stabbed to death by a tall, lean man in his twenties, with thick brown hair and green eyes, dressed like a gentleman. No one had ever seen him in there before last night."

Akoni's eyes narrowed. "And so, you think it is possible that Colonel Scoundrel…"

"Is the murderer," whispered the concierge.

Tears welled in Taiana's eyes. "No," she said, "this isn't possible, it cannot be true. Not Thomas. Not our Thomas."

"Has this been in the papers yet?" Akoni asked.

"No, and it may not be covered at all."

Akoni was surprised. "Not in the papers? How is that possible?"

The concierge smiled. "If every murder committed in Five Points was reported, there would be no room in the papers for any other news. Frankly, the tale of one flea-bitten mick killing another is of no interest to the genteel classes. Kill a Madison Avenue banker, on the other hand, and you'll read little else on the front page for weeks, especially if it was a jilted mistress who pulled the trigger."

Akoni was quiet for a moment. "And this is as much as your friend knows?"

The concierge nodded. "I will ask around and find you immediately should I come into more information."

Akoni and Taiana stood to go. "One more thing," said Akoni. "Is he in police custody?"

The concierge shook his head. "Oh, no, my friend. If Colonel Scoundrel was indeed the man who killed Tarl Sweeney, he is being held someplace far more dangerous than a police station."

Thomas woke to the smell of stale beer, mold, and rat droppings. He was sitting upright with his arms lashed to a post, and the light streaming in from a row of small windows reflected off patches of ice that spotted the rock walls. A pair of boots walked past the windows, which told him he was being held in a basement. His head throbbed, and he could feel matted blood in his hair. Not the best of mornings, perhaps, but the only emotion he felt when he opened his eyes was surprise: why was he still alive? Why didn't they finish the job last night?

He did not have long to wallow in that thought; a door creaked open, and footsteps echoed down the stairs.

"Good lord, the smell," said Harold the bartender. He was holding a lantern in one hand and pinching his nose with the other. Three large men came down the stairs and stood behind him, holding clubs in their hands. "But, considering what is waiting for you upstairs I suppose this was the perfect place for you to enjoy your last good night of sleep." He chuckled at his own joke and nodded to the men, who untied Thomas and lifted him to his feet. They held his arms tightly and marched him up the stairs, through the open door, and out into the center of the tavern's main floor.

He blinked in the bright light and took in the strange scene: The tables that had covered the floor last night had been pushed over against the walls, and a long wooden plank table had been set up in the center of the room. A half dozen men were seated at the table, some with mugs of beer, a few with coffee. Only the chair in the middle of the table was empty. Leaning over the railing above them, four of the upstairs girls still wearing their night clothes were waiting for the proceedings to begin.

The three men who hauled him out of the basement stepped to the side of the room, while Harold stayed beside him. Thomas' arms ached, and he wasn't yet warm enough to feel his fingers.

Harold shuffled side to side, looking and feeling far more nervous than Thomas. Whatever was in store for him, Thomas realized, could also be waiting for the fat barman.

Then a door opened behind the bar, and a man emerged and walked quickly to the table, where he took the center chair.

Thomas felt his jaw drop. The man sitting a few feet in front of him was tall and broad shouldered, with pale blue eyes, a thick mass of red hair, and a shaggy red beard. He was stunned; it was the man he had killed only hours before.

Harold saw the look of shock and surprise on Thomas' face. He leaned in and whispered, "No, it's not him. This is Coutts Sweeney, Tarl's twin brother."

Thomas could only shake his head and stare into space.

A petite woman brought a pot of coffee and a mug and placed them on the table in front of Sweeney. She poured for him, kissed him lightly on the forehead, and then joined the guards watching Thomas from against the wall.

"This has all the feeling of a trial," he thought. It shouldn't be too difficult for the jury to reach a conclusion, of course. Particularly since he had no intention of presenting any kind of defense.

Sweeney took a drink of coffee and talked quietly with the men sitting beside him. Then he directed his attention to Thomas.

"The calling card in your jacket pocket says your name is Colonel Thomas E. Scoundrel," he said in a deep voice tinged with a hint of Irish brogue. "That would be the Civil War Scoundrel, the one pictured in that painting?" He pointed to the colorful 6-foot-wide battle scene hanging behind the bar.

Thomas nodded but did not reply.

"Is that the way it really happened?" Sweeney continued. "Were you surrounded by that many rebs, and did your horse rear back like that in the middle of the fight, and did you hold the flagpole out like that?"

"Some of it is true," Thomas found himself answering in a quiet voice, "the part about my horse, Cornwall, and the flag. Other parts came from the artists' imagination."

Sweeney slapped his hand on the table. "I knew it, damned if I didn't. I fought with the New York Irish, and I have told people for years that real battles don't play out like in your painting."

Thomas was mystified; he saw no grief on Sweeney's face at the loss of his brother, heard no sorrow in the tenor of his voice. He had expected to be facing a firing squad or hangman's noose, and yet here they were talking about a piece of art. He shifted on his feet and wished for a cup of coffee.

Then one of the prostitutes on the upper floor called out. "You can raise your flagpole like that with me anytime, colonel darling." Her friends laughed, and even Sweeny could not suppress a smile. He cleared his throat and said, "Here's the thing, colonel; outside the Five Points you may be a national hero. You may have fully deserved them medals and the invitations to the White House and all the quim that has no doubt been laid down before you, what with the ladies liking to spread their legs for a genuine hero. But here, in my world, you are nothing but a murderer. And that's what we are here to deal with today."

Good, Thomas thought, let's get on with it.

One of the men at the table leaned over and said something to Sweeney. The Irishman shook his head in agreement and said, "It has been pointed out to me that we have a few matters to resolve with our own bartender, who did not perform his duty properly when the dust started flying last night. How long have you been with me, Harold?"

The bartender took two steps forward. "Fifteen years, Mr. Coutts. The best years of my life." Then he stepped back and clasped his hands in front of him.

"Fifteen years," replied Sweeney. "And you have been a fine employee. But last night you had one job to do: pull that damn trigger and send the good colonel to perdition before he gutted my brother like a fish. You failed, and now you must be punished. I can't have people just walk into my joint and kill my family, now can I. What would that do to my reputation?"

Thomas looked to the side and saw a wet stain spreading across the front of the bartender's trousers.

"Here's my judgment," said Sweeney. "Pack your bag and get the hell out of here, right now. I never want to see your face again. Go uptown to one of them Jew saloons, or to Polish street. They'll hire you." He made a dismissive motion with his hand. "Now 'git."

The woman who brought coffee to the table came back into the room with a plate of food, which she set in front of Sweeny. She refilled his coffee, and then, to Thomas' great surprise, she filled another cup and brought it over to him.

Sweeney took a few bites and wiped his mouth with his sleeve. "And now, then, Colonel Scoundrel, to the matter of my brother. My late brother. I hated the bastard, of course. Never worked a day in his life; drank my whiskey, ate my food, banged my whores without paying, and beat the hell out of my customers. I can't count the bribes I paid over the years to keep him out of The Tombs." He turned to the men around him in mid-sentence and said, "Did you know that the government geniuses who built that pisspot of a jail decided to build it over an old sewage pond, and that it started to sink the minute it was finished? They say Five Points was born the day the sewer shit seeped up out of that pond and started to pour down the corridors of that so-called Hall of Justice."

Thomas was confused: was Sweeney going to put a bullet through his head or pin a medal on his chest?

"A man in my position with my responsibilities must be mindful of his reputation," Sweeney began. "Reputation above all. If folks begin to doubt my resolve, if they think for a minute that I have grown soft, all this…" he made a sweeping motion around the room with his arm, "will disappear. Those who wish me ill need to know that they'll have an ice pick up their arse if they so much as look cross-eyed in my direction. Ain't that right, boys?"

The men at the table nodded in unison. "Now, letting old Harold slither out of here with his entrails intact warn't a sign of weakness. He earned his retirement with 15 years of service. But you, colonel, present a bucket load of possible troubles to me for what you did last night. People—and by that, I mean my enemies—would see it as a sign of weakness if my brother's death wasn't avenged. If you'd killed him so much as one inch outside my door, we might be able to come to some kind of accommodation. Oh, I'd have to take a hand or an eye or something just to keep up appearances, but at least you might have been able to live out your life as a live cripple. But you didn't kill him off premise. You did him in my house, in front of my customers. And for that there can be no accommodation."

Sweeney took a minute and finished his breakfast, and Thomas emptied his coffee cup. It would have been nice to sit down, but he didn't think asking for a chair was a good idea.

The Irishman pushed his plate away and pulled a pipe from his vest pocket. He filled it, accepted a match from the man beside him, and took a few puffs before continuing.

"And so here we are, colonel. The fact of your guilt is not in dispute. Do you agree?"

"I do," Thomas replied.

"And the matter of my reputation is no small thing, do you also agree with that?"

"Seems so," answered Thomas without a trace of emotion.

"You know, colonel, you are something of a mystery to me. Here I am condemning you to death, and yet you put up no fight. You are young and strong, and you have been a fighting man, but you are taking this like a child who got caught sneaking a look up his maiden aunt's petticoats. Where is your passion, man? Have you no pride?"

Thomas looked Sweeney in the eye but said nothing. Where was his passion, indeed.

The man sitting next to Sweeney spoke up. "The problem as I see it ain't in the execution part, Coutts, but in how we do it. This man is a national hero, and you don't whack a hero over the head with a club or shoot him in the back and toss him in a ditch. That would be a hell of a thing for your reputation."

All the heads around the table nodded in agreement.

"Well then?" asked Sweeney.

Sweeney's woman returned to the table and took his plate. "He lived as a hero," she said, "so if you want to save your reputation, you're going to have to make sure he dies like one, too."

Sweeney wrapped his hands around his coffee mug and stared at the tabletop. Then he raised his head and said, "Damned if that ain't the smartest thing I've heard all morning."

He stood and walked over to Thomas.

"Die like a hero," he said in a matter-of-fact voice. "How the hell do I make that happen, Colonel Scoundrel?"

Thomas replied with a half-smile. "You're the boss man around here. I guess you'll just have to figure that one out for yourself."

~SIXTY-TWO ~

Thomas was taken to the privy and then led back down into the basement with a plate of cold stew and a half loaf of bread. He was not tied to the post this time, but the men who were watching him made it clear that they would be sitting outside the door at the top of the steps, and he would be wise not to try to leave.

As last meals for the condemned went, the stew was not what he would have chosen had he been offered a choice. Mr. Kwan's paté, perhaps, or Isabella's artful pasta with pesto. A rib eye from Parker Ranch on the Big Island would have been fine, or pork wrapped in banana leaves and slow smoked in an underground oven. Then he thought of Keani's butter and lemon basted parrotfish, and to his surprise the memory brought a smile to his face, not a tear.

His death would not be mourned by many. Even so, he regretted that he had not said goodbye to Akoni or Taiana, his most steadfast friends. Or to Phineas McNab and Winters. They had risked a great deal to help with Aubert's New York art world debut. The good news is that he was certain they would follow through and see to it that the paintings were the centerpiece of Mandleman's gallery at the Museum of Art opening.

He chuckled when he thought about Fitch Donegan and Aata, the two men who had tailed him halfway around the globe and who would now be robbed of the pleasure of killing him themselves. Fate really did have a wicked sense of humor.

Would Sweeney permit him to have a pencil and paper so he could write farewell notes to those he cared about? To Akoni and Taiana, John Hayden and Captain McNab, Princess Noelani, the poet Walt Whitman, and Angela, the nurse who gave him a reason to live when he was at the lowest point of his life.

He ran his hand through his hair. No, not the lowest point, he corrected himself. That was today. What would Angela say about his decision to walk meekly to whatever execution Sweeney had in store for him? She had lost her husband early in the war, who better to understand his overwhelming grief. And yet, he also had to acknowledge that she worked through her pain and found new purpose in living. He chalked that up to her faith and natural optimism; two qualities which he had never spent much time developing.

He began pacing across the room and trying not to think. From the number of feet passing by the basement window he figured it must be midday. Whatever it was that Coutts Sweeney had in store for him, it wouldn't be long now.

The hansom cab driver did a double take when Akoni asked to be taken to Sweeney's Saloon in Five Points. In all his years picking up fares at the best hotels and restaurants on Broadway and 5th and Madison Avenues no one had asked to be taken to the city's most notorious, crime-ridden, and gang-infested neighborhood. Not only that, but the Hawaiian gentleman whose enormous frame was testing the limit of his carriage springs was accompanied by a diminutive young lady for whom Five Points would only represent real danger.

The driver turned in his seat. "Beggin' your pardon sir, and meaning no disrespect, but do you know Five Points? It really is no place for the likes of you and the lass."

"I appreciate your concern, driver," Akoni replied, "but, yes, that is exactly where we want to go."

He and Taiana had spent the past hour with Isabella in her restaurant considering the best way for her to persuade her friends at the Police Commissioner's office to send a squad of officers to Sweeneys to look for Thomas.

"The police won't take any direct action against Sweeney or any of his men, of course," Isabella said. "Every copper from the newest recruit walking Five Points to the Commissioner himself gets a piece of the monthly protection cash Sweeney pays out. The best we can hope for is that they might be able to drag him out of whatever mess he is in."

"That will have to be enough," Akoni replied. "Just do your best."

To Taiana's surprise, Isabella embraced Akoni and kissed him on the lips. "Be safe," she said. "The both of you."

The driver shrugged and tapped the reins. The cab trotted away from the hotel under a cold, clear sky and joined the stream of traffic heading pretty much everywhere in the city except Five Points.

The door to the basement opened, and Sweeney's lady friend came down the stairs with a basin of warm, soapy water and a clean washcloth.

"I noticed the blood in your hair," she said. "Do you mind if I…?"

She stepped around behind his chair, dipped the cloth into the water and began lightly wiping at the back of his head. When she was done, she pulled a chair from the corner of the stone-walled room and sat down in front of him.

"May I sit?" she asked.

Thomas simply nodded.

She settled in and looked him over as if she were making an important decision. "My name is Marie," she finally said. "I manage the books, and, as you saw, I also try to manage Coutts." Her smile was so warm that Thomas had to smile back.

"Why did you come here last night?" she asked. "This isn't the kind of place gentlemen like you frequent."

"Not even for the upstairs entertainment?" Thomas replied.

"From the looks of you I would say that you have never needed to pay for sex, *chéri*."

"Perhaps it was for your menu, then," he said.

Marie wrapped her shawl tighter against the cold. "There is too much here that I find confusing, colonel. Five Points is the last place an important person like yourself would come to for an evening excursion. And yet, here you are, and I am told you didn't even arrive until after 2 AM, and the doorman was certain you walked down the street and up to our door. There were no cabs anywhere in sight, he said."

"Yes," Thomas replied softly, "I did walk.

"From…?"

"Gilsey House."

"On Broadway?"

"Yes."

A look of disbelief crossed Marie's face. "That is nearly five miles from here. And yet you walked all that way, in the snow and ice, to come…here? To Sweeney's?"

"To be honest I didn't know where I was going. Stepping through your door was really an accident."

"In more ways than one, colonel."

One of the guards came down the stairs to check on Marie. She nodded and waved him off.

"I notice that you are wearing a wedding band, Colonel Scoundrel. Does your wife know you are here?"

He shook his head.

"Is she in the city with you?"

"No," he said in a whispery voice.

Marie stared into Thomas' eyes. "Where is your wife?" she asked gently.

He felt tears forming in his eyes. He wasn't ready for this. He did not know this woman. And yet…

"She is dead," he replied. "Halfway around the world."

"When?"

"She died a month ago. We live—we lived—on the island of Moorea, near Tahiti. I did not get the news until last night."

"Sweet Lord," said Marie. "And when you received word, you left your hotel and began to walk?"

He could not hold back the tears. They poured down his cheeks, and he lowered his head in an unsuccessful effort to hide them.

Marie laid her hand on his forearm. "You came in from the cold to have a drink, and within minutes you were set upon by Tarl."

"Yes, that's right."

"Why did you come to the city, Colonel?"

"My friend in Tahiti is a great painter. I brought his work to be shown at the opening of the New Metropolitan Museum of Art later this month."

"Did you come alone?"

"Friends came with me. They are helping to arrange the exhibition."

"Are you in the art business?"

He shook his head, and sniffled. "I know nothing about it. It was more a matter of necessity that brought me here."

"May I call you Thomas?"

"Of course."

Marie pulled her chair a little closer. "Thomas, I am going to get two mugs of tea with honey, and a couple of blankets. Then, I want you to tell me the whole story."

"That could take a while."

She smiled. "We seem to have plenty of time."

Marie stood and walked to the stairs. Then she turned and asked, "What was her name?"

"Keani."

"Keani," she repeated. "Such a beautiful name."

Two hours later Marie gathered up her blanket and mug and prepared to leave the basement. Her eyes were rimmed with tears, and when she hugged Thomas, she thanked him for telling his story.

"Coutts is not an evil man, Thomas, but he lives in a world that is defined by evil rules," she said. "You took his brother's life, and a penalty must be paid. There can be no exception to that. As to what his intentions are, I have no idea at all. I will make my case to him, but I can't promise you anything."

Thomas smiled. "I am ready, no matter what. I am not going to fight."

"I wish you would," replied Marie as she walked to the stairs. "I think Keani would say the same thing."

A half hour later the sounds of a crowd gathering outside seeped through the basement windows, and as he was drifting off to sleep under the warm blanket, the door at the top of the stairs opened and his three jailers came down.

"It's 3 o'clock, colonel. Will be dark in two hours and Mr. Sweeney wants to get this over with now."

"Is that why the crowd is gathering?" Thomas asked.

"Word went out this morning, and it looks like half of Five Points is out back," the man replied.

"They loved Tarl Sweeney that much?"

"Hell, no," said one of the other men. "Half the folks here would have paid good money to see you stick that bag of pus last night, colonel. They're streaming in from all over the city because of the matchup."

"What's that?" asked Thomas as they topped the stairs and went into the bar, which was empty except for a cleaning woman pushing a mop across the floor.

"The match up, colonel. Five Points greatest champion toe to toe against a genuine Civil War hero who's so damn famous that his portrait hangs in our bar. It's like something that Greek feller would have wrote…"

"You mean Homer?" asked his friend.

"Damn straight. Hector against Achilles, that's what it is."

Thomas sighed as they went through the kitchen door towards

the rear entrance to the saloon. "A fight to the death," he said, feeling suddenly weary.

The man who had cited the greatest one-on-one combat at the Battle of Troy 2,000 years earlier opened the back door and they stepped out into a sunlit cobblestone courtyard. It was circular, at least 50 yards in diameter. There were outdoor tables piled high against an outer wall, no doubt to use when the weather improved. Dozens of packing crates and an old wooden bandstand lined the oval wall that separated Sweeney's from a row of tenement buildings. Three beer carts were scattered around the makeshift fence, dispensing the warm, foamy drink from great wooden casks.

That was a lot of beer, Thomas thought. But then, there were already hundreds of people packing the courtyard and more were streaming in through the rear gate. They had climbed up on the crates, they sat on the fence, and they packed the outside stairs to the upper floors. Some had folding chairs, others had stools, but most of the crowd simply plopped on the ground all around the center circle and bided their time until the spectacle began. By the looks of the crowd there were people from every corner of the earth; he spotted Russian fur caps and Jewish felt, Chinese jackets, African pull overs, and stevedores with hob nailed boots mixed in among a sea of raw woolens and homespun cotton shirts and dresses worn by poor working folk. He was bemused to see that there were also a few gentlemen from uptown in expensive wool overcoats and beaver skin hats. As he watched he saw money changing hands among that group; he wondered what the betting odds were.

There was a smattering of applause and a few catcalls when Thomas' guards marched him to the center of the circle. "Ah, pay 'em no mind, colonel," said Rafe, the man holding his right arm. "You get a few good knocks in during the first 25 or 30 rounds, and they'll be eating out of your hand."

Thomas' eyebrows raised. "25 or 30?"

"I seen Paddy York and Big Jim Thorne go 67 rounds at the German beer garden last summer," volunteered another of his guards. "Went on for three hours, and we took a half hour dinner after round 35. Aye, that was a fight."

Thomas started to scan the crowd for any faces he recognized, only to remember that no one knew where he was. Then he saw Marie seated under an awning beside two of the working girls. She made eye contact, shook her head, and then turned away. He wished he could tell her that it was alright. He was right where he wanted to be.

An old man in a threadbare coat and top hat walked to the center of the cobblestone circle and raised his cane for the crowd's attention.

"The contest today will be conducted in strict accordance with the London Prize Ring Rules," he began in a clear, theatrical voice, only to be drowned out by boos and curses. Rules were something this crowd avoided at all costs.

"Now, then, now then," continued the old man, "you can have yer fight today, or not, it's no concern of mine. But them's the rules, and they will be obeyed or the combatant not abiding will forfeit. I will be the judge, and that's all to it."

He waited for the grumbling to subside and then walked over to a white chalk line drawn in the center of the courtyard. "This line will be the scratch," he called out. "When each 30-second round is complete the men will have a 30-second rest in their corner, and then they will have eight seconds to get to the scratch and resume the contest. The first man who does not make it to the scratch in eight seconds will be declared the loser."

"I have a corner?" Thomas asked his guards.

"Just come to us, laddy," answered Rafe. "We're your corner today."

"They'll be no biting," the old man was saying, to more jeers and boos. "No butting, no eye gouging, and no blows or kicks to the balls." At that admonition the crowd groaned with feigned unhappiness. No ball kicking? Where was the sport in that prohibition?

"If we go 20 rounds there will be a five-minute break to refresh your beer, and I have the great pleasure of telling you that your beer will be paid for by good Mr. Sweeney himself in gratitude for attending his great victory today."

Applause and cheers greeted that announcement, and they surged in volume as the kitchen door opened and Coutts Sweeney emerged with two men beside him. Sweeney wore a black, long-sleeve turtleneck above black boxing leggings and laced leather boots. He raised both hands to the crowd and basked a moment in their adulation. Then he walked across the courtyard to within a few feet of Thomas.

"So, this is how it is," Thomas said in a quiet voice.

"I could not allow my brother's death to go unavenged," Sweeney replied. "I am the leader of the Sundowners, and they expect no less."

"I'm guessing they weren't happy that you didn't simply put your pistol to my head and blow my brains out?"

Sweeney turned to the crowd and waved again. "You might say that," he said with his back to Thomas.

Sweeney turned and extended his hand. When they shook, the crowd cheered and began stamping their feet.

"Gentlemen, to the scratch," the old man called out. "Referee, to the ring."

Sweeney turned to go, and then stopped and looked back at Thomas.

"I am sorry about your wife, Scoundrel. May God bless her eternal soul."

The winter sky was pale blue, cloudless, and cold. A breeze came off the river and the scents of beer and cigar smoke mingled with the aromas of the crush of people filling the courtyard.

At the referee's direction, Thomas and Sweeney faced one another and pressed their outstretched fists together. Then the old man raised an iron triangle and struck it with a rod.

The crowd roared.

~SIXTY-THREE ~

Time stood still. There was no wind, no cold, no braying crowd. The decaying tenement buildings with clothes lines crisscrossing the alleys disappeared, the three-story saloon evaporated, and Sweeney himself melted into thin air.

Thomas felt the heat of the tropical sun on his back, and he had to narrow his eyes against the glare from the surface of the cobalt blue water. A spinner dolphin exploded out of a wave in front of him, turned three times in the air, and then sliced back down into the deep Moorea current. Warm water lapped against his thighs, and when he looked down, he caught flashes of rainbow-colored fish darting in and out of clusters of fan-shaped seaweed. If he turned around, he knew he would see the palms behind his cabin on stilts swaying gently in the breeze, and thick masses of greenery spilling up the base of the ancient volcano that protected their cove from the easterly winds.

Then he caught a faint scent of gardenia and heard someone moving up behind him in the water. His heart beat faster, and he held his breath in anticipation of the loving touch he knew was about to caress his shoulders.

That's when Sweeney's first blow connected with his jaw. The Irishman had pulled his right arm back and unleashed a haymaker with the entire momentum of his twisting body. Thomas felt his heels lift briefly off the ground as his head snapped back and his arms flew outwards. He stumbled back, lost his balance, and fell to the ground on his side.

The cove was gone, and the ocean was replaced by a cold, greying sky. Flashes of light rocketed across his consciousness from the power of the blow, and he felt blood dripping down the back of his throat. Searing pain stabbed through his face and neck and for a moment his arms went numb.

He turned to his back and saw Sweeney standing astride him, his arms clasped above his head in victory, but the sound of the crowd screaming their disapproval that the fight had ended after only five seconds of combat nearly drowned out the shouted instructions of the referee.

"You have 30 seconds to get to your corner under your own power, Colonel Scoundrel, and 30 seconds to recover before the second round begins. Can you stand?"

Sweeney's face materialized just inches above his, and he heard the Irishman say, "Damn you, Scoundrel, don't let it end like this. Put on a fight man, or these jackals will tear you to pieces, and probably me and Marie in the bargain."

Thomas blinked hard to clear his vision and pushed to his knees. Something struck him on the back, and he looked down to see the beer tankard that had been flung at him by an unhappy spectator. He got to his legs, unsure of where he was supposed to go. Then he saw Rafe waving a blue kerchief across the arena, and he wobbled his way towards his corner, where his three jailers had set up chairs and a small table with a jug of water.

"That could have gone better, lad," said one of his handlers.

"A sight better," added Rafe. "That your way of suckering Sweeney into thinking you can't fight?"

Thomas shook his head to combat the ringing in his ears. He had 30 seconds to make the most important decision of his life. Did he walk back out like a lamb to slaughter and let Sweeney finish him off in the next round? One more blow like that haymaker would probably do it.

He looked across the compound and saw that Marie was staring directly at him. Her mouth was silently forming a word, over and over.

'Keani.'

He pressed his fist against his mouth, and tears began to form in his eyes. The pain he felt from the blow was nothing compared to the agony shredding his heart into pieces.

Then the old man struck the triangle, signaling the start of round two. He made one last glance in Marie's direction, and when she saw he was looking she held out her hands and began to sign.

Thomas was astounded; she knew sign language? He shook his head and focused on Marie's gestures: 'Honor her and the life you shared,' Marie signed. 'Fight.'

Thomas made his way to the scratch and waited for Sweeney to join him. At the instant they went fist to fist again and the triangle rang out, though, he was not certain what he was going to do. Sweeney seemed surprised he had returned to the ring, but the crowd was shouting and clapping in delight. A boy of eight or nine was doing a line of cartwheels along the fence and Thomas noticed the top-hatted gentlemen once again exchanging money. Someone had faith in him, it seemed.

But it wasn't so much a conscious decision to fight back as it was the primal instinct to live that motivated Thomas to throw his left elbow out under Sweeney's right arm to block the bearded Irishman's next punch. As Sweeney's arm flailed upward, Thomas turned his torso to the right and launched a powerful uppercut to Sweeney's abdomen, just under the sternum. He felt his fist sink in and heard the rush of air expel from Sweeney's lungs.

A look of surprise crossed the Irishman's face, and he doubled over with his hands across his belly, gasping for air. As soon as Sweeney bent down, Thomas cuffed him hard on the left ear, and when his head snapped to the side, Thomas slammed his fist against Sweeney's right temple, sending him crumpling to the ground.

Now it was Sweeney receiving the 30-second warning from the referee and weaving unsteadily back to his corner.

Thomas' handlers were elated. "'ere, another five or ten rounds like that and he'll have to throw in the towel," crowed Rafe as he poured a mug of beer into Thomas' mouth.

Thomas spit the tepid brew onto the ground. "He's your boss, for God's sake. What kind of respect is that?"

The three men laughed as one. "He told us to work your corner, and he made it clear that we were to do everything we could to help you," laughed Rafe. Then the triangle rang out, and Rafe added, "Make us proud Colonel!"

As Thomas walked back to the scratch for round three, he looked over at Marie, who acknowledged him with a half-smile. The crowd was warming up to the combat, and Thomas had no doubt that pickpockets were working their way through the massed assembly, bets were being made at a furious pace, and more than a few new alliances were being drawn. He wondered what price Sweeney's men would really end up paying once the dust had settled.

"Gentlemen, if you please," shouted the referee when they touched hands across the scratch. Thomas noticed a thin line of blood dribbling from Sweeney's right ear, and a new measure of respect in his eyes as he regarded his opponent.

Neither man took immediate action when the triangle rang. They both understood that they needed to assess what had happened so far, and then figure out how to probe and exploit their adversaries' weaknesses.

They circled warily, fists up and elbows at their sides, looking for openings to make a feint and throw a punch. Thomas swung first, high, towards Sweeney's jaw, but the big man ducked and came up with a right and then a left to Thomas' gut followed by a lightning-fast left-hand punch to his jaw and a hammer right to the side of his face.

Thomas was thrown backwards, but he did not go to the ground. Now Sweeney went for a blow to the face, but Thomas sidestepped and launched a series of short, hard punches to his kidneys. The Irishman gasped in pain, but he did not fall back. Instead, he lowered his head and began pummeling Thomas' chest and stomach with short, rapid-fire jabs that took his breath away.

Before Thomas could counter the attack, the sound of the triangle brought round three to an end and both men wove unsteadily back to their corners.

"Ye're warming up nicely, colonel," said Rafe with a tinge of pride. "From my side of things, though, I don't think you should keep playing the inside game with the man. He's got 25 pounds on you, and he can take more abuse than you can…beg your pardon for the offense."

"No offense taken," Thomas replied. "So, move to the outside?"

"Make him come to you, colonel. You have the look of a grappler about you; get behind him, take him to the ground, and have your way with him."

That crude sexual reference caused the other handlers to laugh, but Thomas knew there was a grain of truth to what Rafe said. He was getting winded, and his head and abdomen were on fire from the onslaught of body blows the Irishman was delivering.

He fought off the pain and the bone weariness he was beginning to feel and forced himself to trot back to the scratch for the opening of round four. The crowd cheered his bravado, and he heard beer mugs clanging together and a few chants of 'Scoundrel, Scoundrel!' rang out among the spectators.

Sweeney came up to the scratch with a new, more serious focus. For the first time since the match began, he realized that there was a possibility–no matter how slight–that he could go down to the colonel. He could not afford to have his legion of enemies see that happen; they would take the offensive against he and his men all around Five Points if they sensed he had been weakened and humiliated.

The triangle rang out, and Sweeney muttered, "I'm sorry for this Scoundrel," before drawing himself back to prepare to deliver the most devastating rain of kicks and punches yet. It had to end now.

Thomas had a different plan. The instant the triangle rod touched metal he surged forward and wrapped one hand behind the Irishman's neck, while with the other hand he grabbed Sweeney's left wrist and pulled his arm towards the ground.

He knew exactly how Sweeney would react; with his head and left arm trapped Sweeney would begin pummeling Thomas' kidney with his right fist. It was the most natural of fighting reactions, and one of the foolhardiest.

Thomas pulled down on Sweeney's arm, and, as expected, he felt the first crushing blow to his side. That was his signal to lessen his grip on Sweeney's neck just long enough for Sweeney to try to pull his head back. Thomas sensed when the Irishman's head had moved about a foot and then he yanked Sweeney's neck and rammed his own head forward into Sweeney's with full force.

When he felt hot blood spurt from the gash his forehead had opened above Sweeney's eyebrow, he made his next move. Holding the Irishman's neck and wrist tightly, he began to circle around to the left. Both men were now bent at the waist, and when Sweeney tried to straighten up Thomas let go of his wrist, dropped to his knees, and reached across to grab Sweeney's left ankle. As he made contact with the ankle, Thomas bent lower and drove into Sweeney's body with his shoulder. The Irishman went down in a heap on his side, and Thomas scrambled on top of him and began pounding his right fist into Sweeny's kidney, over and over. Sweeney groaned at the intense pain and sucked in his breath.

Two more punches, Thomas thought, and then I will batter the back of his head until he is unconscious. He raised his hand for another debilitating strike, only to hear the triangle clang. Thomas rolled off Sweeney and got to his feet, but the Irishman stayed down. Was this the end of it?

The crowd stamped its feet, whistled, and jeered, but Thomas avoided the temptation to look back as he walked to his corner. Rafe poured a jug of water on his head, which was the best feeling Thomas had known in days. He hadn't realized how tired and hot he was.

He shook off the water and looked across the ring only to see that Sweeney had somehow managed to stand and was walking slowly back to his corner with his arm pressed against his abdomen. Whatever else happened now, Thomas knew that the Irishman would be passing blood every time he visited the latrine for the next week.

The hansom cab pulled to a stop in front of Sweeney's Saloon and Akoni and Taiana climbed down onto the frozen mud. The sidewalks were deserted but they could hear cheers and shouts coming from behind the brick building.

"Over there," said Taiana, pointing to an open gate through which they could see a mass of people on chairs, atop fences, on stairs and on the ground.

Akoni took her arm. "Stay close beside me, little sister. Do not stray so much as an inch."

They made their way along the side of the building and through the gate. They could not see what the crowd was cheering at. Akoni let go of Taiana's arm and grasped her hand. Then he pushed forward through the crowd, using his massive body as a battering ram.

"Here now…"

"Back off you great ox…"

"Arsehole!"

People hurled curses and shook their fists at the giant Hawaiian, but none were so foolish as to try and stop him. They pushed through several rows of screaming spectators and suddenly found themselves at the edge of a great cobblestone arena. Sixty feet across from them, two men were engaged in close combat; one had the other in a headlock and was banging his face against a wooden crate, while the unfortunate devil being bashed to and fro was trying to keep his footing.

As they watched, the man in the headlock kicked his feet up against the crate and gave a mighty push backwards. Both men fell to the ground and began wrestling around. Then a metal triangle rang out and the men separated and rolled to their backs, exhausted. The first man to stand was the tall, broad-shouldered fellow with a red beard and hair whose head had just been used as a hammer on the wooden crate. The second man's back was to them. He stood and brushed mud and grime from his shirt and turned around.

"Dear God," whispered Taiana. "It's Thomas!"

As Thomas walked back to his corner, Akoni kept hold of Taiana's hand and pulled her along the leading edge of the clamoring swarm of spectators to where Thomas had collapsed on a stool and was being doused in water by a seedy-looking fellow in a garish yellow and purple vest.

When they were just feet from Thomas, a woman stepped out of the throng and placed her hand on Akoni's forearm.

"I know who you are," she said in an urgent voice. "Please, come with me."

She turned and walked into the crowd, which opened a path for her. She was clearly someone important, Akoni thought, and as much as he wanted to get to his friend, he decided he should follow this woman.

She approached the back of the saloon, and the people crowding the back steps made way for her to open the door. She motioned for Akoni and Taiana to step inside the kitchen, and then followed them and slammed the door shut.

As soon as the door closed, they heard the triangle clang and the crowd let out a roar. Akoni looked at her questioningly.

"The fight has begun again," she said. "I think it is round six or seven."

"Who are you?" asked Taiana. "Why is Thomas fighting that man?"

"My name is Marie. That man is Coutts Sweeney, my husband. He is the owner of this establishment, and the leader of the Sundowners. Your friend killed his brother last night."

Akoni's attention was divided between the battle scene outside the window and the remarkable thing this woman had just told them.

"And this is how you resolve such matters?" Akoni asked. "Personal combat? What about the police."

Marie laughed softly. "We are the law here, Akoni. You are Akoni, am I correct?"

Akoni shook his head. How did this woman know who he was?

"And you would be Taiana," Marie continued. "Thomas told me all about the both of you this morning. His great regret was that he did not say goodbye to you before he…" she hesitated, "before he threw himself to the lions."

"I don't understand," Taiana said. "Thomas killed your husband's brother…"

"In self-defense, as it turns out," Marie interjected.

Taiana nodded. "And the penalty for defending himself is that he has to box your husband?"

She and Akoni searched Marie's face. It made no sense to them.

The triangle rang again, and the crowd kept up its cheering and stamping.

"It appears there is no winner yet," said Marie.

"So, you know Thomas's story, and about the news of his wife?" Akoni asked.

"Yes," said Marie. "In fact, it is only because of Keani that this fight is happening."

Akoni looked perplexed.

"My husband's brother was a complete and utter wastrel," she began as the triangle rang out again. "No one will miss him. But he was a Sundowner, and his death must be avenged by family. Coutts had every right to shoot your friend last night and end it all. Believe me, that is what his men expected. Something stayed his hand, however, and he chose to wait until today to pronounce punishment. After I told him Thomas' story, he decided that instead of shooting the colonel on the spot, he would give him a thorough, old-fashioned drubbing."

"To the death?" asked Akoni.

Marie nodded. "If it came to that, yes. My husband has many enemies, inside and outside his organization. Any sign of weakness on his part would be viewed as an opportunity by every gang leader in Five Points, and more than a few of his own men, too. Taking on the man who murdered his brother in a one-on-one battle is something his men and the other gangs would respect."

"And if Thomas loses the fight, will that be the end of it for him and your husband?" Taiana asked.

"I hope so. But we cannot be sure."

Akoni stepped closer to the window and watched as Thomas and Coutts walked slowly back to the scratch for the beginning of the next round.

Then he turned back to Marie. "But what if Thomas wins?"

She gazed down at the floor. "Then God help us all."

<h1 style="text-align:center">~SIXTY-FOUR ~</h1>

"**S**tay here with Marie," Akoni ordered as he swung open the door to the courtyard.

Taiana rushed to him. "No! I must come with you."

Akoni leaned down. "Someone may die out there," he said in a gentle voice. "Thomas would not want you to see." He waved his hand towards the center of the arena where Thomas and Sweeney were wearily trading blows.

Marie came up alongside Taiana. "Your friend is right, child. That is no place for you."

Taiana's face flushed and her eyes teared up. She turned away from the door and leaned against a countertop as Marie wrapped an arm around her and nodded for Akoni to go. He went down the stairs and pushed his way to the front of the crowd just as Thomas landed a solid blow to the side of Sweeney's head. The Irishman started to fall back but was able to grab the front of Thomas' shirt with both hands, and both men went down into the cold dirt.

Thomas struggled to his knees and struck Sweeney once in the gut before Sweeney lashed out with a short jab that caught Thomas on the bridge of the nose. The people in the front of the crowd cheered when they heard cartilage snap and saw blood gush from the colonel's broken nose.

Sweeney struggled to his knees and raised his arms defensively, but Thomas was able to break through with a left hook to Sweeney's jaw, followed by a ferocious right jab to his throat. Sweeney swayed back and forth and then fell to the ground and rolled on his back. Thomas blinked several times against the blood and the sweat pouring down his face and tried to force his eyes to focus, but he was done for, and he knew it. He lay his palms flat on the ground and tried to push himself to a standing position, but the strength was gone from his arms and his legs felt like rubber. He looked slowly around the arena at the hundreds of people chanting for him finish Sweeney off, but it was no use. He ran the back of his forearm across his mouth, closed his eyes, and toppled to the ground.

The wind was picking up from across the river and the first soft purples of twilight were beginning to form as the crowd went silent and all movement stopped.

Thirty seconds passed and neither fighter stirred. According to the London Rules someone had lost the fight. But who? Thomas fell to the ground after Sweeney, but everyone knew that the winner of a bout had to be standing to be declared the victor.

The timekeeper lowered his triangle and looked to the referee for guidance. The referee was also in uncharted territory. He crossed his arms over his chest for a moment and stared at the ground. Then he raised both arms in the air and shouted, "There being no winner per the established rules of boxing, I declare this match to be a draw. We are done here."

The crowd was having none of it. They had crawled out of their roosts and taverns, walked miles in the frigid weather, been cheated out of their free round 20 beer, and deposited their meager pennies with the bookmakers who had been working the assembly non-stop since before the first triangle bell rang out. A draw was an insult. Someone had to lose, and preferably, die. A low rumble broke out in the back, which grew into a torrent of jeers and stamping feet and flying beer mugs. Marie watched through the kitchen window, fearful that a riot was about to break out.

Akoni started to make his way across the arena to help Thomas when four rough-looking men broke away from the pack and ran over beside Thomas' prostate form. Without hesitating they began kicking him in the back and shoulders, cursing, and crying out, "This is for Tarl, he will be avenged!"

Akoni flew across the arena and grabbed two of the assailants by the scruffs of their necks. He yanked them backwards, slammed their heads together, and tossed their unconscious bodies aside like a child's rag doll.

Then a squad of eight blue-clad police officers streamed through the gate and waded into the crowd with their billy clubs swinging. Isabella's pleas to the Police Commissioner had not been ignored. Two of the officers spotted the melee and raced towards Akoni, but by then he had laid the other two men out on the ground with two blows of his ham-sized fists.

Marie and Taiana saw the new fight unfold from the window. "He is the right friend to have in this part of town," said Marie. Taiana could only nod and beam with pride.

"Come," said Marie, and she opened the door and led Taiana down the steps. By the time they made it across the cobblestone arena, Akoni was encircled by six policemen, billy clubs raised and ready to wade in.

"Stop now, you men stop," Marie shouted. "You know who I am… let this man be."

Taiana saw the look of relief in the policeman's eyes when Marie gave them permission to find someone smaller than this giant Polynesian to smack down. They holstered their clubs and trotted off to herd the crowd down the street and away from Sweeney's.

Marie went to her knees and cradled her husband's head on her lap as Akoni and Taiana helped Thomas get to his feet. He wrapped his arms around his friends' shoulders and with their help began limping off the battlefield. When they got to the gate leading to the street, he turned and looked back. The arena was empty, and after the cacophony of the last hour, eerily silent.

Marie was helping Sweeney to sit up and was dabbing a wet cloth on the cuts and bruises that covered his face and neck. She felt

Thomas' stare and gave him a soft smile. Sweeney looked into her eyes with approval and then nodded to Thomas.

Akoni led his friends out to the street and gave a passing boy a dime to find them a cab. Then he sat Thomas down on a bench in front of the saloon between he and Taiana.

"Thomas, my friend," said Akoni, "the next time you want to go to war make sure you tell me first."

"And me," added Taiana softly as she rested her head on Thomas' shoulder.

He managed a bit of a smile before closing his eyes and falling asleep.

~SIXTY-FIVE ~

The man walking across the lobby towards his desk had excellent taste in hunting attire, the concierge thought. He'd worked at the city's finest haberdashery before coming to Gilsey House, and he recognized first quality clothing when he saw it.

It was just after sunrise, and pale winter light spilled across the marble floor as attendants doused the gas lamps that burned through the night. The concierge took a quick sip of coffee and hid the cup on a shelf before turning his attention back to the hunter. He was tall and lean, with a dark felt Stetson hat over a grey wool Mackinaw jacket and wax-saturated canvas duck trousers, the kind that you brush out after wearing but never launder. His brown shirt was made frommoleskin cotton, and the concierge knew without asking that it had come from Moss Brothers Mills, one of Britain's oldest and most prestigious manufacturers. He wore lace-up hunting boots and was carrying a sealskin bag.

The light was still too weak to make out the man's face until he was just a few feet away, which, given the assortment of bruises, swelling, cuts, and scrapes, was probably a good thing.

The man set down his bag and nodded to the concierge.

Struggling to maintain his composure, the concierge cleared his throat and said, "Good morning, Colonel Scoundrel. Are we hunting today?"

Thomas shook his head. Three days after the fight with Coutts Sweeney, his lips were still swollen enough that talking was a bit difficult.

"No, not hunting. I want to spend a day on the shore, somewhere there are as few people as possible. Can you recommend a place?"

Despite the prohibition from eating or drinking while on duty, the concierge reached below his desk and raised the coffee cup to his lips. He needed a moment to tamp down his insatiable curiosity.

"I can," he finally said. "Away from people, you say?"

"Away from everything."

"I would not suggest visiting the Atlantic shore right now. With no headlands or trees to blunt the weather it would be a miserable experience."

He pulled a map of the region from a drawer and asked Thomas to come around the desk.

"This is Long Island," he said. "There are perhaps 10,000 people living there, but they are all concentrated here on the west side, around the new Long Island City. Over here," his fingers picked a spot on the north shore, mid-way along the island near the Long Island Sound, "is the Oyster Bay area. It's isolated, and I can say from personal experience, a splendid location to enjoy the solitude you are seeking. Sand dunes, tree-lined bluffs, rocky promontories, miles of beach, and spectacular vistas. No amenities, alas, so you would need to carry your own water and provisions."

Thomas pointed to his bag. "Taken care of." He looked over the map again and said, "I had hoped for open sea."

"I assure you that you will not be disappointed, Colonel. If you insist on journeying to the open coast, of course I will arrange for that."

Thomas thought for a moment. "How do I get to this Oyster Bay?" he asked.

The concierge smiled. "I will arrange for a hansom to take you on the ferries across the Hudson and East Rivers to the Hunters Point Station in Long Island City. You'll take the Central Railroad to Mineola, here..." he pointed to the map again, "where you will take the Mineola & Locust Valley Branch up to where it terminates at the Locust Valley

Post Office. From there it is about a one-mile trek to the shore of Oyster Bay Harbor. You'll be hiking through thick brush and the remains of last season's windrows, so your choice of clothing is just right."

"Time to get there?" asked Thomas.

"It's about 25 miles, but the trains run regularly all day, and I believe the last return train from Locust Valley departs at 7 **PM**. Figure three hours to get there, the same on your return."

Thomas withdrew his wallet from his coat and handed the concierge a $5 bill.

"That's not necessary, sir, I'm just doing my job."

"You have taken exceedingly good care of my friends, and I appreciate that." He picked up his bag to go.

"Sir?" said the concierge.

Thomas turned.

"Forgive my impertinence, Colonel, but…are you alright?"

Thomas was looking at the concierge, but the man could tell he was focusing somewhere far, far away.

"No," Thomas replied in a voice barely above a whisper.

There were only a handful of passengers on the Mineola to Locust Valley leg of the trip, and as the train wound through fallow farmland and past scattered cottages and outbuildings, Thomas took the time to reflect on what had happened since his bout with the Irish gang leader.

His friends had rallied around him when he returned to the hotel. Isabella had food sent from her restaurant for the first two days, since Thomas did not want to leave his room, and Phineas and Preston Winters visited him each afternoon to report on their progress—or lack of it—in getting a newspaper to agree to review Aubert's paintings. "Don't be dejected," Winters said after the tenth paper in a row turned them down. "There are still more than 50 papers whose offices we haven't visited. Someone is going to have the good sense to want to be the first to introduce the artist of the age to this city."

Tomorrow they were meeting with Mandleman at his gallery to talk about pricing the paintings, and how to best display them in the room they had been assigned for the grand opening, while Isabella and Akoni were taking Taiana to get fitted for a gown to wear to the grand opening of the Metropolitan on the 23rd. Thomas stared out the window to the gray morning sky. What was he going to do? He should reply to Océane's letter about Keani, he should write to Andrew Whitton at the *Chronicle*, and to Kukane at the plantation on Lana'i, and Father Damien at the leper colony at Kalawao. Taiana's parents needed to know that she was well and in good hands. So many things he should do. All that, and there was always the matter of Fitch Donegan and Aata, who by now were surely in the city looking for him. There were over 100 first-class hotels in New York to comb through, so he was reasonably certain they would not have any luck by the day of the grand opening. He patted the revolver in his coat pocket. Reasonably certain was not good enough, of course. They would find him eventually.

The track ended at Locust Valley, where a turntable swung the train around for its return trip to Long Island City. The station master at the tiny stop was surprised to see a tall gentleman with a battered face step out of the coach in full hunting gear, sling his satchel over his shoulder, and march off into the scrub brush and hedges in the direction of Oyster Bay Harbor. The man wasn't carrying a rifle, and since there were no homes, businesses, or farms between the station and Long Island Sound, the station master was mystified. People did not come out here in the dead of winter to picnic or hike.

Thomas smelled the ocean when he stepped down from the passenger coach. He would not need the map the concierge at Gilsey House had sketched on a scrap of paper. He just followed his nose.

It was 11 AM and the dull gray overcast was giving way to scattered patches of blue. A breeze rustled through stands of red cedar, Douglas fir, pitch pine, and bayberry. He passed beneath a canopy of white oaks whose barren branches reached over 100 feet into the sky and when he emerged on the other side and climbed a low sand dune, he could see the deep green waters of Oyster Bay and the red and slate green bluffs lining Centre Island and Cove Neck.

There was just enough wind to set small wavelets rippling across the surface of the water, and he stopped for a minute to watch flights of plovers and terns dive and swoop through the swirling air currents with the grace of circus acrobats.

The concierge had been right about the locale; from his vantage point on top of the dune he could see several miles in all directions, from the expanse of the Sound to the west to the sandstone bluffs above Cold Spring Harbor to the east. What he did not see were any signs of human habitation. That was perfect.

He walked down to the base of the dune and looked along the marshy beach before laying his bag on a tree stump and taking a seat on the branch of a half-submerged oak.

Then he reached deep into his jacket pocket and pulled out a small bracelet made with delicate, multi-colored seashells. It took Keani several days to bore a tiny hole in each shell and thread a dried sinew string through them. She presented the bracelet to him on their wedding day, and he had not taken it off until the night he received news of her death. Now? He didn't know. He could not toss it into the sea, he could not wear it. He turned it over and over in his hand, remembering the glow in her eyes when she slipped it onto his wrist and pulled his hand gently to her breast to feel her heartbeat.

In the five days since Océane's letter arrived, he had become almost numb from grief. His mind had raced unceasingly from one possible course of action to another; should he take his own life and end the pain? It would be easy. Or climb into a liquor bottle and stay there? He had known men who did that when the weight of losing a wife or child was more than they could bear. Perhaps return to active duty in the Army? A full colonel would have his pick of duty stations.

He could also return to Lana'i and reclaim his sugar plantation, work out an arrangement with the bank, and spend his days laboring alongside Kukane's second gang workers in the sweltering tropical heat. At the very least he should go on the offensive against Donegan and Aata instead of waiting for them to appear out of the night to shoot him dead in some New York alleyway.

And what of his promise to Aubert to find representation and sales for his paintings? Phineas and Winters were doing their part, and he knew they would see it through, but he had given his word, and he should not turn his back on a promise.

Keani was the only person he had trusted enough to share his dreams with. They spent hours under the stars on the deck of their cabin making plans for their future, but the razor-sharp edge of a coral fan sliced through those dreams as surely as it had through her leg, and now he could not bear to recall anything they had talked about.

The shrill calls of swooping terns mingled with the sound of waves lapping around the broken trees that dotted the beach. As the last remnants of winter grey gave way to the brightening sun, he slung his sealskin bag over his shoulder and walked midway up a line of undulating sand dunes, where he stopped to get his bearings. When he bent to set down his bag and retrieve his canteen, he suddenly heard the retort of a rifle shot, followed immediately by a zinging sound that whooshed within inches of his head. An instant later a branch on a dead tree ten feet in front of him exploded into a mass of slivers.

He pulled his revolver and went down on his stomach, sweeping the area for the assailant who had just fired on him. Was it possible that Donegan had discovered his whereabouts in the city and trailed him all the way out here?

Then a voice shouted: "Hello! I say, hello…are you there?"

Thomas looked to his left and saw a boy of about 14 coming over the top of the sand dune. He was of medium height and slender build, with a canvas rucksack on his back and a look of fright on his face. An old French breech-loading rifle was cradled in his arms.

Thomas got to his feet and waited for the shooter to approach. The boy rushed to him, and immediately began apologizing.

"So very sorry, sir, I can't tell you how sorry I am. Why, I almost shot you!"

When the boy was within a few feet he looked at Thomas' battered face and added, "Or did I?"

"You did not, but you came damn close," Thomas replied in a gruff voice.

The boy lowered the rifle to the ground and slipped off his pack.

"I am most truly and heartily sorry. Mr...?"

"Thomas. Just Thomas."

The boy brightened. "My name is Teedie, or rather that is, it's Teddy. My parents call me Teedie but I'm getting a little old to be called by a child's nickname, wouldn't you agree?"

Thomas could not help but like the boy. His bright blue eyes and shock of unruly brown hair lent an air of mischief to him, though judging from his clothing, the boy did not come from a poor family.

Thomas motioned to a downed tree a few yards away and they took seats on the weathered trunk.

"Tell me about your rifle, Teddy."

"It's my first, given to me by my father only last week."

Thomas handed the boy his canteen and waited for him to drink.

"And is this your first time shooting a rifle?"

"Oh, heavens no. I've been shooting since I was nine. It's one of the ways I collect specimens for my museum of natural history, along with trapping, of course."

"Your museum?"

"Yes, and I have over 300 specimens, from worms and birds and field mice to fox and racoons and a bear. The showman P.T. Barnum recently gave me a human hand in a glass jar from his private collection, can you imagine that?"

"A museum," Thomas repeated.

"It fills the basement of our home on East Twentieth Street," Teddy said with a note of pride. "You are most welcome to visit."

"How old did you say you were?"

"14."

"Which makes you not only the youngest museum owner I have met, but the only one, too. I am honored."

Teddy beamed. "May I ask, sir, what business you are in that brings you so far from the city?"

"These days I am in the art business. Before that I was a sugar plantation owner, before that a reporter, and before that I was in the army."

Teddy was impressed with his new friend's pedigree. He made a circle around his face with a finger and asked, "Is that where you…in the army I mean?"

Thomas touched his cheek. "This? No, these are only a few days old."

Teddy was bursting to ask what had happened, but he knew that such a question would be beyond the pale. A man did not make personal inquiries of another man without an invitation to do so.

"I am out here today purely to enjoy the natural world," Thomas added. "Rather like you."

"Without a gun?" Teddy asked.

Thomas withdrew his revolver. "Had it been anyone else firing at me I would be answering that question somewhat…differently."

He slipped the revolver back into his jacket. "Tell me what you were shooting at when you nearly clipped my ear."

Teddy's face skewed up in embarrassment. "Over there," he said, pointing to a gnarled tree on which a small piece of blue cloth had been pinned.

Thomas looked at the target, and then at the tree Teddy had hit, some five feet away from the target.

"May I see your rifle?"

Teddy handed over his gun and Thomas opened the breech, checked the action, and then closed it and held it up to his eye. "Sight seems fine," he said as he handed the gun back to Teddy. "Did the wind blow sand in your face as you fired, or did you sneeze?"

"Nothing like that. But…" he hesitated.

"Yes?"

"Things at a distance have been looking a little blurry to me lately."

"Have you ever worn eyeglasses?"

Teddy shook his head.

Thomas thought for a moment and then reached into his bag and pulled out a small, oblong rosewood box. He opened it and pulled out a pair of handsome spectacles.

"Do you wear those?" Teddy asked.

"Not yet," said Thomas with a smile. "They were a gift from my friend, Timothy Boswell. Like you he is a professional naturalist. He currently works on the island of Tahiti."

Teddy's eyes widened. The South Seas!

"He gave them to me when his own needs changed and said I might want them someday. The lenses were ground in Germany." He handed then to Teddy. "They are bifocals. You look at close up objects through the bottom half, and faraway objects through the top."

Teddy held the glasses like they were poison. "I have spent countless hours these past two years strengthening my body," he said. "I have asthma and a host of other maladies that my family thought were going to kill me."

"And you weren't about to let that happen," said Thomas in a fatherly tone.

"No, I wasn't. I can't take any steps backward. I cannot allow any weakness to get the best of me." He started to hand the glasses back, but Thomas stayed his hand.

"Eyes are not like biceps," Thomas said. "You can use weights to strengthen your arms, and there's no shame in that. There's no shame in using spectacles for your eyes, Teddy."

Teddy looked uncertain.

"Try them on at least," Thomas urged.

Teddy sighed and set the glasses on the bridge of his nose. He blinked several times, looked down and then up, and a smile began to spread across his face. He dug into his specimen bag and pulled out the body of a small, colorful bird. He held it up near his face and said, "I have never seen feather detail like this without a magnifying glass." Then he looked at the cloth target on the tree, 20 feet away. He let out a low whistle and said, "or that level of distant detail. Not ever."

"Have you got a reload for your gun?" asked Thomas. Teddy took a box of paper cartridges and musket caps from his bag and reloaded his rifle.

"Now take me to the exact spot where you made that shot," Thomas said.

They walked 50 feet to the crest of the dune and down the back side until they could just barely see over the top.

"Sight in," said Thomas, and Teddy raised the rifle to his shoulder and lowered his head enough to see through the iron sight.

"How does it look with the glasses?"

"Like a whole new world," said Teddy excitedly.

"Fire when ready," Thomas said.

Teddy grinned and pulled the trigger. The muzzle flashed and a second later Teddy let out a whoop of joy: the bullet hit the cloth target square in the center.

"Speaking as the fellow who was almost your last target, I feel pretty good about your future shooting prospects," said Thomas.

They walked back over the dune and Thomas collected his things. Teddy put the glasses back in the box and handed them to him, only to have Thomas hand them back.

"They are my gift to you, Teddy. Use them in good health."

"I can't thank you enough, Thomas. I also can't believe it took this long for me to figure out what my problem has been."

Thomas shook the boy's hand. "I'll tell you what. Promise not to shoot me the next time we meet, and I will call us even."

Teddy looked pensive. "Will we meet again?"

Thomas slapped him on the back. "That we most certainly will, my friend."

"I come out here often, you know" the boy said, "and someday I'm going to build a house near here. You will be a welcome guest."

Had any other 14-year-old in the world made such a bold statement, Thomas would have dismissed it as a child's fantasy. Something about this lad, though, told him that house would be built exactly as he promised.

He smiled and shook his head. Then he took a drink from his canteen, secured his bag on his shoulder, and set off towards the eastern promontory that divided Oyster Bay from Cold Spring Harbor. He liked the looks of the trees on the bluff and the way they shone in the winter light.

He raised his hand goodbye and leaned into the breeze. Teddy sat at the top of the dune and watched his new friend grow smaller and smaller until he was just a dot on the horizon. Then he readied his own bag and rifle and began the hike to the train station for the journey back to the city.

~SIXTY-SIX ~

December 15

New York City depressed and angered Aata, and the Bowery district and Lower East Side made him long to be anywhere other than this cold, gray, crowded metropolis. In his two days in the city, he had spent hours walking streets packed with beer gardens, saloons, cigar stores, dime museums, gin mills, gambling dens, missions, theatres, and cheap lodging houses. Worst of all were the gaudily dressed prostitutes of every age who aggressively solicited any man they passed who looked like he might have an extra 50¢ in his pocket. That was the going rate for a 'tug-and-tickle' as the girls called it, and coincidentally, just enough for her to buy a mug of beer and a decent meal after services had been rendered.

Aata shared one thing in common with the city's whores; he, too, was looking for men, but for an entirely different purpose. He had learned from a fellow traveler on the train out of St. Louis that people from every nation on earth could be found in the city of one million, from places as far away as his native Tahiti. They were in the tenements, on the docks, and in the flesh pots and saloons on every block in the district. Many of the islanders who boarded four-masted schooners and steamers in Polynesia to work as ordinary seamen simply walked away from their jobs when their ships docked in New York harbor to offload passengers and freight. The lure of the gigantic city was too powerful to resist. Of course, within days of walking down the gang plank with all their worldly possessions slung over their shoulder in a sea bag, most of the men had run through their money and were desperate to find any kind of work to survive.

Aata wrote down the passenger's instructions for finding men; Jews from Eastern Europe lived below First Street, Italians settled between the Bowery and Broadway south of Bleeker Street, and Germans and Poles lived from First Street to St. Mark's Place. The Irish, he was told, were sprinkled everywhere. To find native islanders he would have to comb the cheaper saloons and tenements that had sprouted up across the Lower East Side. The good news, the man told Aata, was that he only needed to find one fellow Polynesian. That man would know where to find others.

Aata trudged the crowded streets from midday until late at night, stepping into dozens of beer-soaked saloons, flop houses, and diners in search of a single Hawaiian or Tahitian man who could help him find four or five others. Four men had traveled with him from Hawaii, but after his battles with Colonel Scoundrel at the wrestling match in Papara and onboard the train just over a week ago, he was taking no chances. Scoundrel was a formidable opponent, and Aata would take no risk the next time they came face to face. He would go after Scoundrel with a dozen men if that's what it took.

While he sought out more men, three of his warriors were tracking Donegan around the clock to make sure the assassin did not kill Scoundrel before Aata could wring the bank's money out of him. After that, he did not care what happened to the American. Scoundrel had taken his woman, humiliated him in front of his entire village, and destroyed his reputation as a warrior to be feared by all. Whatever excruciating death Donegan had in mind for the colonel would not be painful enough to satisfy Aata's hunger for revenge.

Fitch Donegan had no need of help. He was going to find Colonel Scoundrel, kill him, and be done with it. Then he would collect his final pay from Colin Stafford in San Francisco and return to Honolulu and the pleasures of the Pearl.

He moved into a businessman's hotel in midtown and immediately put the resources of his employer to work for him. A single trip to Stafford's New York bank provided him with $500 in cash and access to $1,000 more should he need it. Next, he visited the offices of the Pinkerton National Detective Agency. They were hesitant at first about helping to track down a famous war hero like Thomas Scoundrel, but Donegan provided a letter of introduction from Stafford, and convinced them that he was there to see to it that the colonel received a substantial family inheritance that was waiting for him in California.

With their concerns put to rest, the agency agreed to provide three experienced detectives at $10 per day each, plus meals and cab fare. Donegan knew that finding Scoundrel among the hundreds of hotels in the city was a longshot. But as he bundled his overcoat against a sudden flurry of freezing sleet, he also knew that whether the Pinkertons found Scoundrel or not wasn't all that important. Today was December 15th. He knew exactly where the colonel would be eight days from now, and if the brat who had clocked him with the fire extinguisher on the train and the great oaf of a Hawaiian who fought his men were also there, so much the better. He would deal with them, too. It was a shame he wouldn't have enough time to savor the pristine innocence of the girl before he cut her throat, but sacrifices had to be made.

He came to a halt in front of the Dodworth Building at 681 5th Avenue. A wall mounted sign proclaimed the unassuming four-story brownstone building to be the new Metropolitan Museum of Art, whose grand opening, he knew, would take place on December 23rd. Since the brownstone was not large enough to house the combined paintings from the museum's permanent collection and the works that gallery owners would be lending for the event, the Museum's directors had rented out a new hotel that was completing construction next door. The two bottom floors were being specially prepared with 14 showcase galleries that would highlight the greatest works of art that the city— and for that matter the nation—had ever assembled in one place.

Donegan signaled for a passing cab to take him back to his hotel. He would return often in the next seven days to carefully study the perimeter of both buildings, especially the entrances and exits. A few dollars in the hand of any of the workers would make it possible for him to become familiar with the interior of the buildings, too.

Like Aata, Donegan was not going to underestimate Scoundrel's wiles or fighting skills. He would scout the killing ground, make a move on his man as the crowd of well-dressed revelers spilled up the steps for the grand opening, and plunge his knife deep into the unsuspecting colonel's spine.

And, who knew? If he played it smart, perhaps he could lure the girl to his hotel room with a false promise of help. He would pay a whore to deliver the message and bring the girl to the hotel, and then take them both by force.

A surge of heat poured through his body as darkness gathered and the temperature continued to plunge.

~SIXTY-SEVEN ~

December 17

Two carriages trotted across the damp cobblestones on 5th Avenue and came to a stop in front of the brownstone that housed the new Metropolitan Museum of Art. Phineas McNab and Preston Winters helped Isaac Mandleman out of their carriage, while Thomas, Akoni, and Taiana climbed down out of their carriage and joined the other men on the sidewalk.

"Not a terribly impressive structure," Winters said as he looked over the brownstone.

"No, not today, but I promise you that in years to come a magnificent structure will rise to hold our city's great art treasures," Mandleman replied. "In any event, our destination is over there." He pointed to the new marble-columned five-story hotel next to the museum, where workmen were streaming in and out of the front entrance carrying lumber, rolled carpet, draperies, and cans of paint.

"Will they be ready for the opening?" asked Phineas. "That's only eight days away."

The elderly art dealer chuckled. "Ready enough, I am told by the museum official supervising the preparations. Let's go inside."

Akoni carried a folding stool for Mandleman, and Taiana held tightly to Thomas' arm as they walked to the front of the hotel. Since the day he had slipped out at dawn to travel out to Long Island, she had been watching him like a hawk. She was sitting outside his door by daybreak each morning, and she insisted on accompanying him everywhere he went during the day until he returned to his room after dinner. Akoni was amused by her mother-hen attention, but Thomas didn't mind. He had no idea how to manage the demons that roiled his mind every waking—and sleeping—moment. Taiana's presence was calming, and that was enough.

They entered the hotel through a massive set of walnut and cut-glass doors that were propped open for the workers and their deliveries. The two-story-high lobby was large enough to hold a ball in. It had black and white checkered-pattern marble floors, a ten-foot-high Florentine marble fountain, and several dozen sets of oak tables and chairs lined two of the walls. When preparations were complete, they would be spread around the room for the patrons to visit with friends, sip champagne, and talk about the works of art they were viewing in the building's 14 special galleries.

Phineas led the way through the lobby and around a pair of painters who were setting up ladders. "There are seven galleries on this side of the building, and seven on the other side," he said. "Each gallery has its own locking entry door."

He approached the 12-foot polished oak door of the first gallery they came to and waited for Akoni to pull the circular brass handle and open it up. It wasn't easy to move, even for a man of Akoni's size and strength.

They stepped into a rectangular, high-ceilinged room with wood floors, measuring, according to Mandleman, exactly 60 x 45 feet. The walls were painted a dull putty gray, and two gas chandeliers hung from the ceiling. Additional illumination would come from wall sconces that had yet to be installed.

Mandleman sat on his stool and leaned forward on his cane. He gazed around the spacious gallery and proclaimed. "This is perfect."

"Aubert has these walls all to himself?" Thomas asked.

"The expenses for each of the other galleries are being shared among two or even three dealers," Isaac answered. "I chose to bear the entire cost for this one and not share the space."

"That is very generous of you, Isaac," said Preston Winters.

The old man beamed. "Not so generous, my friends. Smart. When people come into this gallery and see every wall covered with Aubert's paintings, and only his paintings, they are going to be overwhelmed. No, this was a wise investment on my part. You'll see." He tapped his cane twice on the wood floor for effect.

"What other artists will be on display in the galleries?" asked Taiana.

"Oh, the best, truly," Mandleman replied. "The Old Masters, of course, along with Alma-Tadema and Edwin Church, Bierstadt and his damnable landscapes, plus Édouard Manet, Whistler, Mary Cassatt, Winslow Homer, and Degas. There will be others, too. A remarkable gathering of Titans, to be sure."

A policeman came into the room and handed a buff-colored envelope to Thomas. He tore it open, smiled, and slid it into his jacket pocket.

"I must excuse myself," he said to his friends. "It seems an old friend has come to town and has asked to see me. I will be back for dinner."

Akoni raised his eyebrows. "And who is it who knows you are in the city?"

Before Thomas could answer Taiana chimed in. "I'm going with you, no arguments now."

"Very well," said Thomas, "but we need to leave right away. It's best not to keep him waiting."

"Him?" asked Phineas.

"The President of the United States," Thomas replied. Then he turned and walked out into the hallway.

Taiana shook her head in bewilderment. The President? Then she raced out of the gallery, caught up to Thomas, and took his arm in hers.

The carriage ride to the Grand Hotel on Broadway only took a few minutes, and they pulled up just as the rains returned. A liveried doorman opened his umbrella over Taiana's head and escorted them to the double-entry doors, where another man in a burgundy uniform swung it wide open and greeted them with a warm smile.

"Welcome to the Grand," he said, "how may we be of service to you this morning?"

"The President's rooms," Thomas replied.

The doorman gave Thomas a thorough look-over. He had been advised by the President's protection squad that any number of favor seekers and ne'er do wells would show up at the hotel when word of the President's arrival made it around the city. The man who had just come in with the well-appointed young woman was suitably dressed, but his face was covered in bruises and scratches.

As the doorman pondered his next move, a tall, thin fellow in a corduroy suit and bowler hat approached from across the lobby.

"Ah, Mr. Cronin," the doorman said, "I was just about to send for you. These folks want…"

"I know what they want," said Cronin with a smile. He stuck out his hand. "Hello, Thomas."

"It's good to see you, John," Thomas replied as they shook. "This is my ward, Taiana. She is from Hawai'i."

"But the prince did not come with you?"

"Akoni will be here for the gala. Will the President be staying?"

"Let's go up to his suite," Cronin said. "He can tell you all about it."

As they walked towards the steam elevator, Cronin turned to Thomas and said, "What the hell happened to you, colonel?"

"A matter of a difference of opinion with an angry Irishman."

"Is there any other kind?" Cronin said with a chuckle. "I do hope your end of the argument prevailed."

"I got a few good jabs in."

They rode to the fifth floor, where two more men from the Washington D.C. Metropolitan police force were sitting on chairs outside a door.

"Have they expanded the protection force yet?" Thomas asked.

"No, there are still only four of us. Makes for some pretty long days."

The other policemen greeted Thomas like an old friend before knocking on the door and waiting to be invited in. Taiana's heart was racing as the door opened and a stocky, rumpled man with a neatly trimmed beard stepped out of the ornately furnished room and slapped his hands on Thomas' shoulders.

'By God, but it's good to see you," said Ulysses S. Grant. "And who is your friend?"

Cronin stepped in with them and shut the door. Thomas introduced Taiana, and then the president asked Cronin to take her down to the hotel restaurant for a cup of hot chocolate. "We'll visit when you come back up, Miss Taiana," said Grant. "Right now, I need to catch up with my old friend."

The president saw the look of concern in Taiana's eyes. He put his hand lightly on her shoulder and in a soft voice said, "He is among friends. I promise."

Taiana nodded and left the room with Cronin.

"Drink?" the president asked as he led them over to two upholstered chairs by the window. Thomas shook his head. "We'll have coffee then," Grant said to the one policeman who remained in the room.

They settled into the chairs and Grant ran a practiced eye over his friend's face. "Recent?" he said, indicating the bruises and cuts on Thomas' face.

"Five days ago. I'm healing up pretty well."

Grant took a cup of black coffee from the policeman and handed it to Thomas before accepting his own. "I'd have hated to see you that first day after," he said with a bit of a smile. "How old are you now? Twenty-four?"

"Twenty three."

"Take it from me, Colonel Scoundrel; get the fighting out of your system before you turn 30. Takes longer and longer for your body to get back together with each passing year."

Thomas had to smile. "Yes, sir. Order understood."

The President took a sip of coffee and set down the cup before leaning forward, his hands clasped together. "Word travels slowly, Thomas, but it does travel. I learned just yesterday about your wife.

I am so sorry."

A look of surprise and puzzlement crossed Thomas' face.

"The news came in a dispatch from our counsel in Hawai'i," said Grant. "He usually reports three times a year, and we had just heard from him a few weeks before. He knew you and I were old acquaintances, and so he marked the letter urgent."

"Does Cronin know?"

"All the boys know."

Thomas didn't know what to say. So many people had offered condolences in the past few days, but the conversations had always ended after the 'I'm so sorry' part. No one knew where to go from there. Grief was a profoundly personal experience, and those who had never known so great a loss as he had gone through, found it impossible to find the right words. So, they just stopped talking, or awkwardly stepped away.

Not Grant. He relit the stub of a cigar and sat back in his chair.

"Tell me about her, Thomas."

"Sir?"

"What was her name, how did you meet, what was she like. Everything."

Thomas grasped the arms of his chair. He had shocked himself when he talked with Coutts Sweeny's wife about Keani. But the president?

"First of all, how the hell did you end up around the world on Tahiti? Last I heard you were in San Francisco."

"I was," Thomas answered in a soft voice. "I worked as a reporter."

"How'd that go?"

"Pretty well, until I wrote the wrong story about someone who is not used to being called out."

"Wrong story?"

"An exposé of a very powerful…"

The president leapt out of his chair. "Hold on a damn minute! Are you talking about Colin P. Stafford? That article in the *Chronicle*?"

Thomas nodded.

"I liked to bust my gut with laughter when I read it," said the president. "Everybody I knew was sending it to me. Stafford is not only one of the slimiest people I know, but the bastard also wants my job."

He looked at Thomas with admiration. "You were the Bayside reporter. I'll be double damned. But," he looked straight into Thomas' eyes, "I find it hard to believe that Stafford would just let something like that drop without exacting some kind of revenge."

"He hasn't let it drop."

"That why you high-tailed it to Hawai'i?"

Thomas looked at the floor. "I stowed away on a German warship. They threw me overboard off Honolulu."

The President had been staring out the window. Now he whirled around, a look of amazement on his face.

"Set down the coffee, Colonel. It's time for a whiskey."

Grant filled two glasses from a carafe on the sideboard and sat back down.

"Let's have it all, Thomas."

For the next hour, Thomas shared his story with the President of the United States. From the voyage to Hawai'i aboard the *SMS König Wilhelm* to winning half ownership in the plantation on Lana'i, fleeing to the leper colony on Moloka'i and sailing to Tahiti, he kept Grant's complete attention. He described his meetings with Captain McNab and Aubert, his fateful wrestling match with Aata, and his courtship and marriage with Keani. Grant was visibly angry when Thomas described the assassins who came after him in Tahiti, and then enchanted as Thomas told the story of building their cabin on the cove on Moorea, their wedding, and the life they led before Thomas had to flee the island.

The president refilled their glasses and Thomas brought the story up until today.

"And this Irish bastard Donegan has pursued you all this way?" asked Grant, "Along with a pack of Tahitian warriors?"

Thomas nodded.

"It's the damndest thing, Thomas. Homeric, that's what your story is. Question is, what happens now, and how can I help?"

"We've got to get through the museum opening and sell enough paintings for me to hold off the bank in Honolulu and pay Aubert for his work, and we have to do that before Donegan and Aata and anybody else out there who is chasing me finds us."

"And then? What about Stafford? That's one polecat who needs a shovel handle crammed all the way up his ass."

The President's vulgar proposal brought a smile to Thomas' face. "I will deal with him in time, sir. However, it's probably best that we don't talk about that situation. Too many…"

Now it was the President's turn to smile. "Yes, too damn many," he said thoughtfully. "Maybe I'll read about it in the newspaper though."

"I hope so, sir."

Grant went over to the fireplace mantel and opened a fresh box of cigars. He clipped the tip, lit it, and took a deep draw. Thomas knew this was the President's habit when he was grappling with something serious.

"You done with the fighting?" Grant finally asked. "No plans to blow your own head off instead of the head of some bastard who deserves it?"

"A few days ago, I would have said no to the first part of your question, and I'm not so sure on the second part. I'm feeling a little different now."

"Fair enough," Grant replied after another pull on his cigar. "But what is changing your mind?"

"Strangely enough, the gang leader I fought a few days ago got me thinking about life. His wife did, too. Two days ago, I met a remarkable lad out on Long Island, and after he nearly killed me by accident, he reminded me of all the wonders that are waiting out there for us to explore and enjoy."

The President nodded but remained silent as Thomas continued. "Taiana, the girl who is with me today…her parents will die from leprosy soon, if they aren't already dead. I promised them I would look after her."

"And you keep your promises," Grant said quietly. "What about the promises you made to your wife?"

"I'm sorry?"

"The promises of all the things you were going to do, the places you were going to visit, the adventures you were going to share."

"She's gone," Thomas said, "and with her, the promises are dead, too."

"Only if you are the one who buries them, son," Grant said quietly. "She wouldn't have given up, and I'm damn sure she wouldn't want you to give up, either."

Thomas' eyes teared up. "It can't ever be the same…"

"No, it can't, and it won't," said Grant in a surprisingly stern voice, "and you will never forget a minute of the time you two shared. Everything will be different." Then his voice grew softer. "Make new choices, Thomas, choose new directions. Little by little, day by day."

Thomas remained silent for a minute. He wiped his eyes with his sleeve, feeling a little ashamed for letting his emotions get the better of him.

Grant stood up again and motioned for Thomas to join him at the window. He parted the curtains and asked, "Which one of us do you suppose has more sons of bitches out there who want to kill him?"

Thomas could only grin. Grant slapped him on the back, "I want you to take Miss Taiana back to your hotel after I visit with her for a minute," the president said. "John Cronin will go with you. Return her to your friends and then have dinner with John. Tell him what he needs to know about the men who are looking for you. He knows every lawman on the East Coast, and more than a fair number of unsavory types, too. Let him help. Do you understand?"

Thomas shook his head in agreement, but the President didn't seem satisfied with his response.

"I'm giving you a direct order, Colonel Scoundrel. You are to get on with life. Honor the promises you made to Keani, and while you're at it, keep from getting your ass shot off. Are my orders clear?"

"Very clear sir."

There was a tap at the door and John Cronin came in with Taiana. The President invited her to sit down, and Thomas shared the President's request that they have dinner together.

Cronin's eyes narrowed. "What the hell kind of trouble are you in this time, my friend?"

'*Someday,*' Thomas thought, '*I hope no one will need to ask me that question again.*'

SIXTY-EIGHT

December 18

The temporary Museum of Art annex in the hotel next to the Dodworth brownstone on 5th Avenue was swarming with activity. The art dealers who were renting gallery space for the grand opening gala had only one day to hang their paintings and set the lighting in their spaces, and as stressful as that was, the Board of Directors had just decreed that each of the 14 galleries would be allowed only two representatives in their respective rooms during the event. More than two would be unseemly, the directors wrote, and make it appear that the event was solely about selling art, rather than achieving the higher purpose of sharing works of transcendent beauty with the only class of people who were truly capable of appreciating them.

The city's leading art dealers also appreciated transcendent beauty, but they were in the business of selling paintings, and this grand opening was both the most prestigious cultural event in the city since the War, and the highlight of the Christmas social season. The opportunity to sell paintings to a gathering of the wealthiest and most powerful inhabitants of America's greatest city was an irresistible lure. They wanted to be present, and they wanted their best sales assistants in the room with them to close as many deals and set as many follow-up appointments as possible.

The physical act of persuasive selling, of course, while the life blood of the gallery business, was considered beneath the dignity of most owners, who fancied themselves as worthy of brushing elbows with the Vanberbilts, Astors, Belmonts, and other members of the city's fabled list of '400.' Those were the select few individuals who were deemed worthy by the social arbiters and doyens of the moment to receive invitations to the glittering soirées, receptions, and costume balls that lit up the mansions along 5th Avenue and 52nd Street during the high seasons.

The board's limit of two representatives per gallery was announced that morning at 9 AM, and by noon a rebellion was brewing. The dealers at first unleashed their wrath upon the board members, but when it became clear that they were not going to back down, those who had made the cost-saving decision to share their space with others soon found themselves in heated shouting matches with their gallery-mates that echoed around the lobby and reverberated down the marble halls. That was especially true of the exhibition rooms who were being sponsored by three or more individual gallery owners. Who would decide which owner had to stand outside the door to his own gallery as if he were some kind of servant?

"It's probably good that Taiana does not understand Yiddish," joked Akoni during one particularly loud argument thundering away in the gallery next to theirs.

"And I almost wish I didn't," said Mandleman, who was seated at a small table jotting notes about the prices they were assigning to Aubert's paintings. "What Mr. Rosenbaum just told Mr. Katz to do to himself is both anatomically impossible as well as forbidden by the Talmud."

Phineas McNab burst into laughter, and stepped away from the center wall where he had been supervising two workers as they hung the first of Aubert's paintings, a three-foot by four-foot gilt-framed depiction of an outrigger canoe beached in a cove. The painting exploded with dabs of sunlight yellow and orange, gloriously colored tropical flowers, and a sky that shimmered with layers of the artist's favorite lapis blue.

"Reserving this gallery to yourself was a very wise decision, my friend," Phineas said to Mandleman, who accepted the compliment and returned to his price deliberations.

Thomas, Isabella, and Taiana were laying out Aubert's framed paintings on the floor along the four walls of the gallery, struggling to make sense of the combination of factors that had to be considered when mounting an exhibition. How should they mix the placement of paintings of different sizes? Should they try to keep paintings of the same general kinds of scenes together, or should they mix landscapes with views of the sea, and evening scenes with morning vistas?

Preston Winters came into the gallery just then with a slightly built young man in tow. The spectacled newcomer was in his mid 20s, already balding and sporting a middle-aged man's paunch that pushed hard at the three-button vest of the tweed suit he was wearing.

Winters called for everyone's attention. "I'm very pleased to introduce the arts critic of the *New York Sun* to you all. This is Tobias Lind."

Thomas stepped forward to intrudyce himself, but the young critic brushed past him wordlessly and approached the Aubert painting that Phineas and his helpers had just mounted on the wall. Lind ran a hand through what little hair was on his head, then put his hands on his hips and stared at the painting without saying a word.

Akoni turned to Winters. "Is it something we said?" he asked with a grin.

"The *Sun* is the third largest paper in the city," Winters told the group. "Over 100,000 subscribers at 4¢ per copy. The Friday afternoon edition contains the week's review of the arts, everything from plays to book readings, and this week, of course, the Metropolitan opening. It is the weekend recreation guide for the monied class."

"Is it possible he could write a review of Aubert's work by this Friday?" asked Isabella.

Mandleman stood and tapped his cane on the floor. "Young man," he said to Lind's back. "Have we lost you?"

Lind turned slowly, and Thomas was taken by the far away glaze in the critic's eyes. "Of course, yes, so sorry, it's just…" He took a moment to compose himself and then turned back to the row of paintings lined out on the floor around the gallery. He began to pace back and forth, his head bobbing, his fists clenching and unclenching.

"I believe that our little exhibit has found its first aficionado," Phineas said to no one in particular.

"Is this normal?" Taiana asked Mandleman as she gestured towards Lind.

"It is most unusual, I grant you that," answered the white-haired gallery owner.

Lind suddenly whipped around and marched to the center of the room like a man possessed. "Again, my apologies," he said in a rushed voice. "This…" he waved his hand around the room, "…is just so much more than I expected."

"And what did you expect, precisely?" asked Akoni.

"This is my second year with the paper," Lind began, "and my third year out of Harvard. Week in and week out I review the same tired landscapes, understated portraits, and washed-out seascapes. I have heard rumors of a new style of painting coming from France, one that puts light and movement and color ahead of the rigid structure so favored by the Academies. But this…" he paused to gather his thoughts. "This is so far beyond what I imagined I would ever see. It really is the biggest leap in painting in the last century—or more. Simply magnificent. And terrifying."

"I think the lad likes the work," said Mandleman with a wink to Taiana.

"Why terrifying?" asked Winters.

Lind went over to the painting on the wall. "Change happens at glacial speed in the art world," he said. "But this…this is going to hit the old conventions like a cannon ball. The old world is going to crumble, and nothing will be the same. Ever."

"Is that a bad thing?" Thomas asked.

"For a while it will be a dangerous thing," answered Lind. "Have you ever seen a wild animal that has been mortally wounded and yet fights more ferociously than ever until its last breath dies away for good?"

Thomas nodded. He had seen bears, cougars, elk, and bull bison do just that.

"The old art world, the one that is being hung in all the other galleries out there for this opening, is going to wake up Sunday morning and know exactly what a dying animal feels like," Lind continued. "And the dealers? My God, the dealers are going to fight you with every breath in their bodies."

"But we mean them no harm," said Isabella.

Lind looked at her like a toddler who wouldn't go down for her nap. "That painting," he said pointing to the Aubert on the wall, "is a stake right through their hearts, and they will know it the moment they step into this room."

Lind pulled a small notebook and pencil from his jacket pocket. "Mr. Mandleman, if you would be so kind, I would like to interview you first. Then you, Colonel Scoundrel, and finally, Mr. Winters." He smiled at the group. "My hands are almost shaking at the thought of seeing this article published in the *Sun*." Then he looked at the floor for a moment, raised his head and said, "I think I can say without exaggeration that the review of Mr. Aubert's paintings will be the talk of the city by the time the doors open for the gala Saturday evening. And a fitting end to my career."

"End? What do you mean?" asked Phineas.

"My editor will approve the article," said Lind, "he knows I am the best writer the paper has, and he does not question my choice in subject matter. But he has no idea of the hornet's nest the publication of the article will cause, or the advertisers who will pull their business from the paper, especially the art dealers."

Mandleman shook his head in agreement. A price would have to be paid.

"But why you?" asked Isabella. "Why should this hurt your career?"

Lind smiled. "In ancient Rome it was not unusual for a messenger who delivered word of a general being defeated in battle to have his own head shorn from his shoulders by order of the aggrieved Caesar, who knew his world was about to collapse. In writing this article, I am that messenger."

He looked around the room at the concerned expressions on

everyone's faces. Then he laughed and said, "And nothing could make me happier. I have a little money set aside; I will go to France and begin to chronicle this movement. There are so many articles and books to be written!"

"Is that what Aubert's work signifies?" asked Phineas. "A movement?"

"I had a letter from a friend in Paris last month that reported what one important critic said when he first viewed work by Mr. Claude Monet," Lind replied. "His style shares some similarities with Aubert's: 'that is not art, the critic said, it is merely a sketch, an unfinished painting, an impression of art.'"

"An impression," mused Winters.

"What better way to turn an insult around than to proudly use it to describe a brand-new kind of art," said Lind.

"Impressionism," said Mandleman in a half-whisper.

"Yes, exactly" Lind replied enthusiastically, "Impressionism. That is a perfect name."

Lind's interviews took three hours and ended when a carriage from Isabella's restaurant delivered baskets of sandwiches, stoneware jugs filled with hot soup, plates of cheeses, and bottles of beer. When lunch was over Lind shook everyone's hand and left to file his story.

Preston oversaw the hanging of the paintings, which they completed at 3:30, one half hour before dealers from all the galleries would begin strolling through one another's galleries to weigh the competition and share the best tidbits of gossip from the season. At Mandleman's suggestion Thomas and his friends would remain in the gallery. If Lind was right, every gallery they set foot in would be enemy territory.

When a bell rang at precisely at 5 PM to signal the end of the visiting hour, the wisdom of Mandleman's advice had proven out; not one of the three dozen owners of the finest art galleries in the city had stepped inside the Aubert Gallery. A dealer would stop at the open door, peer inside, and immediately leave without crossing the threshold. Some shot looks of disgust or anger at Thomas and the others, a few laughed derisively, several just shrugged their shoulders, and one man began cursing in a tongue no one in the room was familiar with.

As they gathered their things to leave, Mandleman thanked everyone for their help.

"It doesn't look so good for us, does it," said Taiana.

"It's worse than that," said the old man through a chuckle. "It is a cataclysm of Biblical proportion. We'll be lucky to make it out with our scalps intact when the opening concludes Saturday night."

"And you can laugh about that?" Akoni asked. "After all of the money this has cost you? I don't understand."

Mandleman turned and shuffled towards the door. He raised his cane high above his head and in a sing-song voice chanted, "You will my children, you will…you will."

~SIXTY-NINE ~

Akoni hailed a pair of passing cabs when they stepped out of the building under a cold, clear sky. Thomas prepared to say goodbye to his friends and return to Gilsey House only to be surprised when Phineas climbed into the first cab with Akoni and Preston Winters without saying a word, leaving him on the sidewalk beneath a flickering gas streetlight with Taiana and Isabella.

"I know that you have no heart for celebration right now, Thomas," said Isabella, "but your friends have worked very hard to make this opening happen, and so I have arranged for a special dinner at *La Villeta* in honor of them and Émile Aubert."

Taiana took his arm. "In other words, you cannot say no. Akoni was certain he would not be able to persuade you, which is why he left that job up to us."

The cab driver flicked his whip in the air to get their attention. Were they coming, or not?

Isabella opened the hansom door and motioned for Thomas to get in. "And also, I have invited a very special and dear friend to join us. He very much wants to meet you, and I promise you will not want to miss meeting him."

She held the door open and raised her eyebrows. "Well?"

Thomas shrugged and climbed in the cab. He did owe it to his friends to toast their hard work and dedication, and it was possible that the distraction of meeting someone new would give him a brief respite from the grief that enveloped him.

As the cab trotted through Vesey Place from Greenwich to Washington Street, Thomas was taken by the dozens of rough wooden booths in which evergreen boughs, wreaths, and trees were being offered for sale. Many of the trees were alight with candles, and street vendors made their way through the crowds of shoppers with tankards of hot apple cider and paper cones filled with hot roasted chestnuts.

"Christmas is one week from today," Isabella reminded him.

"I had almost forgotten," Thomas murmured as the sounds of a group of well-dressed carolers drifted into the cab.

What was the Christmas season like on Moorea and Tahiti? The islanders loved all celebrations, and most he had met had been baptized in the Catholic tradition. He knew there would be endless garlands of white and red flowers, pig roasted in banana leaves, along with games and dancing and hymns sung in Tahitian.

The cab pulled to a halt outside Isabella's restaurant, and the rush of frigid air when he opened the door brought Thomas' gloomy reverie to a close. The front door and window of *La Villeta* were bordered in evergreen boughs, and a wreath with red and green glass ornaments hung above the entry. A hand-lettered sign notified diners that the restaurant was closed until December 26th, except for special parties.

The interior felt warm and cozy, with gaslit wall sconces and candles casting a warm glow around the room. Paintings of the Italian countryside covered the walls, and each linen-topped table was decorated with a tall candle and a wide glass jar filled with small red and green glass marbles. The smell of mulled wine with cinnamon drifted across the dining area, and when the door to the kitchen opened and Chef Niccoló stepped out, Thomas could smell garlic and exotic spices simmering in a broth on the wood-fired stove. He wondered what was bubbling in the huge copper pot.

"*Ossobuco alla Milanese,*" said the chef as he passed by Thomas and read his mind. Niccoló took Isabella aside for a quiet discussion about tonight's menu, which is when Thomas first saw the stranger who was engrossed in conversation at a table with Phineas and Preston.

The man was in his 40s, stocky, of average height, with grey eyes, a long, aquiline nose, and thick, dark, curly hair that melded seamlessly into his neatly trimmed beard and moustache. He wore a stylish three-piece wool serge suit with a diamond stickpin in the lapel, and Thomas was amused to see that while his French-accented English came slowly, he gestured as expressively with his hands as any respectable Parisian would do when holding forth with his friends at the local café.

Isabella came up beside Thomas. "Let me introduce you," she said as she took his arm and guided him across the restaurant. Taiana joined them and a moment later the trio were standing in a semi-circle around Phineas, Winters, and the stranger, who was raising a glass of sherry to his lips.

The man looked up and smiled at Isabella. "Jules Gabriel," she said in a formal tone, "I have the pleasure of introducing Colonel Thomas Scoundrel, the American army officer about whom you inquired."

Jules slid back his chair and stood. He extended his hand and said, "Colonel Scoundrel, it is indeed an honor to finally meet you."

"Thank you, Mr. Gabriel," Thomas replied in French, "but please, call me Thomas."

Jules' eyes lit up at being addressed in his native language. "I will do that my friend, but first I must clear up a little confusion. Gabriel is my middle name, and how the lovely Isabella has referred to me since she was a child visiting my home with her father and mother. My last name is actually Verne."

Thomas was rarely thunderstruck, but this was Jules Verne, his favorite author, and one of the most famous men of letters in the world. How many hours had he spent transported by Verne's *20,000 Leagues under the Sea* and *Journey to the Center of the Earth*, first in the serialized versions that appeared in newspapers, and then in the gloriously decorated hardcover editions in French? Only last month he had read that Verne's newest work, *Le Tour du Monde en Quatre-Vingt jours*, or, *Around the World In Eighty Days*, would soon begin chapter-by-chapter publication in the *New York Sun*.

He could only shake his head and offer a weak smile. "*Mes excuses, Monsieur Verne*," Thomas said. "I had no idea…"

"And it is all my fault," laughed Isabella. "I wanted this meeting to be a complete surprise to Thomas," she said to Verne.

"I believe you succeeded at that," said the author with a chuckle. He motioned for everyone to sit, and a kitchen helper pulled another table over so that they could all be seated together.

Isabella disappeared into the kitchen, and Verne, speaking again in French, said in a low voice, "Thomas, I am so very sorry to hear the news about your wife. It is so very *tragique*…please accept my heartfelt condolences."

Thomas could only nod in response. He was determined to keep his composure; he had been tearing up several times a day, often during the most mundane conversations. He was about to reply when the kitchen door swung open and Isabella and Niccoló swept in with two metal buckets filled with ice and bottles of champagne.

Verne leaned over and placed his hand lightly on Thomas' wrist. "Please do me the honor of telling me about her later this evening," said Verne, "if that is acceptable to you, of course."

"*Oui bien sûr*," Thomas replied, "I would like that."

Taiana placed a Baccarat champagne flute in front of each person and Phineas unwired the cork on the first bottle and allowed the gasses inside the heavy, yellow-labeled bottle to build until they reached maximum pressure and sent the cork exploding across the room.

"Ah, *Veuve Clicquot*," said Verne with twinkling eyes. "A heavenly marriage between Pinot Noir, Chardonnay, and Meunier grapes. It was a wonderful choice, my dear Isabella."

Phineas filled their glasses and held up his stem above the center of the table. When everyone had raised their glass, he said, "To friends, present and absent."

Thomas drank with the others, but he barely tasted the quality of the wine. Verne took note of his discomfort and asked, "Do you not know *Clicquot* Thomas?"

"This is my first taste."

"You read *Vingt Mille Lieues Sous Les Mers?*"

"20,000 Leagues? Of course. It was a marvelous adventure."

"Captain Nemo was a true gastronome who served only the finest and most exotic meals to his guests aboard the Nautilus," Verne continued, "each accompanied by *Clicquot*."

"And did the vintner thank you properly for including their champagne?" asked Isabella.

"A case or two may have quietly shown up on my doorstep," replied Verne with a smile. "It turns out that having more than a million pair of eyes read about their finest wine inside of a grand adventure was good for business."

Thomas found himself laughing along with his friends at Verne's story. He took another drink, taking note this time of the champagne's hints of caramel, citrus, and apple. Verne was right, it was excellent.

Akoni accompanied Isabella into the kitchen and returned a moment later with a platter of cheeses, rounds of sliced, fresh-baked bread, and small dishes of seasoned olive oil.

Thomas watched the faces of his friends light up as they dipped small pieces of bread into the oil and took first tastes.

"What is in this?" Taiana asked. "It is just wonderful."

"Heavenly is more like it," Phineas piped in.

Akoni grinned. "It's a mix from Italy and the South Seas… garlic, oregano, basil, cracked black pepper, red pepper flakes, rosemary, and, of course, olive oil."

Preston Winters was about to take a bite when Akoni finished listing the ingredients in the oil dip. He stayed his hand, and said, "My friend, none of those are native to Polynesia."

"Ah, but they will be when I take them back to Hawai'i with me," laughed Akoni. "Especially if Isabella will come with me and open a restaurant in Honolulu."

The table went completely silent. Everyone knew of the growing affection between Isabella and Akoni, but no one knew things had progressed this far.

Thomas looked over at Akoni, who met his gaze with a soft smile and what appeared to be a blush. "I will be your first customer," Thomas said to Isabella.

"Let us not get too far ahead of ourselves," she said. "There is tonight's dinner yet to finish."

With that she and Taiana went into the kitchen and when Thomas heard Taiana giggling before the door closed behind her, he could only imagine what that conversation must be like.

Niccoló solved the problem of the awkward silence around the table when he wheeled in a cart laden with an iron stewpot and ceramic bowls. "*Ben venga il minestrone*," he said, "Welcome the minestrone." He began dishing up bowls of the savory soup as Phineas opened another bottle of champagne and refilled the crystal stems. The ladies returned with bottles of red wine to accompany the veal, but when Taiana held out her champagne glass for Phineas to refill Isabella clapped her hand over the top and said, "Ah,ah…just half a glass, my dear." Taiana sighed and accepted the partially filled stem.

When the soup was finished, Taiana cleared the bowls and champagne glasses and set red wine goblets around the table. She looked questioningly at Isabella when she set down her own glass. "You may have one," Isabella said as she began to fill glasses.

"This is *Brunello di Montalcino*," she said as she held the bottle up for everyone to see. "It comes from vineyards around my family's home village of Montalcino, which lies in the Siena province of Tuscany."

She waited for her friends to raise their glasses for a first taste and continued, "It is made from the *sangiovese grosso* grape, and I hope you will find it a perfect accompaniment to the *ossobuco*."

At those words Nicoló rolled in another cart on which sat a large copper pot and a thick cutting board. He pulled a veal shank from the white wine broth with tongs and set it on the board, where he began to slice and plate it on beds of saffron risotto.

When everyone was served and the wine glasses were filled, Isabella stood and raised her glass and said, "*Saluti!*"

It was one of the finest meals Thomas had ever eaten, in no small part because of the extraordinary people with whom he shared it. He chuckled when Taiana struggled to extract the sweet marrow from the shank bone with the tiny spoon they were given, and he marveled at Verne's charm and wit. As a dinner companion, he was unparalleled. The author peppered them with questions about Aubert's painting style, about life in Tahiti, and about their expectations for the gala opening in two days' time. Verne was especially intrigued by the term 'impressionism' that his friends had stumbled upon as a way to describe the vibrant new school of painting that was emerging in Paris, and, to his astonishment, also in Moorea, 7,000 miles away from the art center of the world.

"Isabella snuck me into your warehouse last night to view the paintings," Verne said. "I was transfixed; they are so alive I felt I was in the presence of living beings." He stopped to refill everyone's wine, and to Taiana's delight, Isabella did not raise a complaint when Verne topped off her glass.

"And, so, two things," said Verne. "First, I asked Isabella to mark two of the paintings as sold. Please do display them at the gala, and when the show is over, I will arrange for them to be shipped to me in Amiens."

"And second?" asked Preston.

"Next spring, I am going to make the journey to Tahiti. I will meet this remarkable man and his wife, and I will immerse myself in their world. You know, I have long wanted to write a book that would be set in such a place, a mysterious island where the laws of nature and man are tested to their limits."

Thomas clasped his wine goblet and smiled. Were it anyone other than Jules Verne talking, he would dismiss the wild pronouncement as wine-induced hubris. But as he watched his new friend speak, his hands gesturing expansively, his eyes flashing, his smile radiating confidence, he knew full well that Verne's South Pacific adventure would become a reality. He locked eyes with the author and raised his glass.

Across the street from *La Villeta*, a man stepped out of the shadows. He lingered for a moment under a streetlight, pulling a locket from his jacket and opening it to view the photograph inside. He had been watching Thomas and his friends through the restaurant window for the past hour. Now he closed the locket and returned it to his jacket before walking swiftly away.

It was almost time.

~SEVENTY ~

December 20

Dozens of New York's leading art dealers were crowded into the main dining room of a popular Polish eatery on 57th Street as the oversized mantel clock above the fireplace struck 2 PM. Conspicuously absent was Aubert's representative, Isaac Mandleman. Waiters were clearing the last of the lunch dishes and pouring sherry and coffee when the owner of the Gallery on 5th Avenue stood and tapped a fork against his glass for attention.

"Gentlemen, gentlemen," the dour-faced speaker began, "thank you for coming on such short notice. We have business to attend to and given the late hour we have no time to waste. The gala opening of the new Museum of Art is tomorrow evening, but if we do not act now, the show will be a financial disaster for each of us, and more than that, for the entire art business as we know it."

A chorus of 'Here, here,' throat-clearing harrumphs and foot stomping greeted his grim assessment of the situation they faced.

The speaker held up yesterday afternoon's edition of the *New York Sun*. "You have all seen the article by Tobias Lind in this despicable rag; how the piece passed muster with the paper's editors is beyond me." He shook the paper for effect. "There will be a price for them to pay, I promise; I cancelled my weekly ads for the next month this morning, and I expect you all have done the same."

Fists slammed on tables and heads nodded in agreement around the room. Fierce competitors though they were, the art dealers recognized the common threat that the article—and more importantly—the art that it reviewed so positively–represented to them. On this issue, at least, they were united.

"I am disappointed in our old friend, Isaac Mandleman, of course; the idea that he would associate himself with such drivel…" he pointed again to the article, "is simply beyond my comprehension."

"Then why isn't he here to answer for himself?" one of the dealers shouted.

"I'll explain in a moment," the speaker replied. "First, I want to introduce Mr. Martin Graves, a member of the Board of the new Metropolitan Museum."

A tall, thin man with a pinched, bird-like face stood to a smattering of polite applause before sitting down and sipping more sherry. It was clear that he did not want to be here.

"This article is a frontal attack on every value that we hold dear; it celebrates–no it glorifies–this mishmash pastiche of *merde* they are calling 'impressionism,' and seeks to elevate its practitioners alongside the titans whom we are blessed to represent," the speaker continued.

His bold exclamation was met with enthusiastic applause and even a few whistles.

"So, what can we do?" called one dealer.

"How can we stop this obscenity in its tracks?" asked another.

"First," asked the speaker, "by a show of hands, how many of you agree that the style of art that Mr. Lind has referenced in such glowing and reverential tones is nothing more than childish scribbling and smearing of color on canvas?"

Every hand in the room shot up without hesitation, except for the Museum Board member. His participation, even though he was in complete agreement with the speaker, would be unseemly.

"The three dozen of us assembled here this afternoon constitute the foundation of the art world not just in New York City, but in the entire nation," the owner of the Beaux-Arts gallery continued. "For granting us the privilege of making a living in our chosen profession, our public expects that we will be responsible and honorable stewards of the arts. That includes their expectation that we do not allow fine art to be sullied and dirtied by the kind of trash this article seeks to worship."

Another wave of passionate applause ran through the room. The so-called impressionist barbarians had to be met on the field and disemboweled before they were allowed to infect the culture these dealers believed to be their duty to protect.

"I'll ask again," interrupted the man who spoke out earlier. "What can we do? We know this style of painting is abominable. We understand it must be quashed in the womb. We've talked enough—what are we going to do?"

The speaker smiled and called for order. He had been uncertain about the course of action he wanted to propose until just now. They were with him.

"Here is what I suggest," he answered. "The gala begins at 5 PM tomorrow in the museum annex. There will be food and drink and music until 6:30, when the mayor and other dignitaries will speak and take credit for our hard work."

The dealers laughed. Politicians were always either slopping at the trough or taking credit for what the taxpayers had put in it.

"At 7 PM precisely, museum attendants will unlock the gallery doors and New York's patrons of art—our clientele—will begin to circulate from room to room. There are 14 galleries in all, including Mandleman's. I suggest that the attendants unlock only 13 of the galleries. At 7:01 a messenger will hand Mandleman a letter from the Board of the Museum that states that, after careful and due consideration, they have determined that the artwork he wishes to present does not meet the standards of quality and integrity to which the museum aspires. He will be invited to make a protest, of course, but tomorrow night not a single member of New York society will pass through the door of his gallery."

A hush fell across the room. What he was suggesting was an outright act of war, the dealers realized. It was audacious and cruel, but, after barely a moment's reflection, everyone concluded that it was also a brilliant plan.

One dealer began to clap, then another and another, and in a moment the entire room was thundering with applause.

The speaker glanced at the representative of the Board and saw surrender in his eyes. The opening had to take place, too much was at stake for them to allow the dealers to go on strike. If one out of 14 gallery doors did not swing open, what of it? There would still be hundreds of paintings and sculptures to view. Trends in art came and went. Business—and only business—had a sacred right and responsibility to carry on unabated.

Isabella brought a cup of coffee to the table and set it in front of Thomas. Phineas and Winters were completing final details for the gala at a table in the corner, and Taiana and Akoni were just returning from a trip to find the giant Hawaiian a dress shirt that fit properly. Taiana went into the kitchen to brew tea, and Akoni joined Thomas and Isabella.

"I asked you both here this morning because I have news," the owner of *La Villeta* said, "and it is not good."

"These days it seems that's the only kind we get," Akoni replied.

"The Commissioner of Police visited me early this morning. His men have been keeping an eye out for Fitch Donnegan and Aata since Thomas' fight with Sweeney."

"And?" asked Thomas.

"By chance he was having dinner with the managing director of the Pinkerton Detective Agency yesterday, and the man told him that his firm had been engaged to find Thomas."

"Engaged by…?" Akoni asked.

"An official representative of Colin Stafford. The man even presented a letter of introduction from Stafford, which the agency confirmed with Stafford by telegram before they agreed to take the job."

"So, he has found me," said Thomas.

Isabella nodded. "A Pinkerton agent is to meet with the client today to tell him where you can be found."

Thomas took a drink of his coffee. "And with only one day until the gala. Damn."

Taiana returned to the table and poured tea for Isabella and herself.

"We've got to get you out of Gilsey House," said Akoni.

"All three of you must leave," said Isabella. "Thomas, if you write a note, I will take it to the concierge and have your rooms packed up, and everything brought here. Then I will find rooms at another hotel on the other side of town. No one at Gilsey will know where you have gone."

"Isabella, I am so sorry to have brought you into this mess," said Thomas. "I think it would be best if we took care of moving ourselves and kept you away from any possible danger. This is not your fight."

Isabella's cheeks flushed. She stretched her arm across the table and put her hand over Akoni's. "You are wrong about that, Thomas. I have made many choices this past week, each of which will affect where I go in life from today forward." She squeezed Akoni's hand. "This man is my future, and his friends are my friends. We will see this thing through together."

Thomas could only nod and fight back a tear. How was it possible that at this most devastating time in his life, such great friends had rallied around? And as he looked each of his friends in the eye he also wondered, how can I ever repay them?

Fitch Donegan was not terribly surprised that afternoon when the desk clerk at Gilsey House told him that Colonel Scoundrel and his party had checked out only two hours earlier. No, the clerk, said, he did not know where they had gone.

When Donegan turned to leave, the clerk signaled across the lobby to the concierge, and as the Irish assassin walked across the lobby and out the doors, the concierge scribbled a note and slipped it into an envelope. He called for a bell boy and told him to get it to *La Villeta* as quickly as possible.

Colonel Scoundrel's presence in his hotel had provided the gossip-loving concierge with some of the juiciest tidbits of scandal he had encountered in 15 years. His only disappointment was that he might not find out how it was all going to end.

SEVENTY-ONE

December 21

Thomas watched in the bureau mirror as Isabela reached around from behind to knot his mulberry silk bow tie. The bruises and swelling he suffered in the fight with Sweeney were gone, and a slight red line beneath his left eye was the only evidence that remained of the battle. His suit jacket and trousers felt a bit loose because he hadn't eaten more than a few meals in two weeks.

Isabella and Taiana had chosen his clothing, as well as Akoni's. Thomas was much easier to fit than the massive Hawaiian, and it took two tailors working overtime at the haberdashery to ready Akoni's suit in time for tonight's grand opening.

Thomas had turned down Isabella's initial choice of jacket; he wasn't comfortable in the fashionable frock coats that reached down below the knees. Instead, he asked her to select a simple black wool coat that broke at mid-thigh, with matching black trousers. Isabella conceded that fashion point to him but insisted in return that he wear a velvet fronted burgundy vest with black satin trim along the lapels and silver buttoned plackets.

With the tie complete, she pulled his jacket off the coat stand and helped him slip into it. The door opened as she was whisking off a bit of fluff from the tailor's final adjustments and Taiana and Akoni came into the room.

Thomas fought to hold back a chuckle at the sight of Akoni in a formal black frock coat, starched white vest and tie, and beaver-fur top hat, but the sparkle in Isabella's eyes at the sight of her intended in evening dress kept him from laughing.

"Taiana, you look lovely," Thomas said. "I wish your mother and father could see you."

Taiana did a slow turn to show off the contours of her crème-colored satin damask gown with hand-sewn silk flowers on the shoulders and along one side. There was just enough lace and subtle gold embroidery to make a statement, but not so much as to be gaudy. Long trains on evening dresses were the height of fashion this season, but she and Isabella had opted to wear very short trains that they would not have to worry about people stumbling over.

"And you look magnificent," Akoni said to Isabella. Her magenta silk *faille* dress set off her olive complexion, and the high-collared black lace trim with jet black beads and black satin ribbon that extended down in a 'V' shaped form to below her bosom highlighted her hourglass figure.

"Thomas, I believe that we are the most fortunate men in the city tonight," said Akoni as he stepped forward and kissed Isabella's extended hand. The ladies accepted the compliment with curtsies before pulling on their warm woolen wraps for the short ride to the museum annex.

A wave of bittersweet emotion poured through Thomas as the foursome made their way down to the lobby and outside to their waiting carriage. He wasn't sure why he lingered a moment on the side-walk after his friends climbed in. The sky was clear and star-swept, and traffic along 5th Avenue was unusually light for late afternoon. Was it concern about Donegan and Aata, who he was certain were somewhere in the city, or sorrow that Keani was not beside him for this special occasion that had stopped him?

Akoni solved his dilemma. "Thomas," he called from inside the carriage. "It's time."

Akoni pulled the cab's thick buffalo robe from its peg and spread it over the ladies' laps as Thomas climbed inside, pulled the door shut and signaled the driver that they were ready to go. Then he felt for the revolver in his vest pocket. Whatever awaited them at the grand opening of the New York Metropolitan Museum of Art, he would be ready. When he met Akoni's gaze a moment later he knew his friend was thinking the same thing.

Sergeant McIlvaney had never seen so many diamonds in one place. He watched from his position on the marble steps outside the luxury hotel that was hosting tonight's gala, as carriage after carriage rolled up to the curb and disgorged a stream of the city's richest, best dressed, and most socially connected denizens. What a night to be a pickpocket, the sergeant thought as he scanned the glittering diamond necklaces, tiaras, stickpins, and bracelets flowing into the building.

The precinct captain had given his officers explicit instructions for protecting tonight's attendees. In addition to the uniformed officers inside and outside the hotel, several plain clothes detectives would mingle with New York's nobility and patrol along the avenue to head off anyone who looked out of place. McIlvaney was fine with those instructions, they were expected. What he and his fellow officers did not expect was the warning that came next: they were to be especially vigilant and report immediately if they saw any Tahitian men of fighting age roaming around the building and its grounds. Watch them, stop them, arrest them, was the command. When one of the detectives asked the obvious question–what the hell did a Tahitian look like and why had they come halfway around the world to cause trouble at a museum opening–the captain simply slammed his watch book closed and told then to do their jobs.

McIlvaney had no special appreciation for the arts, but he did value his job. He understood that if so much as a single strand of hair was mussed on the head of one of tonight's guests by some hoodlum—or Tahitian– who snuck in off the street he would be transferred from the posh hotel district he had worked up to over the past ten years to a frozen and grimy streetcorner in the Bowery or Five Points. He tapped his nightstick on the ground. No ne'er-do-well would pass his station tonight, and that went double for any miscreant from the South Seas.

Thomas shared many of the same thoughts as he and Akoni escorted Taiana and Isabella up the steps and into the packed chandelier-and-candelabra-lit lobby. He estimated there were at least 300 people in gowns and formal evening wear already in the room, with more pouring through the door. The cheerful din of their chatter mixed with the sounds of the orchestra playing a popular waltz to create a background that he found strangely relaxing.

Akoni stopped a passing waiter and retrieved four glasses of champagne from his tray. As they toasted, Phineas, Mandleman, and Winters found them, and the group moved out of the main traffic path and over to a less hectic corner of the high-ceilinged space.

"Quite an evening," said Phineas.

"Oh, they are all here," Mandelman replied. "The governor, the bankers, the businessmen, and, of course, the arbiters of society. It's quite the stew."

"I saw the President when we came in," said Taiana. "He recognized me and waved!"

"And there is George Custer and his wife with Colonel Kip and Emily Vanderbilt," said Isabella, pointing over to the center of the room.

"Do you know General Custer, Thomas?" asked Winters.

"Quite well, and Lawrence Kip, too, who served at Five Forks when I was at Pebble Ridge."

Mandleman finished his champagne and consulted his vest watch. "We have about an hour before the politicians step to the podium for self-congratulations over the opening, so I believe I will mix it up a bit and get a feel for the crowd."

"Do you mean figure out if they are in a buying mood?" asked Phineas with a smile.

Mandleman flourished his cane. "Precisely, my dear boy, precisely!"

"There are a few people I would like you to meet, Akoni," said Isabella. She nodded to Thomas and Taiana before taking his arm and steering him towards the center of the crowd. That's when Thomas spotted someone he recognized. The grin on his face when he saw the familiar person surprised Taiana. He hadn't been enthusiastic about anything today, especially about this social outing.

"Well, this is a treat," he said to Taiana. "Come meet my new friend."

He led the way across the room to where a handsome, bearded man in his 40s was engaged with an older man who had several medals pinned on the lapel of his suit. The man's wife was chatting with an elderly woman in furs and pearls, while standing between them, looking bored as only a teenager can, was Teddy, the lad he had met out on the shore a few days earlier.

"Thomas!" the boy cried as they approached. He bolted from his parent's side raced up to Thomas and began to vigorously shake his hand. "It is so good to see you. I had no idea…"

"Good to see you, Teddy," Thomas interjected. "Teddy, this is Taiana."

Teddy took Taiana's hand and made an exaggerated half bow, which made her giggle.

"Did I do that wrong?" Teddy asked her nervously. "It was my first time, you know."

"You did it perfectly, just as a gentleman should," she answered, which, for some reason, caused them both to laugh.

Teddy's father had been watching his son out of the corner of his eye. Now he excused himself and walked over to them. He was a tall, fit man with broad shoulders, deep set eyes, a glossy beard, and an expansive smile. He looked at Thomas but clearly did not recognize him.

"It seems my son has a new friend who I have yet to meet," he said to Thomas. "I am Theodore Roosevelt…senior, as it happens. My son is Theodore, junior. It is a pleasure Mr…?"

Thomas shook the elder Roosevelt's hand. "Scoundrel. Thomas Scoundrel. And this is my ward, Taiana, from the Kingdom of Hawai'i."

Roosevelt smiled at Taiana and then his eyes lit up. "That would be Colonel Thomas Scoundrel of Ohio? The hero of Pebble Creek Ridge?"

Teddy's ears perked up. His new friend was a hero!

"I prefer to simply be called Thomas; the war is long over, and the real heroes were buried where they fought."

"You are too modest, Colonel," said an unfamiliar voice. The man who had been speaking with Roosevelt had approached as they were talking. He was balding and portly with a walrus moustache and long hair on the side and back of his head. "I know the story of your heroics well, in fact, my wife purchased a reproduction painting of your exploits on that day. It hangs in my study."

Thomas sighed but kept his expression impassive.

"Benjamin Butler, Brigadier, 8th Massachusetts, now President of the United States Cartridge Company."

Thomas shook the general's hand. "An honor, sir. Your leadership of the Army of the James is a legendary story in itself."

Teddy had stood by quietly as long as he could. "Sir," he asked his father, "may I have your permission to introduce Miss Taiana to some of my friends?"

"Colonel?" asked Roosevelt senior.

"Of course. That alright with you, Taiana?"

Her eyes shimmered and she smiled broadly.

"Off with the two of you then," chuckled Roosevelt as Teddy and Taiana scurried away into the throng. Then Roosevelt reached out to shake Thomas' hand again. "I must rejoin my wife, colonel, before the alarm bells go off. I hope that we can visit again during the evening."

"I will look forward to that, Mr. Roosevelt."

Theodore turned to go, then turned back. "I am deeply appreciative of the kindness you showed to Teedy out in the dunes, Colonel, including the gift of the spectacles. They have opened up a whole new world for him."

Thomas smiled and nodded as Roosevelt and the General rejoined their party. There was still over an hour before the 14 galleries would be opened for viewing by the crowd, which he estimated had swollen to around 500 people.

He decided to take a drink out onto the terrace and wait in solitude until the ceremonies started. He had taken just two steps towards the bar when a hand slapped him hard on the back.

"Thomas Scoundrel, you claim-jumpin', bean-swilling, sad-faced excuse for a teetotalling circuit preacher...how the hell are you?"

He pivoted around to see the mutton-chopped author Bret Harte, whom he had befriended on the journey across the prairie. Standing next to Harte was Jules Verne. It struck him that both authors were drinking something stronger than champagne, and judging from the flush on their faces, they had enjoyed a good head start on everyone else in the room.

Finding a way to pass the next hour was no longer a concern.

SEVENTY-TWO

"Ladies and gentlemen, *Mesdames et Messieurs,* distinguished guests, welcome to the celebratory grand opening of our city's new museum of art!"

The crowded room erupted in applause. Champagne glasses were raised, and the orchestra brass played a brief, rousing flourish to accompany mayor A. Oakey Hall's remarks from the small stage that had been set up in the center of the lobby.

"It is said that the greatness of a city is measured by its commitment to the arts. With tonight's dedication and gallery displays, New York City once again lays claim to the title of America's greatest city!" Chants of 'here, here' reverberated throughout the room.

"We thank the owners of New York's foremost galleries who have lent their finest works of great art for us to enjoy, and we also thank Mr. Van Renssalaer for making his newest hotel available for this evening's gala."

"At a very fair rate, I am sure," Mandlemen said to Thomas with a wink.

The speeches by state and city officials had been mercifully short and the waiters had continued circulating with trays of champagne, sherry, and canapés, which combined to keep the crowd in a festive mood.

"In a few moments the galleries in both halls will be opened," the mayor continued. "Representatives of each gallery will be present to tell you about their works, and I am told that several noted artists are also here. As you step into the halls you will be provided with a printed guide to the galleries and the works they are exhibiting tonight. On behalf of the city, the Museum's Board of Governors and myself, we wish you a wonderful Christmas season excursion into the world of fine art."

The mayor's final sentence was the cue for the orchestra to pick up with a popular holiday tune. Phineas and Preston Winters grabbed fresh champagne for everyone in their party, and Taiana raced off to find Teddy, who had asked her to visit the galleries with him and his family.

"Are we ready, children?" asked Mandleman as he raised his glass to his lips.

"We are," Thomas said, "but before we go to our gallery, I want to thank you all on behalf of Émile Aubert. How I wish he could be here for this event."

"To Émile," said Phineas as he raised his glass.

The crowd was beginning to move towards the two halls, and from where they were standing in the lobby, they could see the massive, 12-foot-high carved oak doors along the halls begin to swing open.

"Shall we?" said Isabella as she took Akoni's arm.

Mandleman's gallery was at the end of the west hall. As they stepped through the doorway a uniformed bellboy pushed his way past several groups of people and approached. "Mr. Isaac Mandleman?" he asked. Mandleman nodded and the boy handed him an envelope.

"This is curious," the art dealer said. "One wouldn't expect a postal delivery here."

He tore the envelope open and scanned its contents. Then he dropped the letter and his cane on the floor and fell back against the wall, his hands clutching his chest. Akoni leapt forward and steadied the old man as Thomas stooped to pick the letter up.

"What is it?" asked Phineas.

As people streamed past them to begin visiting the galleries in this hall, Thomas quickly read the letter. "It is from the directors of the museum," he said. "Signed by each of them. It seems we have been deemed unfit to be a part of this exhibition. Our gallery will remain locked and Isaac's rental fee will be returned to him."

"That's all it says?" Winters demanded.

"Everything," Thomas replied. He handed the letter to Winters and turned to Akoni, who had helped Mandleman to a chair by the door and was leaning over him. "How is he?"

The old man looked up at Thomas and smiled grimly. "Did you know that I was born in 1792?" he said in a weary voice. "I have seen wars and plagues and financial collapses and even pogroms against the people in my homeland. I have seen it, and I have survived. All of it. To have made it to 80 and have this final insult hurled at me…it is unbearable."

Thomas was about to speak when Akoni stood up and said, "Locked door? Do they really think that a locked door is going to stop us now, after everything we have been through to get here?" Then he strode down the corridor, pushing his way through knots of people who were both astonished and frightened by this wild-eyed giant in formal evening wear thundering past open doors like a Titan from Mt. Olympus going into battle.

Mandleman's eyes widened, and he stood up with Isabella's help.

"I think we had better…" Phineas began.

"Yes, we had, before Akoni tears the door off its hinges," Thomas answered. He and Phineas and Winters hurried down the long marble hallway after their friend.

They passed six open galleries. Each room was already filled with well-dressed art lovers who were being greeted by gallery owners and sales associates with fresh champagne and price lists.

When he arrived at gallery seven, Akoni was standing directly in front of the towering oak door. They watched as the Hawaiian took three steps back, turned his body sideways, and then rammed the door as hard as he could. The door did not budge, of course, but that did not deter Akoni. As his friends circled around to try and shield him from the view of anyone in the hall, Akoni smashed into the door again and again. Finally, he stepped back, grasped the aching shoulder he had been using as a battering ram, and silently admitted defeat.

Mandleman arrived on Isabella's arm. "I am sorry my friend," Akoni said to him.

The art dealer laid a hand on Akoni's arm and said, "It was a heroic effort, good friend. No man could have done more."

No one could think of anything to say. All of their efforts, months of travel and danger, one risk after another until, on the cusp of a great victory whose achievement had cost each of them something he or she held dear, a locked door brought their dream to a crashing halt.

Then, in the quiet, a new voice spoke. "To be honest, I don't know if that is true."

Thomas and his friends turned to see that Teddy Roosevelt and Taiana had arrived.

"What do you mean?" Thomas asked.

"I mean there are other ways to open a door. Proper ways," the boy replied.

"Like with a key?" Phineas asked in an acid tone.

"Yes, of course," said Teddy. "That would be the ideal way, but…"

He reached into his trouser pocket and withdrew a pen knife. Then he looked closely at Isabella, and said, "I mean no disrespect, but could I borrow one of those long pins in the side of your hair?"

Thomas was perplexed. "Teddy, what…"

Isabella pulled out a four-inch hair pin and handed it to Teddy, who dropped to his knees in front of the brass lock and immediately inserted the blade of his pen knife in the bottom of the keyhole. Then he stuck the hairpin in above the blade and began working it back and forth. The men gathered behind the boy to hide him while he committed his first burglary.

"You see," Teddy said, "locksmithing is something of a hobby of mine."

Is there anything that isn't? Thomas wondered.

"And these particular locks are relatively simple mechanisms. In fact…" There was a clicking sound and Teddy popped up. "It's done," he said with a wide grin. Thomas nearly laughed at the look of astonishment on Akoni's face.

"Mr. Mandleman, would you like to do the honors?" asked Isabella.

Isaac stepped forward and turned the huge brass handle. Just like that, the door swung open on its perfectly balanced hinges.

"Do you suppose they will call the police?" he asked.

"Let them try," answered Akoni as the group went into the gallery.

The chandelier and sconces lit the room perfectly. Aubert's paintings seemed almost alive against the pale gray walls, their colors shimmering in the soft light. Akoni wrapped his arm around Isabella's shoulder, and Taiana kissed Teddy on the cheek, which set him to blushing and the group to laughing.

Mandleman went to the center of the room and leaned on his cane. "This is perfect," he said.

"Unfortunately, no one knows that we are here," said Winters. "What now?"

"Now I show you *haoles* how Hawaiians call to one another across a valley," said Akoni.

He stepped out into the hallway and put his thumb and forefinger into his mouth. Then he began to whistle, loud and shrill, shattering the decorum of the event and forcing people to turn around to see what the devil was going on. As soon as they looked in his direction Akoni began waving for them to come his way. Taiana and Teddy didn't just wave; they scooted down the long corridor and began to implore guests to come and visit what they promised would be the most interesting gallery they would see that evening.

A few moments later, people began to trickle in. Thomas stood behind the first couple to enter, and when the fur-and-jewel-draped wife took in Aubert's paintings, turned to her husband and said, "I have never seen such remarkable..." in a hushed, almost reverential tone, he knew it was going to be alright.

Issac Mandleman heard her, too. He turned to Thomas and bowed slightly at the waist before going over to introduce himself to the first prospective buyers of the evening.

SEVENTY-THREE

The orchestra played on, and the demi-gods of New York Society wandered the galleries with champagne glasses in hand before clustering in tight-knit conversational groups around the crowded lobby to talk about the holidays, and, when backs were turned and ears were out of range, also about one another.

Isabella and Taiana made repeated trips to all the galleries in the two halls, rushing back to Isaac Mandleman at the Aubert exhibit after each patrol to assure him that the steady stream of people he was seeing was no temporary fluke; Aubert's work was the talk of the opening.

Two of the Museum Board Members who had signed the expulsion letter to Mandleman also paid a visit, but their looks of disapproval did nothing to diminish the enthusiastic chattering in the long lines of people waiting to see Aubert's revolutionary use of light and color. Mandleman simply raised his cane and smiled at the men and then began to whistle a jaunty tune when the Board Members stormed out of the gallery. After all, what could they do?

Thomas was standing at the bar with President Grant and Colonel Kip preparing to introduce them to Teddy, when Aata and 10 Tahitian men rushed up the hotel steps and pushed their way past the guards at the door. He felt their presence before he saw them, a rustling in the crowd, small cries of surprise from startled partygoers, and then the shrill ring of a policeman's whistle.

He knew without looking that whoever had come through the door was after him. John Cronin, the president's principal protection officer, heard, too. He shot a questioning glance at Thomas, who nodded his head in reply.

Cronin took hold of Grant's elbow. "We've got to go, sir," was all he said. Two other members of the president's detail materialized at his side and formed a circle around the surprised executive. As the small group began walking the president towards a side door, Grant made eye contact with Thomas and mouthed the words 'good luck.'

Thomas placed a hand on Teddy's shoulder as Aata and his men surged to the middle of the lobby. "Run to the gallery," he said. "Tell Akoni that they are here for me, and that he must tell everyone to stay inside and close the doors. Can you lock them as easily as you unlocked them?"

Teddy's face shone with excitement. This was an adventure!

"Of course," he said.

Thomas nodded. "Tell Akoni that, once everyone is safe, he should come up the stairs at the end of the hallway and double back towards the front of the hotel. Do you understand?"

Teddy turned and raced off down the left corridor. The crowd was not yet panicked, Thomas noted, but they were moving back to get out of the way of the intruders. That's when he saw that Aata was leading his men down the hallway to the right, with several policemen in pursuit. Of course! The Tahitian warrior had no idea which gallery Thomas would be in. It would take Aata at least two or three minutes to realize they were looking in the wrong place.

As the orchestra picked up a new tune, Thomas made his way to the hall and ran quickly past all seven galleries to the end of the corridor, where a velvet rope blocked off entry to the stairs to the second floor. He hopped over the rope, flew up the stairs and then turned back to make his way towards the front of the building. There was a large double window with a crank opening there that he had noticed earlier. He would go out the window, shimmy down the tree that grew against the building, and wait in the dark alley across the street for the police to get the situation in hand before rejoining his friends. Remaining inside would only make the situation more dangerous for everyone. While he was outside, Akoni would make contact with the police and let them know what was going on.

When he got to the end of the hall, he looked down over the banister to the lobby floor below and saw that the commotion was increasing; to his surprise, police officers were standing at the door blocking attempts by frightened gala attendees to leave. They must have been worried that some of the intruders would also be able to get away. Aata was not there to kill him, of course, at least not until he had collected the bank's money. But where did that leave Fitch Donegan? If Aata had found him, he was certain the Irish assassin would not be far behind.

Then he heard shouts and saw Aata and his men emerge from the gallery hallway on the right and begin pushing through the increasingly frenzied crowd towards the hallway in which Mandleman's gallery was located. He did not see the policemen who had been pursuing them, however. Aata's men must have overwhelmed them, which meant he must have been wrong about Aata's intentions; if they had done harm to the three police officers who followed them down the hall, they would have no misgivings about doing the same to him. He gazed down the corridor towards the stairs and then began cranking the window open. It was time to come up with a new plan. Where was Akoni?

He heard someone running and whirled around to welcome his friend, but it was not Akoni racing his way: it was Teddy. The boy ran up to him, a mile-wide grin on his freckled face.

"Teddy, what…? Where is Akoni, what are you doing here?"

Teddy took a deep breath. "He's staying in the gallery to protect everyone," he blurted out. "He can unlock the door anytime when they want to leave."

Thomas heard the thundering of feet as Aata and his men made their way up the stairs. He could see the flash of knives in several of the men's hands and knew that both he and Teddy were now in mortal danger. There was no time to think. He had to act.

He pulled a $10 bill from his jacket pocket, pressed it into Teddy's hand, and pulled the window all the way open. "I want you to climb down the tree," he said hurriedly, "and hail a hansom cab. Have him take you to Sweeney's Saloon in Five Points. Ask to speak to Coutts Sweeney, and tell him I am in danger, we are all in danger. We need his help. Do you understand?"

Aata and his men were on the landing now and starting down the hall towards them.

Tears welled in Teddy's eyes, but he shook them off. "I won't fail you, Thomas," he said in a stoic tone.

"I know you won't, my friend," Thomas replied.

Teddy hopped up into the open window frame, leaned out onto a branch of the tree, and disappeared into the darkness.

Thomas pulled his pocket revolver and turned to face the Tahitian warriors, who were now halfway down the corridor. As he took aim at the center of the pack, he wondered if he had just put young Teddy in even greater peril by sending him into the most dangerous and unforgiving part of New York City.

The Tahitians were only a few yards away when he fired his first shot. One of the men clutched his stomach and pitched to the floor, and the rest of the group came to a halt. The reverberation of the shot in the enclosed space echoed down into the lobby, and Thomas heard several people scream.

"You men put away your knives," Aata shouted as he stepped in front of the group and turned to face them. "I need him alive!"

"To hell with you, Aata," another man growled, "the bastard just killed Mahana. There are 10 of us, and he has only that one revolver."

Aata was no longer in command of this little ragtag army, Thomas realized. Mahana's friend lunged forward with his long knife, and he fired again, striking the man in the leg. He pulled the trigger a third time, but nothing happened. The hammer clicked, but the round misfired. He drew the hammer back again, only to misfire again.

He had backed up against the railing as Aata's men confronted him, and now, with no place else to go, he swung his legs over the handrail and leapt four feet out into space, grabbing at the folds of a brightly colored banner imprinted with the museum's name that hung from the ceiling to the floor.

When the Tahitians poured through the front doors and raced across the lobby, Jules Verne was in deep conversation with the spectacularly endowed railroad heiress, Liv Vanderholdt. He had just come from the Aubert gallery, where he had seen to it that the two paintings he had asked to be set aside were marked with red 'sold' tags.

As riveting as the effect of Miss Vanderholdt's décolletage was upon his psyche, the author briefly redirected his gaze to the hubbub. He knew instantly that these men were looking for Thomas, and he watched across the room as first the American President and then his friend disappeared into the throng. Then he moved with the crowd as it pushed forward to the exits, only to be turned back by the police before moving back into the center of the lobby.

He held tight to Miss Vanderholdt's arm when Aata and his men came back into the lobby and immediately tore down the corridor leading to Mandleman's gallery. In years to come Verne would pat himself on the back for not losing sight of what was most truly important even as the barbaric Tahitian raiders ran riot through the museum. His focus only drifted from Mlle. Vanderholdt's deliciously creamy bosom twice during the five-minute fracas; first, when two gun shots rang out on the floor above them, and next, when he watched in slack-jawed amazement as Thomas flew over the second floor handrail, grabbed hold of the silk banner emblazoned with the museum's crest and half-slid, half-fell to the lobby floor. He landed in a heap, and just as quickly pulled himself up and raced to the front door, where he knocked down a startled policeman and hurtled out into the cold, dark night.

As Verne and the rest of the gala crowd watched in astonishment, two of the Tahitians tried to follow Thomas' escape route. They jumped together from the railing to the banner, but their combined weight was too great for the fragile silk to bear, and the banner was torn loose from its mooring on the ceiling and the men fell onto the hard marble with the banner fluttering down on their motionless forms.

Two more warriors climbed over the railing and dropped to the ground, while Aata and the remaining intruders retraced their steps down the corridor and the stairs, along the hall, and out into the lobby, where they shot through the transfixed crowd and muscled their way past the remaining policemen.

For the next 30 seconds, the lobby and hallways were as quiet as a church service. People were too frightened, too stunned to speak. Then the orchestra leader pulled a flask from his pocket, took a long drink, and started his musicians in a rousing waltz as servers returned to the lobby with trays of champagne and fresh canapes.

The only raid ever conducted inside the New York Metropolitan Museum of Art by Tahitian warriors was now the stuff of legend, and the only thing left for the crème of New York Society to do was to make sure that the stories of their personal heroism in the face of extreme danger would never be forgotten.

~ SEVENTY-FOUR ~

The falling snow cast webs of golden light around the gas street lamps as Thomas shot out of the building and into the center of Fifth Avenue, where he stopped to catch his breath. Both sides of the Avenue were lined with carriages, and small knots of drivers huddled around the fires they had set in rubbish cans to keep warm while they waited for their employers to emerge from the gala.

He had to move. There was an alley directly ahead that cut across to the next Avenue; he would run two or three blocks and then circle carefully back around to the museum. By that time, he hoped the police would have the situation in hand. After that? He did not know.

He pulled his evening jacket tight against the cold and hurried between two parked carriages and into the pitch-black alley. As he did, he heard footsteps ahead, and then the rasp of a match. The dull light briefly illuminated someone's shoulders and face like a ghostly painting on the wall of an old-world museum.

It was Fitch Donegan.

"Colonel," a familiar voice slowly said. "How nice of you to come to me."

The match dropped to the ground and Thomas heard the hammer of a revolver being cocked. He turned and bolted to the street as Donegan fired twice. Both shots hit the brick wall close to his head, and he was showered with red dust, but the Irishman's aim was off. He knew that the next shots would find their mark. A professional would

505

not miss again.

He flew off the curb and back into the middle of Fifth Avenue just as Aata and eight Tahitians spilled out of the museum and down the steps towards him. There was nowhere for him to retreat.

Aata came to within a few feet of him and raised his hand for his men to stop. "I do not wish to harm you or your friends," he said to Thomas between deep breaths. "I only want the bank's money."

"Funny way to show it, what with a dozen men with knives trying to kill me," Thomas answered.

"Against my orders," said Aata. "They will do what I tell them now."

Thomas looked over the big, rough-looking men lined up on either side of Aata, who he was certain had offered them even more money to do exactly as they were told before they came out to the street.

"It's a dirty business you are in, Aata, especially for a man who used to live by a code of honor."

A carriage approached from down the street and, when the driver realized no one was going to move for him, he brought his horses to a halt and waited.

"That was in another life, Colonel Scoundrel, a life which you ripped from my hands."

A man stepped from behind the cover of the waiting carriage and raised his revolver at the group.

"I am truly sorry to break up your reunion," said Donegan, "but I have waited long enough to fulfill my obligations. This ends tonight."

"Your employer directed you to give me time to collect the bank's money," Aata replied. "Back away now; we will deal with your matter later."

The wind picked up, and gusts of snow began to swirl around the streetlamps. Thomas looked up and down the street, but escape was impossible.

"You can't do anything right, can you son," Donegan said to Aata. "This man bested you in a wrestling match—fair and square, I heard tell. Then he made it under the skirt of that little deaf bitch ahead of you, by which time you might as well have hung your balls up in a closet, being as you clearly had no more use for them."

Aata tensed and a cloud crossed his face. Thomas thought he was going to lunge at Donegan. If he did, it might give Thomas a chance to break away.

Donegan wasn't going to wait. He pulled back the hammer on his revolver, but before Thomas could make out who the assassin was aiming at, a massive form barreled out the darkness behind Aata and knocked him and two of his men to the ground. Akoni had arrived.

Donegan was so startled that he pulled the trigger before aiming, and his bullet bypassed Thomas and Aata and harmlessly shattered a museum window. Thomas leapt forward to help Akoni as Donegan took aim and fired again. Another one of Aata's men fell onto the mud- and ice-covered street.

Six of Aata's men now surged forward as one towards Donegan, who kept his revolver pointed straight ahead as he backed up towards the curb. The Irishman had not planned on having to defend his life tonight, and now he had only two bullets remaining in his pistol to deal with a swarm of attacking Tahitians. At least he would take two of the bastards with him, he thought.

Akoni pushed himself up from the ground where he had been thrashing two of the men he knocked down, only to fall again when two more Tahitians raced down the museum steps and threw themselves onto him. Thomas saw one of them slash at Akoni's arm with a knife, but someone hit him on the side of the head before he could go to his friend's aid, and he had to turn to deal with two attackers who were brandishing long knives.

Thomas stepped towards the closest attacker, took hold of his wrist, and wrenched it hard towards the ground. The knife clattered to the street, but the other man reached around his companion and Thomas felt his blade bite into the top of his shoulder.

It was chaos; he and Akoni were battling at least ten men in the middle of the street, the carriage drivers weren't doing anything to help, and who knew where the police were? Probably inside seeing to the emotional well-being of New York's most important citizens.

Then he heard another shot, and the man who had just stabbed him collapsed, his head smashing against the curb. Donegan brushed snow off his shoulder and took aim from ten feet away.

"One bullet left, Scoundrel, but it's all I need to finish the job."

Thomas took a step back and twisted his torso just as Donegan fired. He felt a searing pain in his side, and he struggled to stay upright. Then he lost his balance and went down to one knee, holding his right-hand tight against the wound. All that was left for Donegan to do now was deliver the coup de grâce. The Irishman preferred killing with a knife, didn't he, so his empty revolver wouldn't hinder him. Thomas looked down the street at the brownstones and storefronts decorated with evergreen boughs and Christmas holly and wondered how he and Keani would have decorated their cabin on Moorea for the holidays. It would only be a moment now…

But his head wasn't jerked back, and Donegan's blade did not slice across his throat. Instead, the shouts of dozens of men and the thunder of their hobnail boots on the snow dusted cobblestone turned everything upside down. The street erupted in a whirlwind of flying fists and swinging clubs, and he watched in disbelief as one after another of the Tahitian warriors were flung to the ground before being kicked and clubbed into submission by men who were pouring into the street from the alleys.

Then the light of the streetlamp directly above him was blocked, and he raised his head to see Aata leaning over him protectively, holding up a knife to ward off any potential attacker.

"I told you I did not want you dead, Scoundrel. I…"

A pistol shot rang out, and Thomas saw a red flower blossom in the center of Aata's white shirt before the Tahitian toppled to his side in the street.

"Thomas? Thomas!"

John Cronin appeared at his side and holstered the revolver he had used to shoot Aata. He went to his knee to check Thomas's wound, all the while keeping an eye on the fight that was still raging in the street around them. One by one, the Tahitians who were lucky enough to break away from their attackers turned tail and raced away from the donnybrook.

"That boy you sent to Five Points?" said Cronin as he pressed a handkerchief against Thomas' side. "Looks like he got the job done. Those are a couple dozen of the biggest, meanest Micks I have seen in one place since the end of the war."

Thomas tried to smile but could only cough at the pain in his side. "Help me up," he said to Cronin.

"We'll do that," he heard Isabella say. She and Taiana stepped off the curb next to Akoni, who was nursing a bloody nose, but looked none the worse for wear after dispatching several of the Tahitians by himself.

As they helped him stand, he saw Coutts Sweeney draw back his leg and deliver a punishing kick to the backside of a Tahitian who hadn't been smart enough to run from the battlefield when Sweeney's men came racing out of the dark to pile on Aata's warriors.

Thomas raised his hand to his brow and nodded to Sweeney. He had no idea when Teddy climbed out the museum window whether the notorious Irish gang leader was going to come to his aid. Sweeney grinned and waved before greeting a well-dressed gentleman who had come out to watch the fight, and soon the two were engaged in animated conversation with several other onlookers. Thomas had no doubt that Coutts Sweeney was the hero in whatever version of the story he was telling.

Taiana took Thomas' arm. "I really want this to be the last time I have to pull you out of a mess like this, Thomas. We could both use a little break."

He smiled. "I'll do my best."

It was starting to snow again. Isabella clutched her evening wrap and pointed across the street to where Aata's body lay.

"Is he…" she asked Thomas.

"Yes," he replied in a soft voice.

"He did want to kill you, Thomas," Akoni said, "and he chased you for 7,000 miles to get the job done."

The fighting was over, and the street was clearing. John Cronin finished giving his report to a police officer, and, as Sweeney's men melted away into the night as stealthily as they had arrived, he came back over to Thomas.

"The President is unharmed?" asked Thomas.

"Only his pride is bruised," Cronin replied. "He saw you fly down that damn curtain, and we had to hold him back from running out here to join the fight."

"Well, the man does know how to win a war," Thomas said with a forced smile. The pain in his side was becoming intense. "I've got to get back," said Cronin. "How about the next time we meet its someplace other than a battlefield."

"That's what everybody is telling me tonight," Thomas answered. He shook Cronin's hand and watched him walk back towards the museum. Then he put a hand on Akoni's shoulder.

"I will always wonder about Aata."

"We can think on that later," Akoni replied, "right now we need to find a doctor. And Donegan got away."

Donegan. Again. Had the assassin been injured in the melee? Was he hiding in the shadows right now, waiting to finish the job? The only thing Thomas could be sure of was that Donegan would not give up. It wasn't in his nature.

He leaned against Akoni and started to walk towards the carriage that was waiting for his group. Then he stopped and turned to look around the street where the battle had taken place. He pressed his hand hard against his side and said, "Give me a minute." As his friends watched, he limped across the avenue and knelt beside Aata's body.

"Who were you?" Thomas whispered into the darkness as he brushed a wisp of snow off the warrior's forehead. "After all this, why did you try to protect me?" With Aata gone those questions would never be answered.

As he pushed himself up, a glint of gold from a thin chain coiled in the snow caught his eye. There was something in Aata's clenched fist. Thomas bent down and gently peeled the Tahitian's fingers open. The great and fearsome warrior who had pursued him halfway around the world had died holding a delicately engraved silver locket. He took it from Aata's hand and carried it over to the closest streetlamp.

A gust of wind sent snow swirling in eddies as he lifted the locket close to his face and undid the clasp in the soft yellow light.

Inside was a photograph of Keani.

Thomas crumpled against the iron lamp post and struggled to stay upright. Akoni and Taiana ran to his side, and he heard the sweet strains of Auld Lang Syne drift out the open doors of the museum and down the steps, joined a moment later by a chorus of voices from the partygoers...

"Should old acquaintance be forgot, and never thought upon..."

The world disappeared.

~ SEVENTY-FIVE ~

Thomas was propped up on the overstuffed velvet couch in Isabella's comfortable brownstone sitting room. The pain in his side was bearable if he didn't move, but the wound continued to seep blood even after the doctor doused it with carbolic acid and wrapped it tightly in gauze bandages.

Before the doctor left, he prescribed a tablespoon of laudanum every hour, twice daily cleanings with the carbolic acid, and two weeks of bed rest.

"Two more inches to the left and that bullet would have perforated your bowel," said the elderly physician. "Your friends would be planning your funeral, and I'd be saved the nuisance of having to make a house call at this hour." He smiled at his own joke before patting Thomas on the shoulder and heading for the door.

It was half past midnight. Taiana and Isabella were drinking tea, and Akoni was pacing the room with his hands behind his back.

"You can't stay here," he said to Thomas when the door closed behind the doctor. "It won't take long for Donegan to put all of the pieces together and come here to find you."

Thomas cleared his throat. "Do you have a plan?"

"I think I do," Akoni replied. "Your friend, Angela, in Boston, the nurse who cared for you after Pebble Creek Ridge. Will she take you in?"

"I haven't seen or talked with her in almost seven years," Thomas replied. "I'm not sure what she would do if I showed up on her doorstep."

Isabella leaned forward on her chair. "Thomas, I am sorry to ask this, but we don't have much time." She took a deep breath and asked, "Was Angela your lover?"

Thomas looked at the floor. Had anyone else asked that question he would have found a way to stand up and strike them.

Instead, he quietly answered, "She was."

"Your first?" Isabella continued.

He nodded his head.

"And she was a recent widow?"

He nodded again.

Isabella looked at Akoni. "I know what a woman goes through when she loses her husband, especially at a young age." She walked over and gently laid a hand on Thomas' head. "She will see you, and she will take you in. Please trust me on this."

Thomas felt his eyes moisten, but he could not find any words.

"So, what do we do now?" Taiana asked.

"The first steamship departs for Boston from the North River pier at 4:00 a.m. Thomas will be on it," Akoni said.

"By himself?" Taiana asked.

Akoni shook his head. "You will go with him. We will book a private stateroom where he can rest until you arrive in Boston in the early afternoon."

"And where will you be?" Thomas asked.

"I must protect Isabella. We will go together to send your friend a telegram as soon as the exchange opens in the morning."

"I don't know her address."

"She lives with her aunt?"

Thomas nodded. "I know her aunt's name and the street she lived on. That's all."

"It will have to do," Akoni replied, "and after we send the telegram, we will go to see Mandleman and Phineas."

"Is that important now?" Taiana asked.

"Child, it appears that every one of Aubert's paintings were sold tonight," said Akoni. "That means Thomas will be able to pay that damn banker in Hawai'i and get his sugar plantation back, not to mention making Aubert a very happy artist."

"I won't be going back," Thomas said.

Akoni raised his eyebrows.

"I can't. There is nothing for me there now." He stared off into the distance for a moment, and then added, "I am sorry, my friend, but I have one last favor to ask. I want you to pay off the note with Wallace Stafford in Honolulu, and then visit your cousin Kukane on Lana'i and tell him that we are out of debt. I am deeding my ownership to him. William Fortnite will not dare return to the islands after stealing all that money, so Kukane will be the sole owner of the sugar plantation."

Akoni nodded somberly. "I will do that, Thomas. And then I will take Isabella to Tahiti with me and see that Aubert gets his money."

Thomas was overwhelmed. So many people had risked their lives and fortunes to help him. He did not know what to say.

Isabella went to the sideboard and filled four small glasses with cognac. She handed them to her friends and said, "Here is what we need to do right now. Akoni and I will go to your hotel and pack light bags for you and Taiana. We will take a carriage at 3 a.m. to Pier 47 and purchase your tickets, and as soon as the telegram office opens, we will contact Angela. Then we will send a telegram each day to…"

"Hell, man," Akoni interrupted, "we will come to Boston ourselves in a few days and sort out the last bits and pieces in person."

Isabella smiled and shrugged. "It seems we have a plan, Thomas. Are you good with all of this?"

He nodded.

"And you, Taiana?" Isabella added. "You do have a choice in all this, you know."

Taiana went to the couch and sat beside Thomas. She rested her hand on his forearm and asked, "Have you not noticed the kind of trouble he gets in when I'm not around?"

At 3:45 a.m. under a clear, cold, star-carpeted sky, Akoni and Isabella walked Thomas and Taiana up the ramp of the steamship *Galatea*. They helped get them settled into their stateroom and then waited on the dock as the steamship pulled away from the pier and slipped into the river.

"You have a choice in all this, too, my love," Akoni said when they got into the carriage for the ride back into town.

Isabella adjusted the buffalo lap robe and then leaned over and kissed him on the lips. "I made my choice a long time ago, my dearest."

~ SEVENTY-SIX ~

Boston

Lunch was delivered to their stateroom by a steward who warned them about what to expect when the steamship arrived in Boston Harbor, but Thomas was unprepared for the hellish landscape of burnt-out buildings and piles of rubble along the docks when they went up on the deck.

He leaned heavily on the cane Isabella gave him and slowly made his way to a bench as the ship berthed. Taiana helped steady him as he sat and then joined him as the *Galatea* skimmed across the calm water and docked at one of the few piers that were still standing.

"Good lord," he quietly said as he looked at block after block of ruined buildings. "How bad was this fire?"

A gentleman standing near him spoke up. "You haven't been here since the conflagration, sir?"

"I have never been to Boston," Thomas replied.

Below them, deck hands were tying the *Galatea* up to her moorings. Passengers poured up from below decks and began lining up to disembark when the gangplank was affixed.

"It was November 9th," the man continued. "The fire started in the early evening in a basement of a warehouse at the corner of Kingston and Summer Streets. By the next afternoon more than 700 buildings and most of the structures along the waterfront were consumed."

"It looks like a battlefield," Thomas said.

The man nodded his head. "I was with Sherman's forces at Atlanta in November '64 when he lit the match. This is every bit as terrible."

The man tipped his hat and joined his party leaving the boat.

"Do you think your friend's home may have been lost?" Taiana asked.

"No telling. I don't know this city, and I have no idea where her street is located. We may end up turning around and taking the next boat back to New York."

A steward appeared beside them. "Your luggage is on the pier, Miss," he said to Taiana, "and I have arranged for a carriage as you asked."

She tipped him and helped Thomas to his feet. 'They do have a wheelchair, you know," she said. "I asked this morning."

Thomas took her arm and began to walk gingerly towards the boarding plank. "I'm not quite ready for that," he said with a half-smile.

When they reached the pier, they saw a middle-aged black man in a dark suit standing next to their luggage.

"Miss Taiana? I am Reginald, your driver."

He slung their luggage into the back of the covered carriage and helped Thomas navigate the step up before helping Taiana in.

"Where to, folks?" he asked.

"There's a problem with that," Thomas said, "and to be honest I'm not sure you will be able to help us."

"Now that sounds like a challenge, sir. I know this city well, and I…"

He hesitated, then turned in his seat to look more closely at Thomas. "Do I know you, sir?"

"I was with the 109th Ohio in the war," Thomas replied. "Perhaps our paths crossed."

"No, sir, it wasn't there. I was an orderly at Mt. Pleasant Military Hospital outside Washington from '64 to '66."

"And I was a patient from April to May of '65," Thomas answered.

Reginald looked more closely into Thomas' face. "I'll be damned— beg pardon, miss—you are Colonel Scoundrel, ain't you?"

Thomas couldn't help but smile.

"I am."

"I was the day orderly on your wing the first week you was there, but every time I came into your room, you was unconscious."

"It wasn't my best few weeks," Thomas replied.

"They moved me to another wing, but I liked to bust a gut with happiness when Mr. Whitman told me you was going to be fine."

"You knew Walt Whitman?"

"Finest poet I ever met," Reginald answered. "Course, he was also the only poet I ever met. A fine man."

"We agree on that."

"So, what do you know about the place you are trying to find?" Reginald asked.

"Do you remember Nurse Angela, who worked on the officer's ward?"

"I sure do, Colonel, she always treated me good."

"She and her mother live on Carmichael Street with her aunt, whose last name is Stewart, but that's all I know."

"If you don't mind my asking, is Miss Angela expecting you?"

Thomas shook his head. "I don't know that, either."

"So, and again, forgive me being forward, Colonel, but if I understand correctly, you are looking up a nurse you haven't seen in seven years whose address you don't know, who may not know you are coming."

Taiana spoke up. "That's exactly right, Mr. Reginald. And we really do need to find her as quickly as we can."

Reginald gave Thomas another once over, and noticed how he was holding his hand against his side. "You be needing a nurse again, Colonel?"

Thomas nodded.

"And there ain't no nurses in New York," Reginald mused.

"Can you help us, or not?" Taiana asked. She was on the verge of tears.

"Miss," Reginald replied, "we will find your friend. And if we can't, I'll take you to a doctor I know who doesn't ask questions. Now, Carmichael Street is on the edge of town. Nice neighborhood, no damage from the fire.

"We'll skedaddle over there, and I'll do a little reconnoitering. If your friend lives there, we will find her."

Twenty minutes later, the carriage pulled onto a wide, tree-lined cobblestone drive with handsome homes on both sides. Reginald drove slowly down the street until he saw an ice-delivery wagon parked along the curb. He pulled the carriage to a halt, got out, and waited for the iceman to come down the drive and put away the huge tongs he used to haul 50-pound blocks of ice.

Reginald and the ice man spoke for a minute and then he returned to the carriage and opened the door on Thomas' side.

"The good lord has done smiled on you and Missy today," he said with a smile. "Seems as how Mrs. Stewart passed last year, but her sister and niece still live in the house."

"Where?" asked Thomas with a grimace. He was being buried in waves of pain and nausea and wasn't sure how long he could stay conscious.

Reginald pointed to a house just two doors from where they stood.

"Right there, colonel."

A minute later they were parked in front of a three-story landscaped home with a Christmas wreath on the front door. Taiana flew out of the carriage and up the walk. She pulled back her shoulders, took a deep breath, and rapped several times with the brass door knocker.

Thomas fought to keep his eyes open, but he was losing the battle. He saw the door open, and he made out a woman's figure and a head of dark hair.

Before he could tell if it was Angela a wave of exhaustion enveloped him, and his eyes closed.

<h1 align="center">~ SEVENTY-SEVEN ~</h1>

Thomas opened his eyes to two familiar sensations: pleasure at seeing Nurse Angela hovering just inches above his head, and pain from the Confederate bullets that tore into his back and leg earlier on Pebble Creek Ridge.

Something was different, though; the military hospital ceiling seemed lower than it was yesterday, and the sparse furnishings he had grown accustomed to had been replaced by a dark walnut highboy, an armoire, and a mirrored dresser. Why had the army moved him?

He turned his head to the side, but the person seated on the chair next to his bed wasn't Walt Whitman. The shaggy-haired, bearded poet with pale blue eyes was gone. So was his omnipresent cigar and brandy glass. In his place, Taiana sat holding a cup of tea, an open book on her lap.

His mouth was dry, and it was hard to form words. "Where am I?" he finally asked.

Taiana chuckled, and then another woman's voice joined in. "You are in my home," said Angela, "and for the second time in our lives it seems you are also in my care."

He tried to sit up, but the pain was too great.

"In a bit, Thomas, dear," Angela said in a gentle voice. "This time you are going to take the doctor's prescriptions to heart; traveling here almost killed you."

His vision cleared, and he felt himself smile as he looked into Angela's eyes. She would be about 40 now, he thought, but she was every bit as beautiful as the day he first met her at Mt. Pleasant Hospital.

"Thank you," he was finally able to say.

"Thank Taiana," Angela answered as she put a glass of water to his lips, "and Mr. Reginald, who carried you into the house and upstairs. And Miss Isabella for her telegram. You had the right friends beside you when you needed them most."

"How long?"

Taiana looked at the clock on the dresser. "You've been sleeping for almost 36 hours. It's 7 p.m."

Angela set down the water glass and pulled a chair close to the bed. "That may sound like a long time to you, Thomas, but Taiana is only now finishing the story of your life for the past year."

"And hers?" Thomas asked.

"Oh, yes, and hers, as well. The two of you and Mr. Akoni have lived an adventure worthy of one of your friend Jules Verne's novels."

"Perhaps so, but I think we could all do with a bit of a rest now," Thomas said with a smile.

"Please?" added Taiana.

"First, is there any news?" Thomas asked.

"Isabella telegrammed today. They are taking the overnight steamship and will be here in the morning."

"Donegan?"

Taiana shook her head. How she longed for the day she would never hear of that man again.

"Your friends will stay here," Angela said. "We have such a large home, and my mother is excited to have company. She loves to cook and bake. In fact, she has been teaching Taiana how to make Christmas bread."

"Christmas?" asked Thomas.

"Is tomorrow" said Taiana."We even have a little fresh snow to go with our Christmas goose."

A tear formed in his eye and rolled down his cheek. He brushed a hand through his hair. "I don't know how…" he began.

Angela leaned over and kissed him tenderly on the forehead.

"There will be plenty of time to talk about that later," she said. Then she and Taiana turned down the gas lamps, pulled Thomas's covers up to his chin, and left the room.

Akoni and Isabella arrived at noon and when they were confident that Thomas was feeling better Akoni helped him get into a dressing gown and down the stairs to a couch in the sitting room. Angela's mother, a plump, apple-cheeked dynamo of energy, bustled in and out of the room with trays of sherry and snacks, which Taiana was helping her to make in the giant kitchen.

Angela took Isabella on a tour of the home and property, an excuse Thomas figured, for them to take the measure of one another and plot their next steps.

"How did it end with Mandleman?" Thomas asked.

"The man hasn't stopped smiling for three days," Akoni answered. "Aubert's paintings fetched top dollar, enough for a handsome commission for him, money for you to pay your banker, and, depending on what your percentage will be, a sizeable payment to Émile Aubert."

"I want nothing more," Thomas said. "Just enough to pay the bank…"

"Which will then leave Aubert with a little over $25,000," said Akoni. "And when Isaac Mandleman visits him in Tahiti next spring to arrange for another trove of paintings, the lad will be able to live in style anywhere in the world."

Thomas smiled at a memory of Émile and Océane sitting on the deck of their home on Tahiti enjoying freshly caught parrot fish cooked over coals with a fine white wine.

"That they already have," he said.

Akoni smiled. "Which leaves us, my friend. Isabella is selling her restaurant and home to her chef. She is coming to Honolulu with me, where we will be married, and, according to her, open the grandest restaurant in the islands."

"A blend of Italian and Polynesian cooking?" Thomas asked. 'That will be a true wonderment."

"And now, what about Taiana?" said Akoni. "She has wandered long enough, Thomas, she needs a home."

"I will give her a home."

Akoni scowled. "A real home, Thomas, not the back of a wagon out on the prairie. A place where she can go to school and make friends and be secure."

"Somewhere like this?"

They turned to see Angela and Taiana standing in the doorway. Angela came over beside Thomas and laid a hand on his arm.

"Thomas, I knew the first night you arrived that I wanted Taiana to stay here with my mother and me. I am content to remain single, but I do long for companionship, for a bright, lively mind with whom I can discuss literature and art and music." Taiana joined them and took Angela's hand.

"She will be my friend, my daughter, and one day, my heir," Angela added."

"And you know all this so quickly?" Akoni asked.

Isabella had walked into the room, and she answered him.

"Women have a way with these matters that you men will never understand, my darling," she said.

"Why do I feel like that statement should frighten me?" Akoni asked.

They were all laughing when Angela's mother came in to announce dinner.

After breakfast the next morning they gathered at the dining table to make their plans. Akoni and Isabella would return to New York and close out her business. Then they would visit Mandleman's bank to secure a circular letter of credit with the proceeds from Aubert's paintings that they could draw upon anywhere in the country, and in Hawai'i.

When Thomas was strong enough to travel, he would join her and Akoni in New York City for the journey back to San Francisco, where Thomas would see them off on the steamer to Hawai'i.

"I will send letters for you to give to Phineas and Winters," Thomas told Isabella, "And also to young Teddy. His bravery made so much of this possible."

"And afforded Taiana the opportunity to meet her first suitor," Isabella added with a laugh.

"She could do much worse," Thomas said as Taiana blushed

Late that night Angela came into Thomas' room with a bottle of cognac and two small glasses. She sat on a chair beside his bed, and after she poured and they had toasted, she said, "This is not quite how we spent our last night together at Mt. Pleasant, is it, my dearest."

He shook his head at the memory of their tender and passionate lovemaking.

"No, but I always wanted to tell you how much you meant to me. You saved my life."

Angela leaned forward and kissed him lightly on the lips. "And you saved mine."

They sat quietly for a long time. Then, in the soft glow from the table lamp, she lay down on the bed, fully clothed. She wrapped an arm around him, put her face close to his, and whispered, "Now, tell me about Keani, Thomas. Tell me about your wife."

The dam inside his heart crumbled, and a river of tears and words poured forth from deep inside his being like a wave cresting over a coral reef on his beloved Moorea.

SEVENTY-EIGHT

Pacific Mail Steamship Docks, San Francisco
January 1873

A steady stream of carriage drivers and porters hauled luggage trunks up to the freight deck of the propeller-driven *SS Ajax* under a gray, mist-streaked sky. First Class passengers made their way up the ramp of the gleaming new steamship for the nine-day voyage to Hawai'i and lined up along the railing to wave goodbye to family and friends.

"I still wish you were coming with us," Akoni said. "I am not comfortable with you knocking around this town for long. Donegan is here by now. You know that."

Thomas nodded. But after spending ten days recuperating at Angela's home in Boston, and a restful four-day cross-country train ride, he felt more fit and capable than he had in months. He was ready.

"I do. Colin Stafford is here, too."

"The man who wants you dead and the professional he hired to do the job," said Isabella. "You have earned a respite from this madness. Come with us. Start over in Hawai'i. Your friends will be there, and the opportunity for a new life. What is there here for you?"

Thomas looked up into the thickening morning clouds. The rain would start soon.

"Justice," he finally said.

"Don't you mean revenge?" Akoni asked.

"Sometimes they are one in the same, my friend."

Isabella dabbed tears away with a handkerchief. "Will we see you again?"

"You will. I promise. And if you wish to write me, please send letters in care of Andrew Whitton at *The Chronicle*. He will know where I am."

Isabella hugged Thomas and kissed him on the lips as Akoni picked up his leather satchel and slung it over his shoulder. Then he wrapped his arms around Thomas and held him tight.

"E maikaʻi mau, my brother," said the giant Hawaiian. "Be well always."

Akoni put an arm over Isabella's shoulders, and they walked to the passenger ramp. They turned to wave when they reached the upper deck, but Thomas had already melted away into the fog. He could not bear another long parting.

Two hours later, a hansom cab dropped Thomas off at the alley-side kitchen entrance to Kwan's *Rue de Paris* restaurant. The driver pulled a heavy wooden crate from the back and carried it to the door as Thomas knocked. A few seconds, later the diminutive chef himself swung the door open.

A smile spread across his face, and he embraced Thomas and shouted, "Bo!" to alert his wife that their friend had returned from across the oceans. The driver set the crate on a table as Mrs. Kwan rushed into the kitchen from the dining room where she was preparing to open the restaurant for lunch.

Her eyes were brimming with tears by the time she wrapped her arms around Thomas' waist. "Thomas, my Thomas," she said, "we had no idea…"

He held her a moment, and when she pulled back and cleared her throat he said, "I am sorry Mrs. Kwan, I wish I could have told you I was coming. I will explain, I promise."

Mrs. Kwan went to her tiptoes and looked into Thomas' eyes. "Mr. Whitton at the newspaper told us about your wife and shared your letters to him with us. We are so very sorry."

Her husband nodded somberly. "Let us go into the dining room," he said. He spoke briefly with one of the cooks, and then led Thomas and his wife to a table.

Almost as quickly as they sat down, a server brought fresh tea and a plate of small sandwiches.

"I have brought you a case of pinot noir from *Burg Ravensburg* in Germany," Thomas said. "I was introduced to it by the commander of a German warship. It is exceptional."

A smile creased Mr. Kwan's face. "Would this be the same captain who had you thrown into the sea off Honolulu? Mr. Whitton has shared everything with us."

"I am not welcomed everywhere quite as warmly as you and your wife greet me," Thomas answered.

The Kwans laughed, and for the next hour the three friends filled in the gaps about what had happened in their respective lives over the past year. A few minutes before the restaurant was to open for lunch, Thomas stood to go. He embraced Mrs. Kwan and promised to see her again as soon as he could. Mr. Kwan walked him through the kitchen and out into the alley.

"Your timing is more fortuitous than you can know, Thomas," said Kwan. "You know that my niece is in the employ of Colin Stafford…"

"For which I owe her a great debt of gratitude. The message she sent to me on Lana'i about the assassin Donegan's arrival saved my life."

Kwan's voice quieted and grew serious. "Yes, Donegan. He is here, staying at Stafford's home. My niece heard them talking about you. It seems both men believe you are on your way to San Francisco to kill them, and Stafford has ordered Donegan to stay close for protection." The chef's eyes searched Thomas' face for an answer.

"I will be honest with you, my friend," Thomas said. "I came back to the city to end this business, whatever it may take. I am weary of looking over my shoulder every time I step out onto the street."

The sounds of cooks and servers shouting orders for the lunch crowd pouring into the restaurant drifted out into the alley.

Kwan's brow furrowed, and his eyes narrowed. Then, in a voice that was deeper than Thomas had ever heard, Kwan said, "Do you truly mean that? Whatever it may take?"

Thomas was unsure of Kwan's motive for asking the question, but there was no point in dismissing it. "I mean it," he said.

"I said a moment ago that arriving today was fortuitous," Kwan said. "In fact, it is more than that, as you will learn. I cannot share more right now. Can you come to dinner tomorrow at 7 p.m? And perhaps take a short trip with me after the restaurant closes?"

Thomas looked into his friend's face. He trusted the man, and knew that there was far more to him than his role as a master chef and owner of a popular French restaurant would suggest.

"Yes," he finally said. "I will be here."

"And you have somewhere safe to stay until then?"

"An inn a mile south of the city, on the coast road. It is safe."

They shook hands, and Thomas turned to go.

"Thank you for the wine," Kwan said as he walked away down the alley. "We must find a proper occasion to open it."

Thomas stepped out of the freezing, fog-shrouded street at precisely 7 the next evening. The *Rue de Paris* was filled to capacity, and the centerpiece lamps and candelabras infused the space with a soft golden glow. He had no doubt that among the wealthy diners there would be friends and associates of Colin Stafford, and probably a few people who would recognize the famous Colonel Scoundrel, as well. As Mrs. Kwan made her way across the crowded room to greet him, he realized that he didn't really care who knew he was here.

She looked lovely in a traditional silk dress with floral embroidery.

"Colonel," she said in a formal tone. "Welcome home."

She took his arm and led him to a small corner table. It was set for two, but one wine glass had been turned upside down. A candle lamp was affixed to the wall, and a bouquet of fresh flowers graced the center of the table.

When he sat down Mrs. Kwan pulled out the other chair and sat across from him. "I will only be here a moment," she said.

He could not take his eyes from the flowers. "You said you would not put flowers on my table until I brought someone special with me," he said, his voice choking with emotion.

Mrs. Kwan reached across the table and took his hand. "But you have, my dear Thomas. Wherever you go, whatever you are doing, whoever else may be in the room…Keani will be with you. I wanted you to feel welcome." She stood up and walked around behind his chair. Then she put a hand on his shoulder and said, "And I wanted her to feel welcome, too."

She left to attend to another table and he watched as Mr. Kwan's starched *toque* emerged from the kitchen ahead of him. "Good evening," the chef said with a smile and a half bow. "I trust you brought your appetite with you tonight?"

"I have been dreaming of this moment for a year," Thomas replied.

A young woman appeared with a silver bucket containing ice and a half bottle of champagne.

"To cleanse your palate," said Kwan as she filled a crystal stem and set it on the linen tablecloth.

The chef crossed his arms and looked thoughtful. "A year is a long time to go without a decent meal," he said, "so we will make tonight's dinner one you will still remember when you are 90."

"To begin, a simple beef broth with caramelized onion, *Gruyère* cheese, and sour dough croutons. A perfect accompaniment to our wet, cold weather. Then, I think, cured *foie gras Torchon* with raspberry jam, grated macadamia, and shaved beet, served with a toasted brioche." Kwan waited a moment and then added, "How are we doing so far?"

Thomas grinned and held up his champagne glass.

"For the main course: a *Canard Rôti*, which is a whole roasted Peking duck with a *sauce bigarade*, duck fat *spätzle*, braised cabbage, and duck bacon. The pinot noir you brought will work splendidly with the duck because of its high natural acidity, which cleans the palate of the fatty texture of the duck skin, and its mild tannins, which do not overpower the delicate meat. You will not go hungry, Colonel."

"Or thirsty," said the young woman who had filled his champagne glass. She uncorked a bottle of the *Burg Ravensburg* and set the cork on the table. "It will breathe as you finish your champagne," she said with a smile before whisking away.

Another server delivered a covered basket of warm bread and a small dish of herbed butter and Thomas found himself feeling more relaxed than he had in months. Then he thought about what Mrs. Kwan said about Keani being with him no matter where he went; he leaned forward, turned over the wine glass on the other side of the table, and filled it with ruby red pinot noir.

From her perch on a tall stool by the front door, Mrs. Kwan watched with a satisfied smile as he poured a glass of wine for his absent wife, raised his glass, and toasted her memory.

~ SEVENTY-NINE ~

When the last guests departed the Rue de Paris, Kwan changed into his street clothes and overcoat while Thomas finished his coffee and a buttery *pain au chocolat.* Mrs. Kwan walked them to the front door, where her two sons were waiting with a carriage. She wrapped a wool scarf around her husband's neck and pecked him on the cheek.

"Keep him safe," she said to Thomas, which struck him as odd. Where would one of the city's best liked and most respected chefs be in danger?

They climbed into the carriage and Kwan's son closed the door before joining his brother on the driver's seat.

"It is a 30-minute ride to our destination," Kwan said. "Just enough time to tell the story." He reached into an upholstered pocket fixed to the side of his door and pulled out a silver flask and two thimble sized metal cups, which he filled before handing one to Thomas.

The men toasted and Thomas started to speak but thought better of it and waited. This was Kwan's moment.

"The first thing you need to know," Kwan began, "is that two men are going to die tonight. Not by my hand or yours, but in such a circumstance that the courts would regard us both as complicit in their deaths and punish us accordingly. Do you understand the seriousness of what I am about to tell you?"

Thomas sat back in his seat. He could not imagine any situation

Chef Kwan could be involved with that would include an execution—or even outright murder.

"I am listening," is all he said.

Kwan had to speak up over the clattering of the horse's hooves on the cobblestone. "We can take you back to your inn right now, and not involve you in any way in this affair; I promise that no one will think the less of you."

"However," he continued, "I can think of no one who has earned the right to be a witness to tonight's proceedings more than you. I tell you this as your friend."

Thomas listened carefully. After months of danger, pursuit, serious physical injuries, and great personal loss, he was ready for some peace and calm. What his friend was suggesting could lead him into something even more perilous.

"I respect you, Kam Sun Kwan," he finally said, "and I trust you. Tell me your story and, if I decide that where you are going is somewhere I cannot follow, I will tell you and ask to be dropped off. But I will never share your story with anyone."

"Fair enough," Kwan replied. He leaned forward and rapped on the small sliding door through which they could speak to the drivers. The door opened, and he simply said, "We are going." When the door closed, Thomas felt the carriage change direction.

"We are traveling to the north," said Kwan, "beyond the wharfs and warehouses to the slaughterhouse and meatpacking district. My brother Mingze, whose daughter, Jing, works for Colin Stafford, owns the largest cloth-dyeing business in the West. Two days ago, one of his employees, a simple laborer who works in the dye-mixing vats, came to my brother for help."

The sound outside the carriage changed as they went from cobblestone street to a long wooden bridge. Kwan held up the flask.

"No thank you," Thomas said. He was being drawn into the story, and something told him that he was going to need a clear head before this night was done.

"The employee, a man named Yuxuan, had run up a considerable gambling debt with one of the Tongs. You know them?"

Thomas nodded. He had encountered the Tongs when he worked as a reporter for *The Chronicle*. Some of the groups were harmless neighborhood associations, others ran opium dens, gambling halls and houses of prostitution.

"Yuxuan's debt became so extreme that the Tong gave him an ultimatum," Kwan continued as the carriage clattered along the rough road. "He would either pay them immediately, or they would take his eight-year-old son hostage until he did."

"And they took the boy?" Thomas asked.

"Yes. It is not an unusual practice for the Tong. They rent the children out as cleaners, seamstresses, any kind of cheap labor. And sometimes, they…"

Thomas nodded grimly. He could only imagine the fate that befell some of those children.

"Yuxuan's son, Wei, was handed over to the Tong last week. Four days ago, he learned that the boy had been sent to a notorious madam who specializes in providing very young children to be the playthings of wealthy businessmen."

Thomas shook his head. Of all the terrible sights he had seen in war, and all the battle atrocities whose aftermath's he had witnessed, nothing compared to the revulsion he felt at the thought of an innocent, defenseless child being violated by a grown man.

Kwan poured himself another brandy, and this time Thomas held out his glass. He felt a sense of dread about where Kwan's story was going.

"Yuxuan combed through the bordellos and alley way lofts," Kwan said. "He talked to everyone he could find who was in any way connected with the business of selling children. And then he happened upon the woman who had purchased his son."

"And this woman told him where to find him?"

"Not willingly," Kwan replied with a half-smile. "But Yuxuan works with razor sharp knives ten hours a day, and he can split the wing of a gossamer butterfly without it feeling a thing. According to my brother,

Yuxuan was getting nowhere with the woman until he drew his knife and began to flay layers of skin from her face."

Thomas shuddered. "And then?"

"The madam told Yuxuan that the boy had been taken to the home of one of our city's leading citizens by a representative who is charged with such tasks and is known to have performed this service many times before."

Thomas looked into Kwan's eyes.

"Yes, my friend," said the chef, "the procurer in this instance was someone you know well."

"Donegan." Thomas almost spit the word out. "And the little boy was taken to…"

"Colin Stafford," said Kwan in a quiet voice.

The carriage came to a halt, and one of Kwan's sons came to the door. They spoke for a moment in Chinese, and then Kwan said, "If you do not wish to come further, this is where we must leave you."

Thomas reached inside his jacket pocket and felt the handle of his revolver. "Close the door," he said, "I am going all the way."

The carriage lurched forward and settled into a steady gait.

"There is more to the story," said Kwan.

"Alright," Thomas replied.

"My brother told his daughter, Jing, what was going on and asked her to find out if the boy was in the house. Her tasks are mostly secretarial, but she has free run of the residence, and from time to time she stays the night in a room Stafford provides for her so that she can work later."

"She found him?"

"She did," Kwan said. "She had retired for the night but decided to go to the kitchen for a cup of tea. On the way back to her room on the first floor, she heard someone crying on the floor above."

Thomas did not want to hear what he knew was coming next.

"Jing went up the stairs quietly and stood outside the room with her ear pressed against the door. At first, she only heard the soft whimpering of a child, but then the boy began to shriek in pain. Jing froze in place.

To open that door would mean being discharged from her job, or worse. Then the boy cried out again, and this time she heard Stafford yell, 'Quiet you little bastard,' followed by the sounds of blows hitting the child."

"Jing could no longer stand there. She flung wide the door and stepped into the room. Candles were everywhere, she said. The boy was lying face down on the bed, not moving. Stafford was nude, astride the boy's backside, pounding down on him again and again and again."

"Jing cried out, and Stafford whirled around. He pulled off the boy, leaned over to a nightstand, and raised his revolver. He fired once and missed and immediately leapt up from the bed. Jing noticed that the boy was still not moving. Before she could decide what to do, she heard a door across the hallway open, and Donegan raced into the room."

"He dragged her into the hallway and began beating her, first with his fists and then with a vase he took from a hall table. As she fell to the floor, Jing saw that a young girl, no older than ten or eleven, was cowering in Donegan's bed."

"Donegan kicked her in the stomach and face, wrenched her arm from its socket, and clawed at her breast through her nightgown with such ferocity that he tore off her nipple."

"Finally, he seemed to tire and turned to go back into his room, probably to get a knife or revolver and finish the business with Jing."

"Somehow, though, she was able to get to her feet and rush down the stairs and out the door. It was very late, of course, and she was in her night clothing, but a Chinese driver in a passing freight wagon saw her stumbling along the street and helped her home."

"My God," was all that Thomas could say.

"Yes," answered Kwan.

The carriage came to a halt outside a windowless three-story wooden building in a warehouse neighborhood. Thomas and Kwan stepped out into a freezing fog. One of his sons held up a kerosene lamp and led them to a wide double door next to a receiving dock.

They stepped inside a storage room that was stacked high with hundreds of bundles of different kinds of cloth, burlap bags of dye powder, steel chemical casks and boxes and containers of all kinds. Supplies weren't the only thing crowding the room, however; Thomas estimated there were at least 100 Chinese men and women standing quietly around the room in the orange light of a dozen lamps. All quiet. All waiting.

He looked at Kwan. "Yes," said his friend, "they have been waiting for you."

"For what?"

"I'm not completely sure. Perhaps to get your blessing."

A middle-aged man walked over to them with his arm around a woman. As they got closer Thomas saw that the woman's face had been nearly obliterated. Her jaw and nose were broken, her cheeks were swollen to twice their normal size, and when she opened her mouth for a moment, he saw that most of her front teeth had been broken out. One arm was in a sling, and she walked haltingly, as if her ankle had been broken.

"This is my daughter, Jing," said Mingze, "or rather, what remains of her."

"The boy?" Thomas asked Jing.

"He is dead," answered a man who had just walked over to them.

"Yuxuan?" Thomas asked.

The man nodded. "My son was found in a heap of garbage behind a slaughterhouse. The doctor who examined him said it was as if someone had shoved a hammer into his little body and twisted it over and over."

"The girl who was in Donegan's room was found wandering the streets the next morning," said Kwan. "They took her to one of the Tong neighborhood associations and she has been reunited with her family. Like the boy, she suffered many internal injuries, and she will never be able to bear children. Her father is here with us tonight."

Thomas found himself longing for another brandy. The entire experience of the warehouse, the nearly silent crowd, and the terribly injured young woman was something out of a nightmare. Even so, the most important question of all had yet to be answered.

"Why am I here, Kam Sun?" he asked. "I don't understand."

"Come with me," Kwan said. He took a lamp from his son and led Thomas, Mingze, and Jing towards the back of the building. The crowd followed silently behind them.

As they neared a narrow, two-story high wooden door, Kwan said, "The next room is where fabrics from around the world are dyed. My brother is famous for his reds and purples and sends the finished fabric all over the country. The dyes are mixed in thousand-gallon vats made with the new Bessemer steel, and many of them use concentrated sulfuric acid and alkali salts in the process. Tonight, my brother is preparing a special red dye."

The father of the girl who had been assaulted by Donegan walked up alongside Yuxuan and Mingze, and together the three fathers swung the huge door open.

The acrid odor of chemicals was almost overwhelming until fresh air from the warehouse began to flow into the room. The high-ceilinged space was lit by pitch torches, and in the flickering light, Thomas saw four enormous steel vats, each about six feet high. A maze of cables and ropes crisscrossed the room above the vats, and pully mechanisms were attached to 10" x 10" oak beams next to each of them. It looked like a straightforward operation: undyed cotton, wool, or silk would be attached to the cables, and the pulleys would lower the fabric into the dye for whatever amount of time a particular color called for. No doubt it was an interesting process, he thought, but what did this all mean?

Kwan led them to the center of the room and stopped in front of the largest vat, under which a fire was burning to heat the liquid dye mixture. The fathers of the children who had been ravaged by Donegan and Stafford walked together to a set of narrow wooden stairs that went up along the right side of the vat. Then they turned and looked towards Kwan and the people who had squeezed into the room behind them. They were waiting for something, Thomas thought.

Kwan climbed three steps before turning around to face the crowd.

"Does anyone here object to the justice we are about to deliver?" he asked in a loud, clear voice.

The crackling of the pitch torches was the only answer he received.

"Then we will proceed," said Kwan.

Thomas knew that he had just heard a judge pass sentence in the presence of witnesses, victims, and jurors.

When Kwan came back down the stairs, he directed Thomas to step back a few paces. Then the three fathers climbed the stairs to a large wooden platform eight feet above the vat and disappeared into the darkness. A moment later Thomas heard the sound of a windlass being cranked. He had used one on the schooner *Kai Douglas* to move heavy freight, but its purpose here tonight was a mystery. He stared hard into the blackness to where the sound was coming from and a moment later saw the end of a thick oak beam swinging out from the darkness high above the top of the bubbling vat.

Then he sucked in his breath and involuntarily clutched Kwan's arm. Dangling side by side on hemp ropes attached to the beam were Fitch Donegan and Colin Stafford. Their arms were stretched above their heads and tied at the wrists,, and in the orange-red light from the torches, Thomas could see that their ankles were bound, their shirts had been removed, and gags were stuffed in their mouths. The three men on the platform pushed the beam out over the vat and Donegan and Stafford immediately began twisting and turning in a futile effort to escape the poisonous, blood red witch's brew of sulfuric acid and dye that was boiling softly just inches below their feet.

"Two men will die tonight," Kwan had said when they got into the carriage. Thomas turned to his friend. "When...how..." was all he could say.

"Early this morning," Kwan answered in a calm voice. "No one on Nob Hill pays attention to a dozen Chinamen in freight wagons pulling up to a mansion. It happens every day. We are the unseen people, Thomas, and some of the time that is an insulting reality." He smiled. "Now and then, however, being invisible has its benefits."

The fathers stepped out of the shadows and stood quietly on the platform a few feet from the condemned men. Thomas thought back to his encounters with Donegan, and about the people the assassin had murdered. His victims had died either at Stafford's behest or simply because the only thing that brought the assassin joy was the sheer terror in his victim's eyes at the moment he took their lives.

Stafford and Donegan began to squirm and vomit through their gags as poison gas filled their lungs, but Thomas took no pleasure from their suffering. He saw no pleasure on the faces of the friends and families of the children they had murdered and abused, either, or on the faces of the fathers who were about to administer final justice.

When he looked back at the men on the platform, he realized they were awaiting his judgment. It was not difficult; his decision neither surprised him or bothered his conscience, and he knew it never would. It was the only one possible. He looked around the room at the people waiting for some measure of justice to be done on their behalf, and then he looked up into the faces of the three fathers who had suffered so greatly. He nodded somberly and watched their heads bow in reply. Then they turned their gazes to Kwan, who also nodded his head, which was the final signal for the three men to place their hands together on the windlass crank and lower Donegan and Stafford into the vat.

Before they did, the father of the boy who had died in Stafford's bed went to the edge of the vat, leaned over, and ripped the gags from the men's mouths. It was not enough for him to watch the men be submerged into the blistering acid and see their flesh melt to the bone, Thomas thought. He wants to hear the depth of their agony and know the same kind of petrifying fear his beloved son had experienced in his last minutes of life.

Thomas felt his blood run cold at the thought of what his enemies were about to experience, but he felt neither pity nor remorse.

Then Stafford began to cough against the black sulfuric fumes that were enveloping his body. "Scoundrel!" he yelled in a hoarse voice. "Damn you man, you can't let these barbarians do this. Please, for the love of God, let us go. I will give you a million dollars, and another million to these Chinese. I will give you everything I own. Everything.

Do you hear me?"

Thomas did not reply. Stafford began to sob, and then, in a plaintive voice barely louder than a whisper, the mighty industrialist spoke his last words. "It was business, Scoundrel, just business. Please, I beg you, let me make it right." His head went down to his chest, and he whimpered, "Let me make it right," over and over.

Donegan had no intention of mimicking Stafford's cowardly performance. He had always known that his death would be an untimely and painful affair; his choice of vocation made that an inevitable fact. For his last act of defiance on this earth he turned his head to Stafford and spat on his former employer. The bastards assembled below were not going to hear Fitch Donegan beg for mercy.

It went completely silent in the room. Then the windlass creaked, and Donegan and Stafford were winched slowly to the surface of the deep red inferno. Donegan's bravado evaporated the instant the acid made contact with his feet and ankles. He shouted an obscenity, followed by a chilling, primal scream that reverberated around the rafters two stories above. Stafford began to howl like an animal caught in a steel hunting trap, but by the time the caustic liquid reached his knees he barely had enough strength to moan.

Thomas pursed his lips as the men instinctively struggled to lift their legs out of the scalding mixture. It was a pointless effort. In a moment the highly concentrated sulfuric acid would begin to penetrate the skin on their chests and shoulders, flow over their faces before blinding them, and then finally, mercifully, pour like a river of molten fire down their throats and stop their hearts.

Thomas watched the tops of Donegan and Stafford's heads disappear beneath the foaming liquid, and a moment later, their arms vanished. Then a flurry of white bubbles rose up through the red poison as the men's lungs expelled their last bits of oxygen. Only then did the ropes holding Donegan and Stafford to the beam go still.

The three fathers came quietly down the stairs. Each shook Kwan's hand, and then Thomas.'

"How long?" Kwan asked his brother.

"When we drain the vat in a week, there will not be a trace of them inside," Mingze replied. "Not a bone or a buckle."

Neither Thomas nor Kwan said a word when they went back out into the fresh, cold air and climbed into the carriage. The fog had lifted, and a brilliant crescent moon hung from the heavens in a sea of glittering stars.

Kwan poured another brandy and handed it to Thomas as the carriage swung onto the road. "No one is looking for you now, Thomas. My sons will take you to your inn to pack your things, and then take you to a nice hotel. One with a good restaurant, of course, but not a great one. For that, you will have to come to see me."

Thomas settled back into his seat and felt inside his jacket for the silver locket with Keani's photograph.

No one was looking for him. The thought made him chuckle, which earned an amused sidelong glance from Kwan.

What was life going to look like now?

It was time to find out.

Ha'apiti, Moorea
April 1873

The schooner *Kai Douglas* anchored outside Moorea reef, 50 yards from the entrance to the pristine blue waters of Ha'apiti Cove, where the crew took in the ship's sails under a threatening sky. Typhoon season almost always ended by late March, but in his 30 years at sea, Captain McNab had learned that when it came to ocean storms, there was no such thing as 'normal.' He scanned the horizon with his leather-wrapped telescope and calculated the path of the towering gray thunderheads piling up to the south. They were headed his way.

Then he watched as Heron and Bembé lowered the skiff into the calm water and stowed three cases of medical supplies and two cases of good whiskey between the plank seats. The medical supplies were a gift to the village, and the whiskey would serve the dual purpose of disinfectant and libation under the supervision of the young resident missionary, Edward Kahale.

When the loading was complete, McNab sent the cabin boy to fetch the schooner's only passenger from below decks. The man emerged a few minutes later and climbed down into the skiff without saying a word. McNab had grown accustomed to his silence on the 17-day voyage from Honolulu, and once again afforded the man the respect of not seeking to engage him in conversation.

There was a light breeze and he could have raised the sail, but he enjoyed rowing to shore over the reef and feeling the push of the coastal swells on the stern of the small boat. They reached the reef in five minutes, gliding over a wonderland of white coral teeming with brilliantly colored fish.

His passenger's gaze remained fixed on the plank seat in front of him as they slipped over the reef and into the smooth waters of the cove. They were headed to a thin strip of beach on which sat a deserted cabin. An overgrown garden fronted the small house, and vines were beginning to take over the two small outbuildings behind it.

A thick wall of green underbrush and trees formed a natural protective fence around the property, and to the south, an outcropping of rock loomed over the southern rim of the cove. To the north, a clear stream fell from the mountains and cut its way past the cabin before spilling into the sea.

McNab took the skiff into three feet of water before hopping out. His passenger joined him, and the two men pulled the skiff out of the water and up onto the beach.

"Are you certain?" McNab asked when the boat was secure. In reply, the passenger simply nodded and slung a small leather satchel over his shoulder. Then he adjusted his slouch hat and walked towards the line of trees that bordered the beach. The captain watched the man for a moment, and then, deep in thought, turned to begin his trek to the village to get help with the supplies.

The passenger made a circle around the cabin and picked his way along a narrow trail that started behind the outdoor kitchen. It wound through a thicket of flowered bushes, over a small stream, and past a fallen tree before it began a steep ascent up the rocky promontory that rose 200 feet above the cove.

He had made this climb many times in every kind of weather, and he reached the top in a few minutes. When he crossed the flat clearing that ran along the edge of the cliff he could see for miles; the jagged volcanic peaks on Tahiti lay 12 miles to the south, and the *Kai Douglas* at anchor felt almost close enough to touch.

As he scanned the deep blue waters, a trio of spinner dolphins exploded from below and whirled six feet in the air before slicing back beneath the waves. Above them a flight of petrels swooped and dipped on the rising air currents and then dove down to skim the surface of the ocean at high speed.

He had journeyed 7,000 miles to come to this place, where a small clearing had been scraped out of the hard red dirt beside a jumble of rocks and an uprooted tree on a cliff overlooking a cabin on the beach.

It was time. He lay his hat and satchel on a flat rock and took a deep breath. When he exhaled, he allowed himself to look at the headstone for the first time since he had reached the summit. It had been fashioned from a slab of local black basalt, smoothed on the front and sides, and left naturally rough on the top and back. The stone was planted a foot deep in the rich volcanic soil and was encircled by polished sea rocks and shells that had been arranged with great care.

Several tiaré gardenia bushes had been planted around the headstone, and someone had strung red and white blossoms across the top of the marker within the last few days. He could still smell their sweet fragrance.

He stepped back and sat on a downed log where he stayed for an hour, soaking in the air, the sun, the sounds of the ocean, and the smell of flowers and massed tropical vegetation.

To his surprise, he did not weep, even as a tidal wave of memories of his life on Moorea flooded over him. Instead, he felt nothing but gratitude and joy for having had the privilege of sharing her love and caring, no matter how short their time together had been.

When the sky began to transform into twilight orange, blue, and rose around clusters of darkening clouds, he stood to go. A storm was coming, and he would be needed on the schooner. Life went on.

He picked up his satchel, put on his hat, and walked over to the headstone, where he knelt, reached into his jacket, and pulled out a silver locket on a gold chain. He opened it slowly, gazing lovingly at the photo inside.

When he was done, he closed the locket and set it gently at the base of the headstone, directly beneath the name the stone cutter had chiseled into the rock.

Keani

THE END

~ ACKNOWLEDGMENTS ~

Crafting a 1,000,000 + word tale that spans six decades, intertwines the lives of hundreds of characters, and is wrapped around some of the most fascinating events in history, is no small feat. And while I have boldly (foolishly, some would say) committed to writing six 'big' novels about the life of Colonel Thomas Edward Scoundrel, no author could complete such a marathon without the support and encouragement of many wonderful and talented people.

To my wife Lesli, whose patience and faith in me (and the work), overflows with love and grace, thank you. To Todd Rhine (who readers got to know in *Scoundrel in the Thick* as major T. Rhine, the firearms and dry-goods purveyor whose bravery was matched only by his generosity), an ongoing thanks for your vision and steadfast support and encouragement. To Anne Marie Levin, consummate wielder of the red pen of 'correction,' a huge thank you for your professionalism and dedication. You stepped up at exactly the right moment, and your contributions have been invaluable.

To Gary Hartzell, my friend and teacher, thank you for showing all of us what it means to stand strong in the face of the storm. Your wit, humor, unparalleled storytelling, decency, and (my wife would insist I note) your charm, have been a source of inspiration and joy to me.

And, to the artist Tyler Jacobson, who once again brings Thomas Scoundrel to life so brilliantly, I give my thanks and respect. Your imagination and talent are extraordinary.

Finally, to Kai Douglas, namesake of the three-masted schooner in this book, thank you for reminding me every day about the things that matter most.

I owe each of you a debt I can never repay.

B.R. O'Hagan
Independence, Oregon /December 2023